As the flatbed wagon skidded wide past the corner of the adobe's front porch, she decided to leap towards the safety of the house and suddenly rolled to the wagon's edge and flung herself over the sideboards. Martha Cox landed roughly on the hard dirt, bouncing on her hands and knees before she rolled over, hugging the Spencer carbine to her chest.

The three Apaches on horseback were too surprised by her rash act to stop quickly enough, even if they were interested in this feisty woman. Instead they chased Jacob and his valuable horses as he careened up to his stable and corral, yanking his tired team to a skidding stop. The Apaches galloped past and slid to stops on their ponies' hindquarters, milling about in the dust, trying to reload pistols and notch more arrows for another run at her brother.

Martha was unhurt as she rolled to her feet and ran to minimal cover behind a porch post to blaze off a last round at the frenzied Indians before running inside their small house to reload her rifle.

THE SERGEANT'S LADY

Inspired by a Short Story by Glendon Swarthout

WRITTEN BY

MILES HOOD SWARTHOUT

A Tom Doherty Associates Book
New York

NOTE: If you purchased this book without a cover, you should be aware that this book is stolen property. It was reported as "unsold and destroyed" to the publisher, and neither the author nor the publisher has received any payment for this "stripped book."

This is a work of fiction. All the characters and events portrayed in this book are either fictitious or are used fictitiously.

THE SERGEANT'S LADY

Copyright © 2003 by Miles Hood Swarthout

All rights reserved, including the right to reproduce this book, or portions thereof, in any form.

A Forge Book
Published by Tom Doherty Associates, LLC
175 Fifth Avenue
New York, NY 10010

www.tor.com

Forge® is a registered trademark of Tom Doherty Associates, LLC.

ISBN 0-765034424-6
EAN 978-0765-34424-3

First edition: February 2003
First mass market edition: May 2004

Printed in the United States of America

0 9 8 7 6 5 4 3 2 1

For Glendon and Kathryn,
for their endless love and support

AUTHOR'S NOTE

Some of the incidents as well as the names of soldiers and Indians herein are real and have been taken from the historical record of this particular time and place. Correspondent Charles F. Lummis's reports about the Arizona Apache War are taken verbatim from the dispatches he wrote that spring/summer of 1886 from the battlefront for his newspaper, the *Los Angeles Times*, which a century later were edited by his daughter, Turbesé Lummis Fiske, into a book, *General Crook and the Apache Wars* (Northland Press, 1966).

We had one war with Mexico to take Arizona,
and we should have another to make her take it back!

—General William Tecumseh Sherman, 1871

THE SERGEANT'S LADY

ONE

The American Indian commands respect for his rights only as long as he inspires terror with his rifle.

—Brigadier General George Crook

Lookout on Square Mountain, Winchester Range, Southern Arizona Territory

He was big for an Indian, especially an Apache. Six feet, one inch; loose-jointed; with long fingers and narrow, almost feminine features, except for his muscles, which ran like steel cords through his arms and legs. His deep chest was another giveaway, a legacy from generations of mountain-dwelling ancestors. His bare chest was covered by a buckskin shirt consisting of only sleeves and a shoulder yoke held down by a blue canvas and leather belt of cartridge loops draped over his shoulder. Beneath his navy blue wool headband, small black pupils in eyes sunk into his handsome face didn't move. They were transfixed, watching a small flatbed wagon rattle slowly toward him from the dusty distance.

He was Naiche, grandson of Mangas Colorado and the second son of Cochise, the legendary leaders of the Chiricahuas and the greatest Apaches of this nineteenth century, now winding toward its hard end. He was nearly thirty years old.

Trail to the Winchester Mountains

Shadows cast by giant saguaro cacti lengthened this afternoon across a rough two-track heading toward Square Mountain. This quartet of rocky peaks comprising the Winchesters rose sixty miles east of Old Tucson and seventy miles north of the border, where it formed the northwest side of the hundred-mile-long Sulphur Springs Valley, the main southern Arizona corridor for Indians traveling down into Mexico.

Jacob Cox was well aware of this ever-present danger as he slapped his horses' rumps with his long reins, urging them to pick up their tired gait now that they were almost home. A gaunt midwesterner on the shady side of forty, Jacob turned to his sister riding the plank wagon seat beside him.

"Another beautiful Arizona spring, sis."

Jacob's free hand swept the air, encompassing the palo verde bushes blooming yellow within their view, a patch of lupines, and Mexican gold poppies alongside the trail. New plant life in spite of the usual wind, which sucked the winter's moisture right out of the ground and contributed to the annual spring drought in this southeastern corner of the territory. "Gosh, I love seeing the country this time of year. So clean, fresh. The Apaches, you know, call spring the season of 'many leaves.' "

"Ahh. To the point, just like Apaches." His younger sibling tipped back the narrower brim of her dark brown cowboy hat to take in the whole grand vista of the big valley, thirty miles across at its widest, its five- to ten-thousand-foot peaks of small mountain ranges providing borders along both of the valley's sides. Tanned and on the sunny side of forty herself, Martha Cox was no woman to wear a sunbonnet.

"What was that poem?" She thought for a moment.

And not by eastern windows only,
When daylight comes, comes in the light,

In front the sun climbs slow, how slowly,
But westward, look, the land is bright!
—Say Not the Struggle Naught Availeth,
Arthur Hugh Clough, 1862.

Jacob nodded.

Her sharp eyes took in all the bright land. Good cattle country were it not for its hereditary caretakers, the Apaches. "I cherish our trips away, Jacob, especially to Tucson for the shopping and someone else's cooking, but the sight of home again after a hard journey always pleases me most."

Her older brother nodded again and smiled.

"You think these latest raids were as bad as we heard at the trader's?"

That wiped off his smile. "Army's been fighting these wild Apaches for twenty-six years now, Martha. Haven't whipped them for good yet, but each time they run off the reservation, seems like there's fewer Indians loose and more soldiers chasin' them. Those long odds can't last forever. Not enough Apaches left."

Atop his pony in a brushy wash lined with desert willow and hackberry, below the fairly flat hilltop over which this rancher's wagon now rolled, a long-haired Apache spit into his palm. He rubbed grime off the silver dollar sewn onto the upturned toe of one of his knee-high deerskin moccasin boots, his *n'deh b'heh.* The turned-up toe was distinctive to the Chiricahua, and the metal kicker protected his elk-soled moccasin from wearing out in cactus country sooner than every few weeks. Perico rubbed more saliva onto the silver coin, brightening it.

Standing nearby, Delkay and Inday-Yi-Yahn passed a willow wood canteen between them, as the former pulled his buckskin shirt from under his rawhide belt, which held up a muslin breechcloth draped down to his knees, and yanked it off over his head. Apache warriors stripped before battle, their bare brown skin blending better with the desert than the white man's colored cloth.

These warriors handed their shirts and canteen and personal items to a sixteen-year-old boy, Zhonne, who stood nearby holding the reins of his pony. Besides his smaller size, the teenager was distinguished from these fighters by his headgear; a leather novice's hat, or rounded skullcap, to which were attached four types of feathers: hummingbird, oriole, quail, and eagle. His trainee's cap had no "enemies against power," for the youth was not a full-fledged raider yet and wasn't even allowed to fight, unless he had to defend himself.

Their youngest warrior-in-training was completing the last of his four required raids with these men, acting as their servant and horse holder, doing what camp chores or errands were required, speaking only when spoken to, before he could finally be invited into the ranks of fighting men. This time Zhonne had to stay behind to bring spare horses, weapons, or ammunition up to the fight if needed.

Perico was Geronimo's cousin, which gave him leadership responsibilities in this little band of raiders. He pushed back the derby hat atop his head and held his silver toe toward the sun, adjusting it to aim some bright reflections up at Square Mountain, the lowest peak in the Winchesters.

Lookout on Square Mountain

From his aerie atop a large boulder halfway up this 5,700-foot pinnacle, Naiche caught the signal flashes from the men far below in the wash. His warriors were ready! The tall Indian untied a long length of horse gut slung over his shoulder and drank sparingly from one end as he watched the wagon rattling toward the ranch nestled at the foot of the mountain beneath him. Nothing else moved on that hilltop or in the arroyos rutting either side. Wiping his mouth, Naiche retied his water carrier and slowly raised his big Sharps hunting rifle over his head and tilted its shiny steel trigger guard and breech back and forth against the sun, answering them. No danger. Attack!

Down in the wash, his warriors caught the flashes from Square Mountain and clambered up on their Mexican mustangs. Inday-Yi-Yahn (He Kills Enemies) adjusted his saddle made from two rolls of rawhide stuffed with grass and tied to his horse's back, while Dahkeya notched a cane arrow onto his mulberry recurved bow, straightened his deerskin wrist guard, and tested the tension of his sinew bowstring. These short, tough men, few of them over five feet, eight inches besides their leader, had the smooth faces, small chins, and strong jaws of Chiricahuas to match their smaller feet and hands common to all Apaches. Narrow white stripes slashed across their cheekbones indicated these Chiricahuas were ready for war.

Perico watched his companions ready themselves as he fingered the buckskin thongs braided into his war charm necklace, which he'd strapped over his right shoulder and under his left arm. Eagle feathers fluttered from this ceremonial strap, fragments of obsidian, pieces of turquoise, and coral beans were sewn into it, also. *Ussen*, the sacred God of all Apaches, would protect them. Perico took a deep breath, exhaled slowly, pulled his stolen black derby tighter down over his long hair, and nodded to the others. Yanking their hackamores braided from horsetails, the warriors jerked their horses' heads around and kicked them up, up the steep dirt embankment of the ravine.

"Will it never end? So many deaths, families, and ranches ruined." Miss Cox rearranged her brown cotton riding skirt over her blue denim knickers. Although not riding this trip, she liked knickers because they gave her the freedom to ride her horse astride like a man rather than sidesaddle like the more proper, citified ladies back east.

"On both sides. Poor Mexicans have suffered far worse than we, Martha. But we've got thousands of troops out here now on patrol day and night, chasin' Geronimo and those renegades over to New Mexico and halfway down into Sonora. General Crook left guards at every ranch and water hole along the border at five-mile intervals from Bisbee to Lang's Ranch over in New Mexico before he got the boot, trader Pertwee told me, so we're gonna be protected." Jacob smiled reassuringly at his sister.

"Heck, I heard Crook's Apache scouts have killed more of their own bad people than our Army's ever been able to. And when you're fighting your own kin, the bloodshed can't go on forever."

The smile she returned was thinner, concerned, as she fiddled with the pins in her hair bun, shaking loose its sandy blonde mass. "Fighting Apaches for over two decades! Hard to believe." Twisting her head about, Martha picked up the flash from the mountain above their ranch. "Oh! Look!"

Her brother saw it and immediately craned about to see who was being signaled. Over his shoulder he got his answer, as three Chiricahua bronchos came boiling up out of the ravine, yipping and yelling, demonstrating their nickname among all the Apache bands as "the chatterers," for the calls they made during battle.

"God Almighty! Get down, Martha!"

Long-reining his two horses, Jacob got their light wagon bouncing faster over the rough trail. His sister leaned forward, pulled a Spencer seven-shot carbine from below the seat, flipped up the rear sight and turned to take jerky aim between them. Her first shot went awry, causing the three hard-riding Apaches behind her to drift their horses apart. The warriors leaned behind their mounts' necks to lower their profiles.

"Sis, ahead!"

Two more Chiricahuas, white stripes under their eyes as well, came racing out from behind a big paloverde, attempting to pinch their trap closed. As Elote and Hacki angled rapidly toward them from the opposite side, they loosed arrows at the

Anglos. One thudded into the wooden sideboard right next to Martha. She whirled round, yanked the breech lever on her repeating rifle, ejecting the cartridge and levering another cartridge into the Spencer, recocked the hammer and took a snapshot at the nearest ambusher.

With a yelp Elote tumbled ass over teacup, bouncing off his pony's rump before he flipped into the dirt, facedown. Angry now, Hacki (He Shakes Something) let fly another errant arrow over the ranchers' heads as his horse curved alongside the racing wagon.

Down the hillside and across a sandy wash the spring wagon bounced and clattered. Jacob crouched, his feet braced against the kickboard, urging his speedy team on as they heaved and slobbered to pull their load up the incline across the dry watercourse.

Taking another shot behind her brother's back at the three Chiricahuas closing in on them again, Martha shot one of the Indians' horses, putting the animal into a careening tumble as its rider flew over its neck.

Hacki took advantage of her distraction and the wagon's slowed climb to leap from his pony onto the heavy sacks of flour, potatoes, and staples they were hauling home in the flatbed. Hacki hit hard on the lumpy sacks but rolled over as he yanked a long knife from the fold of his knee-high moccasin. The Apache lunged at the woman, who had one knee on the wagon's seat to face his attack. Parrying his thrust with her seven-pound carbine's wooden buttstock, Martha swung the barrel rapidly back around to recock the hammer and pull its trigger—right in his chest! The impact of the big bullet blew the warrior backward, sprawling him atop their provisions.

With a thump of a turkey-feathered shaft, Jacob Cox took an arrow in his left bicep. The wagon driver yelled in pain and slumped forward as his sister retaliated, blasting away at the two nearby riders, causing them to duck and swerve their ponies off again.

"Jacob!"

"Get him off! Slowing us down!"

"What?" She was confused, concerned about his wound.

Her brother lashed his team on with his good arm. "Push him off! We won't make it!"

Now she understood. The racing wagon reached flatter ground as the galloping team neared the ranch. Martha crawled back over the swaying wooden seat. Seizing the bleeding Apache's hand, she wrested the knife from his grip and, on her knees, rolled the groaning warrior over to the sideboard. Sensing what was about to happen, Hacki tried to resist. But his fingers were slick with blood from the hole in his chest, and his grip was feeble. She grappled with him, overcoming his waning strength with her own as she struggled to hoist him upright. A big bounce of the rear wheel over a rock and a yank! Martha had him up now and rolled the Apache over the wagon's sideboard with a last kick good-bye! Another arrow flew at her, missing as she ducked down to hold on.

With a groan, the compact Indian hit the ground hard! Hacki's broken, bloody body infuriated his tribesmen as they galloped past, causing Perico to pull his revolver finally and blaze away wildly between his jumpy pony's ears.

Rolling back on a flour sack, Miss Cox snatched up her rifle, jerked the breech lever to insert another cartridge and recocked it to fire again at the enraged Indian, narrowly missing him, too! Perico ducked behind his horse's neck and veered off again.

They neared their ranch house, Jacob lashing his exhausted team for all they were still worth.

"Jump, sis! Jump!"

Martha pulled herself to her knees on the food sacks, steadied as she took aim once more at a galloping Indian.

"No! Staying with you!"

"Going to the stable! They want our horses! Catch 'em in a crossfire!" Bending low over the reins, her brother jerked his head back and forth over either shoulder, frantically eyeing his sister and their hot pursuers.

"Jump!"

As the wagon skidded wide past the corner of their adobe's front porch, she decided and suddenly rolled to the wagon's edge and flung herself over the sideboards! Martha Cox landed roughly on the hard dirt, bouncing on her hands and knees before she rolled over, hugging the precious rifle to her chest.

The three Apaches on horseback were too surprised by her rash act to stop quickly enough, even if they were interested in this feisty woman. Instead they chased Jacob and his valuable horses as he careened up to his stable and corral, yanking his tired team to a skidding stop. The Apaches galloped past and slid to stops on their ponies' hindquarters, milling about in a cloud of dust, trying to reload pistols and notch more arrows for another run at him.

Ranch Near Cox's Tanks,
Below Square Mountain

Martha was unhurt as she rolled to her feet and ran to minimal cover behind a porch post to blaze off a last round at the frenzied Indians.

Leaping from the wagon seat, Jacob Cox pulled the reins between his skittish team and dragged them past his small weathered barn, its arched roof covering a hayloft. Two dogs were out of the barn into the thick of the melee now, bounding around in the dust barking, unsettling both the Indians' and ranchers' horses even more. Throwing open the wooden gate to his corral, Jacob ran the two horses and his wagon inside, between two other horses he kept for riding.

Dropping the reins, Jacob Cox finally pulled his single-action Colt from his hip holster and dodged the stamping, rearing horses to get close to the wagon. Ducking behind its seat's minimal protection, he was able to snap off a couple shots from his .45. His aim was spoiled, though, by his team's nervous jerking about as the Apaches' arrows whizzed by when they dashed past the corral on their ponies.

From a longer distance, Perico's bullets kicked up dust about the hooves of Cox's horses. Their owner was up and down like a jack-in-the-box, firing and then taking moving cover. The Apaches were after his horses, or they would have shot one earlier, so his safest firing position was behind the big skittish animals.

Throwing open her plank front door, Martha Cox dashed through her front room to the kitchen, where she grabbed a spring-loaded tube from a shelf. Yanking the empty out of the buttstock of her Spencer, she rammed a full tube of seven copper rim-fired cartridges up inside her older repeating rifle until it locked. Breathing hard, she flung open the wooden window shutter facing their small stable and began triggering more shots. So practiced was she with this carbine that she could aim and empty all seven cartridges in thirty seconds, even with having to recock the rifle's hammer before each shot.

Three Apaches circled the stable yard, but the few arrows and bullets they had left couldn't hit Jacob as he moved behind his wagon, jerked anxiously about by his still-hitched team. The ranch dogs added to the chaos, scooting from between the corral's rungs to bark at the rampaging Apaches, then dashing back inside again as the Indians cursed and shot at them, too.

Martha's second shot hit an Indian as he galloped past, burning Perico in the thigh. The big bullet bore on through to wound his mount as well, and the horse went down in a flying, squealing fall past her open window, tumbling its wounded rider to the dirt, knocking off his derby hat. His fall panicked Dahkeya and Inday-Yi-Yahn, who realized they were caught in the open in a crossfire. Dahkeya loped his pony over to Perico, now up and limping, leaned down, and thrust an arm out to swing the still-armed Indian up behind him in a rescue carry. Both kicked the mustang's flanks hard, and the three men on their two horses galloped off from that ranch as fast as their tired mounts could carry them.

Martha Cox watched them go, still breathing heavily as she paused to lever a last cartridge into her rifle's breech. She chanced leaning out, sticking her neck from her kitchen window to peer around. Were they safe? Nothing else moved in the stable yard except their two dogs, as the disappearing Apaches' dust settled. Seeing no more attackers, she grabbed a fresh ammunition tube off the shelf and then risked it, jumping right out the window to the ground, still holding her rifle.

"Jacob!"

The Indian pony kicked on the ground, whinnying in pain from its bullet wound as she dashed past it across the stable yard.

Lookout on Square Mountain

The Apaches' leader watched the woman run as he raised his 1860 Sharps, lining her up over his front sight. His index finger hesitated, twitching, before he lowered the long gun slightly. Naiche fingered the blue Anson Mills ammunition belt over his shoulder. He'd taken it off a bluecoat he'd killed, and fully loaded with fifty bullets, the belt weighed at least eight pounds. It was much lighter now, nearly empty of finger-length .50/.70 cartridges in its big loops. Naiche snorted. Little ammunition left to spare, too difficult a long shot. He looked up again to see the damned woman run into the corral where her brother was unhitching his team.

Jacob holstered his revolver as his sister literally crashed into him, overrun with concern. "Jacob!"

"Sis! Good shootin', girl! You saved our carcasses!"

"You all right?" She clutched his shoulder, tearing away his bloody shirt to get a look at the wound.

He winced. "Yes, I guess not!"

"Gracious! They're coming back!"

Startled, he jerked his head to follow her worried gaze. The moment he was distracted, she grabbed his shoulder with one hand and the arrow shaft with her other and pushed—hard!

"Owww!" Her brother was driven straight to his knees in pain. Without flinching, she snapped the feathered tip off and then pulled the arrowhead and remaining shaft out the inner side of his fleshy upper arm. "JESUS, girl!"

Jacob clutched his flesh below his bloody shoulder. "Trying to tear my arm off?" The Apaches' thin steel arrowheads, often made from the hoops of water barrels, were jagged and couldn't easily be pulled from a deep wound. And the pain from pushing the arrowhead through the other side of the skin to extract it was more agonizing than an operation without anesthetics.

"Had to come out quick. Got to wash any poison out and get it dressed. Come inside." She helped him to his feet.

Her brother hesitated. "Got to see to these horses." He patted a gelding's sweaty flank with his good arm. "Good horses got us home!"

"I'll rub 'em down and feed 'em just as soon as I get you doctored." Taking him by his good arm, she led her still agitated brother from their corral before shock set in.

"Didn't see any more Apaches?"

"No, just those last three. Winged one, I think, or at least his horse." They stared at the downed animal as they walked slowly back to their small house. The stallion was sweaty beige in color, and its shaggy mane and bushy tail evinced its wild bloodlines. The horse scraped the dirt in agony with its good rear hoof. Martha Cox reached down to pick up a dusty black derby hat lying nearby. Stolen from some white man? Suddenly conscious of her own head, she shook out her long hair, damp with sweat.

"Don't know if I can doctor that poor horse."

"Oh, my." Jacob wobbled, light-headed suddenly from his loss of blood. His sister reached round under his good shoulder to prop him up.

"In you go, hero, to bed."

"What if they come back?"

Martha walked him slowly on, helping her brother step up on the wooden porch under the eaves of their adobe home. "Shouldn't for a while. Need to doctor their wounds first, just like us."

Jacob looked relieved and so did his two dogs, now that the excitement was over. "And bury their dead and say their prayers. Apaches always do that first, I heard."

The yellow mutt plopped down in the dirt in front of the porch to pant, too tired even to climb up on the porch with them. Jacob reached for a rocking chair next to their front door.

"Let me stay out here, keep watch. Need some fresh air."

Her dry lips creased into a frown.

"Just awhile, please, until things . . . I calm down."

Reluctantly, his sister helped him sit down in the rocker. "Just for a minute then. I'll get my medicines." She put a hand on the door latch, but his pained look stopped her.

"I counted two shot . . . out there," he jerked a thumb toward their back trail. "Did you kill that one you pitched out?"

A deep sigh. "I'm afraid so."

He almost smiled. "Afraid's not part of your makeup, sis."

She caught his look, unspoken thanks, and walked inside.

Her older brother reached down to scratch the neck of the longer-haired, black-and-white mongrel of mixed breeding that took up a guard position next to its master. The younger cow dog looked beat, as it yawned settled down beside the rocker.

"Good work, Buster, boy."

From his vantage halfway up Square Mountain, Naiche could make out the dogs and shadowy figures talking under the piñon poles spaced over the partially open porch. When the woman fighter disappeared inside, the Apache grunted in disgust. His luck in battle was still the same—bad.

His older brother by ten years, Hndaazn, his name shortened by the white men to Taza, had first inherited their father's, Cochise's, chieftainship but then had died on a train trip to Washington arranged by General Crook to meet the Great Chief of the White Eyes. Naiche was immediately chosen by the Chokonen band of Chiricahuas to succeed Taza. He was only twenty years old but suddenly chosen as the hereditary chief of these fierce Apaches! His older brother had received all of Cochise's leadership training, deliberately, so that there would be no rivalry between his two sons. Naiche was the sensitive one in the family, an artist in this all-warrior society, who much preferred to sing and dance and paint pictures and chase girls and drink far into the night.

Of all the Apache leaders, Naiche was also the only one with no special power. Juh, leader of the Mexico-based Nedhni Apaches, and Geronimo, Juh's war chief, could both foretell the future. The stuttering Juh also had the power to handle men. Chihuahua, a leader of the Mescalero Apaches, had power over horses. Chihuahua could gentle and ride the wildest horses, or heal them of sickness or wounds, curing one of a rattlesnake bite. Old Nana's power was over rattlesnakes and ammunition trains. He could always bring back precious ammunition from a raid. Victorio, another Mescalero leader, had a sister, Lozen, who was also famous for her power. Lozen could locate an enemy and even tell how far away they were and had done so on many desperate occasions.

Most medicine men and chiefs-to-be acquired power as adolescents. All Apache boys were required to go alone to the sacred mountains to fast and pray for four days. They could take along a blanket but nothing else. Most did not obtain any special gift on their quest, and the few who did, usually got it the last night of their ordeal. Then the supplicant heard a voice, or saw an animal, even a tree, plant, or stone, which was to be his special medicine. It talked to him, telling the Apache boy what he was to use and how. From that time on he carried a bit of this power in a small buckskin pouch on a thong around his neck. It was his spirit guide and helper all his life.

Naiche was not one of these lucky ones. No power in a deerskin pouch graced his neck. He never experienced any voices or visions as a boy and consequently had never displayed any special insights or abilities to his fellow Apaches as their ceremonial chief. Naiche grimaced as he realized he'd now allowed an easy attack on a wagon to result in the deaths of two of his fierce warriors and the wounding of another, his war chief. By a woman! How was he even to keep this small band together, disgraced like this? He had failed again as a leader in battle, and the Chiricahuas all knew now he had no special power to protect them. Ever! With a discouraged shake of his head, Naiche vanished behind the big boulder upon which he'd been sitting.

Martha Cox took a last swipe with a cloth soaked in carbolic acid around the puncture wound on her brother's upper arm. Jacob's sharp breath and teeth-clenching grimace were the only visible result. She took another bandage she'd prepared by soaking in a smelly yellowish liquid and wrapped it tight around his arm and shoulder, causing him to flinch again. "Poultice should ward off infection, draw the pain from your wound. God knows what Apaches dip their arrowheads in, to kill their game. But this should counteract any natural poisons."

"Mother's herbal medicines?"

"Tincture of goldenseal, stinging nettle, and poke root. One of the many good things she taught me, Jacob. You were too busy with school to learn anything practical."

"Practical. If I were a practical man, I wouldn't be running a cattle ranch out here in the middle of Apache country, no matter how cheaply I acquired it." Jacob Cox took a long swig of water from a canteen, then leaned from his porch rocker to pour what was left into the tin pan between their two dogs resting below them in the dusty yard. Both animals slurped thirstily, then lay tiredly back down. Buster, his longhaired herd dog, sniffed the air carefully first, to pick up any stray scent of the wild Indians who had threatened his life that same afternoon. The older, yellow, shorthaired mutt was just too exhausted from the afternoon's frantic defense of his territory to even venture a sniff.

"No wonder old Morrison almost gave me this ranch. Thought I was stealing it three years ago."

"Gave it up with a deep sigh of relief," added his sister.

"And wished me luck making the Tanks prosper," nodded her brother.

"You've since paid full price, with all the time and sweat you've put into this property, Jacob."

"True, but that's my price, Martha, not yours: I know what mother would say if she knew the hardships I was putting you through, sis. It's just too dangerous out here now. We were very lucky today to save our scalps." He shook his head tiredly.

"If they're that desperate for horses and guns . . . they'll be back."

Silence drifted between these close siblings as the rancher's younger sister wiped sticky fingersful of herbal potion off on her apron.

"We've got this army detail coming to our mountain. They should be able to warn us of any further ambushes." She seemed a bit flustered.

"Besides, I've nowhere else to go. I can't run our old farm in Iowa, with my husband missing and our few relatives moved away. There was really nothing left for me to do but come out to this burning wilderness and look after wifeless you."

The throbbing in his wounded arm intensified, forcing a hard decision.

"It's not fair of me to risk your life and limb, regardless how good a markswoman you still are. I'll make you a promise, sis. If we're attacked again and we make it through alive, we're leaving here, immediately, for good. And if the army's unable to rein in these renegade Apaches, within another year, we're moving out, too." The midwesterner tightened his jaw. "Agreed?"

"Where would we go? What would I do?"

"Further west maybe. Los Angeles, San Francisco. Climate's more salubrious on the coast, and those big towns are booming. We should be able to find decent work. Yet another fresh start for the Coxes, eh?"

"Rowdies don't shoot poisoned arrows down their main streets?"

Her brother managed a slight smile. "I think not. I'll miss this wild place."

Martha smiled back, trying to lighten her brother's defeated mood. "You come inside and lie down. I'll see to our valiant steeds. Maybe I can save that Indian pony."

Jacob laid his good hand upon her arm. "It's been an exceedingly exhausting day for us all. Two handfuls of oats each, okay?"

TWO

Besides George Armstrong Custer, Nelson A. Miles was the only other General in the United States Army to design his own uniforms, being especially partial to extra gold braid, epaulets and sashes.

—Robert Wooster, *Nelson A. Miles and the Twilight of the Frontier Army*

Bowie Station, Southeastern Arizona Territory, April 11, 1886

The officers were impatient. Several senior men paced up and down the wooden platform next to the rail line, raising dust to match their arid opinions of the Apache campaign. Two younger Lieutenants stayed out of their way, wisely seeking what little shade the northwest corner of the undistinguished, three-room train station offered. The Southern Pacific's building was utilitarian: one room for the ticket seller/telegrapher and his freightman to bunk in and conduct the railroad's business from; a waiting room in the middle with unoccupied benches inside due to its lack of fresh air through the few glass windows, which couldn't be opened; and a larger storage room at the far end to hold goods and luggage shipped on the trains. For a small depot way out in the middle of this desert nowhere, Bowie Station did a large amount of business from the six trains that passed through every day headed across the continent between Tucson and Albuquerque. For this was the shipping point for soldiers and supplies passing in and out of Fort Bowie, fourteen miles southeast up the infamous Apache Pass and now headquarters for the entire army of the Southwest.

Charles Lummis decided to look for a new source of information other than these frustrated army officers, so he sat down beside a workman trying to catch a nap under his hat on a wooden bench.

"Look tuckered out, mister. Lots of business through the station these days, eh?"

The hat spoke. "Damned fact. Thousands more troops headed out here, plus all their supplies. Special equipment for 'em coming in on this next train, plus the new general hisself."

The newspaperman was interested. "Thousands more soldiers? Where'd you hear that?"

The freightman opened his other eye to peer at the short stranger in the big sombrero. "Telegrapher. My boss."

"Must be serious about catchin' ol' Geronimo this time, that many new soldiers. What's this special equipment comin'?"

"Guess I ain't gettin' any rest today." The weary freightman sat up to stretch. "Mister, I just move the freight around here, on and off the trains. Not my business what's in it." Instead of adding "or anybody else's," the lanky laborer got up to seek quieter sanctuary in his storage room.

Charles Lummis took out his handkerchief to mop his brow. It was only mid-morning and already the temperature was in the mid-eighties and rising. The army men pacing displayed sweat patches on their dark blue wool dress tunics. The officers were wearing their best today, as the welcoming committee. Theirs was the essence of duty in all armies now, then, and forevermore—hurry up and wait for further orders. The newspaperman leaned forward, straining to pick up their conversation.

"Is it true Miles is the only general to design his own uniforms?"

"Yes. But you couldn't get Crook into a uniform, so I guess it's either full regulation dress or not out here in the wild West." Major Eugene B. Beaumont smiled. "Nelson Miles is an Indian fighter, though. Comanches, Sioux, Cheyennes, Bannocks, Nez Perce—he whipped them all. He was the one made Chief Joseph say, 'I will fight no more forever.' And cowed Sitting Bull and his Sioux. Miles was wounded three times as a volunteer officer during the Civil War, won the Medal of Honor, and was promoted all the way up to Major General for his aggressiveness. Supposedly completely fearless. 'Always advance' is his creed, and I believe General Miles won every major battle he was ever in charge of."

"Can't wait to see what he's wearing. A General of *Volunteers*, huh?"

"Yes. Not West Point. But a spit-and-polish soldier nevertheless." The older Major from the Corps of Cadets looked at his younger brother from the academy. Captain Charles Hatfield turned on his heel, and together they started their slow walk back up the platform.

"Well. . . . Good." A direct descendant of the feudin' Hatfield clan of West Virginia, C.A.P. Hatfield was known for his keen eyesight, and he was the first to see the dark smoke from the Southern Pacific engine rising above the crest of the pass miles east of them. "Speak of the devil, here he comes. . . . Maybe Miles'll be flexible enough in his tactics to capture Geronimo in the Madres or lure him out of his lair back up across the border somehow."

A born Southerner himself, Major Beaumont nodded. "Geronimo is the damned problem. He's become the symbol of all the hostile Apaches back in Washington and the whole territory. We catch or kill him and the rest should surrender."

Captain Hatfield agreed. "Maybe then this thankless, endless war will finally be over."

Although not a Catholic, Major Beaumont crossed himself. "Praise the Lord . . . but pass the ammunition first."

"Amen!" Both Indian fighters laughed.

Charles Lummis also noted the train rumbling down the long, sloping rails toward the depot. Rising, making a display of stretching the kinks out of his limbs, he moved near the two younger officers idling in the building's slight shade, smoking.

"Crook deserved a final chance. Just a few more months, he'd have driven that lying butcher up to the reservation to be trained off to Florida with the rest of 'em, good riddance." First Lieutenant Phillip Fuller dropped his half-smoked cigarillo and ground it out on the platform. Not good to be seen smoking in front of a new Commander until one knew what his personal tastes and habits were.

Although junior in rank, Second Lieutenant Robert D. Walsh was too much a veteran of this interminable campaign to care who saw him smoking. "Crook had his chance. Four years out here again, and he still couldn't get 'em all rounded up. The Gray Fox was a smart fighting man, don't get me wrong, but all those armchair generals in Washington care about is Geronimo. Geronimo, Geronimo, Geronimo. And we lost him. Again. Until he's dead or gone for good, we'll be stuck out here trying to find that son of a bitch forever."

A chuffing of charcoal smoke spraying soot over the station hisses of steam and a squealing of brake metal announced the arrival of the westbound train. From the first passenger car up front a well-dressed older gentleman in a pinstriped suit quickly stepped down and strode across the platform to the two younger officers. Brandishing cigars, the passenger offered them to the military men.

Lieutenants Fuller and Walsh looked the stranger over, then accepted his offer. At their modest pay, small gifts were always welcome. The stranger seemed in a hurry. "Do I have the honor of speaking to a couple of the brave officers fighting the bloodthirsty savages in this wild territory?"

Realizing he wasn't jossing, Lt. Walsh smiled. "You do, sir."

"Ah! Are there any Apaches about? I was hoping to see one."

It was Lt. Fuller's turn to grin. "Not here. But at Fort Bowie, up in the pass, there are a number of Apache Scouts, fairly friendly ones, loitering about."

The mustachioed gentleman looked perturbed. "Damnation! Don't have time to travel up there to see them. This is just a short stop on our way to San Francisco. Why didn't they build the fort closer to the railroad, for passengers' convenience?"

Now the engineering officer looked perturbed at this bumptious man's presumption. "Fort Bowie's a military installation, sir, situated for vantage and defensive position, not for civilian convenience."

"Should be. Our taxes pay for it. How about a real Arizona bad man then? I was hoping my wife could meet one." He jerked a thumb back at a woman who was tentatively stepping onto the platform, adjusting her feathered hat.

Ready to rid himself of this intrusive individual, Second Lt. Walsh pointed at the smaller man in the tapered, Spanish-style, green corduroy suit set off by a red Navajo sash and large felt sombrero standing nearby, seemingly listening to their conversation. "There's one right there. Talk to him."

The passenger touched his derby. "Thank you, sir. I shall."

Motioning his wife to join him, he marched directly to Charles Lummis. "You've been recommended to me, sir, as an authentic Arizona bad man. Don't look much like one, though."

Lummis could see the two young Lieutenants beyond chuckling, watching this fool. "I'm a journalist, actually. But in some quarters, that qualifies me as a ruffian." Charles noticed a commotion at the rear of the second passenger car. "Excuse me, folks. Duty calls."

The newspaperman winked as he tipped his blue-banded sombrero to the tourist and his wife. "No rest for the wicked."

The four officers fell into two rows at the front of the platform, sorting themselves almost unconsciously by rank, with the newsman quickly bringing up the rear.

From the second railroad car a big man in a blue wool tunic with one star in the middle of each shoulder strap and two rows of graduated bullion sewn around them descended the steel steps. Surprisingly, however, the General was dressed more casually for travel in a brown felt, short-brimmed hat with a small screen vent on both sides. Only his leather gauntlet gloves and the ornately inscribed 1860s saber he was wearing gave away his dandyish sartorial preferences.

General Miles is a tall, straight, fine-looking man of 210 pounds, apparently in his early fifties [forty-six actually]. *He has a well-modeled head, high brow, strong eye, clean-cut aquiline nose and firm mouth—an imposing and soldierly figure, all around,* wrote Charles Lummis later in his news dispatch.

"General Miles, I'm Major Beaumont, Commander of Fort Bowie. Welcome, sir, to the Department of Arizona."

"Thank you, Major." General Miles returned the officers' salutes as his aide wrestled his many bags of luggage down the passenger car's steps. "Where's Crook?"

"The General's back at the fort, sir, packing."

"Oh. . . . Guess I would be, too, in his boots."

"I'm sure he'll see you as soon as you arrive, General. Meanwhile, here are Captain Charles Hatfield, Fourth Cavalry, Second Lieutenant Robert Walsh, Fourth Cavalry, and Second Lieutenant Phillip Fuller, Engineer, Second Cavalry. Oh, and Charles Lummis, war correspondent for the *Los Angeles Times*."

General Miles shook hands cordially with all four but focused on Lummis. "Newspaperman." He smiled. "Glad you warned me, Major. They're wilier than the Apaches."

The army men chuckled, but Lummis wasted no time. "Anything you'd care to say, General, as you take over from the famed Apache fighter?"

"Not yet, young man. Let me get my feet on the ground and the lay of this raw land first, then I'll give you my ideas for ending this unbelievably long war. Fair enough?"

Charles Lummis nodded. The General turned to study the last young officer, Second Lieutenant Fuller. "Engineer?"

"Yes, sir"

"Familiar with heliographs?"

"The sun-flashing code system? Not much, sir. That's Signal Corps."

"Well, since we don't have many signal corps officers out here yet, you engineers will have to fill in temporarily. See me later, Lieutenant."

"Yes, sir."

"Gentlemen, this is my aide, Lieutenant Dapray." The Second Lieutenant nodded to the other officers while toting the General's mass of leather luggage toward the platform's edge.

An enlisted man had driven a white painted hospital ambulance around from the front of the train station. A noncom was now afoot, attempting to reposition the six mules pulling it up to the platform. "Back up, mules! Haw!"

Sergeant Ammon Swing cursed as he swatted a lead mule on the backside with his campaign hat. Reverse was not a direction these draught animals were comfortable with, so the husky Sergeant put his shoulder right against the mule's chest and shoved her back in the traces. The mules behind had to step back to get away from this front mule's hooves, and thus the rear door of the army's medical conveyance was slowly pushed back up to the station platform.

Two cavalrymen rode up, pulling along the four officers' mounts. These Privates dismounted, and one held all the horses' reins while the other assisted the General's aide in getting the two officers' luggage into the back of the transport wagon.

General Miles was impatient to get underway to his new command. "Let's go, gentlemen! Daylight's burning!"

Apache Pass, Southeastern Arizona Territory

Apache Pass divided the Chircahua Mountains to the south from the Dos Cabezas Mountains to the north and provided the best route from the east into the Sulphur Springs Valley and on to Tucson. It was tortuous, difficult country for the traveler, with high mountains flanking much of the passageway, snarls of canyons, and a windswept summit more than five thousand feet high—perfect places for an ambush. But this pass offered what easier east-west routes did not—water. Partway through, a spring opened at the foot of a grove of trees. Water gushed from it by the gallons and ran into a pool in the sandy riverbed just below, which remained full even in the dry season. Horses and livestock and weary travelers needed this scarce water on their long journey, which caused a running conflict with the keepers Apache Pass was named after, who also valued that water.

Riding on the front seat next to the driver, General Miles looked up the fourteen-mile trail to the fort near the crest of Apache Pass and spotted a troop of cavalry with their tents pitched among the salt brush and desert broom. Some of the cavalrymen were grooming their horses; others were trying to shave or bathe in several tin tubs. More soldiers were lazing about, sewing clothes or mending gear.

"Which troops are those?"

Riding alongside the General's conveyance, Lt. Fuller spoke up. "My unit, sir. Second Cavalry."

The General squinted into the sun. "Look tired. Why are they camped so far from the fort?"

"No more room at the fort, sir. But there's a well down here at the station. We just came in from a month patrolling the border, Arizona to New Mexico and back. Awful dry out there."

"Any luck?"

Lt. Fuller shook his head. "No sir. Not hide nor hair of any hostile Apaches."

The General almost smiled. "Maybe your luck will change. Where's your Commanding Officer?"

"Up at the fort, sir, briefing General Crook."

"He should be down here, briefing me. I'm in charge now."

Major Beaumont interjected, hoping to head off a dispute. "I'm sure Captain McAdams will, sir, as soon as you get there."

General Miles was curt. "See to it."

THREE

Charles Lummis was the first journalist to christen this vast land "the Southwest," and to coin the phrase—"See America First."

—Mark Thompson, *American Character: The Curious Life of Charles Fletcher Lummis and the Rediscovery of the Southwest*

**Fort Bowie, Army Headquarters,
Southeastern Arizona Territory**

To pass impatient time, Charles Lummis worked on his dispatch about this important change of command, since there was no other news today and he hadn't been able to talk again to the General. Even getting word out was slow, since his writing had to be messengered down to the telegraph at Bowie Station, where it could be wired to Los Angeles. The war correspondent paused to chew the end of his pencil.

Yesterday afternoon the boom of the six-pounder notified us that the ambulance containing the new commander of the Department of Arizona had rounded the bend in the road. In a few minutes more the six mules swung around the corner of the store and trotted up smartly across the sloping parade ground. General Miles crawled out of the inadequate door of the ambulance in front of Major Beaumont's house and shook the kinks out of his legs. General Crook walked up from the office, and the two veterans shook hands unceremoniously. Miles passed most of the afternoon in close conference with General Crook, and this morning there was another powwow,

General Miles gathering up all points as to the situation with which he is now to wrestle. While he and General Crook were talking, the Apache Scouts came over to take their leave. The most prominent and valued ones—Noche, Charley, Dutchy, Stove-Pipe and others—trotted into the office with old Concepción and Lieutenant Maus. They did a good deal of talking, and also had a short speech from General Miles.

He reminded them how much better off they are than the renegades now lying among the mountains of Mexico or the prisoners now in Florida. Every last one of the renegades, he informed them, will be hunted down and taken alive or dead, no matter how long it takes or how much money it costs; so he bade the Scouts behave themselves when they got home. It was a sight to see the Scouts when they came to say farewell to Crook. The common "coffee-coolers" merely shook his hand very effusively, and said good-bye several times over. But the men whom he had trusted and who had proved their efficiency in this campaign were not content with that—they had to hug him.

Apaches fascinated Charles Lummis, with their practical dress and unusual habits. In his youthful travels, the newsman had become an avid student of the Indians of the Southwest and their colorful customs, so much so that he consciously began to embrace the various tribes' ritualistic worship of nature. As he learned more, the Indians' celebration of nature in their religions began to color his writings about the region and its native inhabitants, while his own Protestant upbringing receded into the background.

For Charles Fletcher Lummis, bored with the basic curriculum he had already mastered and interested mainly in whichever "elective" courses managed to catch his attention, had dropped out of Harvard just a few weeks short of his graduation. Writing, however, he was very good at and that combined with this once sickly youth's consuming quest for physical fitness through various college athletic teams, compelled him to set out after three years as an editor of the *Scioto Gazette* in Chillicothe, Ohio, to seek the healthier climes of the Pacific Coast. So Charles walked, with his pet dog and three hundred dollars in gold coins in a waist pouch, across eight Western states and territories, thirty-five hundred miles in four and a half months, with stops along the way to catch up with his luggage and write weekly dispatches about his journey to the *Los Angeles Times*, where a new job as city editor awaited him, provided Lummis ever got there—alive!

He did, and, after another year feverishly building up the *Times*'s circulation to match Los Angeles's rapidly expanding population, Charles needed a break from hurried civilization. He had no trouble talking his Civil War veteran publisher, brevet Lt. Colonel (retired) Harrison Grey Otis, into letting him cover the Apaches' last stand from the battlefield itself.

So here Charles Lummis was, cooling his boot heels in a canvas chair on the front veranda of Major Beaumont's whitewashed frame home.

> *Fort Bowie, headquarters of the cavalry, was founded in 1862 by the California Volunteers. It lies on a rather sharply sloping bench of the mountainside, from which, down through the gap in the hills, one looks across the weird plain to the purple ranges fifty-three miles away. The post stands at an altitude of 4,781 feet and is hemmed in by ranges on every side. Though there is neither fort nor fortification, it is called 'Fort' Bowie. Behind it is the inevitable crag—in this case Helen's Dome—from which a maiden threw herself to escape from the Indians. You know the mountainous country that cannot boast some such legendary cliff is poor indeed. Around the generous plaza stand big, substantial adobes and, at the farthest corner from the entrance, a French-roofed frame building of some pretensions, the residence of Major Beaumont, Commander of the post. Good water is pumped by*

steam power from an adjacent hillside. There are about one hundred soldiers stationed here.

Charles licked the lead tip of his pencil, pondering his description of this isolated place. Should he mention the ice made from the same steam-powered generating plant, which filled their whiskies, cooled their bottled beer, and made their ice cream? No, he wanted Angelenos to think he was roughing it, camping out in the burning desert amongst the savages. If he wrote about Fort Bowie's lawn tennis court, even though it was grassy dirt, rough-surfaced, and angled slightly uphill, his readers wouldn't even believe it. Lummis's thoughts wandered in the midday heat. Wonder what the boys were up to today in the City of the Angels? Murder, land fraud, or gandering bathing beauties at the beach? Something interesting no doubt, exciting. He swatted a horsefly off his ear.

"Mr. Lummis. Sorry to keep you waiting."

Startled out of his reverie, the newspaperman rose to greet the large man in the resplendently gold-braided dress uniform who had just stepped out onto the porch.

"Change of command here, requires all my attention."

"I understand, General, and I thank you beforehand for giving me any of your valuable insight into this endless war with the Apaches."

"We'll see about much insight, yet. What are your observations, Mr. Lummis? You've been here how long?"

"Less than two weeks, sir. . . . Well, so far, it seems to me that here in Arizona, the white people live on the reservations and the Indians occupy the country."

Two officers standing behind him let out startled laughs, but General Miles managed a smile. "You have a keen eye, sir, and a sense of humor to accompany it. I am reluctantly forced to agree with you."

The General stood thinking a moment, evaluating this small impertinent man, a trim one hundred and fifty pounds and five feet, six inches at best in his boots, his reddish skin sunburnt under a large crest of fluffy brown hair. Clean-shaven, too, which wasn't common among men on the frontier. Not a rugged Westerner by any stretch. "Come with me. I'm about to brief my officers on my new strategy to rectify that very situation."

Lummis had been in the large rear room several times before for discussions with General Crook and several of his other higher-ranking officers before Crook departed suddenly, ignominiously. Charles was still struck by the difference in decor between this office and the hallways and the private quarters of Major Beaumont leading to it, which were furnished in modified Victorian style, with dark-patterned, heavy fabricated sofas and chairs, framed family and military photographs of past commands on the walls. No, this back room was the war room and central command of a chain of a dozen forts and smaller army camps throughout the Department of Arizona. General Miles, like General Crook before him, had decided that Ft. Bowie was best situated to serve as headquarters for this campaign.

Brigadier General Nelson Miles walked in to the front of the big room next to a wooden desk and waited until the eyes of all his officers had turned to him and their conversations ceased. Like most famous commanders, Miles was a showman to the tips of his shiny boots and knew well the value of a dramatic pause. He smiled. "Gentlemen. This is going to be the very last Apache campaign, and I expect it to be over by the end of this year, if not sooner."

Nelson Miles paused to let the import of his rash prediction sink in. After twenty-six years of fighting, this brash General expected to end the war with the Apaches within his first year?

"I've requested two thousand more troops be sent, and General Sheridan has given his approval. We will then have six thousand men out here. We will mass overwhelming forces against these renegades and have details posted at every pass, on every trail, beside every waterhole these Apaches have ever used to enter this region, not to mention squads posted at every outlying community that's ever been raided. So the public can see our troops in action and regain their confidence in our protection. We'll have scouting parties of cavalry out crisscrossing Arizona, New Mexico, riding the borderline defensively and aggressively down into Mexico. Sufficient forces will be held in readiness at several of our forts to make punishing strikes at these marauding bands wherever they're located. If we don't capture them, we will chase them for several days for several hundred miles over country suitable for cavalry. Constant pursuit by fresh relays of troops until we wear them down and finish them off. No rest for these renegades. We will find and defeat the wily Apache, gentlemen, this time for good."

Miles's guarantee hung in the hot air as some of his officers looked at each other, nonplussed by their new Commander's announcement: two thousand more troops coming!

"Dammit, where's that orderly?" The big-bodied General slammed his palm down on the hotel bell on the edge of his desk, ringing the brass sharply.

A veteran orderly stuck his head inside the big room, unused yet to the impatient demands of his new boss. "Sir?"

"Whiskey and bitters for everyone. Over some of your desert ice. Quickly, man."

Major Eugene Beaumont stroked his black mustache thoughtfully. "What do you intend to do with the Apache Scouts, General?"

"Disband them." A murmur of disbelief greeted this next startling pronouncement by their new Commander, but General Miles held his hand up.

"I am aware that many of you who have worked closely with these purportedly loyal scouts would disagree with this change. General Crook swore by his Scouts, but neither General Sheridan nor I have ever been comfortably wedded to the idea that it takes an Indian to chase and catch another Indian. I firmly believe that the most fit of our well-trained officers and enlisted men are the fighting equal of any savage, undisciplined Indian on this continent, including these Apaches, and I intend to prove it to the white citizens of America. It is determined pursuits by regular commands that will win the day against the Apache!"

Captain Wirt Davis, a highly experienced Indian fighter commanding F Troop of the Fourth Cavalry, frowned. "That's optimistic thinking, General. I agree that when it comes to actual fighting we can match up with and usually beat the Apaches, man for man. But you mentioned chasing them over terrain 'suitable for cavalry.' In my experience, when the chase gets too hot, the Apaches abandon their horses, run straight up into the mountains, and climb over them, even at night, to get away. They're almost impossible to keep up with in these rough mountains, certainly not on horseback. And when it comes to chasing them, sir, there's not a man among us who can pick up and follow their trail like another Chiricahua can."

"I know that, Captain Davis. That's why we will still use some Indian trackers as our eyes, but they'll mostly be Pimas, Papagos, Yumas, and Wallapais, not Apaches. And only in small groups of three or four scouting for each patrol, not hundreds of them out in front to do most of your fighting for you, such as Crook favored. We will track and chase and fight and win our own battles, gentlemen."

Second Lieutenant Walsh quickly objected. "Sir, those river Indians can't hold a candle to the Apaches when it comes to stamina and skill in scouting. We've seen that time and again in the field."

"Well, they'll just have to do. I want the Wallapais and those other Indians moved in here and the Apache teepees moved out."

Major Beaumont corrected him. "Wickiups, sir."

"Whatever they're called, I want all the Apaches out of this fort and back up to Fort Apache for discharge, immediately.

This is an *intelligence* headquarters, gentlemen, and I don't want *these* Apaches picking up any more of ours."

Looking about the room General Miles saw their hesitancy, the doubt and concern etched upon all his officers' faces. Scowling now, their new commanding officer began to lose patience with their general disapproval of his new strategy.

"General Sheridan and I both think your *friendly* Apache Scouts passed vital information and ammunition along to Geronimo and Naiche and their followers on many occasions when we were close to catching them. So we never did! And God knows *what* your Scouts told Geronimo after he'd promised to surrender to Crook. Probably that he'd be hanged or killed if he was ever caught across our border again, and it sure spooked him, didn't it? Your Apache Scouts might have whispered such nonsense just to protect their jobs! General Sheridan was infuriated when you men were down in the Funnels posing for photographs with those hostile Apaches, already mentally polishing your expected medals and writing your campaign memoirs about how you finally ended the great Apache wars. Then you let Geronimo slip away once more! Right out of your grasp! I have explicit orders *not* to let it happen again! So I will *not* hire any more Chiricahuas to try to capture their own kin, and that's final! It does *not* work!"

Their new Commander's outburst provoked a profound silence among the assembled officers of Fort Bowie. They examined their polished boots, the ceiling of the General's office, and the sweat gathered around each other's starched collars as they cogitated upon their shared blame for letting the war leader of the last wild Apaches escape their army's clutches one more time. The smell of their collective failure was almost palpable.

Thankfully the door opened and two orderlies carrying trays of full tumblers started to enter but hesitated in the stifling stillness.

"Ah! Our drinks. Pass them," ordered the General.

The orderlies circulated, passing out short glasses of the army officers' daily drink—a mixture of whiskey, water, and bitters, with a spoonful of sugar. Their new Commander took a pointer handed to him by his aide, Lt. Dapray, and moved to a large map of Arizona on the wall behind the desk, with a number of locations circled in red.

"One of the things that struck me immediately upon arrival to this frontier is the general ineffectiveness of our communications system. Our telegraph is often slow and unreliable, the Apaches having cut the lines or chopped down the poles, or its operators are often absent. A quarter of the time the lines aren't even operating! So, we're going to set up and operate a new system exclusively for military communications. Heliographs! *Helios*, Greek for 'sun,' wedded to *grapho*, meaning 'I write'—sun writers.

When I was in charge of the Cantonment on the Yellowstone, now Fort Keogh, Montana, we experimented with this British heliograph equipment the Signal Corps had purchased but was not using. I established the first signal line in this country, from Fort Keogh to Fort Custer. Two years ago we set up one of these sun-flashing devices on Mount Hood, fifty miles from Vancouver Barracks, and communicated quite successfully between it and most of the other outposts in my command. I understand there was some preliminary use of the equipment between forts out here a few years ago, but it was discontinued?"

Major Beaumont answered. "Yes sir, some heliographs were shipped out in 1882, and several of our officers, including Lt. Maus here, and enlisted men were trained to use them. They experimented flashing messages between here and several of the camps, Price and Fort Grant, that summer."

General Miles frowned. "But you stopped using them. Why?"

The Major shook his head. "I'm not sure."

Lt. Marion Maus spoke up. "They worked all right, General, but we were nearly at war with our own Apache Scouts over the killing of that Apache medicine man, the Dreamer, at Cibecue the summer before. General Crook was too busy trying to calm the Apaches still on the reservations and chasing other renegades down south to pay much attention to our field tests. I can't speak for him, but he may have felt the mirrors tied up too many soldiers when he could just telegraph messages between the forts and camps. I don't know. But we had our hands full with hostiles right then and just stopped using the mirrors after a while."

"Well, that will change, along with many other former policies around here. Immediately." General Miles's eyes narrowed. "I strongly believe in the heliograph's usefulness, and General Sheridan has authorized our first full-scale test of this equipment under wartime conditions. General Hazen of the Signal Corps has cooperated by sending out eleven operators and a dozen heliographs from Virginia. They should be arriving shortly, and I have placed Lt. Fuller, our engineering officer, Second Cavalry, in charge of them. More heliographs will be sent just as soon as we can round them up from our forts and get new operators trained."

The General paused to move his pointer around the red circles on his map. "We will immediately begin setting up fourteen observation posts on these mountaintops in middle and southern Arizona Territory, areas the Apaches have always roamed. Each lookout post will be staffed by five men, possibly up to eight, headed by a Sergeant and one of these Corporals from the Signal Corps to operate the equipment. They will have water and provisions stored with them to last thirty days, in case of siege."

Several officers smiled at each other over their new Commander's naïveté. No small, unfortified army position could hold out against these determined warriors for three days, let alone thirty, and Apaches were too restless to stay put anywhere for a month anyway.

"Their duty will be to pass along messages and keep a sharp eye out for any Apaches passing below their position. With the marine binoculars and telescopes we're also getting, they should be able to scout out to thirty miles, surrounding. That way we can keep all our troop movements sorted out and our patrols in the field much better apprised of where the Apaches actually are and what they're up to. It is my aim, gentlemen, to contain these renegades within this ring of mirrors until we catch them, or at least keep them from broaching its flashing perimeters with hostile intent."

Another young Second Lieutenant raised his hand. "Sir, is it possible these daylight messages, that anyone can see, might be compromised, too?"

"Not unless you teach the Apaches to read Morse code, Lieutenant."

Stifled laughter. General Miles smiled, too. "Signal Corps field tests revealed that an observer six miles away could not even see these flashes if he were more than fifty yards on either side of exact aim. So secrecy and the speed of the code operators are our weapons with this. Seriously, gentlemen, once we get our lookouts accurately positioned and the system operating well, we're going to expand to another thirteen posts across New Mexico. Lieutenant Dravo of the Sixth Cavalry will be responsible for these others, which we're trying to suitably position right now. Another class of operators is training back at Fort Meyer, and more heliographs and telescopes are being rounded up from our other forts. This is going to be a major field test of our new communications system, gentlemen, which will make newspaper headlines and be of burning interest to all the rest of the world's armies, if it works as well as I already know it can. Geronimo will see us up on these mountaintops he favors, near everywhere he likes to raid, watching him, flashing word of his whereabouts, and he will become very wary about continuing to attack our American citizens. The huge number of fresh troops on their way out to join us, this secure new system of passing messages, and determined pursuit by our regular troops are going to finish off these fierce Apaches, gentlemen, soon. I'm staking my military reputation upon it."

"May I ask a question, General?"

"Certainly, Mr. Lummis. I'd welcome the thoughts of a professional newspaperman."

"This sun-flashing system works only in daylight, right?"

"The mirrors need sunlight to work, yes."

"What do you do at night then?"

"Use signal lanterns, Mr. Lummis. But we will have to test them to see if the lights can be picked up as well and from as long a distance as our daytime flashes. A heliograph supposedly works under full moonlight on cloudless nights, too, but I'm wary of that claim until I see it tested myself."

Lt. Britton Davis interjected. "Apaches don't like to travel much at night, sir, unless it's under a full moon, when they can see better. Like to do their horse stealing then. Nighttime's normally too dangerous; snakes are out, and Apaches have lots of superstitions about the night. So we won't be sighting them after dark or have much need for night communications."

"Even better. These observation details will be rotated every month, with two weeks off for each group to resupply back at a fort before going out again to a different outpost, to relieve boredom. So you infantry commanders start going through your troop rosters to pick out likely candidates. Lieutenant Fuller will begin classes for some of our more trainable soldiers, for we'll need more men familiar with Morse code quickly, as relief operators. Our central heliograph station will be up behind here on Bowie Peak, receiving messages from five other lookouts eventually. Major Beaumont will be in charge of coordinating all the information coming in and keeping the whole system operating properly here, while I am out touring our forts, keeping on top of things."

The journalist was still thinking. "What about carrier pigeons, General? Sent directly from your mounted patrols with the Apaches' latest whereabouts?"

"We tried using pigeons in the Red River campaigns back in '74–'75. They didn't work well."

"Why not?"

"Hawks ate them, Mr. Lummis. There are too many hunters out here that enjoy pigeon. Messenger birds are much more effective over water than across land. Navy uses them sometimes. For now, a couple troopers will be sent off from a patrol passing by any of our observation posts to get the latest intelligence from the field into our network and back here quickly to Bowie. And the Apaches will find our new communications system impossible to disrupt. No wires to cut. Any more questions?"

Lummis and some of the officers shook their heads. General Miles, served last, raised his glass and changed his disputatious tone. "Gentlemen. I want to compliment you on the hard, dangerous work you've already done to rid this wild country of its Indian scourge. I drink to your renewed vigor and enthusiasm for what I guarantee will be the last campaign against these Apaches. I have been ordered by General Sheridan to make 'active and prominent use' of regular troops in this most difficult task, and you will accomplish it. Geronimo and his feared kin will soon cease to be a problem to the good, honest citizens of this vast territory, and this damnably long war will finally be over. And you are the very men who will see to that and thereby be immortalized in American history for your magnificent achievement."

Eyes blazing with righteousness, General Miles scanned the room, looking every one of his fighting men bang in the eye. "To God's luck on your mission and your everlasting good health."

Caught up in the portentous moment, these battle-hardened army officers hesitated for the merest of seconds, then drained their glasses to the very bottoms.

Fort Bowie was abustle early next morning with orders ringing out, soldiers hurrying to pick up rations and more ammunition before heading out to their new postings. General Crook had left late yesterday and this new Commanding Officer was already shaking up their encampment, dismissing the Apache Scouts, bringing out two thousand more soldiers, installing a newfangled communications system, and about to issue new field orders. The veterans wisely knew to obey General Miles now, even with a feigned show of enthusiasm, until the dust settled and the U.S. Army slipped back into its simple, time-honored method of subjugating Indians—pursue and shoot!

Sgt. Swing stepped into the duty Sergeant's small office in one of their adobe buildings. Behind a battered desk rested a burly noncom with hands folded over his big belly. The flies weren't even moving in this sparsely furnished room, compared to all the dust and noise being raised next door in the larger quartermaster's quarters.

"Whatcha got for me, Capers?"

The older noncom eyed his leaner, more active counterpart through smudged spectacles. "Just a little shit, do-nothin' detail. Guardin' one of General Miles's new heliograph stations." Sgt. Capers shuffled some papers and pulled one from the pile.

"Yours is Observation Post Number Four, atop Square Mountain, across the Sulphur Springs Valley, over towards Tombstone."

"Get to pick my men?"

"Lieutenant Davis already done that for yah."

"So you're sweepin' out the fort's trash, right into my detail. Good-bye boys and good riddance!"

The overweight lifer peered owlishly at him. "We resent you slandering our fine army manhood." Sgt. Capers studied his duty sheet again.

"You got Corporal Heintz, big German boy from Texas to help tote your supplies up and down that mountain; Private Takins, veteran from the Carolinas; Corporal Bobyne, signal corpsman to run your new sun flasher; and Private Mullin, kid enlistee just arrived for further training, which I know you'll see to."

Sgt. Swing just looked at him. These lifers were mostly all alike, shrewd veterans who worked the army's system to wangle easier jobs indoors rather than sweating out in the sun, supervising work details or, worse, actually chasing and fighting Indians. "Dandy."

Sgt. Capers smiled. "I could assign a monkey to this easy duty, Swing. All you boys got to do is sit up on that mountain, watching for Apaches, flashing signals, and hopin' it don't rain too hard. The healthy outdoor life! Sleepin' late and playin' cards all night! Beats taking guff from green Lieutenants in here every goddamned day."

Sergeant Swing took the paper the Sergeant handed him. "Thanks for the favor, Capers."

The duty Sergeant flashed big, tobacco-stained teeth. "Remember me in your will."

Loaded down like a mule with extra ammunition belts in his arms, empty canteens dangling from his shoulders, and a wool blanket draped around his neck, courtesy of the quartermaster, the Sergeant didn't hear his name being called as he crossed the parade ground. A second shout got his attention, and he turned to see Major Beaumont waving him over to the veranda of his home. Sgt. Swing shifted his gear and marched over. Then he also saw their new General sipping coffee in the deeper shade of the French roof and slowed perceptibly as he neared. Oh-oh.

"General, I want you to meet Sergeant Swing, one of the finest white Scouts in this whole territory."

Even with his hands full, the First Sergeant attempted a salute.

"Umm, regular army?"

"Yes he is, General." The Major enjoyed showing off his best soldiers. "Sgt. Swing rode with Wirt Davis and the Fourth Cavalry chasing Geronimo all over hell and gone last summer. Killed a couple Apaches himself."

Nelson Miles came to attention. "Excellent!"

Sgt. Ammon Swing shook his head. "Just shot one, wounded another. But he got me, too."

The General's eyes gleamed in the veranda's shade. "Still. Army had more fighters like you, Swing, these wild Apaches would have ceased to be such an ass ache years ago."

The Sergeant of Scouts almost smiled. "They're awful hard to locate, General. But once you finally catch up with 'em, if you can tempt 'em into fighting, you got a fair chance of beating 'em. Moment the odds swing out of their favor, though, they scatter like quail, boxing the compass. Hunting Apaches is very aggravating, General, like trying to sip hot soup. You're bound to get burned."

General Miles snorted. "Hot soup. Put enough Scouts like you on their trail, Sergeant, we'll touch the matches to their moccasins. And then see if they can stand the heat."

Rather than disagreeing with his new Commanding General, Sgt. Swing slowly nodded. Major Beaumont did smile as General Miles waved the noncom off about his business.

"More good luck to you, Sergeant."

FOUR

Those a yas drinkin' to forget, *pay in advance!*

—Roscoe Pertwee, Proprietor

Dos Cabezas Trading Post, Sulphur Springs Valley, Southeastern Arizona Territory

The trader's big adobe sat in the shade of some tall cottonwoods, which were themselves in the shade of a cliff facing underneath the distinctive eight-thousand-foot dual peaks in the Dos Cabezas (Two Heads) Mountains. Well-fortified with mud-brick walls twenty-five inches thick, capable of stopping any bullet, the depot's smaller back bedrooms were used by the occupants, the trader and his Mexican families of employees, while a big kitchen/dining room served meals at all hours to travelers passing on the stage road. For this was a main stage stop on the exceedingly dangerous route through the San Simon Valley bordering New Mexico Territory to the east, on through the infamous, six-mile Apache Pass just south.

This mail route then ran over the Sulphur Springs Valley across to Dragoon Wash, where Butterfield's Overland Mail trail wound through the canyons between the Rincon and Whetstone Mountains west to Old Tucson. This was the old "Oxbow Route," one of two feasible stage trails through the lower southwest to California, starting in either St. Louis or Memphis and running down through Texas. It was shortest distance between Tucson and the settlements east along the Rio Grande.

Stein's Pass, on the western boundary of New Mexico Territory; San Simon; Apache Pass; Dos Cabezas; Ewell's Pass; Dragoon Springs; San Pedro River; and Cienega Springs were the running line of sixteen Wells Fargo stage stops, after it took over Butterfield Overland's operations in 1860, through southern Arizona Territory all the way over to Yuma on the California border.

Apaches attacked every stage stop, repeatedly. The Chiricahua Apaches especially, opposed these intrusions into their sovereignty, and the station at Dos Cabezas bore the brunt of their anger. It had closed any number of times during the long, hard-fought years of the Apache wars, but always reopened for business when more brave storekeepers and stockmen could be recruited to refurbish and resupply the bullet-pocked premises. Darker stains on its plastered mud walls were testament to the valor of its former proprietors, some of whom died fighting to live there. Even the ghosts at Dos Cabezas station were hostile and the Apaches knew it.

The main front room through the big wooden doors was jammed to its twelve-foot ceiling with supplies, foodstuffs, clothing, equipment, and armaments of all types, new and used, for ranchers in the valley. The trader's served as the mailbox for the neighborhood, where orders for more unusual goods and sundries could be sent on to Tucson or picked up off the stagecoach several times a week. Some of the Wells Fargo stage stops had rooms to rent to overnight guests, but not Dos Cabezas, for travelers through this stretch of hostile desert generally didn't linger longer than a quick meal, a dollar per.

Accommodations were safer at Ft. Bowie, a half day's stagecoach ride away, although coaches didn't stop there overnight either, unless for repairs or bad weather. Most travelers never even went to the Fort but stopped instead at Bowie Station nearby to meet a train.

The coming of the Southern Pacific Railroad to Tucson from California in March of 1880 substantially altered patterns of business in the Southwest, even more so when the line was extended east into New Mexico and then Texas later in 1881. Instead of eight exhausting, bone-jarring days in a stagecoach, passengers could now ride from El Paso to Los Angeles in relative comfort in only three, and for much less money. Mail and freight were shipped faster and much cheaper by rail, too, but stages and wagons were still needed to meet the train at its fewer depots to move freight and people on to more remote towns like Tombstone.

The Wells Fargo stage stations suffered from the railroad's new competition, and some of the fifteen stage stops across Arizona Territory had already closed. Dos Cabezas was still open, though, doing business with scattered ranchers and passing patrols from the big Forts Bowie and Huachuca, as well as with people moving between the bigger towns of Tombstone and Douglas, down on the border in the southeastern corner of this vast territory. Roscoe Pertwee, the trader, had gotten a strong monetary whiff of these winds of change blowing down from military headquarters and the railroad north of him and didn't like what he smelled.

The dirt rooftop at the trader's was reached through an interior stairway in the big kitchen or by a trapdoor with a ladder in the bigger bedroom. Up top was a four-foot-high parapet containing loopholes, which were used by all the inhabitants when under attack. Twenty-four hours a day a guard kept watch for hostiles from atop the outpost, warning the inhabitants by bell when he spotted any Indians nearby to drop whatever they were doing and prepare to fight. This round-the-clock sentry system had served the present trader well, for he suffered only a few stock losses and scared deserters among his changing cast of defenders during the decreasing Apache raids of the past few years.

Still, a candle of mourning always burned in the *campo santo*, the temporary mortuary further out back, where the bodies of those not alert or quick or lucky enough to survive were held until they could be interred in the little cemetery next to it. The residents of Dos Cabezas saw that tiny flame flickering out there every night and remembered to beware.

Out back of the kitchen was another storehouse for larger goods and a smokehouse hung with heavy beams, where they cured hams and bacon from the pigs the trader bought from or slaughtered for the area's ranchers. The Apaches did in the pigs, too, and any perambulating pincushions that didn't have their arrows pulled and wounds doctored after their raids were butchered immediately. A long funereal smoke from the smokehouse chimney often meant that Indians had been taking target practice on the livestock again. Long strips of salted beef were always drying for jerky from ropes stretched near the smokehouse's ceiling, to keep them out of reach of the trader's dogs, several of whom had become champion leapers to snatch an occasional treat.

Meals offered to travelers and residents alike by the trader's Mexican cooks were standard for the region—pork or beef seasoned with chiles to the customer's taste, depending upon one's tolerance to mouth fire. Red beans, biscuits, and black coffee completed the fare, sometimes supplemented with onions or potatoes freighted in from San Diego.

The water supply for the trading post was a small creek, which ran down out of the mountains one hundred feet south. It was often dry, though, so they depended mostly on a well dug sixty feet deep, a short distance from the smokehouse, from which sweet water was cranked up in a large wooden bucket by a mule attached to the end of a long rope or hand-cranked by a strong man if necessary. Water was stored inside in kegs to keep the residents hydrated during a fight, but they couldn't sustain a long siege without making dangerous runs outside to the well in the dark. As always in hot, dry Arizona, water was the scarce element that alone made ranching and sheer survival possible.

The log corrals next to the dwelling to the south were home to the mules and stage horse teams, and these were what the Apaches really prized, the first things they attempted to steal on their periodic breakouts from San Carlos. The trader had lost many horses, even with sharp-eyed guards posted up on his roof with rifles through the long nights. But that was just the cost of doing business in these perilous parts, and the trader passed along the cost of restocking his animals through his heavily marked-up goods. Right now, late April of 1886, with so many troops pouring in to defend the few hardy settlers still risking residing in southern Arizona, business at the trading post was better than ever. His saddlery also made money repairing the locals' leather tack and the stage line's equipment. Every possible way to make money besides printing his own, Roscoe Pertwee had investigated and made at least a small profit from. He wasn't a man to let a nickel escape his grasp.

Now Pertwee chanced spending more money to expand those outside corrals to shelter passing cavalry mounts. This sunny spring afternoon, his Mexican handyman was even daubing a fresh coat of mud over the cracks and bullet holes garlanding the front entrance. For hospitality's sake.

Two details of soldiers had stopped to rest on the march out from Ft. Bowie. A couple younger men fed handfuls of grass to the mules in the new side corral, across from the blacksmith shop, where an anvil was being banged on by a sweating Mexican. Several of their fellows had a blanket down in the storeroom's shade out back. The riffling of a deck sounded the call to cards for soldiers too lazy for more active recreation.

A Second Lieutenant idled in a cottonwood's shade, other side of the back buildings from his men. A bit of a dandy in his dark blue flannel officer's blouse, the two silver bars of his rank flashed on his shoulders when the afternoon sun caught their shine. Lt. Philip Fuller used a wet rag to scrub dirt off his black riding boots into which his sky blue wool trousers were tucked.

No room for a tin of polish in his pack, but one could substitute spit and elbow grease to keep up appearances. This blond shavetail was on his first assignment after graduating from West Point, and the giveaway was the brown, linen-covered cork summer helmet he wore so jauntily. Seasoned field officers quickly dispensed with these hard hats for lighter gray felt, wider-brimmed campaign hats that soaked up their sweat and offered more shelter from a mean sun.

Lieutenant Fuller watched from under his helmet as a Sergeant walked out of the store. The private on guard, leaning on his rifle, spoke to the noncom and turned to point his finger in the officer's direction. Sgt. Ammon Swing nodded and limped over.

The Second Lieutenant noted the hitch in his stride, the crossed arrows of his collar insignia, indicating the wearer was with the Indian Scouts. "How's the leg, Sergeant?"

"On the mend, sir."

"Observation duty should be good for you then. Give that wound time to heal."

Sgt. Swing's graying mustache matched the colors in his still-full head of hair, and he straightened it out with his fingers as he eyed this fuzz-chinned officer, calculating how much familiarity he should risk with this young pup. "Beats marchin' after Apaches halfway across Mexico."

"Indeed!" Lt. Fuller laughed. "I've made arrangements with this trader for you to ride one of his horses over to your outpost. Just have the people there send the mount back with the first empty supply wagon. We're lucky; we can come down for our supplies right here, from up in these mountains, but you boys are just too far away."

The Lieutenant passed over the canteen water he'd been using to clean his new boots, and his noncom relaxed enough to take a swallow. "*Good*," thought Sgt. Swing. This shavetail wanted to be a pal instead of an aggravation. It was always wise to be cautious with officers fresh from West Point, though. They were usually too full of beans and gold braid and horseshit regulations to be trusted. If one weren't careful, they could easily issue some dumb-ass order and get you killed.

"Square Mountain's only a day's ride. You'll take your mules down to Cox's ranch several times a week for your food and water. First couple wagonloads from the trader's here will be full—tents and supplies and ammunition and rations. Enough food and water's supposed to be stockpiled for thirty days, in case you get attacked. But you know army quartermasters, Swing. It may take months before you get that many supplies up your mountain."

"Yes, sir, I do. Thanks for the ride."

"You earned it, Sergeant." The Second Lieutenant studied his second-in-command in this godforsaken wasteland. Wrinkles around Swing's eyes told only a little of how much this seasoned Indian fighter had seen and done. "You rode with Captain Davis and the Fourth, chasing Geronimo all over Chihuahua last summer, didn't you? How many Apaches did you kill?"

The Sergeant gave him a long look. Even this new officer had heard about his fight. "One. Wounded another, but he got me, too."

Lt. Fuller was distracted by some loud talk from behind the trader's. "Damnation! I will not have my men getting liquored up while on duty!"

Sgt. Swing followed the Lieutenant's angry glare over to the rear of the general store, where several army men were pushing to get a place in front of a wood plank resting between two big barrels. The trader had just placed it down to indicate his outdoor bar was open for refreshment.

Turning back to his officer, Sgt. Swing fought to suppress a smile. "Not my place to give advice, sir, but I'd let 'em have a coupla snorts before supper. They'll sleep it off. These boys are gonna be a long time between drinks up on these mountains."

The newly minted Lieutenant eyed his noncom. "Probably fancy one yourself, Sergeant?"

Now it was Ammon Swing's eyes that gleamed. "Crossed my mind. You might even think about packin' a bottle a nose paint along yourself, Lieutenant. These cold spring nights."

The former West Point cadet gave his much older Scout Sergeant a hard look. Had he pressed familiarity too far? Finally the young man broke into a small smile.

"For medicinal purposes."

Sgt. Swing nodded. "Little somethun' for the snakebite."

"Stop yer shovin' or none a yas'll get served!"

The curly-haired trader with the red beard pushed back the soldiers crowding against the plank bar, tipping the big wooden barrels toward the bartender and almost crushing him and his assistant against the adobe back wall. Roscoe Pertwee was as broad as one of his barrels and just as hard as the nails in it. The liquor business was by far his most profitable, and he rarely missed a chance to squeeze another four bits from it. Hence, his makeshift bar was open well before the sun set this day.

His Mexican assistant, arms full of glass bottles he was stocking on the shelves set into the post's back wall, nervously eyed the thirsty men pressing toward him under their broad felt hats, but his boss was having none of it. "Hold your mules, boys! Plenty refreshment for all."

The fittest of the enlisted men, who had managed to push his way front and center, jabbed at a bottle of orange-colored liquor Sancho was hugging. "Gimme a bottle a that Indian firewater!"

"Four dollars." The price quieted them all down, quickly. "Greenbacks. Three for silver."

Corporal Hengesbaugh couldn't believe it. "What? That's robbery!"

Pertwee glared at his first customer. "You're lucky I'm riskin' sellin' to you atall. It's il-legal to sell spirits to army boys. President Hayes got that damned law passed back in '81, as I'm sure you remember. I might get arrested."

A thin, longer-haired soldier, Private Slivers, pitched in his two cents' worth. "Sales only prohibited at the forts!"

Corporal Hengesbaugh pulled rank. "Drinks oughta be on the house, protection we're providin'. We're the only armed authority in these parts, mister!"

Pertwee stood his ground, stroking his beard. "'Cept the Apaches. That's why mescal's four dollars a bottle. Delivery's a little occasional." A thin smile appeared amongst his whiskers. "Pay or drift, Corporal."

Looking about at his thirsty companions and seeing no support, the Corporal licked his dry lips. He wanted that first drink. "Damn! Double shot then."

The trader pulled a bottle of his cheapest, with a grizzly bear on the label, off the shelf and uncorked it. With its neck over a glass, Pertwee hesitated. "Four bits."

The Corporal slapped down his fifty-cent piece, took his glassful, and groused off to one of the rickety apple-crate chairs and wooden stools that served as furniture in this backyard bar. Shouting their orders and pulling their money, the others crowded forward to a place at the plank.

Watching their whiskey hunger take hold, Lieutenant Fuller looked at Sgt. Swing, then clasped the veteran's elbow and the two leaders walked over to join their men's revelry. The army's normal drinking hour before supper would extend a little longer this warm afternoon.

Inside the trading post's front room, supplies were stacked about in open crates. This general store stocked mostly canned goods and sacks of staples, but the walls and corners held its luxuries: small plows and farm implements, saws, shovels, axes and hoes. Dirty Navajo rugs and animal skins were nailed to the *vegas*, the poles which supported the thick dirt roof, while loaded rifles and revolvers dangled from pegs, ready for quick use in a fight. Felt hats and a few sombreros were ready to be worn, too, or already had been, and Pertwee had even tacked up some Apache bows, their four feet of juniper or walnut wood wrapped in sinew for strength, with bundles of reed arrows left behind by discouraged or deceased raiders tied to them.

Corporal Bobyne and Private Takins strolled into this gloomy mess of trade goods, drinks in hand. Enlisted men could idle away hours like nobody's business, and these two took their sweet time fingering goods they couldn't afford, until Bobyne walked over to the counter where a half-Mexican teenager slouched behind a metal cash register.

She'd been watching them like a sly cat. A row of *cuchillos*, Mexican long knives with inlaid handles, were stuck right into the wooden counter by their sharp points, next to a big glass jar of souse, pickled hog's heads and feet.

"I'll have a can of peaches, an' one tin of oysters and one of sardines. Please."

The girl moved off to fill his order. Takins sidled over to play with the knives, tipping them back and forth in the wood, testing the temper of the steel blades. "Where'd you learn this code stuff, Johnny Paw?"

Bobyne pulled a *cuchillo* from the counter, checking the sharpness of the blade with his forefinger.

"Signal Corps School, Fort Myer, Virginia. I had practice as a telegrapher before joining up to learn this advanced system. They told us we're the regular army's first 'field specialists.' Heliographs are the newest thing in long-distance, wireless communication, soldier. You'll see."

Takins nodded. "Sweet deal. Better pay and telegraphers get mustered in as Corporals."

The veteran turned to the girl, who came back to ring up the food tins. "Gimme a handful of them Mexican Puros."

She took them from a cigar box beneath the business's embroidered motto tacked on the wall: "In God We Trust. All Others Cash." The Private tucked them into the breast pocket of his grimy infantry blouse, then helped himself to some kitchen matches from a box on the counter and lit one up to smoke inside. Everything about this soldier was dirty, from his long hair to his fingernails, and he smelled as bad as his cheap cigar. Between puffs he nodded at the new Corporal paying for his foodstuffs. "Ol' Virginnie. That's why you like seafood."

Satisfied with his smoke, Takins grinned at the girl. "And a sack of them horehound drops. Pleeease." He bounced a silver dollar on the counter like a big spender, took the small bag of candy the teenager passed over, plopped a couple into his mouth while still smoking. He made a show of offering the sack to Bobyne, who took a candy, and to the girl, who didn't.

"Ever sneak off from yer mama for a walk in the moonlight, sweetie?"

"No." The mixed-blood flicked her fingers back at the glass jars of candy on the shelf behind her. "I get all the candy I want, *Señor*."

"Betcha do, girlie. Me, too." Takins chuckled, clapped the Corporal on the back as he ushered the spit and polished young soldier toward the front door.

"Stick with me, kid, an' I'll teach you how this man's army really works. Maybe you an' me'll even be bunkies."

As he pulled from the older man's embrace, Corporal Bobyne's expression revealed he wasn't real sure about that!

As the two enlistees strolled out the front doors, Bobyne paused to ladle water from a Papago *olla*, a five-gallon pottery jug sweating under the shade of the porch roof. The movement of air and evaporation kept the water inside it cool. He started to drink, then noticed a string of what looked like dried apples dangling from a *vega* nearby. The Corporal squinted, motioned with his gourd dipper.

"What're those?"

"Ears. Warning to any more Apaches wantin' ta try their luck attackin' this tradin' post. They'll wind up collected on a string like their ancestors and have to walk the spirit world mutilated and dishonored. Mexican government used to pay a bounty for 'em, but that ended when the hunters started harvestin' Mexicans, too. Them ears are bad medicine, hombre." The Southerner took the grotesque string of trophies in one hand to offer it to the Easterner.

"Feel?"

Corporal Bobyne did not want to touch dried human flesh. "My God, that's barbaric."

"Tain't nothin' unusual out here. Folks have been collectin' Apache ears for a hundred years." Takins chuckled. "Wait till Mister Apache gets aholt a you with his knife."

He tousled the recruit's hair. "You'll go bare across the top a yer head quick, and won't live long to tell the tale. Cherry-cows like to tie your pretty hair to their lances, just like some of us whites collect their ears."

Bobyne shook his head. "Biblical. Eye for an eye."

The Southerner just nodded. And then grinned.

The two soldiers were distracted then, as Troop D of the Fourth Cavalry trotted up the dusty road from the south. Forty men on horseback, led by Captain Charles Hatfield and Second Lieutenant Robert Walsh, slowed to a walk up to the trader's.

C.A.P. Hatfield looked over the familiar surroundings. "May as well camp here tonight. Give these horses a half day's extra rest."

His Lieutenant smiled agreeably. "Men are always a little butt-sprung till they get used to the saddle again."

The Captain nodded, wiping dust from his mustache with his neckerchief. Lt. Walsh gestured toward the half dozen other soldiers lounging around the makeshift bar behind the store, obviously drinking. "Shall we allow the men a bit of imbibing, sir? After their work's done, a course?"

Now his commanding officer smiled. "Not many chances for a drink in this hot, heathen country."

The men were listening, awaiting the order to dismount, and a rumble of approval rolled back through the pairs of horsemen.

"Cavalry dismount! See to your horses first!"

As the two officers and ass-weary enlisted men swung from their saddles, young Lt. Fuller strode forward, saluting his ranking officers. "Captain Hatfield! Lieutenant Walsh! Welcome to Paradise!"

Three mismatched tumblers of cheap whiskey clinked against the fading afternoon sun where the officers stood, away from the raucous scene that had developed about the backyard bar. Several of the soldiers teased Pertwee's pet billygoat, which bounced about excitedly, trying to butt the men aggravating it.

"Gentlemen, here's to the endless glory of yet another Apache campaign. Let's hope it's our goddamned last." The Captain drank his sour mash halfway off, coughed part of it back up. "Damn, that's vile whiskey!"

"I'll drink to that," agreed Lt. Walsh.

They did. But their newest Second Lieutenant couldn't let such sarcasm pass without an addendum. "Seriously, sir, I think this new heliograph system is going to aid us immensely. The General's right: This may well be the last Apache campaign. Please, let me show you how."

The officers rose to sip and stroll past two Wallapai Indians squatting nearby. The Scouts' blue army blouses were turned inside out to show only the gray lining, the better to disguise themselves against a dusty landscape. These "river" Indians also wore headbands of red flannel to distinguish themselves to soldiers as "friendlies" and, hopefully, not get shot. One of the Wallapais ran his hand over his smooth face, and finding a single stray hair on his chin, pinched and pulled it with a small pair of steel tweezers he'd gotten somewhere—the Indian equivalent of shaving. His companion had gotten a bucket of creek water and was working up soap in it made from yucca roots, with which he was carefully washing his long black hair.

The officers ignored the Indians as they walked to a big cottonwood under which Lt. Fuller had a signalman set up the new communications equipment: the sun mirror on its wooden tripod and the shutter screen on another tripod that was planted just in front of the mirror.

His demonstration hadn't started, however, when the officers saw several more Indians on horseback leading in six more cavalrymen and a dark blue, six-mule–drawn wagon with golden army crossed swords painted on either side. The wagon had squeaked its iron wheel hubs down the same trail east from Ft. Bowie they themselves had recently arrived on. And there on the inside, second seat of the Quartermaster's wagon, sat Brigadier General Nelson Miles.

Captain Hatfield recovered from his surprise. "General Miles! What are you doing here, sir?"

"Touring our fortifications." The General swung down from inside his pack wagon to stretch his stiff limbs. He was dressed less formally today in his field uniform, regular officer's blue tunic, and sky blue trousers, minus his favored gold braid and steel saber.

"Why didn't you tell me, General? We could have accompanied you on your tour, provided better for your comfort and safety."

"Lieutenant Maus and this small detail will suffice. Secrecy will provide our safety, Captain. There's still too many Apaches around our forts scouting us instead of their hostile relatives, and the less they know about our plans and my movements, the better I like it." The General turned to gesture to his twelve-man escort.

"Find a campsite, Lieutenant. Then come join us."

"Yes, sir." First Lieutenant Marion P. Maus issued orders and turned toward the clump of big cottonwoods up the dry wash, his cavalry detail following. As the army wagon turned back, Charles Lummis also swung down from his front seat to join the small coterie of officers. In tan pants, white embroidered shirt, and soiled gray sombrero, the journalist provoked stares from the officers, wondering what this *gringo* was doing along for the ride?

General Miles eyed the commotion over at the trader's outdoor bar, which was calming down now that a few men had noticed their new Commanding Officer's arrival.

"Men fortifying themselves for a long ride, Captain?"

Capt. Hatfield looked a bit sheepish. "Long time between drinks, sir."

The General nodded. "Mister Lummis, Lieutenant Maus and I could probably use a drink ourselves. Cut this dust."

The Cavalry Captain turned to his adjutant. "Get them whiskies."

The General turned his attention to the heliograph nearby. "What's this set up here for?"

"Uh, little demonstration for these gentlemen, General. How we're going to use the heliograph all across the territory," offered Lt. Fuller.

"Fine. Proceed."

Whiskey loosening his tongue, the young West Pointer seized the opportunity to show off his new knowledge to his superiors. "Gentlemen. I've just been reading that the heliograph was invented in the 1860s by Sir Henry Manse as a means of military communication and was first used by the British in India in 1873, in climate and terrain similar to ours here. Our Signal Corps began improving the Brits' equipment at Fort Whipple, Virginia, about four years after that. So here it is, the newest system of frontier communications!"

The green officer almost strutted in front of his new equipment. "All fourteen of the General's observation posts should be up across Arizona by June, and we expect to have thirteen more lookouts strung across New Mexico Territory by sometime in July. We'll then be able to scout the Indians from up high in these mountains and relay that intelligence rapidly down to you fellows in the field, ten to twelve words a minute. Show them, Corporal."

Corporal Hengesbaugh had his mirror aimed properly with the lowering sun and worked the metal shutter's crank bar rapidly, opening and closing the black-painted metal leaves to reveal the long and short flashes of Mr. Morse's famous code—dot/dash/dot.

The cavalry officers sipped and watched, restraining their enthusiasm as Lt. Fuller continued. "Working range of our heliograph's roughly thirty miles, further on a clear day. Signal Corps trials have shown we can flash a thirty-word message four hundred miles over this new system within four hours."

Captain Hatfield lit a cheroot, offering some to his fellow officers. "Faster communication's all well and good, Fuller, but you've got to find the goddamned Apaches first. Just as soon as these renegades murder some more ranchers and steal enough horses and guns to get properly reequipped, they'll be riding hard back to the Sierra Madres."

"I understand that, Captain," General Miles interjected. "So I've wired the Mexican military for permission to extend our observation posts all the way down into Mexico if need be."

Lieutenant Maus had rejoined them, but now raised his eyebrows. "Our Agreement in '82 authorized 'hot pursuit' of Apaches onto their soil, but do you really think the Mexicans will ever allow us to camp down there permanently, General?"

General Miles shrugged. "When we get two thousand more men out here, we'll have six thousand soldiers, one quarter of our entire army massed along this border. That kind of military force, backing up a little diplomacy, can often work wonders."

Captain Hatfield couldn't repress a sigh. "Maybe we'll get lucky with Geronimo. Finally."

Second Lieutenant Walsh spit out the tip of the little Mexican cigar he'd been masticating. "At least maybe now our communications will remain confidential. Son-of-a-bitching railroad telegraphers ought to be thrown in jail, selling military messages to the newspapers!"

This intelligence brought their new Second Lieutenant up short. "I thought we had our own telegraph system out here?"

"We do, Fuller," explained Lt. Walsh. "Only partially completed, though. Many places throughout Arizona, military messages have to be sent over our line gaps onto the railroad's wires. Their civilian operators read a hot dispatch or new general order, even though they've sworn to be confidential, the bastards sell it right out the back door to some reporter. Or even invent dishonest dispatches when there's no news to peddle. Next day, there's the sensation on the front page: 'Indians Attack Again!' Sells a lotta damned newspapers and all hell breaks loose among the citizens, screaming to Washington for more protection. They're after our scalps worse'n the Apaches!" Lt. Walsh was so worked up he spit tobacco flecks rapid fire—*phut, phut, phut*!

Second Lieutenant Fuller looked nonplussed. "That is criminal."

"We do have a war reporter amongst us, gentlemen," cautioned General Miles. "What do you think of newspapermen selling confidential military dispatches, Mr. Lummis?"

"Some of my less ethical brethren have been known to buy news from any reliable source they can find, General, and more than a few unreliable, too. Those that sell this confidential information should be arrested or at the very least lose their jobs. Those that retail this private information, well, it's a journalist's instinct to want a scoop. That'll never change." Charles Lummis didn't look very apologetic.

Captain Hatfield looked as sour as his whiskey. "It's patronage these local businessmen want, not protection. If hostilities ever cease with the Indians and most of our troops leave, half the white residents of Arizona will be broke inside of two months! Keeping the Apaches and settlers stirred up pays very well. Over two million dollars, I'm told, the War Department funnels into this territory every year to keep our army fed and operating. Supplying us is damned good business for 'em, not to mention what extra some make by graft, splitting the proceeds for goods and food never delivered to the Indians, which the reservation agents in cahoots with the suppliers sell right back to the civilians in the nearby towns. The reservation Apaches, meanwhile, live half-starved. That's what needs to change first, or our Indian problem will never be solved."

Second Lieutenant Fuller thought about these surprising revelations for a moment. "Well, as the General knows, our army was the first in the world to establish its own communications branch, and I think the success of our new heliograph system in this final Apache campaign is going to be the absolute making of the U.S. Signal Corps. Gentlemen, from this day forward, our military communications shall remain uncompromised on this field of battle."

Four experienced Indian fighters stared at this cocky green officer and his new equipment. Captain Hatfield, from the hollows of Kentucky, tipped his tumbler toward the young Lieutenant in charge of communications before cowswallowing the last of his whiskey. "Let us pray."

Sgt. Ammon Swing tilted back on his haunches against a cottonwood, squatting Indian-style. He savored the *mescal* from his tin cup as he watched another rosy sunset. Orange-colored from the orange peels dropped into the keg for several months to age this fermented cactus juice, mescal was higher proof than most of the cheap whiskey sold on the frontier. Known as *viña del país*, "country wine," it was the liquor of Sonora. Army Scouts favored it over rotgut American whiskeys.

His soldiers, high-spirited from their drink, laughed and yelled and roughhoused around the makeshift backyard bar nearby, and Sgt. Swing smiled agreeably at their antics. Another weathered Scout in a grimy, long-sleeved undershirt and deerskin britches held up by a "thimble-belt" containing scores of copper cartridges approached waving a half-empty bottle of Indian firewater. Edward "Wallapai" Clark was already a legend across the Southwest for his work with his tribal trackers, as he would have been the first to tell you.

"How's the leg, Swing?"

"Can still drag it behind me. How's your topknot, Wallapai?"

The barrel-thick man squatted down in the dust beside his old *compadre* as he fingered several greasy locks of his long hair. "Still got my beautiful hair." Wallapai laughed ruefully.

"After this monkey chase, though, I dunno. Gettin' a little tired a runnin' Geronimo and his rascally kin all over hell an' Sonora." The tracker squinted at the setting sun as he took another slug of mescal. "Summer's comin'. Gonna be hotter'n the ass end of a Mexican bakery down there." Wallapai rubbed a long undersleeve across his sweaty forehead, leaving a grimy streak.

"You actually catch ol' Geronimo, he'll fix your hair for you good." The Scout Sergeant chuckled as he pushed his pint-sized cup forward for a refill. "They got me on observation duty this hunt."

"You ain't scoutin'?"

"Nope. Retired. Temporarily." Sgt. Swing's sigh was more relief than satisfaction. "Gonna let my leg heal runnin' this heliograph station over in the Winchesters. Let you younger fellas have all the glory a catchin' Geronimo. Again."

Wallapai Clark snorted. "Don't get your hopes up. Since this donkey-ass new General disbanded our Scouts, he's really tied our hands. I begged a couple of my Wallapais for this troop, and Miles did allow a few of the old Apache Scouts to ride as trackers with some of the other patrols goin' out, only 'cause he couldn't find nobody else on short notice. But you damned well know, Ammon, it takes an Apache to catch an Apache!"

Sgt. Swing sucked cactus juice from his mustache. "Don't put much stock in these new tactics of General Miles, then?"

"No sir! Miles's got hisself some carpet knights and ballroom soldiers whisperin' in his ear already. Mouth fighters, alla 'em! We're the ones gonna have hell to harrow flushin' this last bad bunch outta the Madres. Those are all *Netdahe* 'Paches, Ammon, the 'enemy people.' 'Death to intruders,' is their blood oath. Mixed-blood cutthroats with nothin' else to lose. This 'un's now purely a war a who lasts the longest. And without more Apache Scouts to help us catch and kill 'em in the mountains, whal, with these dumb bastards on their trail . . ." The tough tracker dismissed the Fourth Cavalrymen nearby with a backhand gesture.

"You might as well match a bunch a Londoners against the Alpine Swiss!"

The Sergeant couldn't help but smile at his colorful friend. "Maybe this new heliograph system of Miles's will help."

"Hellfire, Ammon, the 'Paches been flashin' bits of metal, not to mention smoke signals, long before the hard thinkers in this army ever dreamed up this piece a bull crap." He belched. "But, with all these troops in the field, maybe the General's mirrors will help keep 'em from surprisin' an' attackin' each other!"

Both veterans laughed as Wallapai emptied the last of his mescal into his pal's big tin cup, then rattled the signature "worm" out of the bottle's neck. Sucking it between his lips, the big Scout crunched it between his mossy teeth, savoring the caterpillar's juicy flavor.

The Sergeant looked at the red sun just setting on the horizon. "*Chigo-na-ay*" (the sun). Apaches won't watch a sunset. Think it'll make 'em sick."

"Let's us get good and sick then!" Wallapai Clark tapped his empty bottle against his friend's cup, as both big men laughed once more.

FIVE

To identify trouble-making mules, packers shaved their tails. Trained mules were called "bell-sharp," untrained mules "shave-tails." Packers irreverently applied these same terms to Army officers, and "shave-tails" for new 2nd Lieutenants stands to this day.

—Donald E. Worcester, *The Apaches, Eagles of the Southwest*

To the braying of mules instead of the bellowing of a bugle, sixty soldiers sluggishly arose the next morning, fighting rotgut hangovers as they crawled from their wool blankets under the cottonwoods and thickets of black willow, several men often bundled together in their clothes against the night's chill. Here and there, cooking fires were started, with several of the men breaking mesquite branches they'd gathered with sledgehammers, so hard had the heat-scorched wood become that it turned the blade of an ax. But mesquite made a hot fire that lasted a long time, so it was the favored firewood.

Sergeant Swing was already up tending his fire, while his drinking companion, Wallapai Clark, wrestled with his blanket. "Oooooh. Who hit me?"

"You poleaxed yourself, Wallapai."

"Jesus, Mary, and Joseph, I'm *crudo* (hung over)."

Trying to remember last night, the hirsute tracker uncorked a canteen and poured the water right over his head, trying to wash the red out of bloodshot eyes. Dripping and sputtering, the famous frontiersman squinted to see what his pard was frying for breakfast.

"Cornmeal mush and molasses."

"Again? My poor stomach churns."

"Standard field rations, Mister Clark. And always delicious."

Wallapai grimaced as Sergeant Swing smiled. "But we're at the trader's. I was hopin' for somethun' better. Like an egg."

"You buy it; I'll cook it."

This brought another groan from the victim. "Already spent my pay on mescal, Ammon. Which you enjoyed."

"A little short in the pocket now myself. Twenty dollars script a month ain't much to live on, even out here." The Sergeant poured his sick friend a tin cup of Rio coffee and passed it over. Army coffee was by tradition as dark and thick and murky as the Rio Grande, after which it was named, but when boiled long enough, some of its strong, natural flavor was gone. "I do owe you one good drunk, though, *compadre*."

His pal nodded, took a sip of scalding coffee, and gargled it cool in his mouth. "Whooo!"

"One of you men Swing?" It was a civilian inquiring, leading two mules, a big gray gelding, and, roped on behind, tied directly to the front mule's tail, a smaller, lighter gray female.

"Present . . . but barely accounted for," yawned the Sergeant, scratching his wild mat of hair. "Who's askin'?"

"Henry Daly. Packer. Gentlemen, meet your mules." He dropped the reins and walked the mules past them and back, giving the boys a good look. Henry showed off his training ability by leading the barrel-bellied front mule merely by placing a hand under its chin, touching no halter at all.

Sgt. Swing noted the Spanish *aparejos* strapped to each mule's back. These were grass-padded, stiff blanket contrivances with small interwoven wooden bibs that could be fitted snugly on each mule's back atop a *corona*, or saddle pad, which, unlike other pack saddles, distributed a pack's weight evenly and did not slip around. A crupper, a band of leather attached to the *aparejo* and passed beneath the mule's tail, kept the pack rig from sliding forward. Ammon Swing didn't like the look of the second animal's shaved tail and roached mane.

"Some sharp trader sold you that Sonora rat."

"No, no, this here's a solid Mexican mule, cross between a Spanish ass and an Arab-blooded brood mare. Just a youngster, though, only a couple years old. Sorry we can't let all the observation details have two experienced mules each, but we need 'em worse up with the patrol. This big ol' boy'll help train your new mare, though. Just tie her behind like this till she picks out her walking gait, and you'll be fine."

"So you say. Okay, packer, take 'em over to my detail, bunked under that big tree, I believe." He pointed to a shady cottonwood, a distance west of the trading post. "Show the fellers how to pack 'em tight. Don't have any desire for that much fun right now myself."

The sturdy Daly mock-saluted the Sergeant. "You bet. Good luck up on your mountain, Sergeant. Sounds like deathly boring duty to me."

Sergeant Swing squinted up at the enlisted man. "But not deadly duty, like you got lookin' you in the eye across that border. Good luck to you, too, Daly. You'll need it."

The civilian packer stared at him for a moment, then led his two mules off through the dust. Wallapai Clark managed to chuckle as he slugged down another swallow of hot coffee.

Soldiers stood in line before the two wooden outhouses out back of the trading post, scratching and spitting as they cleared bodily passages in preparation for another hard day in the saddle. Nearby, blankets were being shaken out and clothing repacked. Dress in the field in Arizona was casual and piecemeal at best, for this was warmer, spring "one-shirt" weather, as opposed to the "three-shirt" coldness of winter. This early in the morning, many of the men had slept in their brown canvas overalls, which were intended to be worn only on fatigue duty, and had on their blue flannel shirts. They'd strip down to ride in their worn blue army trousers and gray undershirts as the day warmed up.

Some of the enlisted men laced up Tonto Apache deerskin moccasins they'd paid as much as six dollars a pair for, instead of their uncomfortable, poorly made army boots. All their clothing appeared hard-used, for wise soldiers purchased the older uniforms of their mates as they mustered out of service. These ragged uniforms were then worn in the field, while a soldier's best clothing was preserved for wearing around the garrison or on parade. This thrifty practice led to some strange uniforms showing up on patrol in these "hobo" brigades, especially in the choice of headgear, with army kepis, campaign hats, felt cowboy hats, even straw boaters in the summer all being worn by troops in the same unit. Comfort and utility were all important in a grueling campaign against the Apache. Kill one and nobody gave a trooper's damn about what you were wearing when you did it.

Officers tended to keep up appearances, but even among them, uniform propriety on patrol was set by the predilections of the commanding officer. Captain Hatfield was too experienced to stand for much ceremony in the field, having earned his epaulets riding with the Tenth Michigan Cavalry during the Civil War. Consequently, he had already dispensed today with his hot tailored tunic for a long gray knit undershirt beneath his suspenders. He did, however, always wear his new brown felt campaign hat with its gold braid and small screen vents on both sides of its crown. C.A.P. Hatfield believed that rank must always be distinctive to be obeyed.

His adjutant, Second Lt. Walsh, passed over an eye-opener of whiskey as they were tying their own bedrolls. "Little hair of the dog, sir."

Captain Hatfield merely nodded thanks, gulped down a big swallow, and then coughed and spit. "Horseshit-t-t-t! How does that trader get away with selling this rotgut?"

"Only saloon open in the wilds between Tucson and New Mexico. Pertwee sells what he wants, charges whatever he pleases."

Remembering his complaint of the night before, Captain Hatfield spilled the rest of his cup without drinking. "Alcohol this unrefined should be fueling lanterns." Their Commander squinched his face. "Ought to be outlawed."

"We should press charges, sir. Poisoning the army."

The Captain nodded emphatically, trying to spit the raw taste from his mouth. An orderly walked up leading the two officers' saddled mounts to assist them in tying on their bedrolls and gear. "Eben, get Fuller and Swing over here before we ride."

"Yes sir."

"Ever think about musterin' outta service a little early, soldier?" Roscoe Pertwee eyed Takins as he rolled up his bedroll in the morning shade of the store's mud-daubed front wall, where this Private had spent the night. The big trader sidled closer, confidentially. "Give you a good price for your weapons and anything you ride in on."

This got the Southerner's attention. "How much?"

"Forty-five dollars for a carbine, twenty for your old rifle, fifteen for a revolver. Animal, depends on its age and condition. Same with your saddle and tack."

Private Takins scratched his sparse whiskers. He didn't shave in the field, water being so precious in the desert. Most of the others sported beginnings of beards, too, because chin whiskers helped protect their faces against sun and windburn. "Only twenty dollars for my Springfield? It's accurate up to three hundred yards!"

The trader was skeptical. "By who?" Pertwee shook his head. "Everybody else wants repeating rifles, soldier. Top price for carbines. 'Sides, I gotta figure in a bit of profit on the resale."

"A bit!" Takins snorted. "Greenbacks or silver?"

"Silver. We discount military script by twenty percent out here."

The Private spit a wad of tobacco juice as he finished filling his haversack with gear.

"I'll keep your offer in mind, mister, case I ever decide to go over the hill."

Roscoe Pertwee reached into his pocket, pulled out a half plug of Battle Axe tobacco and tossed it over to the enlisted man. "Tell your pards, too." The big trader began to chant: "Dollar a day is damned poor pay, but thirteen a month is less."

Takins smiled ruefully. "You're acquainted with that song of ours, too." The Private shouldered his heavy pack, tamped down his Hardie campaign hat, and tipped his free chaw at the businessman. "Thankee."

Takins ambled over to another group of men standing under a cottonwood tree, his detail, including Corporal Bobyne, whom he'd slumbered separately from. Henry Daly had their big gelding mule already packed, the precious heliograph equipment in its three different-sized leather cases tied under a heavy canvas *manta*, or pack cover, on the near side, and their shovel and pick and medical chest balanced and covered across from it. He tied off the last of his rope hitches.

"That's all there is to it, fellers. You can let his ear go now, Corporal."

Big Heintz let loose of the mule's ear on the animal's off side, the right.

"Give 'em an ear twist only if they're a little cranky while you're trying to pack. Distracts 'em from the business at hand. Treat your mules right, boys, and they'll be your faithful servants for life. They're proud of their occupation."

Edgy around unfamiliar animals, Bobyne spoke up. "Don't they kick?"

"Yessir, they have that reputation. But it's only due to faulty handling. Don't curse and beat 'em, and pack them carefully. Each of these mules has already been fitted with its own *aparejo*, so be sure you've got the right cradle on the right animal or you'll have a problem, back sores at least. These Mexican pack rigs weigh about sixty pounds, so you can load another two hundred pounds on 'em fine, but that's plenty. Mules can carry twenty percent of their weight and keep up a six-mile-an-hour pace all day long. Overload 'em for any length of time, though, and they'll turn up lame and sore and mean, and they're done—broke down and spoiled to work anymore."

The packer took out a gunnysack and wrapped it across the smaller mule's eyes, tying it under her long chin. She was not nearly as well-muscled as the leader but was a still-growing thirteen hands high.

"Now this young lady's a bit skittish, so we'll blindfold her till she's packed up. Once she gets used to this daily, she'll be just like the rest, sure-footed as a chamois and as careful with her load as a mother with a babe in her arms."

Henry Daly nodded to the German-American to take hold of the mule's halter as he began to load her up with food stores in crates and sacks under the canvas on the near, left side, where one always started packing. "Watch me tie this diamond hitch, kid, so you can do it."

Mullin leaned in closer. "We used oxen on our farm back home, for work."

"Oxen are good for pulling heavier loads, wagons, and plows and such," agreed Henry. "But they can't touch a mule in carrying a pack. Mules are much faster walkers, for one thing, and longer-lived, too, with marvelous recuperative powers. They can subsist on anything, endure more fatigue, and need only one-fourth as much water, which is a killer of oxen in this desert. They're easier to herd, too, stay together at night, whereas an oxen will just wander off and lie down in the bush till you find him."

"Mules'll run away on yah and are damned hard to catch again. Saw that too many times in the war," argued Takins.

"True," agreed the middle-aged packer. "They can be stampeded by anything, which makes 'em a bit less reliable in Indian country—why we don't graze 'em with horses. Indian steals your horses, mules will follow, willingly. Only way to stop mules fleeing with a horse is to shoot the horse."

The three soldiers looked at each other, smiled in spite of themselves. Young Mullin just shook his head, disbelieving. "What're their names?"

"Don't know, kid. Just arrived. But they're assigned to your lookout, so . . . think some up." Henry Daly moved around to the mare mule's off side to start packing their kitchen equipment, iron pots and pans, and sacks of utensils that clanked and jangled. The she-mule moved her hooves and looked around at the scary noise but couldn't see through her sack blindfold.

"Easy, girl. She'll get used to this soon, strange noises. Females are valued more highly. Sweeter dispositions. General Crook rode his mare mule, Apache, and wouldn't even look at a horse. Just tie her on to that older one's tail every day, and she'll quickly get used to the pace and build her muscles up to handle these loads. Just be patient with her, and she'll learn to love this hard work." The master packer stepped back, pleased with his handiwork. "There. Ready to go, good as gum. Remove the blind carefully and give 'er a moment to get comfortable, and you're on your way."

Heintz carefully removed the young mare's blindfold.

Henry turned back to his students. "You boys ready to try a diamond hitch on this big gelding?"

The smaller mare mule switched her "shaved" tassel of a tail at a bothersome fly, shifted her rear weight a little, and caused a couple skillets in her pack to clank together. Looking around wide-eyed at the new noise right behind her, she suddenly raised both rear hooves and launched a double kick. This really set the pots and pans jangling! Now thoroughly frightened, she leapt sky-high, trying to rid herself of this scary problem. *Eeee-haw! Hee-haw! Eeee-haw!*

"Jesus Christmas, look out!" yelled Takins. The soldiers bailed in a hurry, scurrying to get away from her clicking teeth and mighty sharp-hoofed kicks as she bucked about under the cottonwood, quickly loosening her pack and sending kitchen equipment and foodstuffs bouncing off in different directions with every big buck.

"Wild mule loose!" Bobyne warned some other troopers who'd stopped their own ablutions to enjoy the show.

Henry Daly had the presence to grab the other mule's harness to lead it away before it, too, got a mind to join the rodeo. "Calm down, Buckshot, calm down! Don't you go sky-hoppin' on me, too!"

One of the nearby gawkers couldn't resist the needle, as they all watched the smaller mule bray and buck at a good clip off down the two-track toward the distant mountains.

"Go git 'er, Henry! An' show us how you packed that one again, please!"

Sgt. Swing and his pardner stopped rolling their personals in their blankets to observe the bucking mule contest over under the cottonwoods. The Sergeant held his aching forehead, then shook it to clear the cobwebs. "Knew I didn't have that much fun in me this mornin'."

Wallapai squinted at his friend. "Don't worry, Ammon. God looks after drunks and green mule skinners, too." They both chuckled as they hoisted their bedrolls to carry to their horses.

Sgt. Swing, Lt. Fuller, and the two cavalry officers were mounted and bunched together under a big tree for a final briefing. "Where will your details be positioned, Lieutenant?" inquired Captain Hatfield.

"Sergeant Swing's post is a day's march from here, sir, across this valley, up Square Mountain." Lieutenant Fuller pointed northwest, then swung his arm back and upward.

"We're much closer, right up top of Dos Cabezas Peak here, so we can come down easily for our supplies. I'm supposed to stay only a couple weeks, sir, till this new system's working well in this area, then I'll be traveling around to the rest of the observation posts in Arizona, making sure they're all operating properly, records being kept."

The Captain cleared some morning phlegm from his throat. ". . . I see."

"We should be camped, set up by noon tomorrow, so watch for our test signals, Sergeant," added Lt. Fuller.

Sgt. Swing nodded.

"Have you a man in your patrol, Captain, who can read Morse code?"

Second Lieutenant Walsh thought. "Uh, Timmons, I believe, sir."

"Good." Lt. Fuller nodded. "Have him keep an eye peeled for our flashes. We'll notify you quickly of any Apache sightings and keep you apprised of troop movements and general orders, sir. You know, General Miles is even having a portable heliograph designed by the Signal Corps, Captain, and by your next ride, you may have your own operator right along on patrol, so we'll be able to communicate back and forth directly, instantly. Won't that be something?"

Their Captain was thinking hard, trying to figure instead how this newfangled system was going to complicate his tactics operationally. "You have that map indicating these new observation posts, Walsh?"

His adjutant tapped the breast pocket of his navy blouse. The Captain reined his fine horse out of the gathering. "Okay, then we'll know where to look. We're heading south, for the border. Good luck with the General's new toy, boys."

Second Lieutenant Fuller frowned, but Sgt. Swing suppressed a smile. As he reined his swaybacked old plug, the only horse the trader had been willing to "loan" from his remuda, past his pal sitting his mustang nearby, the Sergeant couldn't resist some sarcasm of his own.

"Watch your beautiful hair, Wallapai!"

The grizzled Scout spat. "Heal that leg, Ammon. You're

replacin' me on scout when I git back. Give my achin' arse a looong rest!"

Sgt. Swing grinned as he plodded on to join his four men lying against their packs in the shade. He watched Henry Daly nearby, finishing repacking the mare mule with the blindfold on, this time with noisy cooking utensils spread widely about in both mules' packs.

"See you boys had your first packin' lesson."

Not a one of them made the slightest move to get out of the shade, so the Sergeant expectorated in their direction. "Let's go, fellers! More fun's awaitin'."

With a collective groan his soldiers hoisted fifty-pound haversacks onto their backs. In the field, such a pack normally contained half a pup tent, rations for several days, a wool blanket, a rubber sheet to be spread on the ground under it, and extra clothes and boots. These men marched with extra rations, for the heavier, canvas A-tents for their semipermanent outpost were to be wagoned out to them shortly. Carrying a rifle, forty-five rounds of ammunition on his prairie belt, and two canteens of water dangling from his shoulders, an infantryman on the march hefted anywhere from eighty to ninety pounds of supplies and gear, mile after endless mile.

The men watched warily as Henry removed the smaller mule's blindfold, but this time she displayed no temper, so the packer cautiously tied her lead rope to the front mule's tail, then handed the bigger one's halter reins to Corporal Heintz. "Just walk easy till they get in rhythm with each other again."

"That I vill do."

Waving good riddance, Henry Daly hustled off to rejoin his pack train now forming near the trader's.

"Will you ride along with us, General, till we hit the border?"

General Miles was on his inside seat, perched in front of his security detail's tents and packs and food supplies stuffed into the rear of the quartermaster's wagon. Now he stood up and stuck his head out from underneath the canvas roof so the men could see him as his wagon came to a stop amidst the assembling troops.

"Wish I could, Captain, but we're moving fast, straight on to Fort Huachuca, southwest—wrong direction for you. I want to quick survey all our forts, see what I have to work with." General Miles stepped up onto the driver's seat while his driver stepped down to steady the six mules.

"Men! I wish you good hunting on this long patrol! I will stand the first unit that brings Geronimo and Naiche and his renegades to heel, two barrels of whiskey!" At a low murmur from the cavalrymen, the General smiled.

"I guarantee that whiskey, for I will be there, too. Sampling that same whiskey and toasting the unit that accomplishes this feat, right from my own cup!" He nodded at several shouts of approval from the assembled soldiers.

"So ride hard, be alert, and let's get this last big task done! Bring these last troublesome Apaches back to San Carlos where they belong, dead or alive! I will use any means necessary to end this final conflict with these renegade Apaches! And soon!"

"Here, here!"

As the huzzahs died down, Gen. Miles saluted the troops and stepped down off his driver's seat back into his own. "Good luck and godspeed, Hatfield!"

"Thank you, General. We'll need it." The Captain saluted his Commanding Officer while his cavalrymen walked their mounts two abreast into a line.

A whip cracked, and the General's six mules moved out at a good clip. General Miles acknowledged the trader's salute as his wagon and security detail sped past. Charles Lummis brought up their rear on a borrowed horse.

"Come visit us anytime, General! Everything we got's at your disposal!"

"For sale, you mean!" riposted Captain Hatfield.

Roscoe Pertwee stood on his store's porch, stroking his tame billygoat's long neck. He grinned. "Well, that, too, Captain."

With a derisive snort, Capt. Hatfield wheeled his pureblood gelding to lead his Fourth Cavalry off to duty.

Pertwee watched the four groups of army men riding or walking off in three different directions: the General's detail and the cavalry patrol and its pack train riding initially south, toward Mexico; and the observation details walking directly east and west, toward the mountains edging either side of the wide Sulphur Springs Valley. The goat seemed content to see the pestering soldiers go, but not its owner, who regretted losing these good topers.

"Good luck, boys! Bring back a few more ears for me!"

Captain Hatfield and Second Lieutenant Walsh, resenting Pertwee's larcenous prices and awful liquor, ignored his wave.

Private Slivers, remembering being overcharged for that same bad whiskey, spit in the trader's direction. "Wouldn't give you the time a day, Mister, from a broken watch!"

The trader chuckled at the riposte as well as at the hard stares from other disgruntled drinkers. The fifty-mule pack train had formed, and its *cargador*, or assistant pack master, led the whitish "bell mare" mule past the outpost. The other mules tagged docilely behind, having established their pecking order long ago and following the tinkling bell single file without being roped together. Packmaster Moore and his assistant as well as their cook, blacksmith, and ten packers all rode fourteen saddle mules to keep this long train moving at a steady pace. Sergeant Moore, though, did nod to Pertwee, and the trader returned his acknowledgment—respect from one wily animal trader to another.

Roscoe Pertwee watched these nearly sixty-five men, mostly mounted, ride off in rising clouds of dust on three separate missions. Hell, good business gone now for a good while, he thought. With a grimace, the trader stepped down and walked round the side of his store to help his Mexicans clean up the mess the soldiers had left out behind.

SIX

*There is an old Spanish word—*apachurar, *meaning "to crush." The Apaches were known for torturing their captives by turning them over to the women and children to crush their bones with rocks. Shortened by time to be referred to as "Apaches" by their usual victims, the Mexicans.*

—Lieutenant Britton Davis, *The Truth About Geronimo*

**Whetstone Mountains,
Southern Arizona Territory**

A Mexican "rock scratcher," his slouch hat shading his dark mustache, led his donkey down a rocky watercourse along the east side of the largest mass of mountains to the north of Fort Huachuca, the army's biggest fort in this territory's southeast corner. His little pack animal slipped on moist rocks in the streambed, still damp from spring rains common to this country. The donkey staggered but righted itself quickly under the canvas-wrapped pack and worn shovel and pickax weighing down either side of its heavy burden.

A giant bird launched itself from the top of the tall rock the Mexican was passing beneath. Its shadow blocked the sun. The hard-rock miner sensed it, and looked up just in time to see Naiche midair, arms and legs spread wide, his mouth open in a silent scream, before he landed on top of the frightened miner with a heavy thud! The donkey bolted, braying in fear at the sudden assault!

The Mexican was stunned, the wind knocked out of him as he writhed on his back on the ground. The tall Apache jumped to his feet, yanked a knife from beneath the ammunition belt holding up his loincloth, and bull-rushed the dazed miner, who pulled his own horse pistol from his pants and from one knee took a wild swing at the onrushing Indian, trying to fend him off! "*Socorro*! (Help!)"

The combatants went down in a heap. The Apache chief rolled atop his prey to stab his long blade into the Mexican's stomach, only to have his thrust glance off a wide belt of thick leather strapped around the miner's waist underneath his threadbare coat. "*Pare*! (Stop!)"

Now Naiche was the one surprised, as the Mexican bucked and rolled away from the big Indian to scramble to his feet. Before he could pull the trigger of his Dragoon Colt, the miner was grabbed by Perico, who limped out from behind the huge rock to pin the miner's arms back. Dahkeya also materialized from nowhere to wrench the pistol from the Mexican's death grip.

To prevent any escape, other Apaches in the raiding party rode up pulling their leaders' horses. Zhonne, the youngest, slid from his horse and began ripping apart the pack on the miner's donkey.

Naiche moved to the man to touch his strange belt, but the Mexican jerked back, aware the Apaches usually aimed for a man's stomach with their dirty knives and poison-tipped arrows, hoping to paralyze an opponent so they could watch him die—slowly. For flinching, he was backhanded across the mouth, bringing blood to his lips.

"*E-chi-ca-say* (Greetings), *tecs-oti*, (miner)!"

Reaching with both hands, Naiche yanked the man closer to unbuckle the belt from under his coat. Amazingly, the six-inch-wide band of brown leather was festooned with at least a dozen American-made pocket watches riveted to it, alternating one gold and one silver. The Apache even smiled as he shook the strange decoration and put his ear to one watch to hear it ticking. It worked! Time was passing on all the watches adorning this unusually ornamented belt as Naiche held it overhead for his fellow raiders to admire.

Having never seen anything quite like this weird watch belt before, the other warriors voiced their approval of their leader's new prize.

"*Nantan!* (literally "wolf," but used to describe a leader)! *Naiche! Nantan!*"

SEVEN

The desert is where God is and man is not.

—Honoré de Balzac

Sulphur Springs Valley, Southern Arizona Territory

Sgt. Swing's detail hiked slowly, following a rough track northwest across a wide basin floor populated primarily by scrub brush, jackrabbits, and fluff grass. Spring rains had already been absorbed by the dry ground, and now there was no water. It was only mid-April but by noon it was already eighty-five degrees, hot enough so the men had to force themselves to breathe through their nostrils so open mouths wouldn't dry out faster and make them even thirstier. The perspiring soldiers had packed their dark flannel blouses away and pushed the sleeves of their ragged gray undershirts way up their arms.

"Keep together, boys! It'll be cooler on our mountain. Should catch a little breeze up there."

"How come you get to ride, Sergeant? Thought only officers were allowed mounts in the field in this man's infantry?"

The Sergeant knew Takins was the one who'd give him guff the moment he set eyes on him. "Lieutenant Fuller kindly arranged for this old hayburner so's I could rest my wounded leg. Horse has to be sent back, though, pronto, and I have to climb that damned mountain same as you, Private. Unless you wanna carry me."

Sergeant Swing turned in his worn saddle to cast a hard eye on the enlisted man skulking along in his old horse's dust. "You look like you were weaned on a pickle, Takins. Maybe when we get to Cox's Tanks, we can talk the lady there into givin' you a bath, so as to improve your disposition."

The other three infantrymen laughed, but a hard look from the Southerner stifled their merriment. Takins stared at the boss of this detail. "Pretty hard-twisted, ain'tcha?"

Sgt. Swing looked back again at the griper and nodded just once. But he attempted to lighten the mood by winking at the others. " 'Sides, a ridin' man always looks more romantic than one on foot, dont'cha think?"

The horseman, four marchers, and two mules finally reached a low hilltop and halted. Corporal Heintz, their big German farmer from New Braunfels, Texas, dropped the pack mules' reins so they could browse while he gulped his water. Sgt. Swing dismounted, unstrapping his Springfield Trapdoor carbine from the cantle of his saddle, as the others tossed off their haversacks to take refreshment.

"I'd swap my tongue for a sun-baked sponge," grimaced Takins, swigging from his heated metal canteen.

Through the distant heat haze could be seen a corral, a small barn, and a ranch house with a wisp of smoke climbing from its chimney. Right behind it raised the eastern slope of a mountain, culminating in several rocky peaks, the Winchesters, beyond.

The Sergeant guzzled some warm water, took his Bausch and Lomb binoculars from his pack, and scouted the forward terrain. "I'm not mistaken, that's Cox's Tanks."

He pointed and passed the binoculars to his men so they could get a good look, too.

The big German perked up. "A woman *ist* there?"

"Sister of the rancher, I was told. Maybe if we're nice, we can get 'er to do our laundry, even a little fancy cookin' come payday."

Mullin sat up. "Suits me!"

Sgt. Swing smiled at their green Private, just out of preliminary training back East and shipped West for polishing. At this early point in his military service, Mullin was fit only for guard duty.

Their Signal Corpsman, also a rookie to soldiering, scanned the distant habitation with his own issued binoculars. "Pretty tough people to ranch out here by themselves, with Apaches raiding hereabouts."

"Or pretty foolish," added the Sergeant. "But there's water down there. See all that green brush around Cox's Tanks?" He pointed toward the water hole this side of a hill before the ranch.

"That's what attracts 'em. Including our friends, the Apaches." Sgt. Swing slung his binoculars over his shoulder, strapped his carbine to the back of his saddle again, and remounted his already tired nag. "Let's go. I wanna be up that mountain before dark."

Sergeant Swing was in a better mood. They were nearly there now, across open country with little cover, to the relative safety of more mountains and a bit of civilization, people his own kind. He would rest his weary bones somewheres up there tonight, peacefully. From atop his swayback bronc, the Sergeant cocked an eye at Takins and sang him a little rhyme: "Oh, if wishes were horses, beggars would ride; if turnips were watches, I'd wear one by my side."

"Mother Goose!" yelled Mullin. Several men grinned as they slogged through the creosote down the long, dusty hill toward their next camp.

Middle Pass, Between the Little Dragoon and Dragoon Mountains

Charles Lummis took advantage of this journey to ride in the army wagon, crammed next to the new Commanding Officer of the whole Southwest, right behind the Corporal driving their six mules. Lummis's cavalry horse was tied on to the rear of the wagon, his felt sombrero lashed to the horn of his Whitman saddle. Without his big hat bumping General Miles, the journalist had a bit more room inside the cramped baggage wagon to pencil notes.

"Which do you see as the principal problems with these renegade Apaches, General, keeping the army from wrapping up this endless war?"

"One big one. Geronimo. My reports say he and Naiche are the leaders of the unrepentant fighters still hewing to the raiding trail, to their predatory way of life. Geronimo's notoriety has made him the symbol, the reservoir of all the fears and anxieties and hatreds of the honest citizens of this territory, both north and south of the border. It's his name that strikes terror into the white man's heart, instantly—Geronimo is coming, Geronimo is raiding, Geronimo is killing again—even if he's not personally responsible for all these bands' latest savagery. That's what my superiors in Washington ask me every telegram, plus you journalists and most of the politicians in congress. What's Geronimo up to, where is he now? That's all I hear. Constantly."

"What's keeping you from catching him, again?"

"Well, he's holed up down in the Sierra Madres, resting, waiting until he gets bored or needs to resupply again, then he lashes out. We'll catch up with him eventually, but ol' Geronimo's a wily one. Gives his word he'll come in to the reservation, even surrenders to our troops, then gets drunk and sneaks off again in the moonlight, back to his sanctuaries in Mexico. Crook said his word, alone among all the top Apaches still out, was not to be trusted."

The General stared off into the shimmering distance, at the

old Chiricahua redoubts strung out skyward toward the border. He picked idly at the gold-fringed braid on his tunic he'd removed due to the midday heat. "Cut off the head and the snake dies."

"Kill Geronimo?"

"If we catch him in a fight. Otherwise capture or talk him into giving up peaceably. But allowing Geronimo to surrender and keep his arms, to be escorted back to our forts under loose arrest, riding his horses and driving his stolen cattle and mules, showing off his plunder back on the reservation and distributing it among his tribesmen with impunity, without our confiscating it, making himself the conquering hero in the Apaches' eyes yet again—that is sheer lunacy! That is surrendering to him, to his conditions and whims. It almost guarantees failure. Those weak terms repudiate anything ever taught about conditional surrender at West Point. Madness!"

"But General Crook told me the Apaches always hide their best weapons and only turn in broken, inferior arms when forced to disarm," argued Charles Lummis. "Crook felt it best not to show fear to the Apaches, even when they were fully armed. They prey on weakness and fear."

"Of course they do! And fully armed, too, since Crook didn't confiscate any of their weapons, whether they worked or not. And look at the mess that resulted. Geronimo escaped again and went right back to war! What was Crook thinking? Such a mistake will not happen again in this campaign, I assure you. Not while I am in command."

Charles Lummis paused to take out his big pocketknife to whittle his two pencils, sharpening their points. General Miles had gotten exercised answering his questions, and the journalist gave him a moment to calm down. Licking the pencil lead to smooth his transcription, Lummis began again. "What really happened at Geronimo's last surrender, General? After which he escaped again. I don't think anyone's really gotten the details straight on that fiasco yet."

The General sighed. "I wasn't there. Lt. Maus was. Ask him." He pointed to the officer conferring with their two Wallapai scouts and Lt. Dapray out front of the wagon. Afternoon shadows were lengthening from the tops of the saguaros, and the four men were looking about, searching for the best place to camp for the night. It didn't look promising. The rough country they were riding through was later described by one veteran as "looking as though at the Creation it had been God's workshop and the scraps had never been swept."

"Several of Crook's officers told me this was the very first instance where Indians have broken their word after formally pledging themselves to surrender."

The new territorial Commander snorted in disgust. "Rubbish! How many times have these Apaches been taken back to their reservation as prisoners or returned on their own and then taken off stealing and killing again just as soon they got bored with farming and stock raising. Their word never meant a tinker's damn! The Apaches are born predators and respect no other way of living. They have no honor. None."

"But I have to say, General, the Apache Scouts I've gotten to know a little at Ft. Bowie seem friendly enough. They try to answer my questions and patiently show me things the few times we've been out hunting together."

General Miles nodded. "That's the hell of it, Charles. They are friendly. When you talk to them without their finger on a trigger. You saw them all trooping in to say good-bye to Crook. Nearly brought a tear to my eyes. The problem comes when these same friendly Scouts get restless after being cooped up on the reservation too long, or after a bout of dancing and drinking their corn liquor. They sometimes take off and go right back to raiding and killing innocents again. A pattern has even developed in which they surrender during the cold winter and draw rations on the reservation, then flee again at the first breath of spring. So we're compelled to go out chasing some of our old friendly Scouts with our new Apache Scouts, who are mostly an assortment of ex-hostiles. It's like they're just changing sides, from defense to offense. No wonder they trade each other supplies and ammunition and information about what we're up to. Chasing Apaches is about as frustrating as a dog chasing its own tail."

The newspaperman didn't dare smile at the General's analogy. "Crook's interpreter, George Wratten, who grew up amongst them, told me the best way to get along with an Indian, is to make a pal of him. Perhaps we whites just haven't tried long or hard enough to treat the Apache fairly, General. Teach him our language and ways and how to raise crops and cattle. So he can assimilate into our society better."

Nelson Miles snorted. "You can't tame an Apache. Not in his nature. He's lived wild and free in his hard land too long. We've given them many chances to settle down, but the bad apples amongst them always taint the whole barrel. Only way to resolve this matter is to lock up the renegades and take them somewhere else, far away, where they don't know the terrain and can't escape back into their old lives. Break them of their bad old habits and they may finally learn some good new ones."

The newsman nodded, finished with questions for now. It was about what Charles Lummis had expected, for scuttlebutt at the fort had most of the renegade Apaches ticketed to distant prisons for a long stay, just as soon as they were caught again.

Their wagon driver began to turn his mules, leading them in a half circle where Lt. Maus pointed, up near some high jagged rocks which would break the wind and keep their cook fire that night somewhat sheltered from interested eyes.

EIGHT

When Iowa Territory was formed in 1838, divorces were granted by district courts on the basis of 'impotency in either of the parties, adultery, extreme cruelty and willful desertion.' In 1842 and '43, bigamy, committing a felony or 'infamous' crime, drunkenness, and the imposition of personal indignities on a spouse were added as grounds.

—Glenda Riley, *The Female Frontier: A Comparative View of Women on the Prairie and the Plains*

Ranch Near Cox's Tanks, West Side of Sulphur Springs Valley

Sergeant Swing rode slowly up to a rope strung between a stunted tree and a big post nail on a corner of the adobe house facing its backyard. A couple chickens clucked out of the way of his slow arrival, while a yellow dog roused from the shade to wander over to give the newcomer a sniff.

Behind him, his four soldiers stopped at the stone well near the small barn to refill their canteens and refresh themselves and the mules from water pails. Green weeds grew from the house's adobe roof, from seeds in the dry grass laid under the mud layer and atop wooden rafters inside for ceiling insulation, giving this frontier home a gay appearance every springtime.

No one seemed to be about, so the Sergeant rode right up to the clothesline, mesmerized by a silk camisole swinging in the slight breeze. Next to it hung a corset, starched white and lengthened for more stomach control, with hooks in front and laces in the back. Ammon Swing looked over this feminine rig, touched the silk, rubbing it dreamily between his thumb and forefinger, trying to recall the last time he'd felt a woman's undergarment. Long ago and far away, his true love, lost, but never forgot. Sergeant Swing leaned forward to relish a whiff of fresh feminine scent, then suddenly realized he was being watched from inside the partially opened window in the back. The Sergeant of Scouts jerked his fingers away from the lady's unmentionables as if they were on fire!

"Ma'am! Beggin' your pardon. I, I, didn't see anyone about. . . . Uh, Mrs. Cox?"

The woman nodded, throwing the wooden window shutters open all the way, almost enjoying his discomfort. Her face looked unnaturally pale, for she had just been rubbing fresh cream from their milk cow on it to relieve her sunburn.

"I'm Sergeant Swing. Detail's filling their canteens." He jerked a thumb backward. "If that's all right, ma'am?"

She disappeared from the window and in a moment strode out the back door, rubbing dried cream off her face with her wet apron, and walked directly up in front of him to unpin her personal items from the clothesline, putting an exclamation point to his offense. If he could have backed his horse away from her threatening presence he would have, but his old bangtail was just too tuckered out.

"We're here to, they should have told you over to the trader's, supposed to man an observation post, heliograph station, up here on Square Mountain."

Sgt. Swing dismounted, putting weight down gingerly on his left leg. "We're supposed to pick up our supplies down here. Thirty days' worth of rations are coming in this month, wagonloads for us to tote uphill. An' we'll send our mail out through the trading post at Dos Cabezas."

She was right in front of him now, placing two ends of a dried bedsheet she had unpinned in his fingers. Quickly the veteran found himself helping fold a strange woman's laundry.

"We agreed to that."

"Oh. Fine." Relieved she'd finally spoken, the Sergeant straightened his sweat-stained hat and regained his composure a little, now that she had folded her underthings in the sheet away from ungentlemanly eyes.

"I'll send a couple men down twice a week with our food requisitions, pick up our supplies, refill our water kegs."

"Why can't you just signal your supply orders over to Dos Cabezas?"

"What?" Her question took him back a bit more. The Sergeant wasn't used to having his plans questioned, particularly by a woman.

"With this new sun-flashing system, why don't you just signal your needs over to the trading post?"

"Oh, no, ma'am. Heliograph's only for official military communications, Apache sightings and such. Not for personal messages or food orders. Besides, no one over to the trader's can decipher Morse code."

Sgt. Swing was aware of someone riding quietly up behind him and he turned.

"Speaking of Apache sightings, Sergeant, we were attacked yesterday on our way home."

The army man was taken aback—a third time. "Attacked?"

"Late afternoon. From right out of that big wash out there." Jacob Cox pointed a long arm, and the Sergeant's eyes followed it.

"Someone was signaling from up on the mountain here, and then we were charged by three bucks. Two more Apaches on horseback jumped us further on, from the other side, trying to run a pincer trap, but Martha shot one from the saddle and killed another who leapt into our wagon. We raced in here and caught 'em in a crossfire. Luckily they rode off."

"You don't say?" It was an amazing story on an already discombobulating day.

"Jacob's always gotten along with the Apaches these past few years, which was why this sudden attack was so surprising."

Sergeant Swing was surprised, too, as he turned back to the woman. "Gotten along?"

Her brother dismounted and ground-reined his stallion. He walked over to shake hands. "Forgive me. I'm Jacob Cox, Sergeant. This is my sister, Martha."

Faces dripping from the cool dousing they'd given themselves at his well, the four soldiers ambled over to listen.

Sgt. Swing took a good look at the lady now, noting the glinting gray among her shoulder-length auburn hair, her sharp-featured, tanned face, which may have prematurely aged her. A trim body inside her blue cotton ranch dress was set off by strong-looking hands extending from her leg-of-mutton sleeves, which were slightly larger proportionally than the rest of her. He'd noticed her big hands immediately when folding laundry. Clearly Martha Cox was a woman who spoke up and could look out for herself. But one who also killed Apaches? He touched his black campaign hat brim.

"Ammon Swing, sir. Ma'am. And these are my men from Ft. Bowie." He gestured. "Corporal Heintz, Private Mullin, Private Takins, and Corporal Bobyne."

The soldiers nodded, half saluted, or murmured greetings. The rangy yellow mutt wandered over to greet all the boys with another good sniff and got a few pats in return.

"Hello, soldiers. Everyone's always welcome at Cox's Tanks, Apaches included." The gaunt rancher gestured. "We've always let them water and camp at the Tanks, over that hill. Martha's fed more than a few who were hungry. I know I've lost some steers to them every year of the last five I've been here, but in return, they've always left our ranch and my horses alone. Until yesterday."

Now Sgt. Swing was skeptical. "Ever sold 'em any ammunition, rifles?"

"No. No weapons. Ever. Or whiskey, either." Put off by the question, Jacob Cox bent to pick up his grulla or mouse-grey-colored stallion's reins, winced a little at the pain, then adjusted his shoulder as he moved to tie his horse to the clothesline tree.

"Arrow. Shoulder's a little tender."

The Sergeant rubbed his chin stubble. "Well, some renegades are rumored to be back up from the Sierra Madres. Evidently slipped through our patrols along the border. They may try to visit their families at San Carlos and recruit more followers. They'll be looking for horses and guns, which is probably why you were attacked. If it was still winter, they'd probably be raidin' for food."

Sgt. Swing moved his tired horse away from Jacob's anxious stallion. "You two did a damned good job standin' 'em off. I'll signal Captain Hatfield's Fourth Cavalry as soon as we get our heliograph set up there, and they'll come search this area thoroughly."

"We'd appreciate that, Sergeant."

"Killed one and wounded another, you say?"

"Martha did. Great, brave shooting, while I raced our wagon home. They left empty-handed and hurting."

The Sergeant eyed the woman again. "Good. Apaches have probably already removed the body, or we could have ambushed them. They're real serious about returning for their dead. Don't like anybody else touching the bodies maybe mutilating them. Our Indian trackers might pick up a blood trail, though. I'll come back down to meet the Captain when he gets here, probably day after tomorrow."

Mr. Cox moved toward the slouched enlisted men, his hands wide. "You're welcome down here anytime, gentlemen. We should all keep an eye out for each other now, for mutual aid."

"Yessir, we sure will." Sgt. Swing tipped his hat again. "Good day, ma'am."

East Coast bred and better mannered, Corporal Bobyne stepped forward to shake Jacob's hand. "Thank you, sir, for the hospitality."

"You're welcome, Corporal."

Sgt. Swing led his swaybacked mount and his men across the stable yard toward the barn. "This old cayuse is supposed to go back to Dos Cabezas with our first supply wagon tomorrow or the day next, so I'll jus' leave 'im with you now, okay?"

"Certainly. Just turn him out in the corral, I'll feed him."

"Would you boys like a dog?" The woman spoke again, and this stopped them all. Martha Cox scratched an ear of the yellow, mixed-breed mutt who sat patiently beside her.

"For mutual protection. He's not spry enough to catch rabbits anymore, but he'll still bark at any Indian comes sneaking around. Jacob's got another cow dog to help him herd. This one's more of a pet."

The soldiers seemed interested, looking to their Sergeant for an answer. Young Mullin piped up. "What's his name?"

"Horace."

Sgt. Swing snorted involuntarily. "Named a dog Horace?"

"After my former husband. Back in Iowa."

Chuckles from the Regulars. Even her brother grinned as he polished his spectacles.

"I'll look after him, Sarge." It was Mullin again.

The Sergeant shrugged. Going to be pretty boring and lonely up on that damned mountain. With a half salute of thanks, he led his tired horse to the corral's gate to turn him in.

Jacob took the Sergeant's reins and began uncinching the borrowed nag's saddle. "Good-bye, boys. Come down and clean up, whenever you want."

"That vill ve do, sir. Tank you kindly." Heintz clucked to the pack mules, and the men followed, waving good-bye, as they hiked toward the mountain.

Private Mullin lingered, as Martha Cox tied a length of hemp around the mutt's neck and handed it to him. "He'll be a loyal companion, Private, if you're good to him in turn."

"We sure will, ma'am. C'mon, Horace. Let's go find your new home."

NINE

The Apaches were the best mountain-climbing guerrilla fighters ever. They were happiest with a mountain at their backs. Scaling cliffs was taken for granted. When closely pursued, they killed their horses and scaled cliffs where they couldn't be followed. Men tied ropes to women and children and lifted them from ledge to ledge until they could take cover or escape. Apaches moved at night only when forced to do so and never fought in the darkness unless attacked. They believed that he who kills at night must walk in darkness through the Place of the Dead.

—Eve Ball, *In the Days of Victorio, Recollections of a Warm Springs Apache*

Square Mountain, West Side of Sulphur Springs Valley

Up the rocky mountainside they climbed, following a scraped trail until they reached the big boulder upon which Naiche had sat looking down on the ranch the day before. Frightening off a Gambel quail, her distinctive blue topknot bobbling along as she herded her brood of chicks away across the mountain, they stopped for a breather. The Sergeant took out his binoculars to survey the mountainside around them.

"We're lookin' for a fairly flat ledge, somethun' recessed far back enough to set our tents up on. We can clear it off some, but it needs a spot nearby to picket these mules safely, sorta out of sight. These two will tempt any wandering Apaches, besides our guns and ammunition."

"Need a clear view to the east and northeast, to pick out

and send along the messages coming in," added their Signal Corpsman.

The noncom nodded. "We'll find it for yah, Bobyne, or break our asses tryin'." Sgt. Swing recased his field glasses and gulped some water. "Only two animals in this desert scale rocks like these every damned day of their lives." Hitching up his wounded leg, their leader limped off again up the mountain, following a trail that no longer existed.

"Animals which, Ser-geant?" their big Corporal wanted to know.

"The mountain sheep and the Apache."

They set off across the face of Square Mountain, angling gradually upward, but not trying to approach its 5,700-foot peak. Elevations in this southeastern corner of Arizona ranged from 4,000 to 10,000 feet above sea level, with the highest peaks fairly pointed. With the exception of the desert valley bottoms, much of the country averaged between 4,500 and 5,500 feet. It was these smaller mountain ranges that kept the country from being brutally hot, despite its latitude only eleven degrees north of the Tropic of Cancer. Apaches liked an elevated coolness, too, which is why they were known as "the mountain people."

The infantrymen broke trail across a slope covered by mesquite, alligator juniper, mountain yucca, and claret cup cacti flowering its blood red blooms in the Arizona springtime. There was no visible path across this smaller mountain in front of three higher peaks, up to 7,600 feet, of the Winchesters behind it. Private Mullin, with his young eyes and legs, and his mutt with its keen nose, were in the lead, while Corporal Heintz and the two mules, roped one behind the other, brought up the rear.

"Lady shot two Apaches from a moving wagon? That beggars belief."

"Not if your life depended on it. You feel a buck's hot breath on your neck, Bobyne, you'll be shootin', throwin' your heliograph at him, anything you can get your hands on, believe me." Sgt. Swing moved across the slanted, rock-strewn hillside, favoring his uphill leg.

Takins stopped to expectorate. "Best use of an Apache is fertilizer."

Mullin halted his panting pooch to wait for the others. "I haven't seen any Apache sign since we left the fort."

The Sergeant shook his head ruefully. "Son, an' ol' Scout once told me, if you see Apache sign, be careful. And if you don't see Apache sign, be extra careful." His frontier truism elicited laughter from all the men except Mullin. Sgt. Swing climbed up to him, then passed the young man and his dog around another big rock.

"I better take point, Mullin. Apaches like mountaintops."

Wide Ledge, Square Mountain

Dusk was beginning to enfold this hard land when Sergeant Swing's sweating brow appeared between several rocks. Grunting, he pulled himself up onto a natural shelf two-thirds of the way up the mountainside, a dip before a ridgeline ran on up to Square Mountain's sawed-off peak, giving it its name. The noncom dusted himself off and unslung his heavy bedroll, then turned back to help others climb up to this somewhat level area. "Didn't think I'd make it, didcha, Takins?"

"Must be the monkey in yah," panted the veteran, not one for compliments.

Heintz and the mules took a longer route around to this spot, avoiding the last little steep climb with their burdened animals. Their circuitous path took them through another patch of Engelmann's cholla, and the smaller mare mule deviated from the trail forged by the buck mule she was tied to. She brushed a cholla, detaching a pad from the spread-out cactus, its sharp pods of needles disguised by pretty orange-colored flowers.

The mule let out a sharp, anguished bray and shot out a rear kick, trying to rid itself of the painful stickers.

Heintz dropped the lead rope and slid back down to grab the kicking mule's halter before she could rid herself of her pack again, too! The little mule was kicking anything within reach of its sharp rear hooves, sending cactus pieces flying. One of the prickly pear joints hit the Corporal right in the shoulder, jolting him with a good sting!

"Oww! *Verdammt* mule, *halt! Halt das minuten!* Stop!"

They all stopped to watch this painful polka. Bobyne and Mullin even laughing. Grabbing a stick, Heinz whacked the prickly pear joint off the mule's flank, barely dancing away from a sidekick for his efforts, but his charge seemed relieved enough to calm down a little. The Corporal brushed the cactus pad quickly off his own blouse with a swipe. "Ow!"

Mullin ran back down the mountainside to help lead the mules out of further trouble and up on top of the ledge. The German muttered along behind, pulling cactus needles from his flesh one at a time. "Ow! . . . Ouch! . . . Oh! . . . *Verdammt* mule . . ."

"Mules in the cactus." Takins shook his head at the comedy. "Worst predicament a man could get hisself into. Besides marryin' his first cousin."

General Miles's Camp, Dragoon Wash, Southern Arizona Territory

Stretched out on his bedroll, waiting for the call to dinner, the journalist caught up on his writing, using what he'd gleaned from General Miles on their long, bumpy ride to this desolute campsite, right in the middle of the Chiricahua's legendary homeland, the Dragoon Mountains. He scanned the dusk around the busy campfire, wondering if they were traveling with a strong enough detail to protect them if it came to a fight. He couldn't convey fear or doubt to his readers, though. Not Charles F. Lummis. Not the man who walked halfway across America just to reach his next reporting job.

The closing work of General Crook's administration has put an entirely new face on the Apache situation. Instead of a hundred and ten dusky raiders, as there were two weeks ago, there are now but thirty-four and these somewhat weary of the fugitive existence they are forced to live. Instead of an army with six war chiefs there is now a handful of men with two leaders—Geronimo, the foxy talker, and Naiche, the hereditary chief, who is but a half-hearted warrior. Having been pursued ceaselessly for the past ten months, it is probable they now lurk in the far vastnesses of the Mexican mountains and will not trouble our side of the line again. This is more likely from the fact that all their relatives have been put beyond their reach by the stroke of sending them to Florida. Had the captives been sent back to the reservation, the outstanding hostiles would probably have raided it and got them out again, but now they have no show of getting reinforcements nor even of recovering their families. This is apt to break the recalcitrants up. In fact I am inclined to believe that if the renegades could be communicated with today and told the exact facts, they would start for Fort Bowie tomorrow—all but perhaps Geronimo and three or four of his intimate followers—to give themselves up. Unluckily, one might as well try to telephone a comet. . . .

As a result of the farcical "news" that has been furnished the nation throughout, we have heard nothing but Geronimo, Geronimo, Geronimo. One would fancy that old Jerry was the only Apache who has been off the reservation; and there is not much question but that it would have made a bigger impression on the public if, instead of the seventy-six prisoners now rolling toward Fort Marion, Geronimo alone had been captured and all the rest were still at large. The fact is, Geronimo is only one of seven chiefs who have been off the reservation with their families and followers. He is not even a Number One chief but merely a war chief, Naiche being the hereditary leader of the Chiricahuas. Naiche is an indecisive fellow, fonder of flirting than of fighting, greatly addicted to squaws, and rather easily led by Geronimo, who is a talker. Geronimo has not been the biggest fighter, the cleverest schemer, or the bloodiest raider in the outfit at any time, until now, when only the dude Naiche is out with him. Chiricahua is smarter; Nana, Kut-le, and Ulzanna more bloodthirsty and more daring. Their bands have done more raiding and more mischief than Geronimo's. The only claim Geronimo has to his unearned preeminence of newspaper notoriety is that he is one of the originators of the outbreak. He is no greater and no worse than several of his co-renegades. History is so fashioned, however, that he will be remembered when his more important colleagues are forgotten.

In spite of his fight to keep them open, Charles Lummis's eyes slowly closed, then shut. It had been a long day wagoning across the desert wasteland, and for a time, the journalist dozed.

Wide Ledge, Square Mountain

Reinvigorated now that he might have found their spot, Sgt. Swing checked the range of view at the wide ledge's edge. "Whadya think, Corporal?" He pointed. "Good view of the Dos Cabezas and Chiricahua Mountains southeast."

The Signal Corpsman had his binoculars out and was scanning the distant terrain to the northeast. "Yup, an' Turkey Flat below Mt. Graham up northeast there in the Pinalenos." Corporal Bobyne glassed the highest peak in all the southeast area, Mt. Graham at 10,713 feet, and scanned the hazy, deep blue shadows moving up the mountain ridges in the falling late daylight.

"We'll see tomorrow, better light, but I don't think we have to go any higher up, Sergeant. Good background against these darker rocks here will make our flashes show up better, too."

"Purty good field a fire. Not a helluva lot of cover for anybody tryin' to come up on us." Takins stepped back from the edge, dumped his haversack and started scraping about with his worn brogan, looking for the softest ground to lay out his bedroll.

"Okay. Camp here for the night, and if we still like it in the morning, we can roll some big rocks down, fortify this perimeter an' give us some better cover," the Sergeant decided.

Heintz idly scratched himself, enjoying the spring sunset. "Yah, *goot*. Apache ve should see, miles avay from here coming."

Mullin slopped water from his canteen into his new pet's mouth. "Hey, doggie. Like your new home, don'tcha?" The recruit took a swallow himself. "Can't the Apaches see our campfire, sneak up here on us in the dark?"

"We'll dig a fire pit tomorrow, rig a blanket up on a couple poles, give us a windbreak for cooking. Not a damned thing we can do about the smoke every day, though."

Sgt. Swing sat down on a big rock to massage his sore thigh. "Apaches don't like to fight at night, Mullin. They think anyone killed at night is doomed to walk in darkness forever."

"You betcha," agreed Takins, and the Sergeant now had their attention.

"They're also afraid of snakes. Too many Indians got snakebit in the dark and died. Rattlesnakes are an evil omen. Only thing spooks 'em worse is an owl. When I rode with the Apache Scouts under General Crook, after we located a camp of hostiles, we always surrounded 'em at night an' then attacked at dawn, soon as we could see. We were usually able to surprise those *heske* Apaches in their blankets and would shoot or capture some of 'em before they could escape."

"They didn't put out sentries?"

Sgt. Swing shook his head. "Apache is too independent. Sure, they have their hereditary leaders like Naiche, Cochise's son, or war chiefs like Geronimo, but the other warriors only take orders in battle or while on raids. Very proud men. Don't like to do women's work such as cooking and farming, either, and they will not stand guard at night, like you're gonna have to."

"Aww, Sarge, you mean it?" complained Mullin.

Tired, sore, and now irritated, too, the Sergeant got up to go over and unsort his pack. "Those folks down there were ambushed yesterday! Damned right we're standing guard up here! Until the Fourth Cavalry comes back and sweeps this area! Takins, you cook, an' I'll take the first two-hour watch. Let's get these mules unpacked and that fire goin' before it's too damned dark to see. I'm hungry, an' foolish complaints don't suit me for supper."

Not wishing to provoke him any further, the others turned quickly, Heintz on one side and Mullin and Bobyne on the other, unlashing the heavy load off its wooden cradle and carrying their special equipment to cache far away from the mules' dangerous hooves. A tired mule brayed in gratitude.

TEN

More than 7 out of every 10 people with an arrow wound would die of shock, blood poisoning, a severed artery, or infection caused by by one of the many arrowpoints painted with snake venom or the decayed livers of animals. All took their toll. The great fatality percentage of arrow wounds to the vulnerable abdomen was well known—and so well known to the Indians that they always aimed at the umbilicus. Thus the Mexicans, who were more knowledgable about fighting Indians, often protected their abdomens with many folds of a blanket.

—E. Lisle Reedstrom, *Apache Wars: An Illustrated Battle History*

Spring Water Canyon, Whetstone Mountains, Southern Arizona Territory

The raiders had dragged their captive down to a lower elevation, a small canyon running from the Whetstones between the two highest peaks on either end of the mountain mass. Unfortunately for him, this canyon was on the west side of this mountain range, the far side from Fort Huachuca, the nearest settlement, and thirty miles north of the border.

Saguaro cacti stood like sentinels along the banks of this dry, sandy watercourse, their crooked, upraised spiked arms seeming to indicate "proceed with caution."

The miner was tied against one of these large cacti. Long strips of wet rawhide bound him tightly at the ankles and the neck to the spiny desert plant. He was a fool for prospecting anywhere near the Chiricahua Apaches' legendary camping grounds, and now he certainly knew better.

The other Apaches sat their horses, stoically watching this

unfortunate suffer. Perico wound two more wraps of rawhide around the victim's chest, pulled them tight about the tall cactus.

The Mexican strained, unable to cry out, his bandanna gagging him between bloody lips. Wide-eyed, he squirmed against the excruciating pain, for he knew when this green, moist rawhide dried, it would tighten further, pulling him even deeper into the long, sharp cactus needles now piercing his shirt and pants the entire backside of his sore body.

The youngest raider, Zhonne, took his ash bow from over his shoulder, notched a hunting arrow, and at a nod from his chief, drew it back against his rawhide wrist guard and drove the three-foot arrow from no more than fifty feet, hard into the Mexican's right arm. This time the miner's squeal was audible behind his gag, pleasing the Apaches.

The bow was passed among them, Fun, Klosen, and Dahkeya all taking their turn, slowly aiming and firing arrows at close range into different parts of the poor man, exposing new areas of flesh as he writhed in agony. One missed, drawing laughter from the warriors, and another feathered, notched tip broke off as it plunged into the Mexican's leg, so deeply was this homemade arrow driven. The scrap-iron barbs pinned their victim ever tighter and deeper into the giant saguaro's sharp needles, making him a human pincushion. But the tough miner wasn't quite dead yet.

Perico was last, pulling the deer sinew string way back to bury a final arrow deep into the man's abdomen, almost up to the turkey feathers guiding its flight. The raider grunted, satisfied with his marksmanship, and handed the bow back to their novice before clambering gingerly atop his pony with his own dirty bandaged leg.

With last looks back at their pierced, barely conscious captive, the Apaches turned their mounts to ride slowly away. Behind them the teenager, Zhonne, led along their next meal, the miner's now unburdened donkey.

A long, agonized groan seeped from the Mexican. It echoed into the nearby mountains as darkness slowly fell and the creatures of the desert began to come out again from their holes to hunt prey.

ELEVEN

General Crook admonished the Chiefs at San Carlos to bring their renegade Tonto tribesmen into the reservation after they'd killed some teamsters taking supplies to Ft. Apache and drunk all their whiskey. The Chiefs sent out spies and located these renegades, then Apache Scouts surprised them and killed all seven of these Apache renegades led by Delche. They cut off their heads and brought them back in a sack and set them up in a row in front of Crook's tent at San Carlos. The General decided to display their heads on stakes about camp as a warning.

—Various sources

General Miles's Camp, Dragoon Wash

The soldiers finished their supper, scraping their tin plates nearly clean in the darkness before going back to their chores, feeding and currying the horses and mules or walking sentry. Closer to the fire sat the officers, smoking now, as they had been served first. General Miles was conscious of rank, and his imperious attitude had quickly been sensed by the enlisted men, who were cautious about speaking to or even approaching their new Commanding Officer. Nelson Miles, too, was reserved in front of the men, measuring everyone and everything, until he'd gotten his bearings out in this vast wilderness. He was not a man who could relax easily, not in front of the troops and not while on duty.

"Corned beef and rice. Again."

"Yessir. That's standard rations, General, what we can carry in cans, whilst on patrol." Their designated cook, a Corporal, scratched his budding beard. "Lessen you can kill us some fresh game."

The General sighed. "No, no hunting this trip around the forts. I don't want the Apaches aware of my presence, if that's possible."

Lt. Maus spoke up. "They're already aware of your arrival out here, General, I'm sure. Perhaps this scout trip, too. Apache telegraph is almost faster than ours."

General Miles grunted, turned to his aide "Remind me to look into the foodstores at Huachucha. Many more troops on the way out here; we've got to have better rations. An army travels on its stomach. The men can travel further and fight harder with better food in their bellies, more variety than just corned beef for supper and hardtack for breakfast every damned day."

The Lieutenant nodded. "You get us better rations, General, that'll go a ways toward raising the men's morale. Long campaigns do get discouraging."

"Indeed. Speaking of discouraging, Mr. Lummis was asking me today about the failed peace parley at the Funnels with Geronimo. General Crook was not very forthcoming on that subject. Probably because it cost him his command." General Miles tossed the stick he was fooling with into the fire, causing a few sparks to fly in the Lieutenant's direction.

"Tell us, Maus."

His First Lieutenant hesitated, thinking a moment before choosing his words carefully. He didn't wish to curry favor too openly, or blacken the preceding General's reputation, either. "Geronimo was up on a protected hillside in that canyon with all his renegades, armed to the teeth. The other chiefs—Naiche, Chihuahua, all of 'em—were wary. No more than five to eight of them came into our camp at any one time. That Tombstone photographer, Fly, was there, wanting to take pictures. I think that was a mistake, to allow him and his assistant to pose the Apaches for the camera, preening, flaunting their weapons. They had good guns, too, repeating rifles better than ours, and all the ammunition they could carry, so we knew there'd be a helluva fight if we got into it with them in the Funnels. It was a volcano crater they had camped atop of, lava ditches running down its sides—easy to defend, difficult to attack."

"Which is why Geronimo picked it." The Brigadier General ran a hand through his curly brown hair. "You don't pose for pictures until a treaty is signed, and they've already turned in their weapons."

"Exactly right, General. Geronimo was very windy, went on and on about how we hadn't treated him or his people fairly, all his grievances. But he was willing to forgive and forget, if we would just wipe his slate clean, not charge him with any crimes from his past. Just take him back to San Carlos and let him return to his peaceful farming and cattle raising."

Nelson Miles actually smiled. "Of course. So he could rest up and then next spring go back on the warpath and start his cycle of depredations all over again."

"Yes, sir. Crook wouldn't hear it. He really lit into Geronimo, calling him a liar, when he said in the Madres back in '83 that he wanted peace. The General accused him of plotting to kill Lt. Davis and Chatto, the Apache Scout. And then said Geronimo had fled and gone back to raiding, killing, and torturing innocent people. Geronimo argued, saying he hadn't tried to kill the Lieutenant and the Scout, but Crook countered that Chihuahua and some of the others had broken away from Geronimo's band when they realized he had manipulated the outbreak. The General caught him in a lie right there, but Geronimo wouldn't admit to it. That gave a bad air to the parley, right from the start. Geronimo was very suspicious, saying the newspapers kept calling for him to be hanged, unfairly, and he didn't want to be seized by civilians and killed."

The journalist couldn't contain himself. "Geronimo was aware of his own press, what the newspapers were saying about him?"

"Don't think he could read them, but people sure had told

him what they said." Now the Lieutenant shook his head. "Told you their Apache telegraph is almost faster than ours."

Their new General nodded. "Crook lost his perspective. When you're trying to get belligerents to surrender, to give up their arms, you don't get angry with them, too. Crook's emotions overrode his good sense, so of course Geronimo no longer trusted him."

"Yessir, that's the truth of it. The next day Crook warned Geronimo he must surrender unconditionally or prepare to fight until he and all his warriors were killed, even if it took fifty years. If he surrendered, his people would face exile in Florida for no more than two years, and then when things quieted down out here, they could return to San Carlos as wards of the government. Or resist to the bitter end. Geronimo said again they didn't want to be killed, but he needed to think it over and talk with his people."

The journalist was rapidly taking notes. "How did you find Geronimo, Lieutenant? His attitude, his demeanor?"

"He was very agitated, Mr. Lummis. When the General chastised him so severely right off, he broke into a big sweat. Looking back on it now, Geronimo was so suspicious, fearful of retribution by white citizens, by Crook, by our army, of course he broke and ran again. He thought he was going to be killed."

The journalist nodded, paused to light another of his hand-rolled *cigarritos* off a stick from the fire. Lummis pulled his tobacco pouch from one of the pockets inside his jacket and offered it around the circle. A Sergeant shook some into a paper to roll into a cigarette. At the General's impatient nod, Lt. Maus resumed his story.

"The third day of the parley Crook didn't remonstrate with Naiche or Chihuahua, and they surrendered easily. Geronimo surrendered last, but you could tell he was reluctant, sullen, didn't say much. They shook hands, but . . ." The Lieutenant's words trailed off, as sour memory washed over him.

Charles Lummis filled the silence. "Where did this Tribolet

come in? How did he get into that Apache camp with his liquor?"

Lt. Maus rubbed his eyes, trying to erase the memory. "Bob Tribolet had a camp he traded from, just barely south of the borderline but out of American jurisdiction. That damned man had a beef contract to feed us in the field, so he showed up with some cattle. He also had barrels of liquor in his supply wagon, which he sold only to officers and soldiers—at first. But that last night everything seemed settled, so he chanced slipping over to the Apaches' camp and sold them mescal, too.

The next morning one of the chiefs, Chihuahua, told Crook about their big toot, but said everyone would move toward the border with me and the Scouts as planned. The General left for Ft. Bowie immediately to telegraph his surrender terms back to Washington. We all set out and met up with Geronimo at Canyon Bonito. He and Naiche and three others were riding around together on a couple of burros, drunk as lords. They'd set fire to the woods behind them, and the grass was burning around these roaring drunks on their mules. It was quite a sight. But we got them out of that inferno and on to San Bernardino Springs a day later. That night, the twenty-ninth of March—I'll never forget that date—it rained, and under that cover, Tribolet snuck back into the Chiricahuas' camp and got them liquored up again."

The newsman couldn't contain himself. "Do you think it possible this liquor peddler was in the employ of the Indian Ring, those Tucson merchants who have large supply contracts with the army and don't want to see the Apaches subdued?"

A large bird, possibly an owl, flapped over the tall rocks they were camped next to, heading for cover, startling the men. After a moment and the night hunter had flown on, the soldiers recovered their poise and put back down the weapons they'd grabbed. The young Lieutenant was a bit flustered. "I . . . I couldn't speak to that, sir. Tribolet was a liquor peddler, like you said, moving back and forth across the border, selling whiskey to anyone, Indian or white, who had any money. He's related to a family of butchers in Tombstone, who sometimes sold meat from cattle of questionable origin. Man had an enduringly bad reputation, all's I know."

"Do you know anything about this Tribolet and his ties to the Tucson Ring, General?" the journalist posited.

"No, I do not. But I'll look into it. Go on, Lieutenant."

"Well sir, they got drunk again that night, in the rain, and later twenty hostiles, led by Geronimo and Naiche, along with thirteen women and about six children, snuck out of their camp and fled back into Mexico. One of Naiche's wives, Eclahheh, evidently tried to run to the scouts, to remain safely with us, but the Chief shot her in the knee for disobeying. Then Naiche had to leave her and his young daughter behind anyway, because she was wounded and couldn't travel well. Chihuahua and a dozen of his braves sobered up next morning and came back with us to the fort."

"And our supposedly friendly Apache Scouts didn't alert you?"

The Lieutenant couldn't meet the General's stare. He ground his teeth instead, grim over this terrible blotch on his war record. "One told me the hostiles were drinking again, so I sent Lt. Shipp to destroy their new supplies and run Tribolet off. Shipp reported the Scouts had smashed all the five-gallon kegs of *mescal* and rotgut whiskey they could find, but Tribolet evidently snuck back in with more after the Lieutenant left and got the Chiricahuas drunk again. I thought they'd sleep it off. I did have sentries out, but it was raining, hard, and everyone was . . . tired. We were on American soil again and the hostiles' surrender had gone fairly well up until then, so I wasn't as vigilant as I should have been, I guess. They got away before dawn. . . ." Lt. Maus swallowed hard. "I'm . . . sorry."

General Miles shook his head. "Thirty-nine Apaches, sneaking silently off into the night. Quite a large number to miss, supposedly drunken ones, too, shooting their women. How many men did you have down there in the Funnels to escort them back, Lieutenant?"

Lt. Maus winced. ". . . Uh, with the Scouts, I guess, eighty, ninety. But some left early, with the General."

"Quite a sizable guard force. Especially if the Apaches had been disarmed, first. Well, not entirely your fault, Maus. I can't believe Geronimo's band could have gotten away without the active assistance of some of your Scouts—blood relatives of his who didn't want to see their kin punished or were doing it to protect their scouting jobs or were even bribed with money or ammunition or liquor, or some combination of all those misbegotten motives. We'll never know. You put dangerous criminals in the custody of their friends and relatives—look out. General Crook should have stayed there with more white troops to supervise this big march of that many hostile Apaches instead of leaving it to two young Lieutenants. He was ultimately responsible."

Lieutenant Marion P. Maus had nothing further to say. Behind him, their cook was unable to suppress a yawn. General Miles pulled his wool coat about him against the spring night's chill. "We'll make Ft. Huachucha tomorrow, men, midday, in time for dinner, if we get an early start in the morning."

Lt. Maus nodded, and the soldiers roused to move to their bedrolls.

One of the soldiers walked past him, tapping another man to relieve him on "running guard," sentry duty of about an hour each until dawn. Charles Lummis bunched his corduroy jacket under his head and wrapped his Navajo blanket about him as he settled into the dirt. Ah, how he missed his warm wife, Dorothea, now practicing as a physician back in California. He pined for his physical romps with Dolly, his pet name for his second wife, which he had taken to recording in his journal. "Dolly *me la cielo*," he wrote, which in his fractured Spanish translated as "Dolly and I went to heaven."

Charles faced the rebuilt fire so he could see to scribble some more notes, which he would soon polish into another dispatch to his newspaper.

Take one single example, the case of the trader Tribolet. "That man," said Crook to me, "is the cause of this whole trouble now. If it had not been for his whiskey, Geronimo's renegades would never have decamped, the whole thing would now be settled, and we should be reaping the results of nearly a year's arduous labor. Oh no, there's no way of dealing with Tribolet. He has been tried before, but bought his way out. If we had shot him down like a coyote, as he deserved, it would have raised a terrible row. Why, that man has a beef contract for our army!"

In those words Crook lays bare a whole section of our national disgrace. The government is obliged to advertise and let the contracts to the lowest bidder. Tribolet got one. "It doesn't make any difference how big a scoundrel a man may be," Crook continued. "That doesn't disqualify him. Punish him by law? We have no laws here! This is a country where the majority rules, and no matter what is on the statute books, no law can be enforced against the sentiment of the community. And such fellows can undo the work of a great government, while we have no recourse. I hope those of us who like to boast of our nation to the detriment of those across the seas will remember what Customs Officer Green told me. Tribolet told him he didn't want the hostiles captured. "Why," said he, it's money in my pocket to have those fellows out." And he bragged how much whiskey he had sold them and how he had given Geronimo a bottle of champagne.

Observation Post #4, Square Mountain, Sulphur Springs Valley

Sgt. Swing had his men up working early next morning before Takins even had their breakfast fire flaming brightly under a couple small skillets. They'd parboiled some salt pork last night, and now he was going to cook it. The grease left over would be used to to fry their hardtack, which had been soaking overnight in water. Takins had some of their roasted coffee beans from the tin bound in an old rag and was pounding them into coffee grounds on a flat rock with the butt of his rifle.

"Coffee in a minute. Hard to cook without a proper fire pit."

The Sergeant stopped helping Bobyne place two wooden tripods on the flattest bit of slope they'd been able to find on this rocky mountainside. Every military unit he'd ever been in contained at least one chronic complainer. Private Takins was already staking out the low ground in this detail. "We'll help dig one, Takins, after we get camp set up. Gotta send this alert first."

"What should I do with this flag, Sarge?" Their eighteen-year-old Private held a two-foot rectangle of white canvas with a large red square in the middle, fitted atop an eight-foot-high wooden pole. This distinctive flag was braced flat for easy identification by wooden rods slipped into its sewn edge sleeves. It was the symbol of the U.S. Signal Corps, required to fly day and night over Observation Post #4.

"Plant it back there somewheres, outta the way. Don't want that damned thing flyin' right on the edge here to guide any passing Apaches right up to us. And watch that mutt, too, Mullin. Don't let him knock over any of this delicate equipment."

"No, no, don't want any of that kind of bad luck, do we, Horace?" Mullin grabbed the dog's rope and a pick. "C'mon, boy, let's get this flag planted."

Heintz swung a shovel at the south end of their ledge, trying to clear a space in the brushy ravine for a makeshift corral for their two mules. He'd had them lariatted out last night, tied at the end of thirty-foot ropes secured at the end of fifteen-inch iron picket pins hammered into the ground. Now he'd let them loose to graze, and as fast as he could whack the creosote bushes off at the roots, the hungry pack animals were into them, nibbling the plants' spring buds.

At the ledge's north end, their Signal Corpsman was involved in a more precise task. After unpacking some small leather cases, upon one three-legged tripod Bobyne very carefully slid the sun mirror, a four-and-one-half-inch square of plate glass supported by sheet brass and cardboard backing in a brass restraining frame. Kneeling behind this adjustable "head," which could be turned at any angle and to every point on the compass, the Corporal began fitting a brass rod, six and a half inches long with a movable bronze collar, onto the mirror frame bar. Looking up, Bobyne realized every man in the detail had stopped what he was doing to watch him fine-tune his equipment. A wisp of smile crossed his face.

"This is my sighting bar." Bobyne sighted through the unsilvered hole in the mirror's center. "Where do you think B and D troops might be right now, Sergeant?"

Sgt. Swing stood, shaded his eyes as he looked down the wide Sulphur Springs Valley. The Swisshelm Mountains were almost in a direct line southeast toward the border, while further to the left were the more massive Chiricahua Mountains, with the area's highest, Chiricahua Peak, at nearly 9,800 feet, right in their middle. Both mountain ranges were designated to host additional heliograph posts soon.

"Southeast—Arizona's roughest corner. Ridin' toward the Sierra Madres of ol' Mexico. Where Geronimo and Naiche like to hole up after they've raised hell and reequipped up here. Army's never had much luck flushin' 'em out of the Madres. Too damned rugged and too far south of the border for resupply. Mexico wears out soldiers and horses somethun' fierce."

Bobyne turned the mirror down and raised the sighting rod until the center of the mirror and the tip of the sighting rod were lined up southeast according to his hand compass and Sgt. Swing's pointed finger. He next flipped a movable disc on his sighting rod and found the "shadow spot" on his own hand, held about six inches in front of the unsilvered center of the mirror.

"Once you get your direction, you have to aim the mirror along that line of sight, too, so the people you're sending to get full benefit of your signal. Fifty yards off to either side, they might not even catch your flash. So accuracy's important, boys, just like when you aim and pull that trigger."

Adjusting the tangent screws now that the mirror bar was firmly clamped to the tripod, the Signal Corpsman tilted the mirror up and down, left and right until the "shadow spot" fell upon the little paper disc atop his sighting rod. The mirror's flash was now aimed correctly, visible directly southeast, so he planted a second tripod with a metal shutter screen atop it close to and in front of the sighting disc, so as to intercept its flash without touching and jiggling the sun mirror on the first tripod and possibly throwing it out of alignment. Opening the shutter's leaves, Bobyne trained the full beam of light on the distant troops' location he'd roughly estimated. This was his "call" signal.

"Since their location's a guess, I'll move the beam around, covering all degrees on the compass southeast, hoping to catch 'em. Obviously it's easier heliographing a fixed location daily, like Post Five, across our valley."

The taut Corporal suddenly stood, pleased by his mates' rapt attention as he self-consciously brushed off the knees of his new pants. "My Manse is adjusted. Guess we're ready to send."

"Okay. Let's see. . . ." The Sergeant rubbed his eyes, composing his first message in his new job.

"CAPT HATFIELD SIX APACHES ATTACKED COXS TANKS TWO DAYS AGO."

The ex-telegraph operator worked the six movable metal leaves on the shutter screen rapidly by hand crank. Via long and short flashes of sunlight, the letters of the brief message from Observation Post #4 were gradually spelled out.

Sergeant Swing nodded with satisfaction, watching his first official message being winked brightly off into the dry desert air. He hoped someone was awake on patrol to receive his warning. "God knows where those raiders are by now. With fresh horses, an Apache can ride up to seventy miles a day, day after day if he's pushin' it. Even takes most of his sleep and food in the saddle. Our cavalry makes twenty-five to thirty miles a day at best. It's a wonder we catch 'em anywhere."

Mouth of Rucker Canyon, East of the Swisshelm Mountains, Southeastern Arizona Territory

Rather than reveille, hacking coughs and loud expectorations were the tune as the men of the Fourth Cavalry got up after dawn, dressed, and rolled up bedrolls, as their cooks prepared a hasty breakfast of fatback bacon and dry bread for another hard day in the saddle. One summoned his messmates with the traditional call, "Soupee, Soupee, Soupee! Without a single bean! Coffee, coffee, coffee! Without a bit of cream!"

One of the troopers, tentatively sipping a scalding cup of Rio, paused when he spotted distant flashes to the northwest. "Hey! That one of them signals?"

Several other soldiers stopped dressing to look where he was pointing. The trooper stood up to get the attention of another stooped behind a large ocotillo, relieving himself. "Timmons! Hey! You read them flashes?"

Corporal Timmons turned to look where this soldier was pointing, shading his eyes against the early morning sun.

Observation Post #5, Dos Cabezas Peak, Southeastern Arizona Territory

Due north of the cavalry, midway up Dos Cabezas Peak, looking down on the trading post of the same name below, another field breakfast was being partaken around a cooking fire. Lounging on his army blanket, Private Slivers also saw something unusual across the big valley in front of him.

"Hey! Ain't that flashin' over to the Winchesters?"

Four heads at Observation Post #5 swiveled.

"Damn! Sons-a-bitches were supposed to wait for my first test at noon!" Lt. Fuller pulled out his pocket watch and peered at it. "Damn! Stopped again. What time is it?"

None of his men knew, for none of them even owned a watch. "Damm it! Can't even keep a watch wound in this blasted heat and dust!"

Sergeant Conn seconded his Commanding Officer. "Tryin' to show us up, sir. We ain't even set up yet."

"Can't read it. Isn't aimed properly," groused Lt. Fuller, as both he and his Signal Corpsman grabbed their binoculars. The Second Lieutenant slammed his cork helmet on, ready for military business.

Corporal Hengesbaugh translated. "A-P-A-C-H-E-S A-T-T-A-C-KED T-W-O D-A-YS A-G-O. That's no test, sir. I think they're trying to signal D Troop."

"Damnation! Let's get ready here, men! Weapons ready, build some rifle posts, set our lines of fire. We may come under attack." As his men scrambled to get their rifles, the young officer allowed himself a small smile. Engaging the enemy, he thought. Now he could put his West Point training to use, maybe even distinguish himself in battle!

Mouth of Rucker Canyon, East of the Swisshelm Mountains

Corporal Timmons stood next to D Troop's officers and their horses, deciphering for Captain Hatfield and Second Lieutenant Walsh through his binoculars a repeat of the message from Square Mountain. "ONE HOSTILE KILLED ONE WOUNDED BY RANCHERS MEET ME COXS TANKS TOMORROW SWING."

The Captain pulled his own ear, helping himself think. "How far is it back to the Tanks?"

The Second Lieutenant had his map out, checking the most direct route. "Umm, forty-five miles now, roughly."

"Tomorrow it is then. We might cut some sign on the way, so get those scouts far enough ahead to flush out anybody trying to set us up for an ambush. Apaches will probably see our dust cloud from a distance, regardless. Let's get moving, Lieutenant."

"Yes, sir!" Lieutenant Walsh nodded to his signalman, as other troopers nearby moved quickly to saddle their mounts.

TWELVE

Liquor was the curse of the Army. Brutal punishments were sometimes meted out by staking drunks out or "spread-eagling" them on the parade ground. Chronic drunkards were sometimes given undesirable "bobtail" discharges, with the character section clipped off, an indication that the recipient had not been honorably released. During the decade of the 1880's, almost forty-one out of every thousand soldiers were hospitalized as alcoholics. In an era when only the most severe cases were treated, for manifestations such as delirium tremens, *this ratio of one out of twenty-five soldiers is evidence of an extremely serious situation.*

—Don Rickey, Jr., *Forty Miles a Day on Beans and Hay*

Fort Huachuca, San Pedro Valley, Southern Arizona Territory

Colonel William Bedford Royall, Commander of the Fourth Cavalry and also in charge of the fort, rode out with Captain Henry W. Lawton to meet the General's dark blue conveyance and small mounted escort accompanying his inspection tour.

General Miles! Welcome to Fort Huachuca!"

Seated on the front seat of the Quartermaster's wagon next to the mule driver, Nelson Miles returned the Commander's salute, then gazed along the rows of wooden buildings. "Thank you, Colonel. A pretty fort you have. I didn't realize it had gotten so built up in such a short time."

"Yes, sir, we've been busy beavers. General, this is Captain Lawton, B Troop of the Fourth."

General Miles nodded. "Captain. Why don't you give us a quick tour before we refresh ourselves, Colonel."

"My pleasure, sir." Colonel Royall and Captain Lawton settled their horses into a walk alongside Miles's wagon. They were approaching four two-storied whitewashed frame buildings on the north side of the parade grounds. "These four are our enlisted men's quarters, two large squad rooms upstairs and down, and some office space downstairs for the noncoms. Latrines out back, and our sewage is piped down to Huachuca Creek about a mile below the post."

"Which units are stationed here now, Colonel?"

"Fourth Cavalry, sir, First and Eighth Infantries. . . . huts up the creek back there, for the laundresses." Colonel Royall turned back in his saddle to sweep his arm along the row of adobe buildings on the far side of the parade ground. "Officer's Row. You'll be staying in that bigger one at the end, General, with me. This is our new bakery we're very proud of, and next to it our new hospital, built last year. Has twenty-four beds. Those are our stables, behind the bakery. We're already expanding them, to get ready for some of those new troops you've ordered out to the territory, General."

"Excellent. This is our southernmost fort, so as our advance base it's going to see much harder use by greatly increased forces. Where does your water come from, Colonel?"

"Permanent springs, about three miles up the creek in some hills. We've got it piped down to our two reservoirs up on that hill behind us. From there the water's piped down to where it's needed, in our buildings."

The General's wagon was approaching the end of the parade ground, and his cavalry escort had now fallen in to amble along behind the officers talking up front. "Where do you intend to put your heliograph, Colonel?"

"Up on that hill, between the reservoirs, General." Colonel Royall pointed southwest. "Highest point near this fort. If line of sight's not adequate up there, once we get our equipment shipped in, we may have to go northwest eight miles, to the Mustang Mountains."

General Miles nodded. "Your heliograph's here, Colonel. Brought several with me. And a couple operators. More of both are on the way from Ft. Myer. Better communications are a priority with me."

"Well thank you, General. That's very prompt. We'll get ours working right away."

Resting atop his horse on the other side of the blue wagon, Charles Lummis interjected. "I just can't think of this place as a fort, General. These southwestern forts are just a series of buildings, no stockade around them, no barrier of any kind from attack."

General Miles smiled at the newsman's impudence, as he turned back to his officers. "Excuse me, gentlemen, for not introducing you. This is Charles Lummis, from the *Los Angeles Times*, checking our facilities on my reconnaissance tour."

The two cavalry officers nodded to Lummis, and Captain Ware took the opportunity to make an impression upon his superiors. "Milled lumber's too dear in this desert, Mr. Lummis, to waste on a stockade. We use it to build strong barracks and adobe roofs instead. If the Apaches were foolish enough to attack us directly, we'd fight them from inside these structures, which they'd have to try to take or burn, one at a time. Meanwhile we'd catch them in a crossfire from our other buildings. Our parade ground would become a killing ground. But the Apaches aren't stupid. They're more interested in raiding our stables, or attacking one of our supply trains, which aren't nearly as well protected."

The General indicated with a finger to turn the wagon around, and the soldier driving whipped his wheeler mule enough to begin making a circle. "Lt. Maus!"

"Sir!" The officer of his detail spurred his horse closer to General Miles's wagon.

"Meet me in Colonel Royall's office in an hour for a briefing."

"Yes, sir!" The Lieutenant turned his mount smartly and loped off toward the stables they had passed, behind the bakery. "Detail follow!"

Returning the way they'd come, Colonel Royall checked his horse at the sight of another rider headed slowly toward them, leading another tired horse with a man in a blue tunic lashed face down over its saddle. The cargo was obviously dead. "Lawton, go see to that," hissed Ft. Huachuca's Commander. With a quick glance at his superior, the Captain spurred his horse toward the problem.

The Colonel, meanwhile, tried to steer the journalist and the General's wagon across the wide parade ground toward his own quarters. "Gentlemen, let's get you settled in and refreshed, before we sit down to a good meal and the latest scouting reports."

But Nelson Miles was impatient. "No, no, I wish to hear what that man says. Is that one of our soldiers over his saddle?"

They rode up to the man in the stained Stetson, now dismounted in front of the single-story adobe building. A wide eave projected over the board porch outside this building, upon which an armed guard walked. The eave also helped keep the few men inside this post guardhouse a little cooler during the summer's heat and the boredom of their confinement.

Captain Lawton was talking intently with the stocky man with a Marshal's dull silver badge pinned to his leather vest, when the General's wagon creaked to a stop in front of him.

"Colonel, Marshal Stevens brought in one of our troopers, Private William Megehee, deceased. Wants the reward. For desertion."

Colonel Royall was already frowning, and it deepened when he saw General Miles hoisting his bulk off the front seat of the baggage wagon. "Where'd you catch him, Marshal?"

"Just outside of Benson. Got drunk and shot up one of our saloons after they threw him out. He was headed northwest toward Tucson when I sighted him. Didn't hang around for the train."

General Miles fingered the dead man's tunic, noting the seeped blood and burned cloth around the gaping hole made by the .45 slug. "Shot in the back."

It was the Marshal's turn to frown. "Winged a couple at me on the run first, before I caught him with a lucky shot, droppin' him from his horse."

"Where's his Springfield?"

"Confiscated. Evidence. Fleeing arrest." The Marshal squinted, focused now on the officer in charge. "Hoped we could settle this quietly, pay my reward, without bringing it to trial, to the public's attention."

The General nodded. "And what is the reward for deserters, Captain?"

"Twenty-five dollars for Megehee, less fifteen for his rifle. Thirty dollars for the horse."

"Dobie dollars?" the lawman asked.

"Greenbacks."

"Pay him, Captain. And get our poor Private buried. He's beginning to ripen." General Miles flashed the law enforcer a very thin smile. "Next time, Marshal, we'd appreciate our missing men returned still breathing. We'll discipline them in our own fashion and set a better example for the rest."

Marshal Stevens tipped his hat. "Do my best, General."

Captain Lawton yelled at a couple soldiers watching to come help move the body. General Miles turned to walk across the parade ground toward officers' quarters, accompanied by the now dismounted Colonel and the General's blue wagon, following behind. "What is your desertion rate these days, Colonel?"

The high-ranking officer winced at the question and looked back anxiously at the journalist riding along behind him.

"It's all right. Mr. Lummis can hear."

"Well, right now, it's about twenty percent of our enlisted men gone over the hill, General."

"Really? Why so high?"

"Well, pay's so low. They enlist to be Indian fighters, something romantic in their minds, then they get out here, and we put shovels and saws in their hands instead of rifles and tell them they've got to build forts and dig latrines. They didn't sign up for a work battalion, and the construction skills they acquire with us are worth more in any town. So they desert, out of boredom and frustration, looking for good jobs, better pay, girlfriends, more excitement. Then we have to issue circulars, and these quick-draw lawmen shoot 'em, like you'd gun down a stray dog. Just to pick up some easy reward money. And no one gives a damn about the poor soldier, just off on a payday toot."

Nelson Miles stopped, halting their little parade. His eyes searched his surroundings, the army buildings, the scattered troops going about their mundane chores. The General sighed as he stared at the bigger mountain range to the south, the Huachucas, right above the border. "Should be a criminal offense, shooting an absentee soldier in the back. Well . . . if it's fighting these men want, to relieve their tedium, they're going to get it. We're going after these Apaches. To the last man." He graced the fort's Commander with another thin smile. "Your construction work, Colonel, will have to wait."

Observation Post #4, Square Mountain, Sulphur Springs Valley

"Losin' the light, Sergeant. Have to be our last message today, unless you want to try a flashing lantern tonight?"

"No, don't want to alert any Apaches to our location, lighting up this mountain. They'll know we're up here soon enough."

With the sun going down behind the mountain at his back, the Signal Corpsman had to bring out a second mirror to clamp at one end of the mirror bar, extended out at an angle from the first mirror. The sun's disappearing light behind him had to be adjusted for and directed from the main sun mirror onto this second mirror so that it could be flashed ahead of him, across the valley, away from the setting sun behind Bobyne.

Sergeant Swing paced, composing. "All right. 'NO SIGN OF APACHES NOW STAY ALERT WILL SCOUT WITH 4TH CAVALRY IF ARRIVE TOMORROW POST 4.'"

Corporal Bobyne began working the shutter, sending the flashes across the valley to Observation Post #5, stopping once to move behind the sun mirror and adjust its tangent screws to keep the "shadow spot" in the center of the paper aiming disc. Only by keeping these mirrors properly aimed and aligned as the sun continued to set on the horizon behind him could its operator maintain the brilliancy of flash necessary for a message to be sent.

Satisfied, the Sergeant moved off to check the rest of the work going on to secure their campsite on this ledge halfway up Square Mountain. At its far end Corporal Heintz was feeding grain to the mules, while Mullin rested, winded, over one of several boulders he'd helped roll up to the edge of their fortifications. Sgt. Swing stopped to survey the slope above them.

"Couple more big rocks up there you can roll down pretty easy. Do that, then you and I'll go down tomorrow to meet the Captain and haul up the rest of our supplies and tents, Mullin, if they've arrived."

"Yessir! I'm tired of this boulder rollin' already."

"Me, too, Private, but a perimeter defense is necessary. Heintz! See if you can't clear out more brush from that ravine tomorrow, so's we can build a brush corral for these mules. Takins can help you. I also want Bobyne to show you fellas where to look for signals, so you can spell him watchin' for messages."

The veteran stopped scanning the mountainside to watch Takins kneeling over the little cookfire he was blowing into flame in his deepened fire pit. Sgt. Swing picked up a canteen, took a long drink, and wet his bandanna to wipe his brow. "What's for supper?"

Their cook stopped huffing his kindling. "Beans, biscuits, and Cincinnati chicken!"

The Southerner noticed Mullin's perplexed look. "Sowbelly to you, sonny. Why'ncha see iffen you can't sweet-talk that lady who ran off from her husband into bakin' us some pies, while you're down there tomorra, Sarge."

That got the German's attention. "Yah! *Goot* idea!"

Sgt. Swing frowned. "I can maybe arrange some help with our laundry, get us each a bath now an' again. Pies an' desserts is pushin' her hospitality a mite, soldier, but we'll see."

The signalman was packing up his precious equipment so it wouldn't be stumbled over by someone trying to find the latrine in the dark. Bobyne grinned at his Sergeant. "Hear, hear!"

Ranch Near Cox's Tanks

Next morning, Jacob Cox was beside his small barn nailing several black and white-striped hog-nosed skunk pelts to it, when he sighted the two soldiers leading mules with their empty pack cradles. "Sergeant! Hey! How you doin' up on the mountain, boys? Seen any more Apaches?"

"Nope. Any more problems down here, Mr. Cox?"

"No sir. Nary hide nor hair of an Indian since their attack." The rancher paused to rap his knuckles on his corral's wooden railing for luck. "Packer who brought in your supplies didn't see any, either, so they've probably fled this section of sand."

"Didn't get what they wanted, your horses and guns, so they may come back yet." Sgt. Swing stopped at the stone-faced well, dropped a wooden bucket into it. At a small splash from the bottom, he began winching it back up to replenish his string of canteens. "I signaled D Troop, and if they got our message, Captain Hatfield should be here today."

"Swell!" Cox hammered a last nail into a skunk pelt.

"Trappin' skunks, huh?"

"Yup. Been after our chickens again. Pelts worth a dollar a

piece over at the trader's, though what they use 'em for, I do not know."

The Sergeant smiled. "Ladies' mufflers for winter back East, I heard. Latest fashion."

"Maybe that's just it." The rancher wiped his hands on his butternut pants, trying to remove some of the skunk stink. "I've had to leave my cattle loose while we were under this threat. I was wondering if you men could help me herd 'em in closer to the Tanks for protection. Shouldn't take more than a couple hours to find 'em all."

The Sergeant poured the bucket water into the mouths of his tin canteens without a funnel, making a muddy mess of his chore. "I've gotta pack up our goods and wait here to report to the Cavalry, Mister Cox. But I can lend you Private Mullin for a few hours."

"Two of us can probably get it done. Do you ride, son?"

Young Mullin looked over the uncut gray stallion frisking about the corral in his new horseshoes. Doubt creased his countenance. "Only plow horses, sir. Back on our farm in Michigan."

"Dandy! Martha's gentle mare will suit you fine then." He pointed to a smaller bay horse. "I'll get her tack."

Jacob disappeared into his feed and tack shed inside the corral, as the Sergeant motioned his new recruit aside while he unbuckled his .45 Army Colt. "Keep your rifle ready, and take my thumb buster, too. Don't let the man outta your sight, Mullin. Any sign of Apaches, haul hell out of its shuck gettin' back here. Don't try to be a hero, kid, or you'll be a dead one."

"Okay, Sarge. Sure."

"And don't dawdle around all day out there, even if you can't find all his cows. I wanna be back up that mountain before dark."

The Private nodded as the rancher emerged from his shed with a smaller woman's saddle and blanket and a handful of horse tack. Jacob whistled sharply. "Buster! C'mon, boy! Time to work!"

His whistle brought his longer-haired, black-and-white cow dog on the bounce from the barn.

The Sergeant led his mules to the horse trough to let them drink the water he'd been slopping into it, then limped toward the house, where he could see the lady inside through the open window facing the barn. "Good morning, ma'am."

"Isn't it, though? Your supplies are on the porch, Sergeant."

Walking to his goods, Sgt. Swing started fingering through the three two-man A-tents the packer had left them, plus several large wooden mess boxes filled with food items and a couple empty ten-gallon kegs to hold their extra water.

Martha Cox came out the front door bearing a glass of water with slices of lemon floating in it. Her stride was straight and stiff, due to the bodice of her calico dress, which was boned inside for extra strength. "Care for some lemonade?"

"Thank you, ma'am." The Sergeant took a long swig of the tart drink, then ran the cool glass over his forehead.

"Where'd you get these lemons, Miss Cox?"

"Come from the mission groves at Tumacacori, over near Tubac. Pick some up at the trader's whenever I can. Helps cut the dust."

"Yes indeed . . ." The career soldier paused for another long draught. "Brave work, fighting off those Apaches. Where'd you learn to shoot so well?"

"My dad taught me, back in Iowa. I inherited the keen eyes in the family, not my brother. Hunted rabbits, coons with my father, even shot rats in the barn at night by candlelight. Jacob did better in school, though. Guess I was more boy than he was." She smiled at the thought.

The cattle herders were mounted. Buster bounded away, eager. Jacob Cox waved to his sister. "Good-bye, Martha! Hold the fort!"

"Don't ride too far out!"

"We won't! Be back fairly soon!"

Mullin casually saluted them with his rifle, cocky like a kid.

They rode slowly off and up the low hill to the east and the Tanks on its other side.

Martha Cox shook her head. "Young men and older. Not a dime's worth of difference, it comes to minding them."

The Sergeant turned back to her. "Don't know about that. These young recruits got more gumption than is good for 'em. Till they meet their first wild Apache. Could use more good shots like you in the army, though, ma'am. Most of my boys couldn't hit a bull in the behind with a bushel basket."

He grinned at his choice opinion and so did she. The veteran gulped the last of his lemonade. "Mighty refreshing. I better get these goods packed so we're ready if the cavalry shows up."

The lady accepted his glass. "You're welcome inside when you're finished, Sergeant. I might even locate a slice of my famous pie."

Curtains of thin, bleached muslin, called *manta*, flickered in the slight spring breeze through her kitchen window. Glass windows were still too much of a luxury for this remote place. Through these curtains the two army mules could be seen moving about inside the corral across the barnyard, tossing some hay the Sergeant had thrown down for them. Nearby sat supply boxes and tents ready to be roped to their pack rigs for carrying back up the mountain.

Sgt. Swing sat across from her at the kitchen table. "Pretty tasty. What's in it?"

"Well, it's too early in the season for fresh fruit, and they were out of dried fruit at the trader's, so I cooked up one of my vinegar pies." She looked directly at him.

The Sergeant's second forkful halted halfway into his mouth. "Vinegar? But it tastes sweet."

"That's the sugar. Vinegar's good for your digestion. Got to eat it fresh, though, or it begins to taste stronger. Ripens right up. My girlfriend, Sadie, back in Iowa, used to tease me that I just cooked up paperhanger's paste and seasoned to taste."

To please her, he scraped the crumbs off her fine china. "Like it lots better than that mock apple pie made from soda crackers. Fresh eggs for the crust, though?"

Miss Cox sighed. "When I can raise enough chickens. Trying to raise chickens out here is just a series of minor tragedies. Every critter in this desert likes chicken for dinner, including skunks."

Sgt. Swing chuckled, causing her finally to smile. She reached for the pie tin to offer another slice, but he shook his head no. Martha Cox had done the best she could to make her brother's ranch house a home, with her pots and skillets on the plank shelves either side of the black cast-iron stove in one corner, its pipe streaked with rust, a pot of cowboy beans simmering atop it. Several other wall shelves were piled with bundles of dried leaves and stalks, glass canning jars filled with various cut roots and ground powders. All her herbal medicines and food seasonings, which she obviously took seriously. For all he knew, Martha Cox could be some kind of prairie witch doctor.

The Sergeant tilted back in his chair, finally able to relax a bit in the presence of this intimidating woman. "So you left your husband back in Iowa and journeyed out here to the burning desert. Must have been hard on you, such a big change."

Now Martha frowned, piqued by his condescension. "I'm used to hard. Don't know any other way. My husband left me, Sergeant, not the other way around. I was his helpmeet, like our marriage certificate said, but Horace got restless. Sure wasn't any farmer. So he headed west to search for gold, to see the elephant, and I was a 'woman in waiting.' Said he'd be back, but . . . After two long years I hired a lawyer and got unhitched. Iowa's one of the few emancipated plains states, like Oklahoma and North Dakota, where divorce is legal for some reasons, and 'willful desertion' is one of 'em. So I sold our family farm, packed up my Haviland china and herbs and a couple bottles of Henry's Invigorating Cordial, and headed west myself, to help my dear brother, who was . . . struggling." She fiddled with her lace collar, made anxious by remembrance.

"Kinda sad story. 'Willful desertion.' " The veteran shook his head.

"When you live so close to the bone, Sergeant, there is very little room for sentiment."

"No, ma'am, there isn't."

She managed a smudge of a smile. "Coming out here, guess I jumped from the skillet straight into the fire."

Now it was Sgt. Swing who frowned. "We'll get the Apache licked. An' make this territory a more peaceful place for everyone to live."

He had another swallow of lemonade, as he probed the woman across from him carefully, changing unpleasant subjects. "Got any other kin?"

"A few aunts and uncles back in New Hampshire. 'Live Free or Die' seems to be our family motto." She shook her head, bemused by the memory, then changed that subject, too.

"Ever been married, Sergeant?"

"Close. Lost my sweetheart to a drummer with a good job and a fancier spiel. So, I joined the army and became the tough old mossyhorn I am. Guess what the Bard said pegs me. 'While I have basked in the smiles of fortune, I have not winced in her frown.' "

Looking down again, he rubbed the back of his hand, uncomfortable at her question.

"Read that in a poem once." He suddenly had the fidgets. Personal revelations didn't come easily to this veteran soldier; he'd rather be asking than telling.

She scrutinized him. "Don't know about that. Little younger, I'll bet you were a ring-tailed tooter."

Ammon Swing raised his head to look straight into her calculating gaze. "Still am. . . . Ma'am."

Through the window behind her, he was relieved to see a

rider appear in the barnyard, then two more soldiers on horseback. He scraped his chair back and rose, breaking their intimacy. "Ah. The cavalry's here." He winked at the still handsome, middle-aged lady. "Guess we're saved."

Captain Hatfield and Second Lieutenant Walsh had dismounted and were drinking from their canteens as Sgt. Swing limped up. Miss Cox followed, smoothing her apron.

"Captain. Lieutenant."

Capt. Hatfield acknowledged the Sergeant's casual, open-handed salute. "Sergeant. What happened here?"

All about them, thirty other soldiers and a few Indian scouts were watering themselves and their horses, drawing buckets from the stone well, while others waited to use the outhouse or stretched out their aches against the rungs of the corral. All of them noticed the woman, though, and had at least one ear cocked to Sgt. Swing's report.

"Lady and her brother were attacked by about six Apaches, three days ago. Miss Cox, Captain Hatfield, Lieutenant Walsh, of the Fourth Cavalry. They'd like to hear about your Apache fight."

The officers tipped their hats. "Ma'am."

"Gentlemen. Well. It was late afternoon. My brother, Jacob, and I were coming back from the trader's at Dos Cabezas when I saw something flashing up there on the mountain. Immediately after that we were attacked by three Apaches riding up from the arroyo out there." She pointed as Lt. Walsh pulled out his binoculars to fix the distant location better.

Wallapai Clark caught the Sergeant's eye and motioned him over to where he was resting against the barn, having a chew. "These people shot a couple broncho Apaches and lived to tell it, Ammon?"

"No reason to lie, Wallapai, unless to get a little more military protection. These folks seem to have gotten along with the 'Paches, feedin' 'em, lettin' 'em water at the Tanks. Raiders wounded her brother, though."

The Scout took another chaw off his plug and offered it to his *compadre*. Sgt. Swing shook his head no.

Wallapai cogitated. "Might be Naiche and some of his bucks, up from Mexico lookin' to recruit some restless ones offn' the reservation, make more trouble." The tough Scout spat. "Hope it ain't Geronimo. Don't know where in hell his ornery ass is right now."

"Well, they got more than they bargained for here. Means they'll keep raidin', till they get all the guns and horses they need."

"Yup." Wallapai Clark spat again. "Keep an' eagle eye out up that mountain, Ammon, and remember us Scouts' rule." He shook hands with his saddle pal. "Save that last one for yourself."

The grizzled tracker ambled off to join the men cooling themselves at the well. Ammon Swing opened his palm to find in it a single .45/.70 brass cartridge.

Cavalrymen were mounting up or taking a quick piss around the stable's far corner, out of the woman's sight. The last of the canteens was being filled and strapped on saddlehorns, when one of the Wallapai Scouts sighted Jacob Cox and Private Mullin riding over the hill from the Tanks.

"Lieutenant!" The Scout pointed his nose toward the riders, for desert Indians never pointed with their hands at anyone. Too impolite. The two men riding in saw the troopers and kicked their horses into a lope.

Sgt. Swing was walking over to Martha to say good-bye, when she spotted her brother. "Ahh, good. It's Jacob."

"Ma'am, I've another big favor to ask of you."

She turned back to him, expectant, her smile fading.

"My men and I are gonna have some dirty clothes, and we really can't spare enough water up there to wash 'em. So I was wonderin' if we could work out some arrangement, for pay, for you to help us out, maybe?"

"Like your laundresses at the forts?"

"Oh no, ma'am, that's their full-time job, for many soldiers.

This would just be once a week, for the five of us, maybe a bit of mending, too, for a fair price?" He was reduced to begging now, for help with his laundry. Such humility didn't suit him.

Martha Cox might otherwise have enjoyed seeing this proud man reduced to a supplicant, but he was asking quite a favor. "Boiling and ironing very soiled clothes is a lot of hot, hard work, soldier, especially in the summer. But I'll give it some thought next time you come down off that mountain with a bundle of filthies."

Sergeant Swing looked hugely relieved. Now he could return to his recalcitrant troops with a smile. "Yes, ma'am! Thank you. The boys will be most grateful."

Mullin unsaddled his loaned horse and the rancher's inside the corral, while Jacob Cox joined the Officers. "Private Mullin and I were out driving my stock in closer to the Tanks, Captain, when we came upon one of my steers, partially butchered. Looked like the Apaches did it, not some varmint. Cuts were too clean for bites. They were in a hurry."

Capt. Hatfield nodded. "Let's take a look. Would you lead us back there, Mr. Cox?"

"Well, duty calls. Thanks again, ma'am, for the lemonade, your famous pie, and the kind offer of help." Sgt. Swing tipped his dusty black hat.

Miss Cox pursed her lips, pondering her new problem. "We'll see how much work your laundry is, first. . . . Don't be a stranger, Sergeant. Might do with a good scrubbing yourself."

Ammon Swing almost blushed. He turned away from her direct, embarrassing gaze to stride off to the safety of the other soldiers now ready to ride.

Capt. Hatfield saw him coming. "Thanks for the prompt alert, Sergeant. Signal us immediately if you see any more sign of them."

"I'll do that, sir. Good hunting."

The Commanding Officer kicked his horse into a trot to catch up with his Scouts. His men booted their mounts to follow.

Wallapai Clark nodded to the Sergeant as his paint horse trotted by. "Peace to your ashes, Ammon."

Cox's Tanks, South End of the Winchester Mountains

The groundwater at Cox's Tanks was actually a *cienega*, a flat alluvium-filled marsh with permanent seeps where water trickled upward and kept the soil at least moist, even in blazing summer. Expanses of sacaton, tall bunch grass, and cattail shoots surrounded the small stands of water, but the rancher had cut back seedlings of cottonwoods that were always trying to tap into the year-round moisture and deprive his cattle. The birds and animals never forgot this location, and the Tanks harbored quite a population of desert dwellers who dropped by for a drink, mostly at night. Apaches did, too.

Resting in their saddles next to the partially butchered steer, the officers looked down to see that someone had recently sliced a haunch off and left the rest. "Rustlers would probably have taken the whole cow. Indians were merely hungry," noted the officer in charge.

"That's what I thought, too. Your men are welcome to the rest, Captain," offered the rancher.

"Thank you." Capt. Hatfield turned to his Lieutenant. "See if the cooks want to pack this carcass up for stew."

"Yes, sir." Lt. Walsh turned his horse away to locate one.

"They'll cut that haunch into strips to dry for jerky, use the cowhide to sole their moccasins," explained Wallapai. "See where the steer's nose is mangled?" pointed their Chief Scout. "Apaches'll cut the gristle out of a beef's nose and eat it raw, 'cause they believe it'll help their sniffers, so they can smell game when it's near."

White cavalrymen grimaced at this bit of Indian wisdom.

Capt. Hatfield turned to Jacob Cox. "Don't hesitate to seek out Sgt. Swing for help if you see the slightest sign of Apaches about again, Mister Cox. He can signal us in the field, and we'll return at a gallop."

"Appreciate the offer, sir. Swing seems a good man."

"That he is. Good day, sir, and be wary." C.A.P. Hatfield kicked his thoroughbred and loped off alongside Wallapai Clark. Turning in his saddle to look back at the butchered steer, the officer frowned again. "This is great country for men and horses, but it's sure hell on women and cattle!"

Trail Up Square Mountain

Favoring his sore leg, the Sergeant climbed slowly up the steeper mountainside nearing their encampment. Mullin clambered along behind, leading their two heavily laden pack mules. "Think they'll catch up with those Apaches, Sarge?"

"You didn't see any, didcha? Well, neither will they. Those Indians are gone from this neighborhood. For now. Evidently they got whupped good."

"Damn. I was hopin' to see at least one wild one." The lead mule Mullin was pulling along by its reins suddenly balked, planting both hooves and yanking the soldier back on his heels.

"What's wrong with you, mule?" The young man looked back to see what was holding up his pack mule, when he heard the warning. A large rattlesnake slithered into a coil next to the big rock he was about to climb past and readied itself to strike! Mullin quickly stepped downhill, pushing his mules backward out of striking distance.

"Hoo, that's a big snake! Thank God this mule warned me."

The Sergeant hauled himself up higher for a safe vantage down on the snake. "Mules'll sense danger quicker than we will and know how to avoid it, so you're wise to pay attention. Go around, off to the far side. Rattler tries to strike, I'll drop a rock on it. Those mules are more valuable than you are, Mullin. Can't afford havin' 'em bit."

"Appreciate the sentiment, Sergeant."

Sgt. Swing hoisted a good-sized rock to his shoulder, prepared to heave it, but the young Private led the mules wide of the climbing path, to the far side of the big rock and slowly higher among the loose rocks on the mountainside. The mules scrabbled and slid, trying to hold their footing under their heavy burdens.

The Sergeant was sitting back down, groaning as he massaged his wounded thigh, when Mullin joined him again.

"Leg's still botherin' you, huh? Decoction of comfrey would be good for it."

"Comfrey?"

"Dried leaves, powdered. Rub 'em in the wound. Healing herb. Maybe we can order some at the trader's, from Tucson. Your leg's not coming around like it should, so you might try something different on it."

"Where'd you learn this, Mullin?"

"Oh, I liked botany in school. Read books about herbal medicines. My dad was a good hunter, too. Taught me some useful stuff about plants."

The Sergeant stared at the Private. Maybe there was more to this green kid than he'd realized. "You'll get along with Miss Cox. She's fond of herbs, too."

With another groan, the noncom resumed his painful climb. "All right, let's get these good California mules up this goddamned mountain."

Observation Post #, Square Mountain

Heintz was sweating profusely, clearing brush with a hand ax from the ravine. "Gover-ment vorkhorse, *ist* what we are."

Picking his teeth nearby, Takins joined the chorus. "Damned lotta hard work for only thirteen bucks a month, ain't it?"

Two tired men climbed up around some of the boulders the soldiers had rolled into position for perimeter defense, and the big Hessian was the first to sight them. "Ser-geant! That purty woman you see?"

Takins roused, too. "She bake us any pies?"

Three men and the dog all dropped what they were doing to gather around the two arrivals, who brushed their dust off.

"Vinegar pie."

"Vinegar?" The Southerner made a face.

"Kinda tart but sweet, 'cause of the baked sugar," explained their leader. "She saved me a slice. For you, though, Takins, it's soon to be your lucky day. Bath time!"

Hoots and laughter from the others at their cook's sour expression. The Sergeant looked round their campsite, noting how much work hadn't been done since he'd left this morning. "Doesn't look like anyone slipped any joints in a frenzy of labor up here. Any messages?"

Corporal Bobyne nodded. "Another station signing onto the circuit."

Their leader suddenly clapped his hands, breaking their languor. "Okay then! Let's get these mules unpacked and these tents up. I wanna sleep inside for a damned change."

Bobyne's fitful sleep was interrupted by Heintz's snoring, so he gave his tent mate a good kick to turn him over in his blankets. Settling back down, trying to get used to sleeping inside a tent for a change, the Corporal next became aware of a rustling, a scratching outside the rear of their tent, like someone trying to get in. Eyes wide open now, Bobyne rolled slowly over to his side to gingerly pick up his Springfield and cock its big hammer. Biting his lip, he was warmed by a thought—at least he'd give those Apaches a fight!

Sliding out of his blankets, Bobyne slipped carefully outside the front tent flaps, where he knelt in dirty socks and longjohns to whisper sharply to their night guard, who was dozing in the shadows beyond the embers of their cookfire. "Sergeant!"

Their leader roused and saw his telegrapher beckoning frantically from his new tent. Sgt. Swing slid his revolver from his holster, picked up a long tallow candle and lit it in the fire, then limped over to his signalman to see what frightened him?

"Something scratching back of my tent. Could be an Apache!"

"Could be a coyote." Sergeant Swing set off in a crouch-walk around the near side of the tent, his candle flickering overhead, his .45 pointed in front of him. Bobyne was right on his tail.

Candlelight caused a four-footed creature to yank its nose from under the backside of the canvas Sibley. Red eyes shone in the darkness and then a beautiful animal the size of a house cat bounded off up the mountain. Its bushy tail was equal to its foot-long body and was ringed with distinctive, alternating black-and-white stripes. Its silky, tawny brown fur shone in the light for a second before the shy creature was gone, like a mystery in the moonlight.

Sgt. Swing relaxed. "Ring-tailed cat. Night scavengers. Eat rodents, carrion, desert fruit, too. Lucky to have seen one, Bobyne. Now you have something to write home about."

His telegrapher sighed. "Lucky, hell. Musta smelled our food, trying to get into our stores."

"Won't bitecha. 'Miners' cats,' they're sometimes called. Prospectors tame 'em to keep mice and rats down around their camps." Sgt. Swing grinned as they shuffled back to the fire. "Maybe you can make a pet outta yours."

Bobyne snorted, rubbed his tired eyes. "Rather have a full night's sleep."

The Sergeant nodded. "I like it you sleep with one eye open, Bobyne. Apache comes, won't make near that much noise."

The Easterner groaned sleepily off to the safety of his tent. "Good night, Sergeant."

Sgt. Swing smiled after his communications specialist. "Sleep tight."

THIRTEEN

Opium pills were a ubiquitous cure-all for wounds, diarrhea, and dysentery, and were often issued in conjunction with quinine for malaria. Many soldiers, especially older veterans with wounds or chronic disorders, became opium addicts, victims of the "Army disease." During the Civil War the Union Army issued nearly ten million opium pills and over two million ounces of various opium preparations.

—*A Dose of Frontier Soldiering: The Memoirs of Corporal E. A. Bode, Frontier Regular Infantry 1877–82*, edited by Thomas T. Smith

Observation Post #4, Square Mountain

The men rested after their noon meal next day, having spent the morning rolling more large rocks into place along the rim of their campsite. Three big tents were now staked behind them. These canvas shelters were nearly seven feet high at their ridgeline and the same in length, and almost eight and a half feet wide with a wall two feet high on either side with laced corners that were rolled up and tied for better ventilation during the day.

The big German dropped a last piece of fried hardtack into his opened mouth and chewed. "*Dis ist* pretty *goot*, Takins."

"It's the brown sugar that does it. Sprinkle on your soaked hardtack, then fry it in the bacon grease from breakfast."

The Sergeant roused from his midday drowse. "Any of that prairie butter left?"

Takins picked a skillet up off a flat rock next to the fire pit and handed it over, then lit one of his Mexican cigars. Sergeant

Swing put the skillet down, unbuckled his pants, and rolled them down to his knees, then rolled the left leg of his dirty longjohns up on his thigh until his bullet wound was revealed.

Mullin also had one of his black army half boots and socks off to examine the blister beginning to boil up on the bottom of his raw red foot. "Damn. New boots are killin' me. I'll be blistered all over."

Bobyne chucked him a piece of soap from his mess kit. "Rub some soap on your foot and in your socks. Cuts the friction."

Their leader weighed in. "Those boots are made at our army prison in Fort Leavenworth, Kansas. Can't tell right from left and why in hell should those prisoners care if we walk straight anyway?"

"Them old brass screwed boots were better, if you can still find 'em," offered Takins.

Facing southeast while picking at his lunch, Bobyne suddenly sat up, alert to a flashing from the distant Pinaleros Mountains. "Picking something up from Rucker Canyon."

The Corporal was on his knees, focusing the 20 × 40 Bausch and Lomb telescope with four-inch refractor lenses on its own tripod to get a better look at the message blinking nearly fifty miles away and not aimed directly at them.

The Sergeant turned to the foot soaper. "Take it down in the book, Mullin. We have to post all these messages. Officer's comin' 'round to check eventually to make sure we've been keepin' busy. You're supposed to record the weather every day, too. Bobyne will give it to you as he flashes it back to Ft. Bowie. Although why they want a daily weather report from everybody in southern Arizona, I'll never figure."

Bobyne, as usual, had the answer. "Signal Corps began as a meterological service, before we even got into long-distance communications. It's our foundation. Weather reporting and keeping records of it is supposed to help military planning, Sarge, for battles, army campaigns. You should understand that."

The Sergeant glared at the know-it-all.

"Signal Corps just set up an office in San Francisco last year to study the weather in the West. Long overdue, seems to me," added the Corporal.

Takins snorted. "Not in this hellish country. It's either drier than an old squaw's dugs out here, or rainin' biblical perportions."

Everyone, even Bobyne, laughed.

The recruit pulled his boot back on over his bare foot, grimacing at the effort, then roused to take up paper and pencil in the leather binder left under the heliograph.

Bobyne was already spelling it out. "RELAY C-O C-A-M-P C-R-I-T-T-ENDEN P-R-E-P-PREPARE . . ."

Only half-listening, the Sergeant daubed three fingerfuls of bacon grease from the skillet and began rubbing it around the pinkish scar tissue on his wounded left leg.

"POST I-N-S-P-INSPECTION AND R-E-V-REVIEW S-O-ON GENRL MILES."

Laboriously printing it down, Mullin licked the pencil lead to help the graphite flow, but the Signal Corpsman relaxed. "'S okay. Doesn't involve us, doesn't have to be passed along."

"Miles is taking a grand tour of the forts, huh?" speculated Sgt. Swing. "Maybe he'll scare up a wild Apache or two and get a taste of what it's really like out here."

Takins watched his noncom rub this morning's breakfast grease into his healing leg wound, and the veteran's discomfort at the sight was palpable. "Oughta try one of my pain pills, if that wound's botherin' you. Better'n dirty bacon grease."

"Apaches rub rendered fat into their achin' leg muscles after a hard day on the trail. Think it feeds them strength." The Sergeant sighed. ". . . What pills?"

"Oh . . . hurt my back ridin' durin' the War of Rebellion. They help some with the pain."

Sgt. Swing stopped his thigh massage. "War of Rebellion? You're an ol' galvanized Yankee, ain'tcha Takins?"

"An' proud of it! Rode in the cavalry with General Wade Hampton, best damned Confederate raider in the whole war. I was only sixteen, but we fought that butcher Sherman tooth and nail all through the Carolinas."

As the Sergeant pulled his pants back up, their dog, Horace, wandered over to lick the last of the grease from Swing's skillet. "But you still joined up with us hated Yankees after the Civil War was over?"

"Nothin' civil about it. Sherman's scum burned our farm outside of Columbia, South Carolina, and my kin was all killed or scattered, so I had nothin' to go home to. Soldierin' was the only life I knew, and I still had some fight left, so I hitched up and come out West."

Sgt. Swing rebuckled his pants. "Romance of the plains. An' you caught the 'Army disease,' too, didn't you, Reb?"

The Southerner bridled at the accusation. "I'm partial to them little blue pills, yeah. But docs keep givin' 'em to me for my bad back. They'll help your sore leg, too, I guarantee."

Sgt. Swing shook his head firmly. "No opium for me. Got enough troubles."

"Hell, them pills ain't nothin'," scoffed Takins. "I seen fellers kill themselves on heart medicine, drinkin' that digi-talis from the infirmary, just to get the war outta their heads."

The Sergeant looked the older soldier directly in the eye. "Well, you've played to some hard luck, Reb. Didn't know."

Takins returned his hard stare. "Nothin' a man can't handle."

Horace idled up behind Takins, smelling something interesting. The dog suddenly clamped his teeth down on the back brim of the reb's sweaty gray campaign hat and pulled it off his head to trot away. "Hey! Come back here with my hat, you damned rascal!"

Takins lurched to his feet to retrieve his sunshade, as the soldiers chuckled at their circuitous, slow-motion chase!

Sergeant Swing pushed himself gingerly erect on his sore leg.

"Okay, boys, look alive. Got more rocks to roll. Make all our backs ache!"

Near the Little Dragoon Mountains, Southwest of Square Mountain

"Wallapai" Clark loped his frothy horse back to the line of dusty cavalrymen plodding along in this spring heat. "Captain! Scouts have found a half-dead horse."

Captain Hatfield rubbed his dry, tired eyes. "Dead cow and now a horse. But no Apaches. Walsh, give the men a rest and come along."

The Second Lieutenant turned in his saddle toward the cavalrymen strung behind. "Troopers halt! Ten minutes!"

Lt. Walsh yanked his curb bit, skidding his gelding into a running dismount, a flashy maneuver of horsemanship eager Lieutenants were wont to try occasionally to impress the higher ranks. The others were too preoccupied with the discovery to really notice him. Second Lieutenant Walsh ran over to where Clark and his two Wallapai Indian Scouts stood with their Commanding Officer, looking down at a panting horse. "Mexican mustang. Maize in its manure."

The animal struggled in obvious pain. Long strips of raw horsemeat had been carved from its flank and withers and evidently cooked over a small fire under the overhang of this rocky hillside they'd stopped next to. The white Scout knelt beside the mutilated horse. "Ate some of the meat this morning, but something spooked them, or they woulda had a real feast. Nice fat, young pony." Clark shook his head. "Sweet meat."

Lt. Walsh was appalled. "They eat horsemeat raw, from live animals?"

"No, they cook it first but like their meat fresh. Apaches think it's more tender when it's still kickin'. Them Indians would rather eat a horse than ride it."

"Good God!"

Wallapai Clark eyed the younger officer skeptically. Mercy was a stranger to this land, and Walsh had been out here long enough to know the vagaries of his mortal foes by now. "They say a white man will ride a horse till it's windblown and staggering and then leave it. A Mexican can mount that horse and spur another twenty miles out of it. An Apache will come along, jerk that same half-dead horse back up on its hooves and scare ten more miles out of it. And then he cooks and eats 'er and is well-satisfied with his meal."

The severely lacerated animal whinnied in pain. Both officers were disturbed by Wallapai's little story and the ghastly sight in front of them. The Second Lieutenant drew and cocked his revolver for a mercy shot, but his Captain stopped him. "Don't. They didn't use a bullet for fear of alerting us, or waste a precious arrow on him, either."

"But we can't just leave this animal here to suffer!"

Capt. Hatfield took the reins of his sweaty horse and hitched up into his saddle. "Use your knife. . . . Ride on, Mister Clark. We're getting closer. I want to track these *heske* killers as long as it's light."

The Indians flung themselves onto the backs of their ponies, and Wallapai Clark mounted to follow them along the fleeing Apaches' horse tracks. Capt. Hatfield looked down at the partially skinned horse one last time and shook his head angrily. "Copper-colored creatures of nature, huh?"

The officer-in-charge kicked his horse into a lope away from the bloody, still moving mess. Lt. Walsh just stood there, deserted, fingering his long-bladed knife from his belt sheath, uncertain whether he could carry out this gruesome order.

The other cavalrymen plodded past, all watching the grim-faced Second Lieutenant, wondering if he would do it?

He wobbled a little, grimacing at yet another pitiful whinny. The sun seemed hot today. The young officer leaned over, wrenched a large rock from the dirt, hoisted it over his head and with a mighty cry of anguish, slammed it down on the horse's head with a loud thud, putting the poor animal out of its misery and Lt. Robert Walsh into his.

Observation Post #4, Square Mountain

The yellow mutt ran slowly across the mountainside, avoiding cacti as it half-heartedly attempted to catch a long-eared jackrabbit. His trainer yelled encouragement. "Git 'im, boy! Git 'im!"

Quickly winded, the dog gave up and halted on its haunches, panting in the heat. At the ledge's edge, Mullin slowly squatted, too, disappointed. "All right, Horace. Next time. C'mon back, boy. C'mon!"

Takins cleared his throat and spit over their campsite's edge. "Yer gonna give that ol' dog a heart attack, runnin' 'im after rabbits."

"Even if he was lucky enough to catch one," added the Sergeant, "he probably wouldn't know what to do with it. That's one dumb dog, Mullin. No wonder she gave it away."

The Private frowned. "Don't say that about our pet. C'mon back, Horace! Don't make me come get you, boy!"

The dog had now spread out on his stomach on the mountainside and was resting heavily.

Corporal Bobyne kneeled behind his telescope, taking down a message coming in from Post #5.

"LOOKOUTS PERILLA AND PELONCILLA MOUNTAINS ON BORDER REPORT NO APACHE SIGHTINGS."

Sgt. Swing stopped restaking the slack ropes on his private tent. "Maybe our raiders haven't left the country . . . yet." His thinking was distracted. "What are you digging, Heintz?"

"Plant sweet mel-lons and squash. *Goot* farmer I was in Texas. Ve be up here long time, yes? So I grow someting." The big German rested on his shovel.

Mullin wandered off to fetch his dog.

The Sergeant was presented too many new problems at once. "How we gonna irrigate melons? We don't have enough water up here to spare for crops."

"Vell, Annie and Gro-ver vill help me vith fer-ti-lizer, and I share some my vater vith der land. May be take ex-tra trip down sometime, fur more vater and our baths."

"Annie and Grover?"

Takins gave him a gap-toothed grin. "What we decided to name them mules, whilst you was down there enjoyin' your pie yesterday. Grover in honor of Mister Cleveland, our Yankee President."

Sgt. Swing dampened their enthusiasms. "I don't give a hootin' holler in hell what you name these mules, but we'll just see about extra trips down to the Tanks. Those folks got better things to do than jaw with the likes of us every other day. You boys are just interested in desserts!"

"Army guar-an-tee me one bath a week, Ser-geant. Reg-u-lation. *Das* voman, she like clean men round, I tink." Heintz winked at his Sergeant.

FOURTEEN

Mules are quite fastidious and will only drink fairly clean water, so always let the mules drink first. Also, most of the grasses and foliage they eat are okay for a man to try as well, if in a pinch.

—Emmett M. Essin, *Shavetails & Bell Sharps, the History of the U.S. Army Mule*

Big Draw, Little Dragoon Mountains, Southwest of Square Mountain

The cavalry officers and trackers stood next to a small water hole at the base of a short cliff rising up into yet another desolate, low mountain range out in the middle of nowhere. Grim faces all around as the men stared at the carcass of a dead coyote someone had inconveniently disemboweled and left floating in the shallow pool of bloody, offal-filled water. Their animal-loving Second Lieutenant was the most incensed by the sickening sight. "Damn! Polluted our water!"

Captain Hatfield groped for a solution. "Probably the only source around, Mister Clark?"

"Only water hole fer miles." Wallapai expectorated into the bloody mess. "Damned Apache trick . . . Don't rain hereabouts till at least the fourth of July, neither."

Lt. Walsh had reason to look distressed. "We're carrying enough water for the men's needs. But the horses are parched."

"Yassir, right now it's drier round here than a pea patch in Patagonia." Their white Scout was peering around in the gathering dusk and suddenly pointed. "Stain on that rock wall there? Means runoff when it rains on this mountain. Seeps all around this regular water hole, soil moist right under the top. Git shovels off our pack train when it catches up and dig down a few feet right there at the base of that water stain and any others we find. Should coax some seepage up from it after awhile. Let the mules try it first. They're finicky about their water, but if it's good we'll dig more and water as much of the stock as we can by morning."

Captain Hatfield agreed. "All right. Nothing else to do tonight. Camp here, Walsh, but picket our horses well away. I don't want any of our stock getting sick trying to drink from this mess."

The Second Lieutenant was down on one knee, scooping his hand in the damp sand below the water stain Wallapai Clark had shown them. "Yessir, I'll set 'em digging just as soon as we set up camp."

The Captain nodded. "Double sentries tonight, too. We're close to those outlaw Indians." The older man tilted his nose in the air, took a sharp whiff. "I can smell 'em."

Observation Post #4, Square Mountain

Next morning, *aparejos* were already on Annie and Grover as several soldiers prepared to go back down the mountain. The Sergeant briefed the lucky two. "Can only afford what we pay laundresses at Fort Bowie, twenty-five cents for a full set of dirty clothes. Don't let her charge you more, Heintz."

"OK. How much ve fur pie pay?"

Two dusty gunnysacks of dirty clothes were tied to both sides of Grover's pack rig. Sergeant Swing and Corporal Heintz lashed empty ten-gallon water kegs to either side of Annie's rig, neglecting to blindfold the younger mule due to her much lighter load.

"Don't bother the lady about treats till we get this laundry goin' first. Have her run a bill till we get our pay vouchers sent out from the fort."

"Been studying your signals, Sergeant?"

"Learned enough to take down any messages that'll hold till you git back up here to send 'em, Bobyne." Sgt. Swing finished a double-diamond hitch on his side of the mule and stepped away to dry off his sweaty hands. His hand rubbing caused Annie to look back and notice the empty barrels now "bandaged" to both her sides. She gave a little hitch and jumped away from the Sergeant, causing a bung plug to rattle inside one of the empty casks. The cork castanet frightened the mule, and suddenly she was bucking and braying and ripping apart the brush corral Heintz had constructed.

"Je-sus, look out!" The Sergeant had the presence of mind to grab Grover's halter and lead the older mule out of the destructive youngster's way.

"Grab her, boys!" The noncom was concerned as one water keg flew loose, while the mad mule was trying to buck off the other rattling cask as she careened back toward their tents. Heintz grabbed Annie's lead rope and Takins was dangling and bouncing from the free side of her pack rig, while Bobyne hurried to snatch up his mirrored heliograph equipment! Eeee-haw! Hee-haw!

"Keep her away from my equipment!" yelled the signalman, as huge Heintz managed to yank Annie's head around away from their tents and stores. Takins hung onto the whirling mule with one hand, while he got the tie-rope unlashed with his other and the rattling cask flew free. Freed from the fear-making noise at last, the live merry-go-round stopped, breathing heavily. Takins let go, staggering away. "Whose goddamned idea was that?"

Sgt. Swing led Grover over in hopes its presence would calm down the female. "My fault, fellers. Anything possibly noisy ain't right for that mule. I forgot."

He unlashed the bundles of laundry and dumped them on the ground. "We'll try the water kegs on this one instead. What'dya call 'im?"

Takins was still panting hard. "Grover. After President Grover . . ."

"Yeah, okay. Just git 'em lashed on again and this rodeo underway, will yah."

Little Dragoon Mountains, Southwest of Square Mountain

High on another mountainside looking down on a sandy wash below where several soldiers worked their shovels, two black-haired heads rose slowly up behind a boulder. They watched horses and mules suck up the source water that had pooled overnight in the sump holes dug at the bases of the cliffs by the troopers. Beyond them, the rest of the patrol was busy with their morning ablutions, eating breakfast, currying and saddling their mounts.

Perched high above, Yanozha and Fun looked at each other. Yanozha shook his head quickly, then the two heads slowly lowered again and disappeared.

Ranch Near Cox's Tanks

Martha Cox stood in the back doorway of her brother's adobe, wiping her hands on her apron as she looked at the two smiling soldiers in front of her, each holding a gunnysack full of dirty clothes. "Fellows, I've been giving your Sergeant's proposal some close thought, and I've decided to let you boys wash your own clothes."

Both Corporals' mouths inadvertently dropped open. After a dumbfounded pause, the signalman recovered. "Do our own laundry?"

Now it was her turn to smile. "Sure. You fellows cook your own meals, don't you? Well, you can learn how to do your own laundry, too."

She pointed a long finger at her washing equipment on a

wooden bench against the house's back wall. "Tub and scrub board are right there. Use some lye from the can to get them clean."

Martha reached behind her inside the house, lifting out two big tin pails of steaming water she'd prepared when she spotted them coming down the mountain, and handed them over to the flummoxed military men. Reaching back inside once more, she pulled out a big bar of soap and a pig-bristle brush.

Heintz finally got his tongue working again. "Your pardon begging, ma'am, but . . ."

"No buts, Corporal. Take turns scrubbing while you do your other duties. By the time you're finished you'll both be half-bathed, so I'll heat some more water and you can finish the job."

She handed one soldier the soap, the other the brush. "Don't fret over it, boys. You can't go back up to camp with a load of dirty drawers, and you can't pay me enough to do your own hot, hard washing, either, so just reconcile yourselves to the work."

Martha Cox turned back into her house, leaving the Corporals gaping at each other like fish that had just been landed. "Get yourselves nice and clean and I'll have some lemonade for you when you're done."

Bobyne broke ranks first, grumbling under his breath as he kicked aside several squawking chickens to dump his bucket of hot water into the galvanized tin washtub and throw the soap in after.

Observation Post #4, Square Mountain

Swing, Takins, and Mullin were stripped down to their undershirts as they strained over a large rock they were grappling in a three-sided hoist. Sweating, they staggered with it to the edge of the ledge they were camping on.

"Careful! Don't bump my bad leg!"

"Golly!" grunted Mullin.

Takins yelled, "Losin' it!" They suddenly dropped the rock. *Whump!* It landed next to several other good-sized boulders they'd already moved this afternoon to extend their defensive perimeter.

The noise set off the dog, who dashed across the ledge and down the mountainside, howling as if his life depended on it.

Brushing dirt off, panting, the three turned to watch Horace go, then sat down on their big rocks for a water break. Mullin admired his pet's perseverance. "Lookit 'im go. Musta saw another rabbit."

Takins picked up Bobyne's binoculars to scan the mountainside after the bounding mutt. "Don't see any hare."

"Aww, he musta sensed sumpthun', or he wouldn't a gone howlin' off like that."

This observation roused their curiosity. The three got slowly up to amble over to the far edge to check after the dog. Sgt. Swing took the binoculars from their cook to survey the whole mountainside.

Mullin was concerned about his distant, disappearing dog. "Horace! Come back, boy! Horace! Don't make me come git you again! C'mere, boy!"

They spotted their mutt again, running out from behind some distant rocks down the mountainside, still howling and racing off to God knows where.

The Sergeant just looked at Takins.

Ranch Near Cox's Tanks

In his soaked undershirt, Corporal Bobyne poured water from a bucket into a tin funnel in the keg he'd placed atop the rock wall about the well at Cox's ranch.

Jacob Cox and his cow dog trotted in from out on the range, where they'd been working cattle.

"Afternoon, Mr. Cox! Seen any Apaches?"

"Nope! Or scalped cows, either!"

Jacob walked his horse up to the small barn, dismounted, and began unsaddling.

"How you boys doin' today?"

"Just fine, sir. We came down to replenish our water and do some . . ." Their educated Corporal couldn't even bring himself to say the demeaning word—laundry.

Miss Cox peered out her back door to see how Heintz was doing. A pile of wet laundry was stacked atop an old apple crate and next to it, the big Hessian stood barefooted in his longjohns in the tin washtub sopping wet, as he scrubbed himself and his dirty underwear all over with the hard brush and soap. Biting her lip to keep from laughing at the sight, Martha sauntered outside to begin pinning his wet wash up on her clothesline.

"Should have told me you were ready for your bath, Corporal, and I'd have gotten you some clean water."

"*Das* OK, ma'am. I vet get, I finish."

"Well . . . I'll heat some more water for your partner."

"*Goot*. He not vant his vash to do, I tink."

She pursed her lips. "Is that right?"

Heintz scrubbed his dirty undershirt under his arms. "You not now married, ma'am?"

The question was bracing in its directness. ". . . No, I'm not."

"I just vonder. Must lonely out here be . . . alone."

Clothespin between her teeth, Martha stopped hanging wet clothes to pin him with a sharp eye. Her cold stare halted Heintz's scrubbing.

"Well, I've got my brother and our animals . . . for company."

Heintz tried to get soapsuds out of his ear with a stubby finger. "Ya, but . . . no hus-band or *kinder* after to look."

It was time to put the big man in his place. "This Arizona desert's a rough place to raise kids, that's for sure. But I figure it's up to me and my brother to tame this rugged part of America. For if we don't do it, soldier, who will?"

Later, Corporal Bobyne, his wet hair slicked back and his uniform damp but much cleaner, too, drained his mason jar glass and handed it back to the smiling woman on her front porch.

"Thanks for the lemonade, ma'am."

"You're welcome, Corporal. You boys smell nice and fresh, clean as your clothes."

Bobyne frowned and without another word, strode off to join Heintz with the mules.

Filled water kegs were roped onto Grover's *aparejo* rig; gunnysacks of damp laundry tied on the smaller mule. "*Goot*-bye, Miss Cox! Tanks fur the bath!"

Bobyne said nothing, didn't even look back at the woman who wouldn't do his laundry. Pulling reluctant mules along by their lead ropes, the men trudged off, headed back up Square Mountain.

Martha Cox gave them a big wave. "Good-bye, boys! Next time I'll teach you how to work a flatiron!"

Observation Post #4, Square Mountain

"Learn to work a flatiron!" Sergeant Swing laughed so hard he spilled his coffee and had to refill his wiggling cup from the pot in the ashes of their evening's campfire. "That's rich! That's a real good one."

Mullin grinned. "Damned sure a feisty lady. Take two."

Takins dealt the recruit two cards off a greasy deck. They were playing draw poker for nickels and pennies, except Heintz, who was tight with his meager pay. "Sounds like a bitch ta me. I ain't doin' my own laundry. That's woman's work."

Sgt. Swing smiled. "Then we'll just have to throw you *an'* your laundry into the tub together, Takins. Certainly your turn for a bath. Gimme three."

The Civil War veteran arched his back. "Don't give a trooper's damn about any bath! Not right in front of her like Heintz did, no ways."

"You gotta do something, Takins," Bobyne chimed in. "All you have to do is walk by the pot and you season the stew."

More laughter as soldiers scratched or spit into the fire. Takins didn't enjoy being the butt of their jokes but dealt cards out to the other two players. "I'm gettin' beat on here worse'n a redheaded stepchild."

Nearby, the big Corporal cleaned out his tin cup with his finger. "This des-sert *ist goot*, Takins. Any more?"

"No. My 'spotted pup' is the best, though, ain't it? It's the slow bakin' of the rice and raisins with the brown sugar makes 'er sweet. . . . Take four to keep my ace company." The Southerner dealt himself new cards and slowly unfolded them in his hand.

The mention of "pup" turned Mullin gloomy. "Wisht I had my pup back. Walked all over this damned mountain lookin'. . . . Hope the coyotes didn't git him. Bet two cents." Mullin clinked a two-cent coin into the tin mess cup they were using to hold the pot.

"Or the Apaches. Understand they eat dog." The signalman tossed several coins into the pot. "Raise you a nickel."

Sgt. Swing tossed in his cards instead. "They eat dog if they can't find any other game and they're hungry enough. So would you. That's not what happened to Horace, though." The Sergeant yawned and stretched. "Mountain madness. Animals just can't take it after awhile without the company of their own kind."

Bobyne was skeptical. "You mean dogs just go crazy and howlin' off to nowhere?"

Sgt. Swing nodded. Takins lit another of his cheap cheroots. "Seen it happen in the war, too. Soldier boys would just wander off, clean outta their minds. . . . See your nickel and raise a dime."

Young Mullin disagreed. "I don't believe our dog went mad. He's just lost."

"Ya. Hor-ace come tomorrow back, first ting. You see," agreed Heintz.

Bobyne couldn't resist his seven cents' worth. "Meanwhile, you've still got Takins to sleep next to, Mullin, so you shouldn't be lonely. Fewer fleas, too."

Chuckles from everyone except the cook. "That's fifteen cents to you, sonny. . . . You're liable to wake up with a rattler for company, you're lucky."

Suddenly edgy, Mullin threw in his cards. "Rattlesnakes will crawl into your bedroll?"

Takins nodded. "Like your body warmth."

"I'll see your dime and bump it two bits." Bobyne clanged his change into the cup. The others paid attention now, for this had become a significant poker pot to men who only made $13 a month.

The wily Southerner upped his ante. "Make that four bits."

"Rattlers will not crawl over a horsehair rope, though. Old cowboys know that an' sleep with their lariat spread around their bedroll," added the Sergeant. "Good snake stopper."

Bobyne dropped his last quarter into the mess cup. "Here's where you land in your narrow grave, Reb, just six by three, and the wild coyotes will howl with glee," he chortled as he turned over three queens.

Everyone leaned forward, expectant, as with a toothy smile, the Civil War rebel turned over, one at a time by lantern light, a spade flush!

Hoots from the boys. Takins jingled his winnings into his big hands.

The Corporal objected. "No goddamned chance."

"Questionin' my luck, telegrapher?"

"I am! When I get three queens beat by a four-card draw, I have misgivings about the deal."

Takins dropped his change and launched himself right

across the fire, hands outstretched for Bobyne's throat. "Yankee bastard!"

"Poker sharp!"

The two struggled and rolled around in the dirt, wrestling. The others were quickly on their feet, ready to intervene, especially the big German-American. "*Nein!*"

But the Sergeant held them off with an outstretched hand, willing to let his men burn off a little pent-up aggression. With Takins on top and choking him, Bobyne's face began to turn beet red in the old reb's grip. When they rolled over again into the embers, Sgt. Swing gestured to Heintz, and both men jumped in to pull the combatants from the fire. He couldn't afford to have his Signal Corpsman seriously burned. "You men stop this nonsense right now!"

Within the big Corporal's grasp, Takins was still trying to land a punch. "Called me a cheat!"

Sgt. Swing pushed the struggling Bobyne back down onto his pants seat.

"Before I take you over my good knee and give you each an old-fashioned army skinning!" Campfire reflected in his angry eyes as he stomped about it, determined now to put out the flames among his troops.

"Alla yas get to bed right now! I will make all hell howl if this nonsense continues!"

Bobyne was back up on his feet brushing himself off, fastidious as always, but Takins crawled about in the dirt, trying to recover his winnings from the folds of the mussed-up blanket.

"Leave that damned money right there, soldier! I'll return it in the morning!"

The reb came off his knees. "Ain't so high and mighty now. Special-trained, bullshit! You're just a common . . . mouth fighter!"

Heintz collared Takins to lead him back to his tent, keeping his large self between the combatants. The Sergeant was still worked up. "And no more cards . . . for a month!"

Mullin lingered near his leader, hoping to calm him down. "I'll take first watch, to wait up for Horace, Sergeant. You fellers go dream about your rattlesnakes."

Sgt. Swing hesitated, but the sight of his boyish, concerned face caused him to lower his hackles. After a moment, he nodded. "Wake me in two hours."

By the light of a lantern, Mullin rummaged in the storage area next to the temporary brush corral, where their two mules were picketed in the ravine at the south end of their ledge. Groping under one of the pack rigs, the young recruit pulled out one of the lariats they used to catch the mules. Examining it in the light, he saw this rope was made of hemp, not horsehair, but maybe it would still work.

The Private walked back to the tents with his lamp, rifle, and rope and stopped at the Sergeant's. Bending inside the noncom's big A-tent, Mullin shook the sleeping man by the shoulder. "Sarge. Your watch."

Rousing to clear his throat, Ammon Swing rolled out of his blanket to pull on his boots, then his tunic against the night's chill.

At his tent, trying not to wake their snoring cook, Mullin dropped the lariat around his own bedroll, then arranged the snake guard about the rubber pad under his wool blanket. Hopefully no crawly critters would be out looking for bedmates tonight. Just thinking about rattlers again, the teenager shuddered.

The Sergeant poured himself a tin cup of hot coffee from the pot. From his tunic he pulled a pint bottle and held it up to shake the contents in the moonlight as he growled at the kid moving about in his tent back of their fire pit. "Join me for a taste a Dutch courage, son?"

"Huh?" Then he whispered. "Oh, sure, Sarge."

Mullin took his lantern and shuffled back to join the Sergeant atop one of the big rocks they'd rolled to the front of their camp's ledge for protection. Sipping his strong coffee to wake up, Sgt. Swing handed over the bottle of cheap whiskey. "Snakebite medicine. . . . Don't tell the fellers I got a bottle up here or someone will sneak it."

"No, I won't." Mullin took a slug, choked and sprayed a little through his teeth, and handed the pint back.

The Sergeant was still grumpy over the fight. "This is damned boring duty. Hard to keep the boys occupied, somethin' else on their minds besides their hats. Boredom, close quarters—lead to foolish trouble like tonight."

The young soldier nodded but looked preoccupied. Somewhere up the mountain they heard the weird, dismal call of the ravenlike Sierra hermit bird. The kid was nervous again, looking about in the darkness, so the Sergeant kept talking. "So you came out West to fight wild Indians?"

"I guess. Always had the army fever."

Sergeant Swing grinned. "That fever will run its course long before your first five years are up, son." He stared out over the dark Sulphur Springs Valley below and at the wounded moon rising over the Chiricahua Mountains to the southeast. The corners of his smile drooped slowly into a frown. " '*Gotchamo.*' Apache moon tonight."

"Apache moon?"

"Apaches like to raid when there's a full one, 'cause it helps them see the best horses and mules to steal. Spring months especially, after their winter supplies get low. Full moon lets 'em see well enough to ride all night, without runnin' their stolen horses into ravines or off cliffs in the dark while they're tryin' to get away."

"Huh. Makes sense."

The First Sergeant took another drink, wiped his mouth, and offered the Private one, too, but the teenager raised his hand to decline. They both tasted the raw liquor in their throats as they stared at the reddish tint to this rising full moon. "Yup. An' there's blood on this one.

FIFTEEN

In Oklahoma, a generation or two later, according to a pioneer's granddaughter, "When my mother was growing up, parents would threaten their children, 'If you don't behave, Geronimo *will get you!'* "

—*Geronimo and the End of the Apache Wars,*
edited by C. L. "Doc" Sonnichsen

Peck Ranch, Santa Cruz Valley, Just Above the Mexican Border, Southern Arizona Territory, April 27, 1886

A dark, stealthy hand pushed a heavy wooden front door, testing it. Finding it barred from the inside, Perico gestured to several others who came gliding from the darkness carrying small lit torches made of long strips of juniper bark dipped in creosote sap. The Apaches smeared this flaming juice around the wooden door frame, setting it slowly burning.

Dahkeya and Inday-Yi-Yahn moved again, one daubing flame along the mesquite logs framing the window as well as smearing the wooden shutters themselves, the other setting fire to one end of the wooden porch, before stubbing out their torches in the dirt and retreating back into the night to await developments.

This smaller adobe ranch, owned by Arthur L. Peck, was isolated in the Santa Cruz Valley six miles west of the river of the same name, twenty miles east of Nogales, and only ten north of the border itself. A dangerous location notwithstanding the advantages of raising cattle in such a grassy river valley, for the southern halves of the Arizona and New Mexico territories were among the liveliest places on God's footstool during the past three decades of unceasing warfare with the Apaches.

Several horses wheeled skittishly in the corral, frightened by the first scent of smoke. A door to a feed and tackle shed beside the corral suddenly slammed open and a cowboy in boots and pants came storming out into the night.

"Hey! What's a-goin' . . . Jesus to Genoa! Fire!"

Seeing fire burning the front of the ranch house, the neighbor Al Peck had hired to help him brand mavericks fired a warning shot from his revolver, then started running toward the conflagration.

"Fire! Al, look out! You're burnin'!"

Two arrows struck Charlie Owen from different directions, front and rear, spinning him around the stable yard. The hired hand gasped at the shocking pain from the sharp metal points slicing deep into his chest and back, then toppled backward, impaled like a stuck pig.

Behind him, several shadowy Apaches ran inside his lamp-lit tack shed to plunder.

Inside the small house, Al Peck lurched up in bed. Instinctively he sniffed. "Christ, honey! Smoke!"

Throwing off blankets, the rancher grabbed wool pants off the bedpost to yank on over his red flannel longjohns.

His pregnant, Mexican-born wife was groggy. "Al?"

"Heard a shot, maybe Charlie yelling." The lean man pulled boots over his bare feet in his hurry.

"I'll get the kids. Al, be careful!"

Her husband was up and grabbing his "yellow boy" Winchester off the pegs above their bedroom doorway and clomping out without even a last look at her.

Petra was frantic, throwing on a cloth robe over her cotton nightdress as she hoisted her ripe belly out of bed. She could hear their two children whimpering behind the stitched-together blankets curtaining off another smaller bed in the rear of this big room.

Through the darkness, Al Peck could see the latched wooden window smoking around the leather straps anchoring it to the adobe bricks. Lurching toward the front door, he saw it also had flames licking around the edges of the door frame. "My God, we're on fire!"

Trying the metal door bolt, he burned his fingers. Panicked, he tried again with the butt of his rifle, ramming the hot bolt aside, then kicked the burning door open with his boot. It hung in flames on its hinges, and Al Peck hesitated, wondering how, before he charged out into the cool night air.

The cattleman stumbled into his hard-packed dirt yard, rifle butt against his hip, whirling about, blinking, waving his hand in front of his teary eyes so he could see what in hell else was burning? Through the smoky, fiery darkness, he saw an Indian standing tall right in his front yard, nearly empty bandoleers crossing his bare chest and a buckskin breechcloth extending down to his knees. The tail feather of a red-shafted flicker stuck from the blue cloth headband holding his coarse black hair from his eyes. Watching the activity over at the corral, rifle dangling from his hand, Cochise's second son turned toward the rancher and smiled.

That ghost of a smile was the last thing Al Peck remembered for a while, as a shot from the night grazed his head, knocking him unconscious. From behind a corner of the house Perico fired at him, too, but missed as Al was falling down. Naiche walked to the rancher, turned him over with a moccasined toe to check his bloody scalp and raw head wound. The Chiricahua picked up the white man's repeating rifle so that he had one in each hand as he knelt and pointed them toward the adobe's burning front door, waiting to see who else might come running through it?

Fun and Zhonne ran from the tack shed, dumping three saddles before approaching the three whirling horses inside the corral with ropes and bridles they'd also helped themselves to.

Impatient, Naiche stalked onto the ranch's burning porch, both rifles cocked and ready. Dahkeya and Inday-Yi-Yahn moved in behind him, sticking their gun barrels right in the burning front window and busted door.

Rifle barrels preceding him through the flaming doorway, the tall Apache stepped slowly into the ranch house's only room. After a moment he saw movement as he emerged from the smoke and gloom. The rancher's wife was standing next to her bed. Her ten-year-old niece cowered behind her. Trying to steady the big revolver she was holding in both hands above her extended stomach, Petra Peck fired!

A .45 bullet sprayed mud plaster off the wall above Naiche as he ducked. He cut loose with both rifles. Blood bloomed on the breast of her nightdress as two high-powered slugs knocked her backward, banging the woman into the screaming young girl and tumbling them both to the dirt floor.

Naiche sprang to the fallen woman, snatched up her six-shooter as he saw that she was dead. Jamming the wife's revolver in the waistband of his breechcloth, the Chiricahua grabbed the crying girl's arm and dragged her across the smoke-drenched room to push out the front door.

The ten-year-old lurched into the dirt in front of their burning porch with Naiche right behind her. Hysterical, Trinidad Verdín crawled to her uncle and tried to hug some life into him, oblivious to the smoking hem of her sleeping gown, which smoldered from the fire.

The Chief watched her a moment, saw his warriors now saddling three agitated horses in the corral. Behind him Dahkeya and Inday-Yi-Yahn jumped through the burning door frame to loot inside the house.

Klosen (Hair Rope) rode up leading their other two horses

by their rope hackamores. Buckskin had been tied around these horses' hooves to muffle the sound, and their long noses were muzzled with rawhide thongs to keep them from whinnying. The horses still stamped about in the blurring, smoky chaos, as the girl's strident keening added an eerie, high-pitched edge to these bloody events.

Inside, two Apaches pilfered in frenzy, ripping drawers out of a big dresser looking for weapons and ammunition they were desperately short of. Only one box of cartridges and a revolver came out of a storage cabinet, but Dahkeya ransacked the small kitchen, stuffing food and sacks of coffee into a flour sack, along with a butcher knife. Under the noise of the house burning and china smashing in the kitchen, Inday-Yi-Yahn heard a baby whimpering. Ripping aside the blanket curtain, he saw the Peck's two-year-old boy trying to stand up in his crib. One sharp blow to the head with the butt of his lever-action Marlin silenced that annoyance.

Outside, Fun and Zhonne ran over, leading three saddled horses from the corral. Two Indians stood over sobbing little Trini as she clutched her dead uncle. Perico yanked the girl's black hair back, extending her brown neck as he put a sharp blade to it. The warrior looked to his leader, his eyes wild. "*Zas-tee*? (Kill?)"

"*Dah!* (No!) Take her with us!" Naiche gestured sharply toward the downed man, and Klosen and Fun quickly ran to him, Perico pulling the girl away while the others began yanking off the dead man's boots.

Al Peck coughed. The two warriors leapt back, pulling knives from their waistbands, as the others swung their rifles to cover the suddenly alive rancher, who moaned as he touched the side of his head. The sight of a hate-filled Apache holding back his crying niece with one hand while poised above him with a long knife in the other, shook something loose in Arthur Peck's mind. He started screaming and didn't stop.

This startled Perico, and he pulled the now silent but shaking girl away from the screaming man, who, running out of breath, began to spray spittle from his lips. His knife pointed out for protection, Klosen darted in to snatch Peck's boots, then jumped back again as the once dead man began to twitch.

The three Apaches closest looked to one another questioningly, not quite understanding this strange man with the bloody head, who just sat there panting, spittle condensing to foam in the corners of his mouth. White women sometimes screamed when captured by these Apaches, before they raped or killed them. But few brave or even scared white men said much, until they strung them up by their ankles and lit small fires under their bare heads.

The long blade of his Mexican *cuchillo* flashed in the firelight as Fun moved toward the man, who now twitched uncontrollably. Realizing he was about to have his throat slit, Al Peck rose once more and began to scream. Spittle flying, the rancher twitched and jerked unsteadily toward the Apache, stopping him cold. Fun began to back away from this disturbed man, once dead but now on his feet and screaming at a high pitch, right in his ears. All the Apaches were a bit unnerved by this human wraith in red underwear, head bleeding dark red in the firelight, screeching and lurching about in a half circle, seemingly trying to catch them to fight barehanded.

Naiche remounted his pony, and Klosen held Perico's for him as he yanked young Trinidad Verdín up in front of him onto his rawhide-covered, straw saddle. Fun still dodged the shrill Mister Peck, dancing just out of his reach, sweeping his knife dangerously close to the deranged American, keeping him at bay. The fiercest fighter among these renegades, Fun looked to his leader. "*Zastee tetiye?* (Kill this poor person?)"

"*Dah!* (No!)" Naiche shook his head sharply. "*Heshke!* (A crazy one!)" Apaches were afraid of *bini-edine* (people without minds) and wouldn't touch them, worried that their craziness might be catching. Cochise's son couldn't risk any more failure on this misbegotten raid, or none of these fighters would ever follow him again.

The last two Apaches ran from the smoking house with their plunder, coughing and distracting the others from the wounded man's fate. Dahkeya and Inday-Yi-Yahn handed up their sacks of food and fresh ammunition, then Dahkeya leapt up behind another man, to ride double on his horse.

"*Ugashe!* (Hurry!) We still don't have enough horses!" Naiche wheeled his pony and booted it away from the carnage.

Fun didn't have to be told twice as he ran away from the raving rancher. The warrior literally vaulted into the Mexican saddle atop a fine horse he and Zhonne had just stolen from him. Then the two young *shee-kizzen* (close friends) hightailed it after the other *netdahe* (blood oath) renegades. Six sets of muffled hoofbeats echoed, as seven wild Apaches galloped off into the smoke-scented darkness under a blood-red moon.

Al Peck stood panting hoarsely in the moonlight, hopeless, watching them go.

SIXTEEN

As fierce warriors, most Apache men felt it beneath them to engage in any physical labor. Society dictated that their one and only responsibility was to their weapons—caring for them, whether bow and arrow or occasional firearm, and using them when necessary. Apache men were very careful not to be seen doing anything that could be considered women's work.

—E. Lisle Reedstrom, *Apache Wars: An Illustrated Battle History*

Observation Post #4, Square Mountain

A loud whisper. "Sergeant! Wake up! They've come!"

Bobyne rudely shook Sgt. Swing where he slept alone in his supply tent, head toward the opening, ready for trouble. "What? . . . Who?"

"Apaches!"

The Sergeant sat up quickly to yank on trousers and boots, groped in the dawn's dusty light to locate his Springfield, then hotfooted it after his Corporal to the far edge of their ledge, facing north.

Flopping down beside Bobyne, Sgt. Swing peered cautiously out from behind a large rock to where the soldier pointed.

Sure enough, several hundred yards away, along another ledge just below a ridgeline running north from Square Mountain toward a peak several thousand feet higher in these Winchester Mountains, he saw several Indians moving about with a covey of little kids.

"Jesus! Gimme your field glasses."

The freshly minted signalman handed over his binoculars. Behind them, the other soldiers were beginning to rouse, awakened by this early commotion.

In the lightening distance, one Indian woman was building a warm-weather *ramada*, or "squaw-cooler," out of four wooden poles stuck in the ground and roofed with cross poles she had covered with brush and old skins. Another woman scraped a wide hole in the ground with a large, sharpened stick. A third scooped loose dirt out of this hole with a wicker basket and was lining the rough pit with flat rocks a couple of the kids carried to her. In front of the open-air shelter being built, two younger girls had a fire going into which they fed sticks.

"One, two, . . . three squaws, an' a covey of kids . . . Don't see any bucks . . . yet. Wake the men, Corporal, quietly."

At Bobyne's whispered warning, Takins and Heintz jumped from their bedrolls half-dressed, yanked on boots and jerseys, and grabbed their rifles as they hurried over to the others.

Mullin took his time, carefully coiling the lariat he had encircling his bed site and hiding it under his rubber ground cover before pulling on his boots and joining them.

The five men of Observation Post #4 were all sprawled at the northern end of their high ledge, nervously watching Indians across from and a little below them, going briskly about their early morning business.

Takins rubbed sleep from his eyes. "When'd they get here?"

Corporal Bobyne looked a little uncertain. "Sometime in the night, I guess, I didn't see 'em until dawn, when I heard their kids squealing."

Sgt. Swing punched him in the shoulder. "You were sleeping!"

"No. Resting my eyes a little maybe but not sleeping."

Now Takins was awake. "You dumb bastard! We coulda been scalped in our tents!"

"No, no, I would have heard anybody tried to climb up here."

Playing mediator again, Heintz interjected himself between the antagonists. "There no men are, I vunder?"

The Sergeant passed the binoculars along to the others. "Probably out huntin', or raidin'."

They watched one of the squaws put something into a metal can she hung from cross-sticks braced over her cooking fire. This piqued their own cook's interest. "Wonder what they're havin' fer breakfast?"

"Horace probably," surmised Bobyne.

"Oh no! They wouldn't stoop to that, would they?" The young Private was up on his knees behind one of their perimeter rocks, grabbing the binoculars away from Heintz to get a closer look at the distant stewpot.

"Mullin, settle down. Too late to worry about the mutt now. Takins, you and I are going down to find out where these Apaches are from. You boys cover us and don't shoot unless we're fired upon, or they try to take us hostage. An' Bobyne, keep your eyes open for a change and don't let any bucks sneak up behind here or get position on you from above. Then we'd all be breakfast."

The Southerner checked the cartridge in his Springfield's chamber before he crouched to slink off around a boulder. The others hastily loaded and aimed their weapons.

Sergeant Swing, however, stood straight up to loop a belt filled with .45/.70 cartridges across his chest, checked the Army Colt in the holster at his waist, and picked up his Springfield carbine. Ammon Swing then stalked off, a hitch to his stride, over the edge and straight downslope, headed boldly toward the Apaches. "Come on, Private. They know we're up here."

Lower Ledge, Square Mountain

The three Indian women saw the two soldiers climbing down toward them from two hundred yards off and called their little kids as the armed men approached. Three of the kids hid behind one mother's dark green calico skirt, which was cut in a wide, pleated pattern reaching almost to her instep. Her blouse had wide sleeves and was cinched at the waist with a leather belt. Another had on a blue paisley cotton print, high-necked and decorated with white trim, now dirty.

The youngest woman wore a more traditional buckskin shirt with a V-shaped neck hole and matching skirt. *Hoddentin*, the Apaches' sacred pollen from the tule reed, had been rubbed into this deerskin dress and then heated, turning the treated leather brown and making it somewhat water repellent. The women's hands and feet were quite small, like those of all Apaches, but their legs and arms were well muscled and their backs strong. All three Apache women had small buckskin bags tied to leather belts about their waists, probably filled with dried venison, piñon nuts, mesquite screwbeans, or their delicacy, fried grasshoppers, or perhaps even a bone awl and deer sinew for repairing clothes and ripped moccasins on the spot.

Sgt. Swing strode right into their camp, carbine dangling from his left hand, his right palm upraised in the peace sign. Takins nervously covered the enemy with his rifle, its long barrel moving about, his finger on the trigger.

"*I-chi-ca-say* (Greetings)." The Sergeant pointed to himself. "*Schichobe* (Good friend)."

The oldest, stoutest of the three women, nodded. Somewhere between thirty and forty, it was hard to tell, her hair worn loose and parted down the middle like a long-married woman, this heavyset lady's most distinguishing feature was the tip of her nose, which was missing. Standing next to her, the youngest woman's black hair was tied up differently, in a flat, beaver-tail shape, and covered in red flannel studded with gilt buttons, *nah-leen* (maiden) style, to distinguish her from her married friends.

The Sergeant continued his hand gestures and rough Apache. "What tribe you? Where from?"

Mrs. Cutnose replied in rapid Apache, which he strained to

understand. "*Chokonen Chiricahua.* No reservation. Belong to no one."

"Who fathered your children? Where are your men?"

Mrs. Cutnose merely shrugged, looked at the other women on either side of her, who also had no answer.

On his knees, Takins poked about the blankets lying inside their half-finished brush shelter, looking for weapons. The Southerner rifled several fringed rawhide saddlebags for personal items, sucking his teeth sharply as he pulled out several long Mexican knives.

Their oldest boy, skinny-looking in only a grimy loincloth, maybe twelve, stood apart from the women on the other side of their cooking fire, watching Takins.

Sgt. Swing was not letting them off that easily. "What are you doing here?"

"Baking mescal. Apache food."

He walked on to look at their seven-foot-wide baking pit lined with flat rocks. They were digging it deeper and had started a fire on criss-crossed pieces of wood, which they were laying more big stones on top of. Next to this pit were a number of wide-mouthed, woven willow burden baskets filled with ten-to-twenty-pound crowns of century plant cactuses, severed from their roots. These cacti's spiky, several foot long leaves were tied at the top to give them handles for taking in and out of the hot pit. Agave cactuses' juice, fermented in various ways for different lengths of time, produced *mescal*, *pulque*, and *tequila*, the potent liquors of Mexico. Baked *mescal* hearts, however, were also the main staple of the Apaches' diet.

The Sergeant shook his head. "You can't stay here."

The Apache matron put both hands together in a gesture of obeisance. "Please, *señor*. Let us bake our *mescal*. Our children are hungry. We need our food. Then we will go."

Takins hadn't had his breakfast, either, and was back out of the *ramada*, checking their cooking fire, where he was startled to find the Indians using some kind of big bones burning among the kindling to provide heat. He poked in the five-gallon coal oil can they were using for a stewpot with a stick to see what was cooking. Some kind of flower buds, it appeared to be.

Pegged crossways between duty, compassion, and personal safety, Ammon Swing frowned, kicked at a rock with his boot and rubbed the stubble on his chin, groping for a decision, the right answer. Clearing his throat, he spit instead.

The older Reb completed his reconnaissance by pulling out the leaves plugging the mouth of a *tus*, a wide-mouthed water jug made of sumac coils wrapped in cottonwood strips and caulked inside and out with heated pine pitch to stop leaks. Takins tipped it with his boot, so some of its precious water spilled out.

"Didn't see any weapons, Sarge, but a cuttin' knife or two. Their menfolks must be out somewheres with their guns."

Sgt. Swing nodded, turned on his boot heel without a further word, and started walking back the way they had come, his limp now more pronounced.

Takins started to follow, then bent to pluck a blue corn tortilla off a stone *metate* placed in the fire next to some ash bread baking in the embers. He also helped himself to a couple Indian figs from a black pottery dish. Walking away, head turned warily to keep an eye on the women behind them, he sampled the dried fruit of the prickly pear cactus. Liking its sweetness, Takins didn't notice the boy until he suddenly jumped atop a boulder he was passing, giving the war veteran such a fright he dropped his fruit. "Dammit, kid! Be careful!"

Seeing the older soldier's fear as he jerked his rifle up to cover him, the Apache boy grinned, unafraid, squatting atop his big rock.

Sgt. Swing frowned as he waited impatiently for Takins to catch up.

SEVENTEEN

Revenge, for an Apache, was not a lawless rampage of individual will, but a sacred social duty. Nor was it necessary to kill the particular enemy who caused the harm; others of his people would do. What we call torture had for Apaches something of a sacramental act. It was a test of courage of an enemy warrior. Apaches appreciated great bravery in a hopeless cause, and a white man who fought vigorously to the end was sometimes accorded a special honor: his slayers skinned his right hand and stirrup foot in testimony to his prowess.

—David Roberts, *Once They Moved Like the Wind: Cochise, Geronimo, and the Apache Wars*

Peck Ranch, Santa Cruz Valley

K Troop of the Tenth Cavalry, seeing the distant flames of the burning ranch against the night sky, had ridden hard several hours from Ft. Huachuca. The Tenth were the famed "Buffalo Soldiers," and Captain Thomas Lebo had led this unit composed entirely of black cavalrymen for almost twenty years, chasing Kiowas across the plains of Kansas and Kickapoos across the Rio Grande. In the late 1870s Lebo's black troopers successfully fought Victorio, leader of the Mescalero Apaches, all the way across west Texas, and now here they were again, chasing the last renegade Chiricahuas around southern Arizona Territory.

K Troop fanned out about the acreage, men poking through the still-smoking embers of the burned adobe ranch house.

The Captain and his First Lieutenant, John Bigelow, Jr., walked their horses about in circles, bending over their necks in this dawn's dim light, trying to read the tracks leading away from the devastated ranch.

Across the yard, two soldiers carried a charred Petra Peck out in a blanket to lay her down next to her burned baby.

Second Lieutenant Powhatan H. Clarke rode up, breaking the tragic spell. "Lieutenant! Found tracks of six horses headin' east. Three unshod and three shod—horses they stole here probably. But there were moccasin prints of seven bucks, so some of 'em may be ridin' double."

Lt. Bigelow frowned. "Then they'll continue raiding till every damned one of them is well-mounted."

"Prob'ly." Stuffed up with dust, their junior officer blew his nose with his fingers.

His Commanding Officer walked up leading his horse. "Send two men back to Huachuca to warn the territory the hostiles are back, and killing.

"Yessir."

"Maybe headquarters at Bowie can spare us another troop to help track these killers. Make that request."

The rookie officer nodded as his veteran Commander motioned over a non-com. "Sergeant . . . Let's get these poor folks buried here. A mother and her baby?"

"Yessir. And that cowboy, over to the corral."

The officers looked around until they spotted the human pincushion propped against a fence post, arrows sticking from him. Captain Lebo shook his head. "Well, let's leave him above ground for now. Strap him over a horse to take back to Huachuca for identification, so his kin can be contacted." The Pennsylvania Civil War veteran exhaled sad air.

"No use taking these other bodies over to Nogales and enflaming the populace any further."

One of his troopers strode briskly up. "Found some other feetprints, sir, like offen a chile."

* * *

The trooper led the three dismounted officers near the house's smoldering front porch. They could see by torchlight where a smaller person had gone down hard on their knees, and then crawled over to where someone else was lying. The cavalryman pointed.

"Blood here, someone wounded. Then the chile's feets disappear over there."

The officers paced the path, pondering. "Probably took a kid with them. Apaches like to raise child captives as camp slaves." Captain Lebo swung around and pointed to the man sitting against the corral with the arrows in him.

"If that's the husband, then whose blood was back there?"

"Husband shot an Apache," offered Lt. Bigelow.

The Captain tried to scratch his ass. He'd had one of the laundresses at the fort "fox" his worn britches, sewing a heart-shaped piece of tanned buckskin into the seat and extending it down the inseam for longer wear on a hard saddle, but that made it difficult to get purchase on an itch. "Didn't see a weapon."

"Apaches stole everything of value, sir, arms, ammunition, his horses."

The Captain nodded, thinking hard, when his answer suddenly staggered around the rear corner of the smoking ranch house.

"Sir!" Lt. Clarke blanched at the sight of the wraith wandering out of the darkness. His shocked warning startled the others. Arthur Peck did indeed look like a walking ghoul, arms outstretched for balance and one side of his head messy with dried blood. Eyes wide, mouth open, he started to howl again, frightfully. All the soldiers backed away from his lurching path.

Thomas Lebo, however, took command. He stopped the howling zombie in his tracks with an outstretched hand. "Sir! Who are you?"

Alfred Peck was drooling. ". . . House . . . my . . ."

"Apaches? Did they take your child?"

His progress halted, the rancher suddenly introverted, lowered his arms, and ceased his eerie wail. "Trini? No. . . . Niece. . . ." He seemingly had regained a little of his wits. "Stayed . . ." he gestured toward what used to be his home, "here."

"But she's gone now. Indians took her?"

Al Peck looked confused. "Don't . . . know . . ." He shook his head. "Dunno."

He was still shaking his head as Captain Lebo took his two other officers aside.

"Strap this poor man on a horse, too. Maybe our doc can calm him down. Clarke, take him and that dead man back to Huachuca with your detail. Get the message telegraphed that the Apaches are raiding. We'll get these poor people buried and be tracking these hostiles within the hour."

EIGHTEEN

The heedless influx of whites into what they considered an "empty" land, little knowing or caring that already the place was settled to its approximate capacity in terms of a native culture that depended for survival upon hunting and food gathering over huge expanses. When considerable portions of these lands were seized upon and made unavailable for native use, the aboriginal people were faced with slow starvation—or else seizure from the invaders of the requirements for survival. This caused inevitable retribution for these "depredations" and "thievery." Vengeance was then levied for this punishment, and soon there developed what many believed an endemic "war," as implacable as it was considered unwarranted.

—Dan L. Thrapp, in an introduction to
Martha Summerhayes's *Vanished Arizona*

Observation Post #4, Square Mountain

Four soldiers chewed a late breakfast around their cooking fire as they pondered their problem. Takins had satisfied his curiosity about the Indians' edibles. "Liked their corn tortillas, an' that fruit was sweet, too. We should pick some of that stuff."

"Nopal. Dried prickly pear cactus fruit—their favorite dessert, though I didn't hear 'em askin' you to a meal, Takins," said the Sergeant.

"They was usin' big bones, steada firewood to cook. Prob'ly some poor soldier's."

"Prob'ly a cow or a horse," explained Sgt. Swing. "Fat in those bones makes 'em burn slow. They'll do when wood's scarce."

Mullin was eating his breakfast atop a boulder at the north end of their ledge, posted to keep an eye on their new neighbors. "Weren't eatin' my dog, were they?"

"Checked their stew pot but couldn't really tell what they was cookin'? Some kinda plant buds, maybe yucca, in that mess. Smelled a bit like Horace, though," mused Takins.

"Damnation!"

"Prob'ly acorn stew. Grind nuts and sunflower seeds into a flour, add vegetables and beef, whatever they can hunt. Regular Apache fare," growled the Sergeant. "So don't go gettin' these boys riled up, Takins, about soldiers' bones and such nonsense." Sgt. Swing thought aloud, trying to figure out what to do about their new neighbors. "*Mansos* Apaches maybe. Tame."

Takins snorted. "Can no more tame an Apache than you kin tame a tarantula."

"Well, those women were wearin' calico, a sure sign they've been on a reservation at some time," argued the Sergeant. "But they could be wild, *netdahe* Chiricahuas up from Mexico. She lied she didn't know where their men were or who fathered their kids."

"How come the big one had her nose cut like that?" inquired the Southerner.

"Apaches like to snick off a little, they suspect their women of fooling around with another man."

Bobyne was quick on the draw. "Maybe she wasn't lying then, when she said she didn't know who fathered her kids."

The laughter relieved their tension.

"Suppose we should flash headquarters we've got Apaches up here," the Sergeant mused.

Takins objected. "Ain't you gonna look foolish, worryin' about a few women and little kids?"

"What the hell am I supposed to do with 'em then? Run 'em off? Christ, everybody's gotta eat. Springtime's always when they harvest and bake their *mescal*. Without that and their mesquite beans, they'd never make it through the winter."

"We feed them on the reservations," argued Bobyne.

"Not very well. Indian agents are so damned crooked, most of 'em, Indians only get half of what little they're supposed to. Without venison and what traditional foods they can gather, the Apaches would starve." Sgt. Swing rubbed his forehead hard, trying to think. "They know we're under orders not to harm their women, and they take advantage of that."

For the first time, the men saw their Sergeant looking worried.

"We probably should at least warn the boys over to Dos Cabezas we got more Apaches around."

Feeling responsible, Corporal Bobyne got up to go over to his equipment to transmit.

Heintz was troubled with a thought. "How long this cactus bakes?"

"Ohh . . . mescal takes several days to cook. Chiricahuas' main food. Then that big woman said they'd be movin' on." Frustrated with indecision, the Sergeant threw another handful of coffee from a sack into the simmering pot, then splashed some water from his canteen in to settle the grounds. Behind him, he heard the heliograph's shutter working. "What are you sendin', Bobyne?"

"POST FIVE THREE SQUAWS AND THEIR KIDS HAVE COME SARGE DOESN'T KNOW WHAT TO DO."

The others grinned, but didn't dare laugh. Sergeant Swing turned a hard eye on his signalman. "Smart aleck Easterner. Only got that second stripe because you were special trained to send code, Bobyne. Didn't earn it the hard way, out here in the field. But I can sure bust you down from that extra pay, Corporal, you get too sassy."

A hostile pause while the men digested this breach of authority. Bobyne, surprisingly, chuckled at this threat, but his eyes were on the distant mountain, not his Sergeant.

Angry, Sgt. Swing saw flashes coming from Dos Cabezas Peak, thirty-six miles away.

"What do they say?"

"HAVE DANCE INVITE US."

Unable to hold it, all the others did laugh. And Ammon Swing finally lost his temper, jerking to his feet to slam his coffee cup down!

"Goddamn you men, you don't know straight up! Stay shy of them women! Where there's squaws there's bound to be bucks showin' up, sooner or later! Apaches often send their women in first to scout or draw fire! So nobody go down there callin', and if they try to come up here, you treat 'em warily, like somebody who's just waitin' their chance to depredate!"

"Can't tell 'em apart from their menfolks anyways, at long range, especially when they's shootin' arrows an' yer duckin' 'em," agreed Takins.

The big German-American was brave enough to disagree. "*Dat*'s too stiff. You tink them squaws vill really at-tack us?"

Mullin piled on. "You mean we can't even be decent to the kiddies?"

Their leader's expression, even in the morning's rising heat, was ice cold. "Not as you love your mother, Mullin. And calculate to see her again."

Commander's House, Ft. Huachuca, Southern Arizona Territory

Captain Henry Lawton hurried into the office in the rear of Colonel Royall's home, where the Commander of the fort was enjoying a post-breakfast whiskey with General Miles and his aide. The Captain had already caught the General's eye due to his size, six feet, four inches of brawn and muscle, matched by his enthusiasm for military work.

"Patrol just came in, General. Apaches attacked a ranch in the Santa Cruz Valley, killed a ranch hand, the rancher's pregnant wife, and his baby boy, but left the rancher behind and took his young niece along with them. A Mister Peck."

Nelson Miles grimaced. "Killing women and babies. Were they . . . violated?"

"Lt. Clarke didn't say, sir. But they've got this rancher with them, this Peck fellow. Seems to be a bit out of his head. Doctor's looking at him now."

Colonel Royall weighed in. "In my experience, General, Apaches don't usually molest women, besides sometimes killing them, when they're on a raid. Believe sex drains their strength and endurance, spoils their luck."

"Umm . . . Was it Geronimo?"

"No mention, sir."

"Why would they take a girl hostage, let a man go?"

"Well, Geronimo usually kills everybody he encounters, that's why I wonder." pondered the Captain. "Often Apaches take young Mexican boys and girls as captives, even white kids sometimes, to train as future warriors or wives. But to let a grown white man go, without even torturing him first, is rather unusual for them."

The Colonel had a thought. "Perhaps Peck was let go to raise a ransom to buy his niece back?"

General Miles pondered that. "Kidnapping . . . For later slavery or torture . . . Scares the civilians even more." He got up, moved to a map hanging on the office wall.

"Where is this ranch?"

Captain Lawton pointed out the location. "Roughly twenty miles east of Nogales, and then north, right across the border, ten miles or so up the Santa Cruz Valley. Good ranching country near that river."

"Apaches attack there regularly?"

"Not that often. Usually further east, riding back and forth to their hideouts in the Sierra Madres. Can't remember a raid down in the Santa Cruz for awhile."

The General struggled to make sense of the Apaches' tactic. "Why would they risk this now, with all our patrols out, squads staking out their watering holes? They are taunting us, by God, daring us to catch them!"

Colonel Royall rose to join the officers studying the large

map. "Possibly. But I think they are also coming up here for ammunition. Those Apaches have stolen the very best guns they can find, General, our Colts, Winchesters, Springfields, which require heavier, machined American cartridges. God knows what they find to shoot down in Mexico for whatever weapons they can steal or trade for all different calibers, hand-made bullets, inferior ammunition. Better horseflesh up here, too, oat-fed and well cared for. So they sneak across our border to plunder all our good stuff they need."

The Brigadier General snorted. "Not exactly sneaking, slaughtering defenseless women and children. And will continue to do so, until they're all caught or killed."

"Yessir."

He turned to Second Lt. Dapray. "Tell my escort we'll be riding to Camp Crittenden tomorrow. I want to get closer to the fighting."

"Into Mexico?" queried his aide.

"Oh, no, no. Don't think I need to go into Mexico."

The Colonel eyed his superior officer. "Crook went into Mexico. Right into the Sierra Madres after the bastards."

"Well, maybe eventually. After I get these commands better organized, our heliograph network fully operating. But if there were a capture or surrender, I wouldn't mind a look at that noxious country. Eventually."

The towering Captain couldn't contain his energy. "Noxious, sir? I find those mountainous deserts beautiful. *La espinosa del diablo* (the devil's spine)—that's what the Mexicans call their infamous Sierra Madres. Harsh, savage maybe, but strangely beautiful, too."

"Yes, and devilishly hot as well. Damned sand gets into everything—eyes, clothes, your food. Awfully irritating." General Miles pondered his new problem a moment longer, more interested in strategy and politics than nature's wonders.

"That newspaper over in Tucson, the *Daily Star*, its editor has already been after me for an interview. We must calm the citizenry here now, so there's no panic. Meanwhile, Colonel, let's clear out the forts, get every damned cavalry unit we've got out on these renegades' trail or headed south. Flash those orders. Perhaps we can scare them back below the border. This raiding and killing for ammunition must not be allowed to continue . . . not in our country anyway."

Colonel Royall nodded sharply. "No sir. A teased snake often strikes back, eh?"

Observation Post #4, Square Mountain

The telegrapher had his telescope focused on Post #5, now flashing a message across the Sulphur Springs Valley. Bobyne related the gist of the warning. "Sergeant, there's been an attack on a ranch down in Santa Cruz Valley. Peck's ranch. Let's see, three people killed, last night."

"Santa Cruz Valley."

"Seven Apaches they're chasin'. Stole horses. We're on alert again."

"Could be our same bucks, still lookin' for horses and guns as they head back across the border."

"Yes, sir. Probably cut any telegraph wires they've come across, so our heliographs will be even more important."

"Apache splices. They cut the wire, fellers, tie the ends back together with rawhide. Devilishly tough to locate when they hide the break in trees." Sgt. Swing thought aloud. "Poor folks. That ranch is right on the *Camino de los Muertos*. Little white crosses all the way up to Tucson. The Dead Men's Trail."

He picked up his binoculars and wandered over to their ledge's north end, while Bobyne recorded the message in his notebook. Higher up on the mountainside, Heintz watered his melon bed, irrigating from a canteen.

Takins sat on a barrier boulder, cradling his rifle. Down the mountainside below him, Mullin appeared to be playing with two of the Indian kids, the older boy and one of the little girls, as they ran and jumped around, seemingly chasing something. The Sergeant took a long look. "The hell's he doin'?"

Takins had been watching them romp. "Kid's got a baby turkey they's playin' with."

"Mullin! Shoo those kids off! Back to their mothers, where they belong!"

"Aw, we're jus' playin', Sarge!"

"Get back up here! Don't aggravate me, boy!"

With a frown, their young recruit gestured for the Apache kids to leave. "Okay, okay. . . . Bye, kids. Go along home now. . . . Bye-bye."

The little girl stopped playing, rubbed her cloth doll wistfully against her cheek. Her twelve-year-old brother recaptured his pet bird and quickly read Mullin's intent, his arm pointed toward their campsite. Grabbing his sister's hand, the Indian boy scampered off with the girl toward their lower ledge.

Sgt. Swing scanned the Indians' campsite several hundred yards away. The heavy squaw was positioning a grass mat over the cactus crowns now baking in their four-foot, rock-lined pit, as the two younger women started to scoop loose dirt in on top of the mat to cover it.

"Got their cactuses bakin'. Day after tomorrow those mescal hearts oughta be cooked. Then I'm shooin' 'em on their way."

The Sergeant saw the young soldier climbing back up on their ledge. "Jus' can't stay away from pets, can yah, Mullin?"

"I love animals, Sarge."

The noncom took the binoculars back to Bobyne, now flashing the surprise attack message on up to Turkey Flat. "You're goin' down with me to the Tanks tomorrow, Mullin. The Coxes need to be warned there's wild Apaches up here and their kin jus' killed three ranchers eighty miles south of here, only last night."

"No foolin'?"

"Remember that, son, next time you go playin' with their kids."

* * *

Early next morning the new recruit slept sweetly with a lasso encircling his blanket. A hand reached into his tent's opening and shook a set of mule's chain traces right next to his ear. "WHOA!"

Mullin jerked upright at the sudden jingling, thinking he was about to be run over. Takins, on dawn duty, chuckled as he stood up and turned back to wedge another dead cholla branch into his breakfast fire. "Almost got run over there, sonny."

"Damn you, Takins."

"Rise and shine, soldier. Say hello to another wonderful day in the Regular Army O."

The kid rolled grouchily from his blanket. "'Hello,' my heinie."

Their cook smirked as he took his frying pan full of roasted coffee beans and poured them hot into a canvas sack. Chewing on the stub of last night's cigar, Takins set the thick sack on a flat rock next to the fire and began pounding it with his rifle butt to grind up the beans.

Behind him, the other three were beginning to rouse from their bedrolls. Sgt. Swing sat up to stretch. "Our Indians?"

Private Takins jerked a thumb. "Already havin' their breakfast."

"Well, ladies can enjoy one more, then they're *adiós, amigas*."

"Hope they go peaceably," added Bobyne, standing up to pull on his blue pants.

"Lookit him with his snake guard." The Southerner focused their yawning attention on Mullin, now with his pants on, too, as he coiled up his lasso from around the rubber mat beneath his blanket. "Sleep tight, kid? No rattlers come out to bite?"

Several of the fellers grinned sleepily. Private Mullin, however, didn't. "You're the only snake that bothers me around here, Takins."

The older reb laughed. The young Private bent to pull on his black half boots, as Heintz ambled off to take a leak from ledge's edge. "Ow! Jesus! Owww, I'm bit!" Hopping about on one foot, Mullin sat down in a hurry, yanked his boot off, and shook it empty. "Oooo! It hurts! My God, what's that?"

The others gathered round to see. Clinging to Mullin's dirty sock was a six-inch brown centipede, curling and uncurling, its front pincers intact. The Sergeant whacked it away with a stick, then pulled off the rookie's dirty sock to inspect the angry red bite on the arch of the lad's foot. "Centipede. . . . Venomous."

"Christ it hurts!"

Sgt. Swing frowned. "Bite's gonna swell up, be sore for a while." He turned on Takins. "Did you put that bastard in his boot?"

"No sir, I did not! I like teasin' the kid, sure, but I wouldn't do somethun' mean like that to my bunkie."

Mullin was rolling on his back, holding his wounded appendage. "Je-sus. . . ."

"Ain't gonna kill yah, Mullin." The Sergeant looked around for some kind of salve to help soothe the kid's pain, then noticed the reb masticating his cigar. "Spit some tobacco juice there, right on the bite."

"What?"

"Just do it!"

The Southerner bent, removed his cheroot, cleared his throat noisily several times to work up some good phlegm, then spit a brown gob on the reddening arch of Mullin's bare foot. Sgt. Swing rubbed it into the puncture with his thumb, until a little blood flowed.

"Tobacco juice is strong enough to kill anything. That'll have to do, kid, till we get down to Missus Cox's. Maybe she'll fix you a poultice to draw out the poison."

The centipede crawled toward Heintz, its many feet flailing to get away, but the German punctuated the painful moment by crushing the wormlike arthropod beneath his big boot.

Later, Mullin was dressed and seated atop Annie, a haversack of dirty laundry tied onto the mule as a makeshift saddle. His bare left foot dangled against the California mule's stomach, a swollen reddish reminder always to shake out one's boot—first.

Takins was back to his old self. "Don't go spurrin' that mule, Mullin, or she might leave you barefoot in the cactus."

The Sergeant held Grover's reins, two empty water kegs riding the *aparejo* cradle on its back. "Stay shy of those squaws now. General Crook warned us to treat the Apaches as 'children in ignorance, not innocence.' So look sharp, boys, while we're undermanned up here. We'll be back before supper."

He winked at the other three. "Unless we have to amputate."

The mule rider grimaced.

"Feel better soon you vill, Mullin. Nice lady to help."

Takins perked up. "Ask Bachelor Bess if she's got any more pie to spare for our desserts, Sarge."

Bobyne couldn't resist a smart comment, either. "Yeah. I eat much more corn mush up here, I'm gonna turn into a mule."

"Thought you already were, Corporal." Laughter from the men as the Sergeant set off, leading the two mules and their unwieldy cargo down the noticeable trail they had begun to wear in the mountainside.

Takins nudged Heintz. "Must have Cupid's cramp. He's findin' excuse to do more business with that woman than a rooster with only one hen."

Trail Down Square Mountain

Mullin groaned when his swollen bare foot accidentally banged into the mule's belly. To distract his poisoned man, the Sergeant broke into an off-key song, one of the many ditties the soldiers made up to lift their spirits on the long, wearying marches across an endless desert.

Oh we went to Arizona
for to fight the Injuns there;

We came near being made bald-headed,
but they never got our hair.
We lay among the ditches, in the dirty yellow mud,
And we never saw an onion, a turnip or a spud.
On the telegraphic wire, we walked to Mexico,
We bless the day we skipped away,
From the Regular Army O.

—*From* "Forty Miles a Day on Beans and Hay,"
by Don Rickey. Jr.

Sgt. Swing looked over his shoulder at his young charge, who was almost smiling, in spite of his pain.

NINETEEN

A Dr. LaCroix of Albany, New York, wrote a book, Physiological View of Marriage, *which was widely advertised in prairie newspapers. 25¢ for 250 pages of a guide promising to provide women with a "confidential medical adviser in regard to any interesting complaints to which their delicate organization renders them liable."*

—Glenda Riley, *The Female Frontier: A Comparative View of Women on the Prairie and the Plains*

Ranch Near Cox's Tanks

The Sergeant tied Grover's reins to the corner porch post and helped the teenager down from his perch. Martha Cox was standing in her front door, sweeping dirt out with a homemade broom—big, feathered turkey wings lashed to a pole. She pulled on a "Spencer," a form-fitting jacket, over her blouse and man's-style canvas pants, and walked out to her company.

"Sergeant! Your supplies and mail are late again. Packer hasn't shown up from Dos Cabezas yet."

"Maybe won't for a while, ma'am. Was a raid on Peck's ranch last night, down in the Santa Cruz Valley. Killed three people."

The news visibly distressed her. "Oh. Apaches?"

"Probably. Maybe the same ones tangled with you. They're chasing 'em now, but everybody smart's stayin' home while we get more troops out on patrol."

An arm around his waist, Sergeant Swing assisted the young soldier to limp up onto the porch. "Mornin', Miss Cox."

Her distress turned into a frown. "What's wrong with you?"

"Private Mullin got a hello from a centipede this morning. Wondered if you might have a pain cure?"

"Come in. Let's lay him down on the bed." She moved to the

young man's other side, and together they helped him inside her house.

The Sergeant first helped her move her bed out from the wall so she could tend the victim from both sides, carefully sliding the tomato cans filled with water in which she had placed each wooden bed leg to keep the ants from crawling in with her every night. After daubing a colored liquid on the bite, Martha wrapped it in a bandage of old sheet. She then propped Mullin's sore foot atop a pillow on her linen sheets. A smelly, yellowish fluid stained the bandage over the wound.

"There. Tincture of echinacea, skullcap, and Virginia snake-root. Should draw the pain and relieve the swelling." She put a china cup in his grateful hands. "Drink this tea, Private, all of it. Root tonic to flush the poison from your veins."

"Echinacea, skullcap, and Virginia snakeroot. I'll remember that." Mullin took a swallow of medicinal tea and smiled. "Thank you so much, Miss Cox."

"Certainly. Come, Sergeant. Let him rest."

Sgt. Swing was seated once again at her kitchen table, bracing himself for another inquisition, as she replaced her teapot on the iron stove. "What was in that tea you gave him?"

"Sarsparilla, as a spring tonic to cleanse his blood, mixed with butternut extract for worms."

He gave her a hard look. "You worming one of my soldiers?"

"Can't help but do him a world of good."

Her smile defused his irritation at her presumption. "You don't believe in home remedies, Sergeant?"

"If they help."

"They do. The desire to take medicine is perhaps the greatest feature that distinguishes man from the animals, Mister Swing." She smiled again, taking the edge off her nursing demeanor. "Care for some sarsparilla tea?"

"Uh, no. Thank you."

She cocked an eyebrow. "No poisons need flushing from your blood?"

The veteran smiled ruefully. "Prob'ly, ma'am. But it's a little warm today, for tea."

"Lemonade then?"

"Please . . . So you're well-versed in home medicines, too?" He fidgeted at the table while she sliced a lemon and squeezed it into two glasses of water, then spooned some sugar in. This woman of many talents and wide knowledge disturbed him, threw him a bit off balance, never quite certain what she would say or do next.

"Some. My mother was very good with herbs. Thought I needed some nursing skills to go along with the hunting and fishing tricks my father was teaching me."

"Befitting a good wife."

She served and sat down across from him. "Yes. But I liked the woodcraft better." Martha Cox laughed and he did, too. Her humor, always lurking behind her bossy exterior, her sometimes viperish tongue, relaxed him a bit.

"You are a pioneer in petticoats, Miss Cox."

"Martha. Or a saint in a sunbonnet, as they sometimes called us ladies back in Iowa. I can't abide sunbonnets. They're an obstruction to sight and an impediment to hearing."

Sgt. Swing grinned. "No, ma'am, can't see you in any sunbonnet."

"Call me Martha. Please."

"I'm afraid I have another favor to ask . . . Martha. We're running low on supplies up there already. Regulations say we're supposed to keep a thirty-day supply, but we haven't gotten close to that. Could you loan us a little flour, coffee, beans, any beef or bacon, until our packer gets here? We'll pay you back, naturally, as soon as our pay and supplies arrive."

"Of course. Whatever we've got. I'll see if Jacob will butcher a steer when he gets back from moving his cattle. I'd like to jerk some fresh beef for *carne seca* anyway. My brother has developed a fondness for spicy, Mexican seasonings."

"Me, too. Fits this hot country. Most gracious of you, ma'am." He looked relieved, constantly having to ask her for big favors.

"And a bath, too?"

"What?" He reddened.

She shook her head at his foolishness. "Mercy. Men and little boys . . . I promise not to look."

Observation Post #4, Square Mountain

Perched on a boulder whittling a long stick sharp for gardening while ostensibly on guard, Heintz looked off to the north where the Apaches were camped and didn't see them. Perplexed, he put down his knife, picked up his rifle, and looked around, only to suddenly see the three Indian women down the mountainside, quietly climbing right up toward him.

"Hup! Vimmen! The *Indianer*! They come!"

The big Hessian was on his feet, pointing down in alarm. Bobyne hurriedly put down the telescope he'd been polishing to grab his rifle and run over, while Takins roused from inside his tent where he'd been napping.

Peering down, they watched as Mrs. Cutnose puffed up toward them, quite agile for a brute of a woman. Behind her clamored the two younger women. Haozinne, the last and loveliest, had a woven willow burden basket on her back, secured by a tumpline around her forehead. All three women wore buckskin moccasins folded over at the knee with bullhide soles turned up at the toes, decorated buckskin so thick as to make their small feet look smaller by contrast. Simple strings of colored Mexican bean beads, shell beads, and other fetishes hung from the ladies' necks, embellished by pendants made of flattened, polished metal from discarded tin cans, in the biggest woman's case, in such gaudy, heavy profusion that Heintz wondered how she could even hold her head up for any length of time.

"*Nein! Nein!* Back! You go." Heintz swept his arm toward them, gesturing hard. "Avay you must!"

The ladies stopped to stare up at the big man trying to brush them off with a large forearm jerking in the air. Their leader smiled, held up her empty hands in a gesture of openness. The two women behind her giggled, and on they came.

Takins arrived on a three-legged tear, cocking his rifle. "Get ready, boys, for trouble!"

"Keep your eyes-peeled above and behind us, for their husbands, just like the Sergeant warned," added Bobyne.

Heintz was confused. "But ve cannot them shoot?"

"We can if they attack us. Apache women always got a knife about 'em somewheres, even hidden in their hair," admonished their war veteran. "Shoot first, fellers, an' we'll straighten it out with the officers later."

Mrs. Cutnose pulled herself up between several boulders, her girlfriends right behind her. The ladies were wearing their finest today, like they were coming to a party. Besides their medicine-token necklaces, several of their earrings were made of pieces of iridescent shell from the Pacific Coast, and their arms and wrists were decorated with trade brass, silver bracelets, and beaded wristbands.

As the three soldiers stepped back protectively in front of their precious signaling equipment, rifles raised. Haozinne unstrapped her burden basket with the buckskin bottom and swung it down in front of Mrs. Cutnose. Smiling, the big woman motioned like she was putting something in her mouth.

"*E-chi-ca-say Nda* (Greetings, white man). *Mescal. Eyanh.* (Eat a little.)"

The pretty young woman reached into her grass basket as Bobyne, too, cocked his Springfield. Oblivious to the threat, Haozinne (One Who Is Standing Out from the Crowd) pulled from it the baked crown of a cactus, holding it out for them to see. "*Mescal.*" It resembled an oblong mass of golden brown, pulpy mush.

Mrs. Cutnose mimed eating again, but the reb waved her off. "Don't want any. Not today."

The hefty woman reached down into the burden basket again and pulled out an old flat-bladed knife, its wooden handle wrapped in deer hide. Instantly Heintz cocked his rifle, and now all three men had their weapons leveled, pointed straight at her.

"*Hai*! (Wait!)" Mrs. Cutnose gestured palms up that it was okay, then reached to scrape off some of the charred outsides of the *agave palmeri* and sliced off a hunk of the baked cactus. She offered the golden mush to Heintz, the big appetite in their midst.

Takins was still suspicious. "Don't. Might be poisoned. Mescal's liquor, not some ol' piece a cactus."

Seeming to understand their reluctance, Mrs. Cutnose ate it herself. She chewed, still smiling, then carved two more hunks of the fifteen-pound agave heart to give to her girlfriends, who began enjoying them, too. Another slice she offered again to the large Corporal. Heintz's appetite was sorely tempted. He accepted it, tentatively.

The other two soldiers watched their comrade sniff, then lick, finally tentatively chew a bite of baked cactus. "Hmm. Sweet. Sweet po-ta-to *ist* like."

The two holdouts watched the rest of them enjoying the treat. Mrs. Cutnose sliced off two more sticky chunks of mescal mush, passed them over to Bobyne and Takins. Nadezba (She Crosses to Go to War) took the knife from her, sliced off bigger pieces for herself and the others.

Takins grudgingly watched them all eat, his fellows chewing and nodding, before finally, hesitantly, he tried a bite himself. His frown brightened slowly into a smile as he, too, began to enjoy the juicy sweet taste of the heart of a freshly baked century plant cactus.

"Is like candy."

Ranch Near Cox's Tanks

Sgt. Swing was enjoying his bath. He settled back into the big tin tub in the Cox's backyard in the shade of the house. His hair was wet as he stretched his left leg out over the side of the tub to soap his slow-healing, wounded thigh.

"What kind of a name is Ammon Swing anyway? German?"

The soap slipped from his hand as he pulled his leg back in the tub with a splash! Startled, he hadn't heard her come from the house.

"Thought you wasn't gonna look."

She lounged in her backdoor, watching him with a sly grin, like a coyote snatching mice from beneath a haystack. "I fibbed. Want some more hot water?"

"Nope. Just some privacy."

For emphasis, he reached behind the tub to his dirty clothes, plucked his dusty campaign hat from the top of the pile and plunked it back on his wet head, further shading his upper body.

"How about some hot tea?"

"Depends on what you slip into it. Ma'am."

"Oh, perhaps some damiana leaves. They're a tonic for 'lethargy of the sexual organs.' "

The Sergeant couldn't help himself, he chuckled. "Don't think I need that."

"Well, maybe a tincture of skullcap and lady's slipper then. A nervine for 'persons troubled by undue sexual desire.' "

Martha smiled at his frown but changed the saucy subject. "Cox is English. Several generations off the boat. Your kin are from Germany, I'll bet. Where your stubborn streak originates."

Resigned to not getting any peace from this nosy woman, the Sergeant continued lathering up. "Nope, got that from my mother."

"Really? Seems to me settling down would suit you then."

He cocked his head round to fix her with an inquisitive eye. "Ma'am?"

She straightened up, leaning into her proposition now that she had his undivided attention. "Sure. Marry and raise a family and whittle your own stick out here in these Western wilds. Someone's gotta civilize this perilous desert."

He frowned and fingered some soap out of his ear so as to not misunderstand her. "Naw. Afraid I'm wedded to the army. Too old for kids now, prob'ly."

"Too old?"

"Old as you."

He knew his blunder immediately when he saw the turkey red under her tan. Martha Cox marched directly over to the bathtub, giving him a granite eye in return.

Ammon Swing sat up and swung round in the water to face her, alert for trouble as he tried to cover himself modestly with soapsuds. "Ma'am. Please! You have me at a disadvantage."

"Good! Mister Swing, if ever you alter your mind, I know the very one would have you."

Flustered, he tipped back his black hat to get a good gander at this provocateur. "Who?"

She pointed a sharp finger at the corral across the stable yard, where Grover and Annie were contentedly munching hay. "Your mare mule."

Martha Cox snatched up the gunnysack full of dirty soldiers' clothes lying next to the tub and dumped them right into the soapy water with the now thoroughly discombobulated Sergeant. "Enjoy your scrub!"

Observation Post #4, Square Mountain

Up at Post #4, festivities were in progress. Heintz leaned against a boulder, being fed more baked cactus by the coquettish Mrs. Cutnose. Corporal Bobyne sat atop another rock, trying to communicate by hand signs with the youngest and prettiest Apache, Haozinne.

Takins sat in the opening of his A-tent with the third woman, stroking her thigh under her thin calico dress. Nadezba smiled and pointed to herself. "*Schicho*. (Lady). *Nah-to*. (Tobacco)."

The Confederate veteran just smiled and winked back at her.

Mrs. Cutnose jabbered away at the big German-American, miming drinking something. "Whis-key."

"*Nein*. Whiskey *nein*. Ve haf none."

Takins overheard. "Sergeant does. He'd scalp us hisself if we let them git after his bottle, though."

"Ve haf any food to share, Takins?"

"No. We're low on supplies already. That's what they went down for." Takins suddenly snapped his fingers. "Hey! Got jus' the sauce for 'em."

He hustled into the Sergeant's tent, where he could be seen rummaging around inside their unlocked medicine box.

Bobyne, feeling responsible, stood atop his rock, shading his eyes as he scanned uphill and down, all around them, still alert for enemy attack.

Takins came back out of Sgt. Swing's tent and walked over to his own, where he knelt next to his Indian lady friend in the tent's opening, showing her the brown bottle of darker brown liquid before he poured a spoonful. "Here, girlie. Try some of this."

Nadezba tentatively tasted the dark liquid with her tongue, liked it, then greedily swallowed the whole spoonful.

Takins nodded and grinned. "Good, huh?"

His spoon-feeding caught the other ladies' attention, and they came over to the tent to see what treat was being offered.

Bobyne couldn't figure. "What is it?"

"Castor oil."

"Don't give 'em that!"

The ragged Southerner in dirty clothes gestured at the buttoned-up Easterner in his clean uniform. "Good for their digestion." Takins grinned as he fed the squaw beside him another spoonful of the purgative oil, while the other two Apache women crowded in behind her for their dose. "An' they'll be runnin' for the bushes tonight!"

Ranch Near Cox's Tanks

Private Mullin was back atop his mule later that afternoon, resting upon a gunny sack of moist laundry, his bandaged foot dangling below Annie's belly.

"Thanks again, ma'am. Feels better already."

Martha handed the young man some pieces of old sheet and a small, stoppered bottle of greenish solution. "Change your bandages the next couple days and use all of this tincture, right on the bite. You'll be fine."

Sergeant Swing contradicted her. "Apaches hardly ever change bandages in order to prevent that extra irritation, and their wounds seem to heal up pretty quick."

"They have to. They're Apaches. Okay, try not changing your bandages regularly and see what happens, Private. Just don't call me again if your foot gets infected."

"Oh no, ma'am. I'll do exactly what you say." Mullin nodded vigorishly as she handed a sack of canned goods and food to a freshly scrubbed and shaven Sergeant. Even in the gathering heat of May, there was now a frost between them.

Sgt. Swing accepted the bundle gratefully, sheepishly, having difficulty looking at her directly, after his grievous insult earlier. "Thank you, ma'am. This'll do fine. Somebody will be down day after tomorrow to pick up our own supplies. Should be here by then. And please warn your brother about that raid on that Santa Cruz ranch. We gotta stay alert, 'cause we've got some Apaches up our mountain now, too."

"What?" She was suddenly concerned, her irritation with him temporarily forgotten. "I saw that extra smoke, but we just figured you'd spread out your camp."

"It's just three women and their kids, bakin' mescal. Can't tell whether they're wild ones up from Mexico or tame Apaches off the reservation." He avoided her worried eyes by looking up Square Mountain. "I'm shooin' 'em away soon as their mescal is cooked. Don't want 'em scoutin' our defenses for their menfolk, wherever they are."

"No, indeed." Martha looked off anxiously in the direction of the Tanks. "Wonder what's keeping Jacob?" She turned back to the Sgt. with a worried frown. "Anything goes wrong, Sergeant, give us three quick flashes with your mirror, several times, and we'll come up on the run."

"You read signal code, too?"

"No, but three flashes should get our attention."

"We're already on guard, ma'am. Thanks again for the hospitality." He thought as he turned away, *The U.S. Army in Arizona had yet to need rescuing by homesteaders!*

Sgt. Swing led Grover away, their refilled water kegs sloshing against either side of his back, trailed by Annie and his rider, Mullin, who waved. "Good-bye, Miss Cox. Say hello to Jacob for me, and thanks again!"

"I'll do that, Private. You'll find some comb honey tucked in there, too, Ammon. Perhaps it'll sweeten your disposition."

Walking off, Sgt. Swing turned his head to give her a thin smile and a touch of his hat brim.

Observation Post #4, Square Mountain

The big mule packer heard them first, climbing slowly back up to the ledge as a dusty desert sun lowered to the horizon. The Sergeant was singing again, if you could call it that, to cheer up the bitten Mullin, and his ditty echoed up the mountainside to the workmen above.

Oh I'd like to be a packer,
And pack with George F. Crook,
And dressed up in my canvas suit,

To be for him mistook.
I'd braid my beard in two forked tails,
And idle all the day,
In whittling sticks and wondering,
What the New York papers say."
—From Forty Miles a Day on Beans
and Hay, *by Don Rickey, Jr.*

Heintz leaned over the far side of his mules' brush corral, nearest the ravine, to see the trail. "Hullo, fel-lers! Still yer foot got, Mullin?"

The others were ostentatiously busy with various chores, but Heintz walked over to help Mullin down from his mule and limp him over to his tent.

The Sergeant rubbed his sore leg to massage out some of the tiredness. "Anything important pass?"

Bobyne made his report. "Troops are on the move. Two more patrols coming down from Ft. Apache on the chase. Haven't caught those raiders yet, though."

Sgt. Swing sat back on a perimeter boulder a moment to take a load off. "Damn. Good Apache can track a shadder on a rainy night, but I don't know about those Wallapai Scouts. What about our Apaches?"

"Still cookin' their cactus," answered Takins.

Heintz unloaded the heavy water barrels from the mule, manhandling each down by himself. "Where *ist* food?"

Their leader excused the problem. "Rations still haven't come in yet. So many soldiers out chasin' Indians, supply details are runnin' late."

"Unless the 'Paches caught them, too?" countered the war veteran.

Anxious, the soldiers looked glumly at one another.

Sgt. Swing was having none of it. "You boys know how disorganized those quartermasters can be. Don't fret. Miss Cox lent us some canned goods. We can even hunt us up a whitetail or muley, anyone wants to get up early enough."

"I spotted a bighorn sheep, near the top a thet other mountain, when I was pickin' up firewood yesterday. Sure like to kill me one a those," agreed Takins.

"Fresh venison suits me. Hell, you boys been eatin' better up here than you do at the fort, where it's nothin' but beef, beans, bread, and coffee. We won't starve, fellers, before our supplies finally get here. I promise." The Sergeant limped tiredly over to drop the sack of canned goods next to the fire, then moved on to flop down inside his tent to rest before supper.

Watching him, the Southerner leaned toward the telegrapher to mutter, "An' two gimps now, to help guard us."

TWENTY

One old bear hunter told an informant in the 1890's that his crippled, clenched and stiffened fingers, resembling a bear-like claw, were the result of eating bear in his youth. Bears were of the brown and black varieties. Bears were hunted on horseback or foot by 4 or 5 men, all of whom had to be medicine men with "bear powers" due to the danger and possible mauling from cornering them.

—Winifred Buskirk, *The Western Apache: Living with the Land Before 1950*

Little Rincon Mountains, San Pedro Valley, Southern Arizona Territory

A pinch of sacred yellow tule powder, *hoddentin*, flew in the opening to the shady cave, followed by another, rousing the beast from his midday stupor. Several bayonet-pointed lances were suddenly thrust into the mid-sized hole and rattled around against the rocks, further irritating the inhabitant.

A dark-skinned, painted face framed against a blue sky appeared in the mouth of the hole for a quick peek inside before jerking back out of sight.

With a loud, guttural snarl, a large bear erupted from its summer den, which was little more than an underground hole in the sandstone escarpment below a mesa. Four Apaches antagonizing the four-hundred-pound, six-foot-tall animal jumped back as the yellowish brown bear foolishly chose to defend its turf rather than flee to safety. Growling and huffing, the bear slashed its sharp claws at the lance pokers on either side, then tried to run back into its hole, only to be blocked by two crossed lances across the entrance. These lances were nine-foot-long sotol cactus stalks with foot-long steel bayonets or Mexican lance points wrapped firmly in each stalk's notched tip by the skin of a cow's tail.

The brown bear bounced off these guard spears with a frightened roar and whirled on its attackers. A flint-pointed arrow thudded into its stomach, and the big bear reared up on its back paws with a squeal! It sprang at the nearest lancer, cuffing its curved claw across Fun's shoulder and outstretched arm, knocking the lance from the warrior's hands. Blood instantly bloomed in three gashes on the Indian's torso. Fun saved himself from a deeper bite by spinning and leaping out of the enraged bear's way!

Another reed arrow flew into its furry neck, doubling its hurt, provoking the wounded beast into another outraged charge right into the lance of their leader, Naiche.

A heart strike! The sharpened steel bayonet penetrated the brown bear's chest, impaling him right on the end of Naiche's lance. The other end was rammed into the dirt after the tall Indian holding it firm was bowled over by the force of the bear's charge.

Perico screamed! "*Haldzil shoz-litzogue!* (Strong yellow bear!)"

The Apache leader sprang back up to watch the big bear wobble on its metal skewer, then topple slowly over, dead. Naiche's victory cry erupted! "*Yah-tats-an!*"

Dahkeya yelped and raised his lance in respect. Fun-held his spread fingers across his bleeding shoulder but managed to join Perico in crying out. "*Diyi* (one with extraordinary supernatural powers)! Naiche! *Diyi*!"

It was the Apache's highest expression of respect, acknowledgment of a man's supernatural ability, and Cochise's second son finally smiled. At last he'd found his special power, the one extraordinary gift he alone among all the chosen Apache chiefs possessed. The ability to kill the sacred bear, which Apaches were normally afraid of and shied away from hunting.

Diyi! Bear killer! Naiche!

TWENTY-ONE

In an attack, Apaches tried to kill the horses first, so that the cavalrymen were trapped and could then be picked off as they starved or tried to escape. Another trick was to have an Apache pretend to be wounded or injured and limp away from a fight so that the soldiers would rush after him for a capture. These foolish soldiers would then be led into an ambush. Quail do this in the brush to lead pursuers away from their hidden family.

—Eve Ball, *In the Days of Victorio, Recollections of a Warm Springs Apache*

Observation Post #5, Dos Cabezas Peak

At their sister heliograph station across the big valley, things weren't going smoothly this noonday, either. Turning to his officer, Corporal Hengesbaugh was all frown. "Tried sendin' it three times, sir, but can't get 'em to acknowledge."

"Probably takin' siestas in this heat," opined Sgt. Conn. The veteran Sergeant was on temporary duty from the Sixth Cavalry, assigned to take over this observation post when this engineer Lieutenant soon moved on to supervise the rest of Miles's heliograph stations. Sgt. Conn used to be in charge of issuing rations to the Sixth's Apache Scouts, who warmly referred to him as "*cocke* sergeant" (hog, or ration sergeant).

Second Lt. Philip Fuller took off his cork campaign hat, mopped his sweaty brow with his neckerchief. "Well, keep trying; it's important. Captain Hatfield's lost those raiders' trail. Those murdering Apaches could be any damned where by now."

Their heliographer turned back to his mechanical shutter and began flashing the message again.

The young Lieutenant wrung his hands. "How will I ever get out to check all the other outposts now? I will never get off this son-of-a-bitching mountain!"

Listening from his guard perch on a big rock above Post #5's mountain campsite, their veteran couldn't resist tossing in his two cents' worth. "You know, an' old Scout once told me, 'When Apaches are in sight, be careful. And when they aren't in sight, be durn careful." Private Slivers laughed at his own witticism, but quickly ceased.

His four camp mates just stared grimly at him, unamused by his tired jest.

Observation Post #4, Square Mountain

Across the big valley, the reason for Observation Post #4's non-response was apparent. A social gathering was in full swing. Heintz and Bobyne were munching baked *mescal* that Nadebza sliced for them with her knife.

Mullin had the twelve-year-old boy and several of the little Indian girls mesmerized by his steel harmonica, on which he was blowing a passable rendition of "Turkey in the Straw."

Nearby, Haozinne bent curiously over the mirror on the tripod, reaching to see her reflection in it. Bobyne anxiously tried to keep her hands off the delicate equipment. "No, no. Don't touch that, ma'am. Please."

Mrs. Cutnose picked up a spoon from a pile of cooking utensils and confronted the Sergeant, who stood right in the middle of the goings-on, exasperated. The hefty Indian woman poked the spoon into her opened mouth, mimicking eating, as she flirtatiously wiggled the necklace of red beans and white seeds dangling about her thick neck. Sgt. Swing eyed her warily. "Whaddya want with that damned spoon?"

Takins merely relaxed, watching. "Wants some castor oil, Sarge."

Now pulling his arm, Mrs. Cutnose continued sucking on her empty spoon, insistent.

"Castor oil? Don't think we . . . oh yeah, the medicine kit. How would she know about that?"

The Southerner smiled. "Well, first she asked for whiskey, but castor oil seemed to suit her jus' dandy instead."

"When was this?"

"Yesterday. Ladies come over with their fresh-baked cactus to share."

The Sergeant pulled away from the eager lady to stride to Takins, who was lounging, smoking one of his cheroots in his tent's opening. "Yesterday! So now they're back for more fun? A castor oil party every day, is it?"

"Now, Sergeant. Jus' calm down. We're purty near out of food, admit it. I'll trade 'em castor oil any day, for sumthun' to eat."

Ammon Swing was really perturbed, stalking about with his hands on his hips like an angry rooster, trying to decide how to handle this unwelcome invasion of their camp.

Heintz, meanwhile, was in the Sergeant's tent and stuck his large head back outside, holding up the bottle of digestive aid. The women saw it and came running to him. "I may them some give, Sarge?"

Takins shrugged at the Sergeant. "Jus' bein' neighborly."

Sgt. Swing glowered at him but finally nodded sharply to the big Hessian, in the interest of camp peace.

Bobyne jumped to attention, finally spotting the winking flashes across the valley. "Message comin' in."

Only Sgt. Swing paid him any heed, the others being too busy playing with little kids or feeding giggling squaws laxatives to bother.

"Captain Hatfield's lost all track of the Apaches, Sergeant."

"They aren't lost, dammit! They're right up here, linin' up for their daily dose! All right, goddammit, get these women the hell outta here an' let's try to get back to something resembling military order, shall we?"

Heintz's castor oil bottle was empty now, but the Sergeant limped over to take it from him anyway and throw it far over the ledge. Then he started running the Apaches off with two-handed swooshing motions. "Let's go, ladies! Good-bye! *Ugashe!* (Hurry!) Off this mountain tomorrow, *comprende*?

The soldiers moved to the edge to watch the Indian women and their little kids skedaddle back down the mountainside toward their campsite. But their leader still fumed.

"Next damned soldier I catch up here fooling around with any Apache, I'm sending straight back to the guardhouse at Fort Bowie!"

"You will, Sergeant?" Private Takins grinned, sucking his cigar. "Nothin' I'd like better'n to git off this cussed mountain!"

TWENTY-TWO

As early as August of 1885, according to C.A.P. Hatfield, an Army officer who participated in these campaigns, Apaches had taken "a position on a conspicuous, lofty mountain called Sierra Azul, in Sonora about 75 miles southeast of Fort Huachuca, and kept up a brisk signaling to parties in Arizona. The signaling was done by torch at night and could be plainly seen."

—Odie B. Faulk, *The Geronimo Campaign*

Cochise's Stronghold, West Side of the Sulphur Springs Valley

In a cave under a rock overhang in a narrow canyon twenty-five miles north of the notorious town of Tombstone, a different celebration was in progress. Dahkeya pounded an *escadadedne*, a buckskin drumhead stretched over an iron pot partially filled with water for more reverberation, with a drumstick also wrapped in buckskin. Young Zhonne accompanied them with rapid trills on a three-fingered cane flute.

No enemies could be close enough to hear this music, for any dust clouds horses raised could be seen forty miles away from the summits of this natural sanctuary, a range of low peaks standing in severe isolation, surrounded on all sides by sagebrush desert and alkali flats. Cochise's Stronghold, lower than the Little Dragoons behind it to the west and less massive than the main range of Dragoon Mountains to the south, had been carved by sun and wind and rain into a labyrinth of thousands of weathered granite spires, cliffs, and crevices, making it an ideal place for concealment and ambush.

Its slopes were covered by piñion pines, mesquite, alligator juniper, and scrub oak trees. Besides the small game they hunted there, the Apaches ate its piñon nuts, juniper berries, the fruit of the banana yucca, acorns, and mesquite beans. More crucial, the Stronghold's springs seeped reliably year-round. The legendary Chief of the Chiricahuas was buried somewhere in this labyrinth, safe from treasure hunters and the U.S. Army, who never dared attack him in his stronghold when he was alive. Indeed, Cochise's Stronghold was the safest place in the whole Southwest for Apaches, and they continually put it to good use.

Three warriors danced about a bonfire in their *kabuns*, deer-skin boots worn round a *kuhn-gan-hay* (campsite), shaking war clubs made from hardwood sticks shoved into peeled cow's tails. Round, fist-sized rocks were sewn loosely with deer sinew into floppy ends of these clubs so they could be swung with deadlier force.

Naiche wore a blue wool tunic that had been taken off a dead soldier. Eagle medicine feathers were tied into his long hair as he led his victorious men in a bear hunting song, chanting and dancing, holding the cured brown bearskin over his head. Klosen danced next to him, waving his family's small war shield of rawhide painted with yellow suns.

Resting his wounded leg nearby, Perico tossed tule pollen into the fire, causing it to blaze up as these healthy Apaches danced to exhaustion to steel themselves for the final battles for their still-free way of life.

Their tall leader turned the greasy bearskin over to Inday-Yi-Yahn, as the warriors continued their determined shuffle stomp in what might be their last time together.

Fun was propped against a rock, enjoying his comrades' celebration as best he could. Green nopal (prickly pear) leaves had been split open and their needles singed off, so the sticky cactus juice could run into his wound. These moist cactus strips were tied directly onto Fun's clawed shoulder with buckskin thongs, restraining his arm movement. But the curative unguent provided some relief from the throbbing pain and kept the gashes carved by the bear from becoming infected.

Perico saluted his leader with another pinch of tossed *hoddentin*. "*Yah-tats-an!* Naiche!"

Naiche rattled the bear-claw necklace around his neck, acknowledging his second-in-command's victory cry. He flopped down in the sand near the fire, spent. The Chiricahua rubbed bear grease on his hands up and down his bare legs, "feeding" his tired muscles and ligaments. Breathing deeply, Cochise's second son questioned his friend. "What will you do now, *te-iltcohe* (troublemaker)?"

Perico smiled thinly at the jibe. "I have *chin-da-see-lee* (homesickness). Fun and I must heal our wounds, and Zhonne wishes to ride with us to our *che-wa-kis* (stronghold) in *Cima-silq* (the Sierra Madre Mountains of Mexico).

"Zhonne?" Naiche was surprised by his younger brother-in-law's intended defection. "This is Child of the Water's fourth raid. He has passed his novice test and is ready to become a warrior. *Ijanale* (Let him die) there, instead of here."

"*Unhuh!* (To hell with it!) We will all be ridden down some day soon," argued Naiche. "The *Pen-a-lick-o-yis* (White Eyes) took my older brother east on the iron horse with John Clum to meet their Great Chief and then poisoned him with their sickness. They can never be trusted. They will never become *shee-kizzen* (close friends) of the Apache. This may be our last chance to fight well here. *Ijanale* (Let me die) like an Apache in my homeland!"

Perico, the most violent of all these fierce Apaches, shrugged. "*Na-tse-kes* (a deep thought), but I will go back to Mexico, where our *Ga-ns* (representatives of the mountain spirits) have always kept us safe."

The drummer and dancers stopped. In the sudden silence, Naiche looked around. Down the narrow canyon toward their ceremonial cave plodded a string of horses ridden by more Apaches. Four men and two women were returning from other raids further north, all the way up to *Ojo Caliente* (Warm Springs) on the Mescalero reservation in New Mexico Territory.

To shouts of greeting, Chappo, Geronimo's son, and Tsisnah and Yanozha slid off their mustangs to help the women untie a small buck deer, which a young Mexican-American boy held balanced over the horse's back he was riding. These renegades had kidnapped this boy a few days ago from a ranch south of Tucson. The men helped drag the deer to a small tree and tied it up to a branch by its rear hooves so Shega, one of Geronimo's wives and Yanozha's sister, and Tahdaste, a handsome young woman who often served the band as a messenger, could disembowel it and get its freshly cut meat onto their cooking fire.

Naiche got to his tired feet again to welcome the broad-shouldered older man in his early sixties who ambled toward them on bowed legs. "Goyahkla! (One Who Yawns!)"

These fighters paid deference to this aging warrior because of his fierce reputation and the number of scars visible on his body—the third finger of his left hand bent backward by a bullet, a rifle slug still lodged in his bare left thigh, and the bullet that had creased his forehead and left a vivid scar. Geronimo grabbed his younger, hereditary chief by the shoulder and laughed. "Where is *tizwin*?"

As they relaxed about the campfire waiting for their meat to roast, Geronimo poured some water from his willow wood canteen onto the red bandanna he'd been wearing as a head cover, and used the wet rag to wipe his face clean of the deer's blood he'd rubbed on to protect his dark skin from sun and wind.

Naiche used the lull to present his new problem to their veteran war strategist. "Perico, Fun, are wounded and wish to return to Mexico."

"*Anzhoo* (Good)," grunted Geronimo, preoccupied with his face wash. "After this fast ride, I am ready for rest."

"But I wish to stay at this *kunh-gan-hay* (campsite) awhile longer," argued the current Chief of these Chiricahuas. "We need more *thlees* (horses) to get our wives and children back down to Mexico. We need more bullets and *petilows* (Winchester rifles)."

Perico interrupted. "Ahh! We can always find *nah-lin* (sweethearts) among the *Nedni* (the southernmost band of Chiricahuas, from the Sierra Madres)."

Naiche frowned at his wandering friend. "Our wives are *Chokonen* from these lands. Haozinne, my favorite wife, and several other women gather mescal for us nearby right now."

Geronimo offered his counsel. "Then wait for them. We can split up again, as we have on this raid. Too many soldiers moving about now. Smaller groups will make us more difficult to track leaving." Their war leader fingered his medicine necklace. Small *mescal* beans had been sewn into buckskin strips with small holes cut in them so these beans could be shown off as charms to promote the good health of the wearer. Geronimo pointed to the Mexican-American boy conversing nearby in Spanish with little Trini Verdín. "We need to get these little *nakai-yes* (Mexican people) safely to *cima-silq* (the Sierra Madre Mountains of Mexico)."

Naiche gestured at the rock walls hemming in this warrior band. "These mountains were my father's *che-wa-kis* (stronghold). *Ocha* (I pray) his spirit rides and fights with me here. Since Skinya and his warriors came to quarrel in my brother's camp and I killed him, my luck has been bad. But it will change, for I have my *diyi* (supernatural power) now! *Yah-tats-an!*"

Cochise's son shook the bear claw necklace his followers had awarded him, showing defiance to the vengeful gods.

Klosen interrupted their leader's tirade by bringing them chunks of bear meat sizzling from the spit. "*Eyanh!* (Eat a little!) *Itsi!* (Meat!)" The tipsy warrior adjusted the white-striped skunk's tail he was wearing as a headband, which had fallen over one eye.

Naiche put the hot meat in his mouth, held it with one hand, and cut off a bite-size piece with his knife to chew ravenously. Perico joined him in eating the bear, for this might be the last feast these two warriors would ever enjoy together. Between bites, Naiche's second-in-command defended his decision to move south.

"Too difficult in this country now. The *Nda* (white men) guard their *wohaw* (cattle) and water holes closely, and their soldiers increase like *ka-chu* (rabbits). And they use spirit lights on our mountains, watching us with their long eyes."

"Not spirit lights! Another *pesh-bi-yalti* (telegraph) to pass messages, as we use a silver glass to signal with the sun. Nothing for us to fear." Naiche swallowed a bite of meat. "Tasty *shoz* (bear)!"

"I wonder if those *sun lights* work in the rain?" questioned Klosen, grabbing a drink of *tiswin*.

Tsisnah, who had once been a Scout for Lt. Britton Davis, joined them with another hunk of sizzling bear on a skewer, offering it deferentially to their most famous warrior, but Geronimo waved it away. "I do not eat *shoz*. A bad spirit may enter my body and poison me, if I touch bear meat."

Perico laughed. "A bad spirit cannot hurt an already bad man."

Naiche was insulted the older Apache leader wouldn't share his victory feast.

"*Shoz* is my *diyi* (supernatural power)! He will not hurt me!" Their Chief shook his bear claw necklace again.

Shegha brought her husband some seared venison instead. Geronimo stuck it in his mouth to slice off a big bite with his knife. Tahdaste came with several flattened tin cans upon which she'd cooked *zi-gosti* (ash bread), corn meal mixed with salt and water and then cooked in the coals of their *kuhn* (fire). Ashes shoveled over these bread cakes allowed them to bake without burning. The Apaches devoured them, washing their meal down with water or their fermented corn liquor.

Inday-Yi-Yahn, a smaller, lizard-dry Chiricahua, weaved toward them waving a hollow gourd. A bobcat skin around his neck kept the night's spring chill off, as he sat down heavily with the aid of his prized war club, made from a man's thighbone.

"Tizwin! Ish-lan-y-ag-itna is-d-ah! (Drink now, talk later!)"

Naiche took a big swallow of the corn liquor, then passed the gourd along. Yanozha joined them for a drink and began rolling a cigarette with tobacco carefully poured from a pouch made from a horse's testicles. He was Geronimo's fiercest follower, and in appreciation of his loyalty, the old war leader had awarded him a silver star beaten from a Mexican *peso*. Yanozha had sewn it proudly onto the lapel of his stolen wool coat.

Relaxing back against the rock cliff, these fighters watched a rising orange, almost full moon. The *klego-na-ay* (moon), especially, was enjoyed by Apaches, for it ruled their weather and was thought responsible for the procreation of all animals and Indians.

The youth watched these men enviously, wishing he too could drink *tizwin*, no matter how bad it tasted. But Zhonne, on his final training ride, was not a warrior quite yet and had to content himself with quietly sipping water from a drinking tube in a smaller *tus*, a corded Apache canteen. Water or fermented cactus juice was not allowed to touch this young man's lips, not while still a novice on a raid.

His hunger slaked, Perico turned to his leader again. "Where will you find more *thlees* (horses) and *besh-she-gars* (guns)? From those soldiers up on the mountain?"

"No *thlees* up there. But those soldiers will be out in the open, undefended. That rancher and his woman we chased nine suns ago, still have *thlees* in their corral," argued Naiche.

"*Ahn* (yes), but two warriors were *zasteed* (killed) there," Inday-Yi-Yahn added. "They shoot good! Don't make your young wife a *bijan* (widow)."

Dahkeya wandered up to the group drunk, spilling more *tizwin*. The bloodstained silver crucifix about his neck swayed with his wobble. "Or any of your stray *ish-kay-nays* (boy children) *yudastcin* (bastards)!"

The other Apaches joined in his laughter at their leader's expense. *Perhaps they should all enjoy a good drunk, a full-blown borracho,* Naiche thought. They'd all certainly earned one from this hard raid back into their homelands.

"You see that ranch woman, ask for my round hat back," grinned Perico. He attempted to rewrap a bandage of fairly clean cotton about his wounded thigh, but tipsy fingers fumbled with the knot. "Then shoot her for me, too."

Naiche was not amused. His *enthlay-sit-daou* (warrior's pride and countenance) was being supremely tested by his closest companions. Cochise's son sat up straight and scowled.

"I have my *diyi* (supernatural power) now. I am bear killer! I will kill this fighting woman and her man, too, and take their *besh-she-gars* and bullets and *thlees*, to avenge our dead warriors. Then we will join you in Mexico to hunt and raid together again. For as long as we have left."

From nearby in the *si-chi-zi* (twilight), a *bu* hooted. All Apaches, drunk or sober, were instantly alert to its haunting call, for an owl's cry was the spirit of a person who was bad during his life and continued to be vicious after death. Hearing an owl was extremely bad medicine, especially at night when ghosts were out as well, spreading "darkness sickness." These Apaches would move this camp the very next day to get away from this messenger of death who made "blood in the throat."

The warriors quickly reached into the fire to take ashes to rub on their faces and toss in the direction of the hooting call to ward off bad luck or even imminent death. Nothing was said about this evil night bird of prey, though. They would not speak its name.

In the solemn silence they could hear the ticking of the many pocket watches tied to the leather belt about Naiche's waist. *Per-*

haps this noisemaker was not such a good trophy from a kill to keep, he thought. Then again, Geronimo had admired it, even wanted to trade for the strange watch belt, so maybe he should keep this war trophy, at least for a while.

The Apaches involuntarily shivered, adjusted their sleeveless coyote-skin shirts against the chills down their spines, and hoped the night owl would fly away quickly. Maybe the *Ga-ns* (spirits) who dwelt in these mountain caves would then be appeased.

Chappo inhaled deeply of a cigarette he had lit in the campfire. The flames revealed its rolling paper was actually a greenback dollar bill he'd acquired in some robbery. The broncho Apache offered it to his *nantan*, but Naiche wiped his knife off in the sand first, bloody from the bear meat, and put it away before taking a ceremonial puff. Blood and tobacco were considered incompatible by these superstitious people, and the wisest ones observed all their traditions and fetishes, especially when on a dangerous raid.

Dahkeya took some sand in his fingers to rub the blood off the silver crucifix about his neck before taking a puff on the dollar-bill cigarette as it was passed along. He didn't need any more bad luck, either. Zhonne, their novitiate at the end of the line, also took a final smoke of the communal cigarette, something he was proudly allowed to do, since he had already hunted alone and killed several buck deer with his bow. The teenager didn't have a warrior's shirt yet, so he unwrapped the Navajo blanket round his waist and threw it over his shoulders for insulation against the night air.

"*Heci* (a word of disgust)!" Naiche suddenly rose to his feet. He nodded formally to Geronimo, his rival for this small band's loyalty.

"*Yadalanh* (formal good-bye). May *Ussen* (the Apaches' supreme being) see you safely back into Mexico."

The hostile old warrior stared at him for a moment, then shrugged and slugged down another gulp of *tizwin*.

Naiche pulled a flaming faggot from the fire, snatched up his buffalo gun, and strode from their hideout without another look back at his companions.

Geronimo wanted a last word. "You stay here, you will only ride a ghost pony (death) into a *intchi-dijn* (black wind)!"

Their leader's answer echoed off the narrow canyon's walls. "What matter? We are already *yah-ik-tee* (gone)!"

Wooden torch between his teeth, the Chiricahua's youngest hereditary Chief climbed atop a large boulder at the mouth of the narrow canyon they were hiding in, which opened out onto the western side of the long Sulphur Springs Valley, ten miles due south of the heliograph post atop Square Mountain. Exposing himself by holding a torch against the night, Naiche put down his big Sharps rifle and poured some tule pollen from an amulet tied to his neck onto the flame, sending up a small cloud of pure white smoke. The flame reflected off this whitish smoke, making the white stripes on Naiche's dark cheeks gleam in the torchlight. Reaching high, he waved the burning ember back and forth overhead twice, before turning his back to hide the fire behind the Mexican serape he'd brought along. After a pause, Naiche turned around once more to wave his burning signal overhead twice again toward the mountains to the north. In two days. Did they see it? From this far away?

Naiche turned to snub out his torch when he saw Zhonne waiting below the boulder, hugging his striped blanket about himself as he scratched his hair with a five-inch stick given him by a medicine man, trying to figure what to do. Inexperienced fighters weren't allowed to touch the long hair on their heads with their fingers, or their face whiskers would grow too fast. So many commandments to remember, tribal rules not to break. But soon he would be finished with all of them, and become a fighting Apache for life!

"I will tell your sister, Haozinne, of your decision to ride back down to *Cilm-silq*." Naiche gave the young warrior a hard look. "Without her."

Zhonne returned his stare. A response was clearly called for, so he was allowed to speak. "We must all live first . . . to fight another day. On ground of our own choosing, *shikis* (my brother)."

"I choose to fight . . . and die, on this ground where I was born."

Naiche's young friend, the brother of his newest, youngest, prettiest wife, nodded once, understanding perfectly. It was settled.

Naiche stubbed the burning torch out on the big rock, jumped to the ground, and brushed past him without another word before disappearing into the darkness, leaving just the slightest sound of ticking behind.

TWENTY-THREE

It is an invariable rule that the visits of Apaches to American camps are always for sinister purposes. They have nothing to trade for; consequently, it is not barter that brings them. They beg, but in no ways comparably with other Indian tribes, and scarcely expect to receive when they do. Their keen eyes omit nothing. One's arms and equipment, the number of your party, your cohesion and precaution, your system of defense in case of attack, and the amount of plunder to be obtained with the least possible risk, all are noted and judged. Wherever their observations can be made from neighboring heights with a chance of successful ambush, the Apache never shows himself, nor gives any sign of his presence. Like the ground shark, one never knows he is there until one feels his bite.

—John C. Ceremony, *Life Among the Apaches*

Observation Post #4, Square Mountain

The troopers of Observation Post #4 relaxed the next day for their noon meal—heated deviled ham from a can Martha Cox had sent up, with cooked rice. Soldiers were used to eating at the sixes, six A.M., noon, and six P.M., and just because they had drawn relaxed duty, Sgt. Swing saw no reason to alter army routine. He noted the dark smoke curling from their smoldering campfire with a scowl. "Go easy on that creosote, Takins. Makes too damned much smoke in the daytime, tellin' everybody for miles around we're home."

"Already used up most of the ironwood, mesquite around

here, Sarge. Now them 'Paches are grabbin' it up, too. Gotta forage further off."

"Well, save the creosote for night. We'll lay in some better stuff for day use."

"'Preciate that, gettin' some help with the cookin' for a change." The reb smiled toothily around at his squad.

"Any more of that 'lick' left?" Heintz held out his plate with a lone biscuit.

Sgt. Swing passed over the canning jar of honey Martha had sent up with them. "Easy on this. Gotta last, and the way you like to eat, Heintz . . ."

"Vhat? Veight I lose."

"Believe that when I see it."

"No, true it is." The Corporal pulled a long face. "I vish *bier* ve had here. New Braunfels, *dis* time every year, ve our *Kindermaskenball* had. A parade of *kinder*, little childs, in costume, marching to an omph-pah band! After, *bier* and sausage, *für* everyone. I good food miss . . . and friends." For a moment it looked like the big German-American was almost going to cry, longing so for his Texas homeland.

"We're all a little homesick, Heintz," the Sergeant commiserated. "To be expected, stuck up here. But this easy duty beats chasin' Apaches to hell and gone every day, boys, believe me. One long patrol into Mexico, you're buttsprung for a month, if you even get back with your horse and saddle intact. I've seen fellers return from below the border barefoot, boots torn apart after months in the field, horses dead or lost. Officers so damned exhausted, they resigned their commissions on the spot. Apaches just wore 'em out. And the Chiricahuas chuckled about it later, for that's how they like to live."

Their young Private changed the grim subject. "You should go back to Texas when your five years are up, Heintz. Bein' a farmer seems what you were born to do, not soldierin'. I heard that Texas hill country is awful pretty."

The big Corporal nodded. "Avful pretty. Better for cattle and sheeps, not crops. Irish po-tato, maybe. I tink I go home, too. Better land there than this dust. No vater. Nothing here *goot* grows."

Sergeant Swing nodded ruefully. "Except trouble."

"Uh, our Indians are coming back." Bobyne was on watch, sitting atop a boulder, keeping an eye out for Morse code flashes from the north and east.

"Damn!" The Sergeant put down his coffee cup and sat up. "This is the day those ladies need to be on their way."

"Oh-oh. Looks like a newcomer, a man, is with 'em!" warned the Signal Corpsman.

This got everyone's attention, with Sgt. Swing looking around, scrabbling for his field glasses, the others hurrying to grab Springfields and ammunition belts from their tents.

The three troopers quickly joined Bobyne and the Sergeant at their rock perimeter, who were eyeing through binoculars the little group of three Apache women and one smaller man climbing up the mountain again toward them, the man swinging something over his head.

"Is an old man with 'em now," reported the Sergeant. "See any more bucks about?"

All the men's heads swiveled, checking Square Mountain up and down in all directions.

Takins was perplexed. "What's that noise?"

Sgt. Swing watched the little old man bounding uphill after the ladies. He didn't need binoculars now, they were close. "Bull roarer. Apache medicine men use 'em to make the sound of rain and wind in their ceremonies."

Mullin didn't understand. "Medicine men?"

"Get ready, boys. Stay alert." The Sergeant was edgy, unbuttoning the flap on his holster. "Prob'ly want a better look at our mules. Mule meat's their favorite."

The Indian party clambered up onto the ledge, climbing past the soldiers' rock defenses. One of the women, Nadebza, unslung the tumpline from her forehead and lowered her burden basket to the ground. All the soldiers' eyes were on the newcomer, though, who smiled broadly as he stopped swinging his rhombus on its rawhide cord. It was an eight-inch oblong piece of pinewood, shaved down to a quarter inch thick, etched and painted to represent serpent lightning, raindrops, and the cross of the four winds. It was a *tzi-ditindi*, or "sounding wood."

The diminutive stranger wore little more than a dirty loincloth and deerskin boots, with a round yellow buckskin war cap decorated with three golden eagle feathers and centered by a big metal concho with brass tacks stuck onto it to form religious symbols perched like a beanie atop his long gray hair. Striding right past them to their fire, the little old man stooped to light a hand-rolled corn husk cigarette in the embers.

"Is a medicine man," stated the Sergeant, pointing at the hunk of pea-green malachite attached to a thin piece of cedar wood carved into human form that was dangling from a leather thong about the Apache's neck.

"See that green amulet around his neck? Badge of office. That's a medicine cord over his shoulder, too," Sgt. Swing added, indicating a three-strand leather cord colored dark brown from walnut juice, red from the bark of mountain mahogany, yellow from soaked algeita roots. Tied among these three dyed cords were bits of abalone shells, crystal quartz, turquoise, flakes of obsidian, and coral "medicine beans." This medicine cord was looped over the little man's right shoulder across his skinny chest down to his left hip. "That's his charm to promote good health and keep witches away."

"Witches?" Mullin squinched his face.

"Yeah. Apaches are very superstitious about snakes, owls, all kinds of stuff. They'll even kill their own kind, if they believe one's a witch."

Sucking deeply on his cigarette, the shaman turned to face the East and blew a big puff of ceremonial smoke. Pausing to inhale again, the old man moved slowly clockwise, puffing smoke once in all four directions.

"Gonna summon the spirits today."

The old man dipped into the small leather pouch attached to his waist belt and pulled out a pinch of *hoddentin*, which he threw up in the air toward the sun, chanting several words repeatedly.

"Tule powder. Praying for his safety."

"Like he should, with all our guns here," added Takins.

The Sergeant moved close to the medicine man, almost accosting him. "*E-chi-ca-say, Ostin*! (Greetings, honored patron!) Where in hell did you come from?"

Smiling and nodding, the little gnome spat out some words, pointing to the rhombus and his neck amulet. "*Tzi-daltai, tzi-daltai!*"

"Yes, yes, I know you're a big *diyi* (medicine man). You still can't be up here today." Sergeant Swing raised his voice in case the old man was hard of hearing."YOU MUST GO BACK WHERE YOU CAME FROM!"

The old Apache pointed to himself. "*Beela-Chezzi* (Crooked Fingers). *Beela-Chezzi*."

Sgt. Swing looked at his men. "Something about his fingers. Maybe his name."

Nadebza rummaged in her burden basket and hauled out a bundle of a half dozen ears of blue corn tied with bear grass. "The boss of all corn," blue corn was the Apaches' favorite food and used in their few ceremonies as well.

Takins brightened. "Fresh corn!" Licking his dry lips, the Southerner accepted the armful of food before his Sergeant could protest.

"Mighty tasty roasted."

"*Tudishishn!*"

Sgt. Swing frowned. "Wants coffee. Do we have much left?"

Private Takins shook his head. "Not much."

"Give him just a little anyways. Our gift."

Takins frowned, but walked off with the corn to their crate of foodstores.

The old Apache was now down on his knees, reaching into the woman's woven basket to pull out a huge ancient cap-and-ball pistol, which he pointed into the air and waved about.

This rash act startled all three soldiers, and the men stepped back, leveling their single-shot rifles at the Apaches. Their Sergeant hastily pulled his .45 revolver from his service holster to aim from the hip.

"*Dah!* (No!) Drop the gun! *Dah!*" growled Sgt. Swing.

"*Dah! Dah! Schichobe!* (Good friend!)" replied the little shaman, waving his free hand like everything was okay, before reaching back into the basket to pull out a small powder horn and two small round balls which he held up in his fingers like a magician. Assessing they were not going to shoot him, Beela-Chezzi half-cocked the 1851 Navy Colt, poured powder down two chambers of its cylinder, and popped the two soft lead balls on top of these charges. He then rotated the cylinder slowly so that a metal lever beneath it mechanically rammed these balls down inside their narrow tubes.

"He's loadin' up!" yelled Takins from the Sergeant's tent.

To finish loading, the elder Apache took out two nipple caps and inserted these carefully into the rear of each filled cylinder, "capping" its ball and powder charges.

Bobyne looked distressed. "He's not going to fire that old horse pistol, is he?"

Their Sergeant was perturbed. "He better not. But I don't want to shoot the old bastard, either. We killed the Dreamer over on Cibecue Creek, summer of '81. Our Apache Scouts deserted us in that battle and set off a ruckus lasted for months. Killing an Apache medicine man is very, very bad medicine."

Sgt. Swing stepped toward the old man, his free hand out imploringly, the other holding his Peacemaker. "Dah. Give me the gun."

Still smiling, Beela-Chezzi turned his back on the Sergeant, suddenly pointed his pistol uphill, away from the man, and fired!

At the percussion the squaws winced and three soldiers jerked their Springfields to their shoulders, fingers on triggers and long barrels aimed straight at the old Indian.

The old Apache's lead ball clipped a pad off a prickly pear cactus at which he'd been aiming.

Takins ran back to the group with his coffee offering to snatch his rifle up, too.

Delighted with his marksmanship, the shaman clapped his hands in glee and skipped in a tight circle, doing a little dance of victory. Sgt. Swing stood frowning at these shenanigans, hand on one hip, revolver in his other. "Christ on a crutch. . . ."

The old medicine man turned his still-loaded pistol over to Mrs. Cutnose and proceeded to march fifty feet away from the gathering to the near end of the ledge, throwing *hoddentin* from a pouch into the air and muttering incantations for luck. He turned there, put a final pinch of cattail pollen on the crown of his head and presented his bare chest to them. Jerking a bony finger at his chest, Beela-Chezzi shouted to the stout woman. "Shoot *besh-she-gar*! (Gun!)"

Realizing what was about to happen, Sgt. Swing lurched toward her to grab the old revolver. "No!"

But she was too quick for him, extending the big revolver in both hands, squinting down the barrel and jerking the trigger. Another loud bang and puff of black smoke!

The elderly Indian rocked back on his heels with a groan, as though buffeted by a blast, froze a moment, then slowly straightened up to feel about his chest for a wound.

"She missed!" yelled Takins.

"I didn't see any dust, hear any ricochet," argued their signalman.

The Sergeant didn't know what in hell to think as the old shaman strutted back toward them unharmed, arms extended, grinning, wiggling his crooked fingers, doing everything but taking a bow.

The Apache women were impressed, bowing and yelling excitedly. "*Diyi! Beela-Chezzi! Diyi!*"

Mrs. Cutnose discreetly put the Navy Colt safely away again in the grass basket.

Ammon Swing was weary of this interruption. "Okay, get 'em out of here. I've had enough nonsense for today."

The soldiers used their rifles as prods to herd the Apaches back toward the ledge's edge. Mullin turned to Heintz. "Musta pulled her shot over his head."

The big German just shook his head, confused by the whole strange incident.

The Sergeant reholstered and stalked over to their fire pit to pick up one of the tins they'd emptied for dinner. Striding back, he saw the Apaches were reluctant to leave and started waving them away with swooshing motions. "Let's go, ladies! *Ugashe!* (Hurry!) C'mon, *Ostin* (honored patron)! Time to go!"

Nadebza strapped her basket back on, and the other women moved slowly away in front of the soldiers' thrusting rifles, Mrs. Cutnose mimicking spoon-feeding castor oil again.

Old Beela-Cheezi walked backward, smiling and pointing proudly to his unmarked chest. "*Diyi! Beela-Chezzi. Nah-to* (Tobacco)!"

To prick his vanity, Sgt. Swing walked up to confront the old shaman, thrusting the red tin can of deviled ham in his face. "*Diyi! Diyi!* Me, too, *diyi!*"

At the sight of the red-garbed Mephistophelian figure with a pronged spear on the can's label, the old medicine man looked frightened. "*Chidin-bitzi* (Ghost meat)!"

"*Ugashe*, you old charlatan! Good-bye!"

The old Apache turned tail and hurried in surprisingly sprightly fashion after the nervous women now clambering down the rocks to get away.

The Sergeant slowed his pursuit, pleased with his ploy. "Afraid of the devil's picture on this canned ham. Reminds them of their *Ga-ns* god, their own devil. Red's a warning to Apaches. Think it attracts lightning."

Struck by an afterthought, he dropped the empty can and climbed up on a rock to shout. "I want all you Apaches off this mountain by tomorrow, *comprende*?"

The women just kept going at his warning, hurrying back toward their campsite and kids a hundred yards away. But the little shaman turned back to wave at the noncom, still smiling and happy, impervious to bullets or threats.

The other soldiers just watched them in wonder, mesmerized by the medicine man's visit. "How you think he managed that bullet business, Sarge?" asked young Mullin.

Sgt. Swing just shook his head. As he got down off his rock, however, he spied a scrap of paper fluttering toward him on a slight breeze. Catching it up, he saw the powder burns on the little bit of parchment. "That tricky old bastard. I heard about something like this bein' done once, by a magician. He'd cast his lead shot with a piece of paper inside, right in the mold."

The Sergeant held it up for them to look at. "See the powder burns on this scrap? When that special bullet's fired, under percussion, the paper inside it causes the soft lead shot to split apart, break in half, missing its target."

"May-be," said Heintz.

"Maybe is right," added Bobyne. "One heck of a dangerous trick to try."

"Just to show us bluecoats bullets can't even kill an old Apache," nodded Sgt. Swing. They all turned again to watch the women meeting up with their running kids. And moving right along behind them, a little hop to his step, was the old medicine man.

The Sergeant shook his head again, ruing the day. "Turning into a damned circus."

Ranch Near Cox's Tanks

Martha Cox leaned inside their stone well, hoisting a bucketful of water up to pour into one of the tin pails tied to either side of the wooden neck yokes they used to carry bucketfuls of water inside the ranch house for cooking and bathing.

Jacob walked out of their barn, where he'd been tending the horses. "Need some help, Sis?"

"Could carry a couple pails inside, for my bath."

He strolled over as she dropped the bucket back down the well to winch up a few more pailfuls for another yoke load.

"How come the soldiers' supplies haven't come in, Jacob? They're several days overdue, and we're running low now ourselves, since I had to lend them some stores."

Her brother straightened his mustache with his fingers, thinking. "Disruption in service due to the Apaches runnin' loose around here again. Don't think they ambushed the packer or surely we would have heard of it?"

"Okay, but what do we do?"

"Well, that freighter doesn't show by tomorrow, when the soldiers come down again, hungry, I'll ride over with 'em to the traders' and see what's the holdup?"

"And leave me here alone?"

Jacob Cox permitted himself a small smile. "Apaches won't come back here again after you ran 'em off with your sharpshooting, Sis! You put the fear of Annie Oakley into 'em!"

His chuckle contradicted her frown. "It's difficult for one person to defend a ranch, Jacob, even a woman."

His eyes twinkled. "Okay, maybe I can get one of those soldiers to come down and stay with you while I'm gone straightening out their mix-up. There's five of 'em. Shouldn't take more than two troopers to run their equipment up there, so which one shall I ask?"

Now she was embarrassed she'd brought the subject up. Martha sloshed the last of the water into the buckets and helped him into one of the neck yokes, being careful of his wounded arm.

"How about that tough Sergeant? With the limp? Sergeant Swing, isn't it?"

She hoisted the other curved wooden bar with two filled pails tied to either end over her shoulders and started off across the barnyard, her brother awkwardly following.

"That's his name, I think."

"You think? Isn't he the one you've been entertaining with lemonade? Sure you aren't just a little bit sweet on him, Sis?"

"Me? No . . ." She was hurrying now, to get out of range of his sharp jibes. "He's probably too old for me anyway. An' married to the army." She halted at the back door to catch her breath and jab a finger. "Bring the tub inside for me."

"Yes, ma'am!" Jacob chortled, assured his choice remarks had hit their mark. "Those supplies don't show up, I'll sure request Sgt. Swing be your bodyguard."

He winked. Reddening, his sister disappeared inside, leaving only her embarrassment behind.

TWENTY-FOUR

By the time Geronimo and his band first surrendered in January, 1884, the Apache had become a deadly warrior indeed. With his modern arms and his newly acquired knowledge, he had become a near-even match for the troops. In ambushes he no longer fled swiftly after the first blow to escape superior firepower and weapons; now he could stand his ground and make the soldiers retreat.

—Odie B. Faulk, *The Geronimo Campaign*

Observation Post #4, Square Mountain

Because of all the dust in the air, an unusually reddish sun rose the next morning across the valley. Private Takins laid sticks into the warm ashes to prime their breakfast fire and emptied several canteens of water into his coffee pot. He paused a moment to savor the quiet, taste the early morning's freshening breeze, then took a small tin from the inside breast pocket of his blouse and slipped a blue pill from it. Draining a canteen, the Reb washed his daily backache medicine down. Then he took the corn in their shucks the Apaches had given them and laid them carefully in his now flaming fire to roast the ears.

The others began to stir in their tents, awakened by the harsh light up on Square Mountain. Heintz wandered sleepily out barefoot in his longjohns, to go take a prebreakfast piss in the ravine. The mules saw him coming and greeted their keeper from afar with brays of welcome!

Pulling on his pants and boots and picking up his field glasses, Sgt. Swing ambled past the campfire over the edge of the ledge to check on his Apaches.

"We're outta hardtack and salt pork now, Sarge, and I'm usin' barley to stretch the coffee, even though those Injun beggars didn't get none yesterday. *Pinole* for breakfast today, from that corn they gave us. Runnin' short on water, too. Three pints in these canteens and most of 'em are empty. We'll be boilin' shoe leather an' drinkin' our own blood if we don't get some supplies up here. Soon."

"I'm sending you an' Heintz down today" replied Sgt. Swing. "Food should have come in by now. I'll see our friendly Apaches are gone by the time you get back."

"Dandy fine by me." The Southerner began scratching inside his dirty, buttoned undershirt, alternating hands. "Need to get these clothes scrubbed. Mighta picked me up a pet coon or two."

Behind them, Mullin crawled out of the tent he shared with Takins, tied open a front flap and sat down in the entrance to unwrap the bandage from his sore foot.

"Hey, swelling's gone down. Bite don't hurt so much anymore, either."

The Sergeant turned back from his morning surveillance, put down his binoculars to find his tin cup and help himself to what they were pretending was coffee. "Home remedy's workin' then. Bobyne! Help Heintz with the water kegs. Let's pack those mules!"

Train Depot, Tucson, Southern Arizona Territory

"It's a shame you're leaving us, Mr. Lummis, so soon." General Miles clapped his new friend on the back. The journalist stood next to his dusty carpetbags in his field uniform: tapered dark canvas pants tucked into his big Texas, high-heeled boots and dirty white cotton shirt tied with a red Navajo sash around his waist under his corduroy jacket, topped off by his large felt sombrero.

"I'm sorry, too, General. I was just starting to get a feel for the problems with the Apaches out here. Captain Davis even offered to let me ride with him on his patrol that's about to leave Bowie."

"That would have been exciting for you. Onto the field of combat."

"Yes, sir. But my newspaper needs reorganizing. Los Angeles is growing so rapidly the *Times* is having difficulty expanding fast enough, training new reporters, to keep up with the boom."

"We have a similar logjam here now, Charles, digesting all these new troops coming out to the frontier." Both men smiled at each other. The General was resplendent in his starched blue dress uniform with extra gold braid on the jacket and red pantstriping on his trousers.

"You're looking very distinguished today, sir."

"Mayor's holding the presidential suite for me over at the Orndorff Hotel—dinner with the city fathers tonight. Tomorrow I'm meeting with reporters from the *Weekly Citizen* and *Daily Star*. They'll all want to know my plans for ending this endless war."

They shook hands. "Give 'em hell, General."

"Expect it will probably be the reverse. The number of soldiers, civilians, Mexicans, and Indians killed and wounded in this endless war is absolutely staggering. I don't even want to give you the estimates so far, Charles. Most of them south of the border we don't even know of and never will."

They were standing on the wooden platform of this large railroad station in Tucson, the "Old Pueblo," which the Southern Pacific Railroad had turned into its main depot and switching station in the Arizona Territory for trains coming from Texas. Civilians who weren't staring at the formally uniformed officer and his aide, or at Lt. Maus and their horse escort waiting next to the General's Quartermaster wagon, were bustling about, climbing into the passenger cars or saying good-bye to family and friends.

"This is the end of the game for these wild Apaches still loose, Mr. Lummis, I promise you. This raiding and indiscriminate killing will cease, for good, and the army and I shall see to it."

"Hope so, General. I hope you take Geronimo alive, too, for history's sake. He'd be a helluva interesting interview."

"No doubt. But alive or dead, Geronimo will soon trouble us no more. And then, sir, all this rough country will need is water and good society like we see here, and it will bloom."

"General, you could say the same about Hell."

Soldier and scholar both laughed and shook hands once more. "When this war's over and I get to Los Angeles again, Charles, we'll go out for drinks and I'll tell you how I ended it."

"That would be a pleasure, sir, but those drinks will be on the *Times*."

The big engine chuffed steam as its whistle blew. "All-l-l aboa-a-a-rd!"

Charles Lummis picked up his bags and climbed up the steel steps to his train car, where he turned and paused, enjoying his association with this famous military man.

"Watch those sneaky reporters, General. Just remember, if a man knows how to use the lemon squeezer of philosophy, he can punch a power of good juice out of adversity." He threw Nelson Miles a salute.

The Brigadier General saluted back. "Saying of yours? I'll try to remember it! Safe journey!"

Passenger Car, Southern Pacific Railroad

Inside the passenger car, the newspaperman stuffed his carpetbags under his second-class seat amongst the traveling salesmen, the parents trying to herd squabbling children, and several cowboys journeying with their saddles. Before the train even started rolling, Charles Lummis had his notepad out and was licking his pencil. He intended to telegraph his last dispatch from the battlefront from Yuma, next stop west before the train's final leg north to Los Angeles.

The North American Indian, by and large, has never been notorious as a failure in war. Crude his methods may be, but they are effective. It has taken the "superior" white man's best efforts to subdue him, and it would never have been accomplished but for infinitely better weapons; for, later, superior numbers and a judicious use of whiskey. Some tribes have naturally inclined to peace and endurance of wrong; some have fought fearfully at the pinch; and some are born butchers, hereditary slayers.

Foremost in the latter class has always stood the Apache. For warfare in his own domain he has been and is today without a peer. From time untold he has been pirate by profession, a robber to whom blood was sweeter than booty, and both as dear as life. Untold generations before the Caucasian outpost encroached upon his Sahara, he was driving his quartz-tipped shafts through the agricultural Aztec or peaceful Pueblo. The warlike tribes to his east and north too suffered from many a wild foray. From Guaymas to Pueblo and from San Antonio to where the Colorado laps the arid edge of California, he swept the country like a whirlwind. Of what he has done to keep his gory hand in since blonde scalps first amused his knife, I need not remind you now.

Not only is he the most war loving of the American Indians, he is also the supreme warrior. The Bedouin of the New World, he is strong to an endurance impossible in a more endurable country. He has the eye of a hawk, the stealth of a coyote, the courage of a tiger—and its mercilessness. His horse will subsist on a blade of grass to the acre and will travel a hundred and ten miles in twenty-four hours without dropping dead at the finish. He knows every foot of his savage realm better than you know your own parlor. He finds food and drink where we should perish for want of both. Wherever you may strike him, he has a fastness, and one practically impregnable. Lay siege to him, and he quietly slips out some cañon back door and is away before you know it. The menace of the Indian moreover is in inverse ratio to his food supply. His whole life is a ceaseless struggle to tear a living from nature, the Apache is whetted down to a ferocity of edge never reached by an Indian of a section where wood, water, and game are ready to his hand. Why, a six-year-old Apache will ride a broncho farther in a day, and over rougher country, than you could ride the gentlest steed. These youngsters who were out with the hostiles were doing it right along.

This is not all that puts the Apache at the head of his class; he has comrades to stand in with him. From the outstretched hand of pursuit he slides down into Mexico as if the hills and valleys were a greased pole, taking time to murder, rob, and ravish in transit. Once safely in Sonora, he sells his stolen stock without any trouble; caches the stolen arms, ammunition, and money; enjoys a genteel holiday in the Mexican Sierras until he is rested; swoops down upon hacienda and village, killing a few people and gathering up all the loot he can pack or drive; and flits back like a shadow to his Arizona strongholds. The better class of Mexican desires his extermination; even the lower classes sometimes organize against him; but he finds plenty of degraded natives to help him. The Mexican line is not only a boundary; it is a wholesale "fence." And sad to say, some poor, mescal-corned paisano *is the Apache's only ally. In Tombstone, Tucson, and many another place on either side of the line, you will find white Americans who fatten on his bloody booty. If the list were published, certain Arizona merchants would writhe. At $20 a gallon, however, they willingly take their chances.*

Observation Post #4, Square Mountain

After a breakfast of roasted, crushed corn kernels soaked in water and sweetened with the last of their sugar to make the staple meal of Mexican travelers, *pinole*, they lashed their empty kegs to Grover. The cook walked over to Annie, rolling up his dirtiest shirt and trousers into his blanket to stuff into a gunnysack of dirty laundry to go down the mountain.

Sgt. Swing saw what he was doing. "Don't tuck your lousy laundry in with ours, Takins!"

"What the hell kin I do with it then?"

A little stiff this morning, Sgt. Swing limped over to their woodpile to select a long stick, then hiked on toward a big anthill he'd spotted uphill from their ledge.

Curious, the other four followed. Their Sergeant looked the ant colony over, then jammed the long stick into its middle and stirred it around. Big red "harvester" ants immediately came boiling out of the wreckage of their home, ready to repair it or fight. Picking Takins's shirt up on the end of his stick, Sgt. Swing placed it right atop the broken anthill.

Red ants swarmed quickly across the filthy blue infantry blouse, isolating the small white lice and attacking them savagely in heavy numbers, biting them with their pincers. Even the shirt's owner was taken aback. "My gawd, lookit those red devils swarm. They're bitin' those bedbugs to death!"

Mullin, like the rest, leaned in, fascinated by the red ants' war. "Kinda reminds yah of redskins attackin', doesn't it?"

The Sergeant frowned at the rookie. Takins snatched up his shirt to shake the ants off, as they all took a thoughtful walk back.

Takins rolled his lousy clothes up in his wool blanket again and tied it separately to Annie's cradle pack. Heintz scratched his lead mule under its hairy chin and started Grover down the mountainside. The animal was now so attached to his packmaster he'd follow him anywhere without necessity of a lead rope.

"Bring some food back, fellas, or we'll be reduced to mule meat," ordered their Sergeant.

"We used to eat mules during the War of Rebellion. These long ears make a tasty stew!" choused Takins, plodding after the big German.

Heintz switched the topic to one that had been lingering on his mind. "I talk with lady last trip about marriage, Ser-geant. *Dis* time I form-ally ask her, an' I tink she say yes."

Sergeant Swing was astounded at this sudden confession. "What? . . . Why?"

His big Corporal answered over his shoulder. "Because *goot* farmer I am, an' more help dey need on that ranch. Alzo, she is nod much young. Nod many chances more vill she get." Heintz stopped their procession to turn back and address his leader directly.

"Change your mind about com-ing, Ser-geant?"

Ammon Swing just stood there, emotionally confused, looking down at the two soldiers standing below on the mountainside, now looking up at him. His other two troopers watched him keenly, too, awaiting an explanation. "No. . . ."

Bobyne and Mullin looked at each other, then down at their laundry detail, now moving away again. "Boil your clothes separately, Takins! Please!"

"An' throw in some tar soap, too!" chorused Mullin.

Downhill, Pvt. Takins, bringing up the rear, acknowledged their pleas with a backhanded wave.

Orndorff Hotel, Tucson, Southern Arizona Territory

"Well, they like our show of force, additional patrols, the extra troops stationed at the ranches and water holes down near the border," said General Miles.

"Yessir, they do," agreed Lt. Dapray. "Taxpayers like to see their army in action. Our boys in blue, dashing about, has a calming effect on the citizenry. Presents a better picture of us as soldiers, rather than layabouts at the forts doing little but drinking and gambling on paydays."

"Larger forces also fatten the profits of these Tucson merchants selling us goods," added Lt. Maus.

"That, too," mused the General.

The officers languished against the balcony of the Orndorff, the Old Pueblo's finest hotel. General Miles had been given the presidential suite downstairs free for two nights by the town's grateful fathers, while his two aides were billeted in cheaper quarters elsewhere. The three men sipped their whiskeys from the bar at the Masons', who had commandeered part of the hotel's newer second story for their lodge. Already on his second drink before lunch, Nelson Miles grew expansive as they watched a twelve-mule team pulling a heavy freight wagon down the street, carrying supplies to some outlying town like Tombstone. "That's exactly what this hard country needs, more commerce, mining, cattle raising and shipping, town building, to trim its rough edges, drive its two-footed predators off to wilder climes."

"Tucson will become more civilized, General, now the railroad's come through. I've noticed big changes already, just in the few years I've been stationed in Arizona," opined their veteran First Lieutenant.

"Indeed. . . . What is that about?" The General pointed to two strings of men shuffling up Pennington Street toward them. Some of this scruffy crew were shoveling dirt in the ruts the heavy wagons and stagecoaches had left in the hard-packed street, smoothing them over. The other string of men were using straw brooms to sweep trash and horse pucky from the alleys and off the boardwalks in front of the businesses lining the town's main thoroughfares which crossed at this corner. The men were getting fresh dirt from and pitching the refuse into the back of an open wagon slowly following these work crews. What caught the military man's attention, however, were the metal shackles clamped around one of each workman's ankles, linking each gang together on two long jangling chains.

"Judge Meyer's chain gangs, sir. One of the salutary changes I was talking about. Tucson's streets used to be filthy, dead animals left about, sewage draining. Now the judge fines these boys for vagrancy or public drunkenness, and if they can't pay immediately, a few days in leg irons in public, cleaning the streets, seems to have a sobering effect. Quite a few scroundrels have moved out of town, I'm told, just from the humilation."

"Capital!" smiled General Miles. The officers on the balcony watched Tucson citizens walking by, horsemen in the streets, all seeming to pause for a moment to watch their public offenders at work, or at least to give them wide berth. One young scamp suddenly threw a rock at one of the miscreants and got chased a short ways with a swinging broom before the chain caught up with him and the shotgun-toting guard stepped up to prod the struck party back in line. "That's exactly what some of these proud Apaches need, clamp 'em in leg irons and put 'em to work until we can ship them off to some prison, far, far away."

Lt. Maus lit a short cigar, tossed the burnt match over the balcony for the cleaning crew to deal with. "Reporters were rough with you, sir, about Geronimo."

"Yes, yes. Until that bastard's caught the white citizens will be after me as relentlessly as the Chiricahuas. Why can't we find him, Maus? We don't even know if he's involved in these new attacks up here, do we?"

"It's rumored he and Naiche are leading these renegades, General, but we're not certain yet. We're not getting good intelligence from the field. You've taken most of our Apache Scouts off the payroll, sir, so there's no motivation for the old Apaches on the reservation to tell us anything. They probably know what's doing with their kin."

General Miles's brow furrowed deeply. "So what are you saying?"

"Hire some of the old Scouts back, sir. Then we'll be paying them for good information about Geronimo's whereabouts. Our white Scouts just aren't up to tracking these wild Apaches, General. It's been proven for decades out here that the old saying is true, 'It takes an Apache to catch an Apache.' Now you've seen that, too. Unfortunately."

The three officers stopped sipping to watch a rider whip his lathered horse up Main Street, probably headed for the Sheriff's.

"What do you think, Dapray?" asked their Commanding Officer.

"I'm a practical man, General. I would always be willing to change tactics to solve a big military problem, until I found something that worked."

Nelson Miles scowled, slugged down the last of his whiskey. ". . . Me, too. My Plains War tactics, with our white Scouts locating the troublemakers, then leading us into pitched battles against them, are having no effect whatsoever against these elusive Apaches. We only find their bloody trails, not where in hell they're headed next." Thoroughly frustrated, the General lashed out at his underlings. "But these Apache Scouts will only be employed as guides, scouting trail. I will not have them fighting our battles for us like Crook did!"

Lt. Maus was quick in support. "No, sir! Once we catch up with Geronimo's bronchos, our troopers can fight them just as well as any hired Apache."

"If not better!" chorused his chief aide.

"All right. Let's rehire the best of these Scouts as soon as we get back to Bowie. But attach them quietly to our patrols and units. I don't want this new tactic going out over our heliographs or showing up in these newspapers. Maybe we can still surprise these murderers, with their friends leading the chase after them again."

His two officers nodded. General Miles sighed. "I find it ironic that it takes his turncoat tribesmen to catch Geronimo, but I will kill that son of a bitch if it's the last thing I ever do in the service of my country."

The two Lieutenants finished their drinks, satisfied. Now *it was back to the army's old ways out here,* they thought, *and better days.* Below them a horse broke wind loudly, punctuating the

General's crucial decision, as the chain gangs moved up the street.

Slim Canyon, East Side of the Winchester Mountains

Jacob Cox rode his gray stallion slowly through dust kicked up by the twenty steers he'd collected from the upper reaches of a canyon leading out of the Winchesters. Winter rains had left water pockets and expanses of black grama and fluff grass browse for these winter-wild cattle, but with summer's bake coming on, these moisture sources would dry up, and his livestock would need the regular water available at Cox's Tanks to survive.

Buster, his cow dog, was his only help, moving these cattle along from behind with nips at their hooves and an occasional bark!

As they passed another ravine angling into the narrow canyon's far side, an unshod horse walked slowly out from it to join the herd in front.

Jacob noticed this strange horse, but lost sight of it amongst the cows and steers in their traveling dust cloud. He was momentarily distracted by a red-tailed hawk hovering overhead, but when he looked down again, he caught another glimpse of the unfamiliar horse heading his cattle along. Craning up and down for a better look, Jacob kicked his horse into a trot to get closer.

He looked around as he trotted, for he was wary of a loose horse in these remote parts. Belonged to whom? Jacob pulled his .44/.40 carbine from its saddle scabbard. Rifle cradled in the crook of his arm, Jacob Cox leaned forward over his mount's withers as he rounded the front of his small herd to get a look at this new horse's brand.

From its far side, an Apache pulled himself up by the horse's long mane onto its back, using the moccasin he had hooked over the gelding's rump for leverage.

The rancher was startled to see a tall Indian directly in front of him and reacted by swinging his carbine defensively over to cover him. Naiche was even faster, pulling his .45 from the ammunition belt about his waist and jerking its trigger, shooting Jacob Cox just once, right in the stomach!

Ranch Near Cox's Tanks

Martha Cox blinked as she heard a single shot echo from a distant canyon, sounding like a kid's firecracker going off. She stood in front of her dresser-top mirror buttoning up the neck of her magenta-colored, silk taffeta dress. Magenta was an affectation, a favorite color of her youth, but more suited to a saloon than affairs in formal society. It was her "second-day" dress, saved for debuting the day after her wedding, while leaving for her honeymoon. The fine cloth was well preserved since she'd had so little chance to wear it out West, its multiple folds giving it fullness in the front and its padded shoulders still stiff. Abruptly agitated, Martha fumbled the last couple of buttons, took a last glance at her trim figure in the mirror, slightly amazed that the dress still fit, then hurried from her bedroom.

Slim Canyon, Winchester Mountains

Jacob's surprise as he looked down at the blood burbling from his wound slowly turned to anguish. His rifle slipped from his hand to the ground as he clutched his bleeding stomach.

"Why? . . . We were friends . . ."

Both Indian and white were distracted by Buster, who barked and dodged about after the cattle that had started running off, frightened by the gunshot.

Leaning from her back door, Martha shaded her eyes and craned her neck, but couldn't see anything in the distance, where the shot might have come from. "Jacob!" Silence, blanketed by an early summer sun. "JACOB!"

Nothing. No answer to her urgent cry. Unconsciously she began to unbutton the high neck of her dress, uncomfortable in the heat as she tried to figure out this mystery.

Shock quickly set in as Jacob Cox slid slowly, agonizingly, from his saddle to the sandy wash beside his anxious, mouse-gray stallion. Naiche sat quietly watching him from atop his shaggy pony, revolver cocked, unperturbed.

Back inside her kitchen, Martha Cox pulled the rifle off its pegs on the adobe wall next to her iron stove. Feeling its heft in her hands, she checked the seven-shot load of cartridges in the tube in its rifle butt to see if it was full, hesitated, then laid the carbine back down on the table.

Picking up potholders, she opened her oven and pulled cornbread in a square pan and then a baking vinegar pie in a round one and put them both atop the stove to cool. She stared at her brown, bubbling handiwork as she sprinkled some nutmeg across strips of piecrust, still trying to decide what to do. Finally, she picked up the old Spencer carbine and levered its breech decisively, mechanically inserting a long cartridge into its chamber.

Spread-eagled on the ground, looking down along his legs, Jacob could see the tall Apache pulling the boots right off his own feet! "Hey. . . . Don't take. . . . Leave me. . . . like this? . . . I'll die. . . ."

Naiche picked up Jacob's carbine to jam into the scabbard tied alongside the saddle on the rancher's restive horse, which was stamping its hooves nearby, aware something was wrong. The Indian stuffed Cox's cowboy boots into a saddlebag, then gazed expressionlessly at the man dying painfully on the ground right in front of him.

Clutching his stomach in a vain attempt to hold in his seeping blood as he rose up on an elbow, Jacob summoned his failing strength.

"Apache . . . I'll see you in hell . . . with your back broke. . . ."

The Chiricahua Apache nodded, then bounded up onto Cox's saddle without using the stirrup. Naiche took the nervous stallion's reins and leaned to grab his own pony's rope hackamore he had put on as he kicked his new horse away from the dying cattleman.

Still wearing her purplish red silk taffeta dress, Martha Cox stalked across their ranch's wide dirt yard, dusting her crème-colored, kid leather, high-buttoned shoes, also the best she owned. It was amazing they still fit, too. Many more years of hard ranch work, she'd probably be broken down and flat-footed, making it difficult to wear a shoe with any kind of heel, she thought gloomily. Probably just have to give her horseshoes. No time to think about that, though, with this new worry. Where had that shot come from in the middle of this hot day? From one of the canyons Jacob was working his cattle out of to the north? Or from up on the mountain where the Sergeant said Apaches were now camped? And where were that Sergeant and the men from his detail?

Moving into their dim tack shed, she slid her carbine into its leather scabbard and pulled her saddle off its wooden tree, grabbing her mare's bridle and a saddle blanket on her way out the doorway again. Her good horse wickered as she paused in the little shade the barn's roof provided, looking up to scan the mountainside above her. No movement, no sound across the rocky slopes of Square Mountain. Soldiers must be taking a *siesta* in this heat. But they were running low on supplies and here their's finally were, cans stacked in small wood crates outside the corral, plus another labeled "ammunition" and some sacks of flour and spuds, dropped off by the supply wagon late yesterday. Why weren't those hungry men down here already, washing their clothes and bathing, refilling their water kegs?

Her bay mare nosed her hand, looking for a treat. Even without a food bribe Martha had no trouble saddling the horse, but her long dress and tight corset and the voluminous petticoats underneath it made mounting and sitting her saddle awkward. Now where to go? Ride around this dangerous desert in her second-best dress looking for her brother, or climb up to Sgt. Swing's camp and see what his problem was? At least she knew there were people up on the mountain and about where his observation post was. Maybe she could spot her wandering brother from up on the mountainside?

She booted her bay gently from the corral, turning at the entrance to rehitch the gate's rope loop. Miss Cox presented quite a sight in her high-fashion dress and flouncing petticoats, astride a prancing steed. All dressed up out in the middle of this desolate desert and nowhere decent to go.

The horse began to pick its way up the discernably worn path leading higher up the oddly topped mountain behind their adobe ranch house. She hoped maybe that stoic Sergeant would finally show a little more appreciation when she suddenly showed up gaudily gowned for a visit. Martha Cox almost grinned at the thought.

TWENTY-FIVE

Torture among the Apaches was often committed by the women to avenge the death of a spouse or a family member of their clan. A hostage would be taken and brought back to camp, then cared for and danced with in a victory celebration. Then next morning one of the Apache women would run the prisoner through with a spear.

—Grenville Goodwin, *Western Apache Raiding and Warfare*

Observation Post #4, Square Mountain

The soldiers sat on the boulders ringing their campsite on the mountain ledge, munching what little was left to eat. Sergeant Swing pressed his stomach with his fingers, puffing out his cheeks. "This mescal's startin' to give me the bloat."

From the pocket of his blouse, Bobyne pulled out a small tin, passing it over to his noncom.

"Sardines! Where'd you get these?"

"Trader's." The Signal Corpsman chuckled. "Been savin' 'em for a rainy day."

"Too long a wait, huh?" Sergeant Swing got the tin's top rolled open with its metal key and helped himself to several overripe sardines before passing it on to Mullin.

"Thanks, Bobyne. . . . Cochise once told an army buddy of mine he'd never eat 'little fishes out of tin boxes.' Didn't know what he was missin'." The Sergeant grinned at the recollection. "Apaches believe fish are taboo, like snakes, and they ain't too sweet on pork, either. Think pigs are dirty animals."

"Oop. Message comin' in." Rousing, he helped himself to an oily sardine, then their heliographer picked up his binoculars to focus on the flashes from across the big valley above Dos Cabezas.

"G-E-N-GENERAL MILES R-E-Q-REQUESTS P-L-E-A-PLEASURE M-A-J-O-R AND MRS B-E-A-U-MONT O-F-F-OFFICERS BALL H-E-A-HEADQUARTERS FORT BOWIE 15 JUNE."

"Officer's Ball. . . . And ladies' punch will be served." The Sergeant spit to punctuate his distaste for General Miles's affectations, then washed the fish flavor from his mouth with warm canteen water.

Corporal Bobyne unlimbered from his perch to align his heliograph equipment with the sun and relay the social invitation up to Turkey Flat in the Pinaleno Mountains to the north.

Mullin licked his oily fingers. "Sarge, how come these Apaches keep fightin' so hard? So many troopers out here in the field now, they can't possibly win, right?"

"Fightin' for the only way of life they've ever known, Mullin. Other warrior tribes pushed 'em into this hot, dry, mountainous country nobody else ever wanted until now, so they adapted and became just like this desert—harsh, pitiless, and cruel."

Corporal Bobyne smiled. "You're a philosopher."

"No, just passin' along a little wisdom I learned out here. The hard way." The Sergeant settled himself against his rock, trying to get comfortable.

"Apaches never were gourd growers like the Pimas, or sheepherders like the Navajos. They're raiders, pure and simple! Don't consider it stealing; it's what they do for a living. Shoot, they never even learned to breed horses. They're wanderers. Survive by trickery. They've always lived like coyotes, off what they could thieve or kill. Hell, the name *Apache* comes from the Zuni word *apachu*, for 'enemy.' All the other tribes hate and fear 'em, and the few wild ones still loose up here or down in Mexico with Geronimo are fightin' to the last man to protect this homeland, their raidin' ways. I was in their moccasins right now, I probably would be, too."

"Indians killing each other, fighting amongst the tribes, just awful, isn't it? Barbarian. They're savages!" added Corporal Bobyne. "Much different than us cultured white folks going at each other tooth and claw in our own Civil War."

Sgt. Swing gave the best-educated, most sarcastic member of his little detail a hard look.

Mullin disagreed. "But Apaches torture their victims, scalp or burn 'em alive, Bobyne."

"Nothing we haven't done to them, first. Or the Mexicans have," explained the Sergeant. "I've seen a white man using a horse bridle braided from Apache hair. Decorated with teeth knocked from the jaws of live Indian women. You see, Mullin, revenge for an Apache is his sacred duty, and he doesn't have to inflict it on the particular enemy who caused the outrage in the first place, any white or Mexican or another tribesman will do. Yes, they do multilate their victims sometimes, because they believe a dismembered enemy will travel through the afterlife in that bad condition. So multilation, to an Apache, is the ultimate punishment."

The young soldier grimaced at the thought. "Their gooses are cooked, though, right? War's pretty much over for 'em?"

"Yup," nodded the experienced Indian fighter. "Just too many damned troops chasin' 'em now, both sides of the border. Too hard to steal horses, get ammunition, with everybody they run into wanting to shoot 'em on sight. These are their last moves on this great big checkerboard." Sergeant Swing gestured expansively out at the Sulphur Springs Valley beneath them. "In a way, I gotta admire 'em. Man for man they are the fiercest, most cunning warriors this army's ever faced. In all our nation's Indian wars, no other tribe has ever fought us so hard, so savagely, for so long as these Apaches. That's why they've dominated this wild country for over two hundred years. Couldn't believe another tribe or race could be as powerful as themselves . . . They have proven to be a most superior foe."

"Gosh." Their rookie was impressed by his superior's knowledge. But Mullin suddenly sat up. "Speak of the devil, here they come again."

The Private pointed, directing their gaze to the north, where the three Apache women walked along in front of their four kids, all followed by a little old man, as they climbed slowly up the mountainside again from their campsite on the other ledge.

"Damnation! I ain't havin' another castor oil party or medicine show up here again! I told 'em today was the day they had to leave!" Sgt. Swing jerked to his feet, limbered up his wounded leg as he belted on his holster and walked over to the north end of their ledge to watch the Indians coming on.

Mullin got down off his rock to grab his Springfield and hurry over to join him.

"*Dah*! (No!) *Dah*, ladies! *Dah-e-sah*! (Disappear!) Off this mountain! Now! Back to your home! Go to San Carlos!" Sergeant Swing thrust his palms out in front of him to halt, and the ladies and kids did, momentarily.

But the old shaman, smiling broadly, bounded right past them from the rear to lead the party on. Mrs. Cutnose followed him, walking the group across the mountainside to maybe twenty yards below Observation Post #4.

Finished with his sun flashing, Bobyne, too, grabbed his rifle and joined the soldiers watching the Apaches from above.

All the Indians carried long sticks, and Nabedza had an armful. Mrs. Cutnose led them to a large bush, which the others quietly surrounded. She Crosses to Go to War dropped her sticks and began to start a fire in the pile with a burning torch one child carried.

"What in hell?" exclaimed Mullin. "Are they gonna start smoke signaling?"

Trail Down Square Mountain

Heintz lumbered along in front, leading his mule down the mountainside along the trail through the cactus and brush and rocks they'd created by their comings and goings from Cox's ranch, below them in the distance. Grover suddenly balked, digging his hooves in. The Corporal turned back to grab the mule's lead rope to yank him forward again. The instant he did, an arrow whistled straight into his back, driven so hard and deep its metal arrowhead came out the front of Heintz's blouse. "Ooooo. . . . *Verdammt*. . . ."

The big Hessian blanched in shock as he crumpled to his knees, fumbling, tugging to try to pull the three-foot shaft out through his chest.

"Jesus to Jerusalem!" Catching up to his comrade's mule, Takins stopped short as he saw what had happened to Heintz, face down now in the dirt with a hawk-feathered arrow sticking from him. The reb quick unlashed his rifle from Annie's pack and cocked it as he peered nervously about in every direction. "Oh no, oh no. You thievin' bastards ain't gonna get me!"

Consumed by fear, Takins turned tail and scrambled back up the mountainside as fast as his scrawny legs could carry him, the mules and his arrowed Corporal left to fend for themselves. "Not me! . . . No siree-E-E-E-E!"

A squeal of fright as an Apache, white war stripe blazed across his face, jumped out from behind a rock above him. Sliding on the steep ground, trying to take a fighting stance, Takins swung his rifle up to fire, but Inday-Yi-Yahn ripped it right out of his hands with one hand and lunged with his other, sinking his knife up to the hilt in the soldier's gut. He Kills Enemies twisted the steel blade and ripped it out sideways, disemboweling the trooper.

The two fighters were face-to-face a fatal moment before the Apache pushed him aside, wiped the bloody blade on the downed man's filthy undershirt, and snatched up Takins's

Springfield to run downslope to help Dahkeya and Klosen secure the mules.

Blood spurted from Takins's lips as he struggled to speak. . . . "Not . . . me. . . ."

Observation Post #4, Square Mountain

The large creosote bush had brush piled against its trunk, and, looking closely, one could see mounds of dirt cast up under it by some animal burrowing tunnels beneath its roots. The squaws and their kids began to shout as they poked their rat sticks into this brush pile. When they pulled their notched sticks out and saw hair on the sharp ends, they knew they had their prey trapped beneath and thrust down into the dirt holes even deeper.

Beela-Chezzi danced about on his scrawny legs, a mad hatter in a buckskin cap, playing a shrill song on his wooden flute.

A small brown head popped from one of the dirt holes the girls weren't wiggling sticks in, but the twelve-year-old Apache boy jammed his notched stick over the rodent's head, twisting its fur as he reached down to pull it from its escape hole. The boy quickly bashed its tiny skull on the ground to kill it, then hoisted the small animal into the air for all to see. The field rat still quivered!

Standing up on their camp's ledge, maybe twenty yards away, three soldiers watched these goings-on, fascinated.

The Indian boy hurried his trophy over to Nadezba's fire, which had burned down to coals. Mrs. Cutnose grabbed the rat from the kid, eviscerated it with a slash of her knife and gave it a good squeeze to pop its little guts out, then flipped the rat, fur and all, onto the smoking fire.

Indian girls squealed round the bush as more rats were rooted out, pinned, killed, and run over to the fire for cooking.

Corporal Bobyne's mouth was wide open. "Well I'll be damned. A rat roast."

The troopers watched as Haozinne impaled a roasted critter on a stick, lifted it from the embers, shook it to cool, and then picked at the juicy tidbit with her fingers.

"You ever eat one, Sarge?" asked Mullin.

"Nope. Apaches consider 'em a treat, though. Wood rat's one of their favorites."

"Really?" mulled Bobyne. "Damn. Haven't had a full meal in two days."

Hungry but sort of horrified by this messy business, three soldiers were drawn toward the banquet in spite of themselves. There just seemed to be no end to the victuals or the fun.

"Salty sardines just made me hungier," said Mullin.

The action was fast and furious now around the big bush, with all four Indian kids gleefully catching their meals as the old shaman egged them on.

Cradling his rifle, Bobyne's scientific curiosity drew him down off his rock for a better look. Mullin, the amateur botanist, also limped down from the ledge on his sore foot, using his rifle as a cane.

A little Apache girl ran up, offering a roasted rodent to the Corporal. Bobyne sniffed it, looked back at his two fellows. The Signal Corpsman put down his rifle, accepted the rat-on-a-stick with a smile. "Thank you, young lady."

Twisting skin aside with his Barlow knife, Bobyne gingerly picked out a seared morsel with his fingers and tasted it. Bobyne chewed a bit, then swallowed hard.

"Umm . . ." He turned to give his fellows a grin. "Tastes like rodent to me."

Bobyne dug in hungrily as Mullin was next to be served by another little girl. The young Private was quick to try his scorched rat. He held his stick up for Sergeant Swing to see, licking his lips with a smile. "Little sagebrush flavor."

Naiche's wife, Haozinne, brought a roasted rat up to the Sergeant, perched now atop a perimeter rock on the ledge, still on guard. The plump offering was done just to his liking, medium-rare. Ammon Swing could no longer resist. He smiled thanks, closed his eyes, then tentatively tasted a small piece of meat. Its odor and flavor reminded him of the woodchuck he had shot and cooked as a sprout back in Indiana. What opened his eyes again was a terrible silence, slashed suddenly by a scream!

For an instant as the cooked rat fell from his hands, Sgt. Swing was stricken with fright. The kids seem to have vanished. As his head jerked round to locate the piercing cry, he saw a dying Mullin staggering toward him, screaming again! A red-banded arrow transfixed his body, driven with such force through his chest that the steel arrowhead pierced him completely. "SARGE! Jesus, Sarge!"

Haozinne, the younger woman who had fed the Sergeant, ran full speed toward their tents to find weapons and plunder, her grimy calico skirt held high.

Like deer, three Apache bucks leapt from hiding places behind bushes and cacti below the south end of the ledge behind the soldiers, where their mule trail started down the mountain. Whisks of palmilla grass were tied into dark flannel headbands, and clay was smeared on their bare upper bodies for camouflage, which had allowed them to crawl undetected right up to the observation post while the soldiers were diverted.

Bobyne dropped his snack and grabbed his Springfield to fire at the oncoming Apaches.

Nadebza leapt onto the ledge behind the Sergeant and ran right through their heliographic equipment, giving the tripod a kick and toppling the main instrument onto a rock, shattering its mirror!

Dahkeya and Inday-Yi-Yahn sped toward the Sergeant on his boulder, letting loose arrows from mulberry bows held waist-high with the sinew strings drawn back against their stomachs.

A cane shaft guided by eagle feathers whizzed toward him, suddenly skewering the thigh of his already wounded left leg! Sgt. Swing yelped in pain, wobbled, then toppled off his boulder, falling behind it. Groaning, sweating, pulling himself upright again onto his good knee, he managed to draw his revolver.

Twirling a buckskin sling made from two-foot lengths of sinew several times over his head, the Apache boy unleashed a stone that hit Mullin hard in the back, buckling his knees and hurting the crying young man even more.

Bobyne reloaded and fired again! Klosen, the youngest and nearest attacker, dropped like a bloody rock, dead immediately from a bullet right through the neck!

The little medicine man darted about the rat bush, his war-charm hoops and wooden crosses clacking about his neck as he banged ineffectively away at the troopers with his big cap-and-ball pistol, the kick from its recoil nearly knocking him over with each wild shot.

Bobyne was hurriedly reloading when he was abruptly seized from behind in a powerful embrace. Mrs. Cutnose hurled him backward onto the fire of hot coals as if she were barbecuing another rat! Jumping upon the surprised Corporal, the heavy Apache woman managed to set his hair on fire as she stabbed the helpless soldier repeatedly in the chest with her small skinning knife.

Balancing on his good knee, Sgt. Swing swiftly raised his Colt .45 in the air, cocked it, and lowered his extended arm in one motion, letting the hammer slip. Snap-shooting was like throwing the bullet out of the barrel, and he brought down the closing Dahkeya at fifteen yards. He quickly turned to shoot Mrs. Cutnose right in the back, dropping her flopping atop the dying Bobyne, extinguishing his flaming hair.

Wounded in the shoulder, Dahkeya got back to his feet to shoot at his nearest target with Takins's reloaded rifle, putting down the whimpering, crawling Mullin for good.

The Sergeant took this determined Apache out with a second shot near his heart, spinning him into a teddy bear cholla, leaving Dahkeya spiked among its prickly limbs. But that still left one warrior alive. *Where in God's name was he?* he thought desperately.

Out of arrows in the mountain lion-skin quiver across his back, the wily Inday-Yi-Yahn had gotten around to the side of him, out of the Sergeant's sight, and suddenly leapt right up over the big boulder Sgt. Swing was crouched behind, sweeping a butcher knife out of his hide moccasin!

Sgt. Swing brought his revolver up to brace himself against the attack. Going down under the onslaught, the Sergeant glimpsed the contorted brown face with its ghostly white stripe under bulging dark eyes and heard the death yell before a large caliber bullet slammed the wind out of the warrior. "Aiiiieeee!"

He Kills Enemies fell heavily upon him. Ammon Swing lay wondering if he was further wounded, stupefied that the last bullet had not been his own. The Sergeant saw a pair of crème-colored, high-buttoned, kid leather shoes near his face, and then the dead Apache was dragged off him by Miss Martha Cox.

"You all right?"

". . . I guess. . . . My leg. . . ."

She shouldered her Spencer again to trigger off several more long shots for effect in the direction of the two Indian women scrambling down Square Mountain's rocky slope, braids flying, one carrying off several empty army canteens on slings, the other a long-handled spider skillet held high, to make sure they didn't circle around to attack again. Her breathing heavy, Martha lowered her carbine and looked around. "Soldiers and women. . . . Look at this carnage."

She picked up the dead Apache's knife, knelt beside the Sergeant, and slit his pants leg up to his newly bleeding wound to examine it. A thin steel arrowhead was buried in his leg. Sgt. Swing let out a deep groan. "You shoot him?"

"Sure."

He levered himself up on an elbow, gasped in pain again as

she suddenly whacked off the feathered tail end of the shaft in the front of his left thigh with the dead Indian's butcher knife. "OWW!"

"Gotta get this arrow out soon. Deer sinew they use to attach the arrowhead loosens and you can leave the point behind to fester. Where's that honey I sent up?"

"What?" Then the question registered, and he gestured with another little groan. "Stores. My tent. Middle."

She strode off to get it while he looked around at the bloodshed. Both his troopers were dead, arrowed or stabbed, and Mrs. Cutnose lay sprawled face down in the fire pit, dead, too. Below and about their campsite, three *netdahe* Apache renegades were also shot to death. Sgt. Swing shook his head sadly, stunned by the fierce engagement. "Jesus Christmas. . . . Why didn't they fire their guns, kill us all quick?"

Martha reappeared from his tent, toting the leftover comb honey in her mason jar and some scraps of cloth. "Didn't appear too well armed. Probably trying to save the few bullets they had and yours, too."

The Sergeant thought, then nodded. "Maybe so. We count our cartridges at the fort and have to destroy any shells we empty in the field, so they can't reload 'em."

"Much gunfire up here would have alerted us down at the ranch, or any patrols in the area. They wanted their killing quiet. Here, let me help, so I can bandage it." Lifting him under a shoulder, she helped him up on his good right leg and propped him against a boulder.

"Ah! Careful. . . . Oh! Christ. . . . Heintz and Takins? They—"

"—Dead. Ambushed on the way down. By these three, I bet."

"Damn. Never heard a thing. . . . Arrows." He blew sorrowful air, began getting a little misty. "Those boys were as brave . . . as any ever shouldered a rifle. . . . Well, hell, somebody will have to relieve us up here now, bury these . . . good men."

She pointed. "Oh! There they go!"

The Sergeant jerked his head round to see far below them, Nadezba and Haozinne and old Crooked Fingers herding the four kids away as fast as their short legs could carry them down the mountainside toward a mounted Apache riding toward them leading a spare horse. "JESUS! Oooo. . . . My God, girl. . . ."

He seemed to swoon, and she thought for a moment he might pass out from the pain. Distracting him, she had pushed the arrowhead through and then yanked the rest of the shaft out the backside of his wounded thigh. Martha kept talking to keep him alert and immediately began to smear the bleeding wound with fingerfuls of comb honey. "This sticky honey will help stop the bleeding and start the healing, till we get you downhill. Then I'll have to clean it with alcohol, stop any infection."

"You'll enjoy that . . . I bet."

She frowned at him, threw the bloody arrow away and began wrapping his leg wound in a strip of old linen. "This is not my pleasure, sir. Saving your life was."

"Oww!" He was sweating profusely at all this wrenching pain. "Least that damned Indian didn't stick my good leg."

They both paused to look down the mountainside again. Haozinne jumped atop the spare pony and yanked a couple little girls up behind her. Naiche pulled a third child onto his lap, then looked up and raised his stolen .44/.40 carbine high, toward the armed white man and woman halfway up the mountain, watching him.

"*Indah*! (White man!)"

A salute to their valor, he wondered? Sgt. Swing responded, putting his right hand holding his pistol into the air. "*Teneh!* (the Apaches' word for themselves, the 'People'!)"

Whatever his meaning, Naiche, last son of the legendary Cochise, reined his mouse-gray stallion around and trotted off, the twelve-year-old Apache boy and Nadezba jogging along to follow, holding on to the two horses by their tails to help themselves keep pace.

Martha fretted. "Worried about my brother. I heard a shot from the direction where he was rounding up strays . . . but I rode up here to get help first."

"Just one shot?"

She nodded, anxiety etched around her eyes. "Can't be sure, but that Apache might have been riding Jacob's gray stallion."

The Sergeant stared at her, then looked away, speculating. She finished her bandaging with a hairpin fastener. "I'll get my mare."

He measured her appreciatively as she returned, leading her horse from where she'd left it on the trail down from the south end of their ledge. She was wearing probably the best she owned—a long dress of silk taffeta and high-button shoes—about as inappropriate as a woman could possibly choose for a rescue mission, so she must have been planning something else. When fully furbished, however, Miss Martha Cox was right near handsome.

He managed a grim smile through his pain. "Pretty dress."

She ignored the compliment, walking her skittish horse about, trying to calm her down amongst the smell of all this death.

"Heintz was intending to ask you to marry."

She glanced at him self-consciously. "Well, I didn't put all this on for him! . . . Haven't had my fancies on in five years." She managed a half smile herself. "Least they still fit."

She halted her bay mare, unstrapped and reached inside her saddlebag to take out a bottle of patent medicine, and handed it to him. "Help deaden your pain."

The Sergeant uncorked it, ready for some relief, but paused to read the label. " 'Henry's Invigorating Cordial. For women's complaints.' " He looked at her. " 'Contains morphine, quinine, and alcohol.' Well, if your decoctions don't kill me, this might actually help."

He took a couple big gulps and exhaled. "Whoo! That'll put hair on a Mexican dog." He offered it to her.

She accepted. "I guess. Been an awful afternoon. . . . Are your men dead?"

Sergeant Swing turned grim again. "Yeah. Shot, arrowed, stabbed. Several times. Apaches don't leave much to chance."

Turning to survey the bloody landscape again, he caught a flash from the mountains across the big valley to the north. "Oop! Message coming in . . . from Turkey Flat. Ain't fully trained to decipher it yet, but it better be put down."

Martha took a swallow of her medicine as she squinted northward at the sun flashes. "It better not."

"No, it's my duty. Get a pencil and paper from my tent. . . . Please."

She glared at him a moment before digging into her saddlebag again to pull out pencil and paper. Sgt. Swing squinted. Diligently, he recorded the signals according to length. She watched him, helping herself to a couple more invigorating swigs.

"Short, short, long. Long, short. Short. Okay."

The flashes finally ceased as he cast a glum look over at his own shattered heliograph mirror nearby. "Oughta relay this. It's maybe important."

"Mister Swing, infection won't wait. You army around up here much longer, and you might have to do without that leg. Unless I get my herbs on that wound."

He wasn't really listening. "Have you a mirror with you, ma'am? Or anything shiny in those saddlebags? Our pots and pans are burned, an'—"

"—No, I do not." Now she was really impatient with this ungrateful, exasperating man. "Apaches, you know, poison their arrowheads. . . . With rattlesnake venom or something nasty. Blood poisoning is a gruesome death."

He snapped his fingers. "My apology, ma'am. What do you have on under that dress?"

"Well I never!" She colored up real ripe.

His eyes crinkled with doubt, if he should dare be so bold? "Would you please remove it?"

"Oh!"

"Government business, ma'am. . . . 'Sides, you saw me in my bath."

This time she really did stamp her foot before she reluctantly obeyed, hoisting the heavy taffeta dress over her head. Above she wore a white corset cover laced with pink ribbon and below, ruffled muslin petticoats so overstarched they were as stiff and glittering as galvanized tin, touching evidence that it had been a long time since she'd made starch.

He pointed downslope. "Get me that rifle, and help me over to the edge."

Frowning, she picked her way carefully down the mountainside a little ways in her underthings, retrieved Takins's long Springfield, and brought it back. With him using the rifle as a crutch, she grudgingly helped the Sergeant limp slowly over to the edge of their campsite's ledge, facing east across the Sulphur Springs Valley.

"We're in luck, ma'am. We have a clear day and the whitest unspeakabout this side of Heaven, so I calculate they will see us. . . . Right here. Face forward, and hold onto me. Please." The Sergeant took her magenta dress and reading slowly from his paper, began to transmit the message using her dress as a shutter, shading her with it and then sweeping it away like a bullfighter, for long and short periods, corresponding to the code letters he had just transcribed. "Lessee. Short, short, pause, short. Short, pause short. Ver-r-r-y long. . . ."

Her frown deepened into a grimace, as the tough frontierswoman was near tears. "This is the most embarrassing thing . . . anyone's ever asked me to do."

"Stand still, please. . . . Short, short. Long, short. Short. Ver-r-r-y long. Stop fidgeting!"

"Can't help it! I'm dying of shame!"

Observation Post #5, Dos Cabezas Peak

Private Slivers, dozing against a rock below Dos Cabezas Peak above the trader's, roused from his mid-afternoon stupor as he saw something white winking against the distant mountains across the valley. "Somethin' winkin' over to the Winchesters. Don't look like any heliograph, though."

His alert roused the idle curiosity of the rest of Post #5's bored detail, napping about their campsite right below his perch.

"Give me the glasses," ordered Lt. Fuller. He looked through them for a long moment. "Damn, it's indistinct. Something white. Is that the right location?"

"Nearabouts, sir. Post Four," answered Sgt. Conn.

"Put the telescope on it."

His heliographer had already gotten the 20 × 40 Bausch and Lomb aimed, and Corporal Hengesbaugh focused his sighting equipment in. "Something large and white standing against that mountain, Lieutenant. Can't make it out . . . real good, but it disappears, and then reappears, sort of like a . . . coded message."

"Try to translate it. . . . Why in hell wouldn't they use their heliograph, if that is Post Four?" Frustrated, Lt. Fuller rifled some stones downhill.

"Lessee A . . . C . . . C . . . E . . . dammit, I think P . . . T. . . . Maybe W . . . I . . . T . . . H. . . . Christ, this is hard to decipher, P . . ."

"Open the shutters all the way on ours and aim it at them, so they'll know to adjust their sight and repeat the message."

Observation Post #4, Square Mountain

Up on Square Mountain, poor Miss Martha Cox was forced to stand five thousand feet high in plain sight of half the military department of Arizona, being alternately covered and revealed, a living heliograph, flashing in the sun like an angel descended from above and blushing like a woman falling forever into sin. Her ordeal and her glory finally ended when Post #5 blinked rapidly on and off to signify receipt of the message.

The Sergeant blew some relieved air. "There. Done. Thank you, ma'am. For everything."

She snatched her dress back and covered herself with it. To his confusion, a tear splashed down one of her cheeks, while at the same time she drew up breathing brimstone.

"Ammon Swing! No one has ever in all my days displayed me in such a state out-of-doors for God and all mankind to see! Either I put my brother on your evil trail or you harden your mind to marrying me this minute!"

He blinked. "Already have."

She caught her breath as she pulled on the magenta dress. "We better kiss on it then."

". . . Okay."

So they did, tentatively at first, then with all the passion pain and sudden death and frustration and heartache and loneliness could bring to one long, very intense kiss.

Sgt. Swing paused to catch his breath. "You know . . . you put me in mind of one of your vinegar pies: sorta tart on the outside but sweet within. . . ." He smiled, almost tenderly, and she managed one as well.

"You've got some juice left in you, too. But when trained, you'll rein."

Observation Post #5, Dos Cabezas Peak

At Post #5 that late afternoon, the exasperated junior officer stopped pacing. "Got it deciphered? Finally?"

"Think so. Just about burned my eyes out gettin' it." Corporal Hengesbaugh rubbed his, to emphasize his hardship. "Never did acknowledge their aim was off or give a station call sign. Must be a new operator."

"Okay, okay. What was the damned message?"

"'RELAY MAJOR AND MRS BEAUMONT ACCEPT WITH PLEASURE OFFICER'S BALL FORT BOWIE 15 JUNE.'"

Their young Second Lieutenant contemplated. "I'm going to have a talk with that damned Swing about these monkeyshines, we meet again, down at the trader's." Lt. Alvarado Fuller rotated his stiff neck, letting out a long sigh. "Officer's Ball. And I'm stuck up here . . ."

Observation Post #4, Square Mountain

Sergeant Swing painfully pushed himself up with both hands into her smaller saddle, while she pulled on his shoulders from the other side to help right him atop her horse. Groaning, he caught his breath while she slid her Spencer rifle into the saddle scabbard.

"Martha. We'll go locate Jacob now, if he's not back at your ranch."

She hefted his light Springfield carbine, took the reins in her other hand.

"Yes. Regardless of how we find him, Ammon, promise me one thing."

"What's that?"

"After your leg heals and we're married, let's leave this bad luck place, put down new roots somewhere else."

"Leave the territory? For where?"

She pulled on the reins leading her horse and her man across ruined Observation Post #4, down the mule trail from the south end of the campsite, hiking in her kid leather shoes.

"Anywhere but this godforsaken country."

"What? And give up the pleasures of army life?" Sergeant Swing managed a chuckle, which echoed a little across the Winchester Mountains, as the groom and his bride-to-be disappeared into the gathering dusk, moving slowly down Square Mountain toward her ranch below.

Horse Stables, Ft. Bowie

Taking the train back from Tucson to Ft. Bowie the next day, the General barely paused in his inspections, walking right to the stables at his headquarters to check the fitness of his cavalry units' mounts, who would immediately be tested in the longer patrols he wanted his cavalry troops to be conducting with the reinstated Apache Scouts. Major Beaumont accosted him from around a corner as he was striding through the post's extensive horse quarters.

"General Miles! There's been an attack on Observation Post #4, yesterday. Four of our men including the heliographer were killed, but their noncom fought back and killed three Apaches and a squaw. He's wounded but coming in with the ranch woman at Cox's Tanks, who lost her brother as well. Sgt. Swing thinks it was Naiche who rode off with some other Apache women."

The General was taken aback. "Lost four of our men? And a rancher?"

Major Beaumont nodded. "Yes sir, sounds like quite a fight, but he drove them off that mountain."

"Sergeant Swing? Didn't I meet that man here? Big, strapping fellow, gray mustache?"

"That's him. Ammon Swing's a tough man, General."

"A hero!" General Miles paced, thinking hard. "When he gets here we must make something of this, bring in reporters, hold a full-dress review, give him a medal for godsakes, the Medal of Honor. We need to divert attention away from these raids, these random killings. Here's one of our own who went toe to toe with these Apache bastards and won his fight, drove them off! Yes! The public craves heroes."

The West Pointer almost smiled. "Maybe a battlefield commission, General?"

Nelson Miles's eyes lit up. "Second Lieutenant Swing! We did that all the time during the Civil War!" The General was so delighted by his idea that he hugged a bay horse. "Enough scrappers like this new Lieutenant, and we'll have this hellish war over in two shakes of Geronimo's tail!"

AFTERWORD

Captain Thomas Lebo and K Troop did indeed chase down Geronimo and his band on May 3, 1886, in the Piñito Mountains, a short distance southeast of Nogales in Sonora, Mexico. After fleeing two hundred miles, Geronimo realized he couldn't shake the famed Buffalo Soldiers and their Apache Scouts, so his warriors laid an ambush among some boulders up a semicircular cliff. But Captain Lebo was alert and didn't walk into their trap. His black troopers attacked up the slope, where one was killed and a Corporal had his knee shattered by a bullet. Second Lieutenant Powhatan Clarke rushed through withering fire to drag his trooper to safety, winning a Medal of Honor for his brave act.

Captain Lebo's men, running low on water and with dusk approaching, staged an orderly retreat to the Santa Cruz River. Geromino's band retreated, untouched, and five further days of pursuit by the Tenth Cavalry was futile.

On May 12, the Chiricahuas partially defeated Mexican troops near Planchos, Mexico. On the fifteenth, Captain C. A. P. Hatfield and thirty-six Fourth Cavalrymen surprised nearly thirty Apaches south of Cananea and got into a running fight, wounding several Indians and capturing all twenty of their horses and camp gear.

Backtracking with their prizes that afternoon, the Fourth Cavalrymen were in turn surprised by these same Apaches, who snuck around and hid themselves between the front skirmishers and the main body of D Troopers herding the captured Apache horses. In a lengthy fight, Captain Hatfield had several soldiers badly wounded, lost some of the cavalry's horses back to the Apaches, and emerged with his military reputation tarnished. It's rumored Geronimo turned up for his final surrender parley with General Miles at Skeleton Canyon wearing Hatfield's cavalry blouse, which during the fight the Captain had tied to the saddlehorn of his own horse, which he also lost.

After another battle on May 16 with a different troop of U.S. Cavalry, the Chiricahuas split into two groups, one fleeing west, the other north. For the next month and a half, the military documented a "series of outrages, with fatiguing chases by troops." On every occasion the Apaches avoided a decisive action against them.

Until June 21, 1886, forty miles southeast of Magdalena, Mexico. There the Apache raiders were surprised by a posse of about seventy Mexican vaqueros. The much smaller band of Chiricahuas managed to escape with few casualties, except for a single warrior who was carrying ten-year-old Trinidad Verdín on his horse. The Mexicans shot the Indian's horse, and the girl fell off and ran to her rescuers. The irregular troops surrounded the bush the warrior was hiding under but couldn't dislodge him. Perhaps it was Geronimo himself, as one story goes, or Fun or Yanozha, but the unknown Apache was extremely brave and a superb marksman. He shot seven Mexicans dead, panicked the rest into fleeing, and made his getaway. When Captain Henry Lawton reached the battlefield the next day with his cavalry, he found all seven vaqueros killed by headshots.

The Mexican-American boy kidnapped near Tucson was also

saved from this fight. Alfred Peck picked up little Trini and took her back to the States. He never returned to his ranch near the Santa Cruz River to relive his temporarily mad moments of fear and grief when his wife was raped and killed by the Apaches right in front of his eyes.

Al Peck eventually remarried and became a stable owner in Nogales. "Dad Peck never talked much of the Indian raid," said his daughter-in-law, "and we never pressed him for details, for even thinking of it upset him badly."

The Geronimo campaign ran from May 17, 1885, to September 3, 1886, for fifteen and a half months. In it 35 men and 8 half-grown boys, encumbered by 101 women and children, eluded the pursuit of hundreds of veteran soldiers in a flight of almost unbelievable endurance. They accomplished this with no regular base of supply, in a hostile territory some eighty thousand square miles in size, against 6,000 soldiers (*one quarter* of the entire U.S. Army at that time), 500 or more Indian scouts, and an uncounted number of civilian vigilante groups searching for them in two countries. In their fifteen months of freedom, these last hostiles killed 75 citizens of Arizona and New Mexico, according to official records, including 12 White Mountain Apaches, and 8 army troopers. The number of Mexicans killed is incalculable and probably ran into the hundreds. Geronimo lost only 6 men, 2 boys, 2 women, and an infant. Two of his six men weren't killed in combat but in a Mexican village where they had gone on a peace mission. The difference in kill rates between these warring groups was phenomenal, making this final Apache campaign one of the most remarkable sagas in military history.

By September 8, 1886, after twenty-six years of exceedingly bloody, mostly hit-and-run guerrilla fighting, the last of the great American Indian wars was finally over. Casualties among army men would top those of Custer's lost battle at the Little Big Horn. When civilian casualties, especially the horrific loss of lives among the Mexicans, were included, the long fight for the control of Apacheria was by far the most costly, in human lives, of *any* Indian war in America's history.

Geronimo, Naiche, and the other renegades, as well as former army scouts, including the two who had negotiated Geronimo's surrender, and any Apache who was even partially Chiricahua were put on the train headed east to two prisons in Florida, many still believing they would be returning to their desert homelands in only two years. But General Miles hadn't told them the terms of their surrender to General Crook had been quickly nullified by the federal government. Now it was unconditional.

When Geronimo and Naiche departed in the heavily guarded wagons for the railroad station that morning, the Fourth Cavalry band at Fort Bowie broke into "Auld Lang Syne." The Apaches didn't understand why the soldiers singing along were laughing and jeering at them, too. "The wickedest Indian who ever lived" was on his way to prison for the last time.

After selling bootleg whiskey to Geronimo and Naiche and encouraging them to go back on the warpath in the spring of 1886, Robert Tribolet established a ranch near Fronteras, Sonora. He was arrested there for a stage robbery and "shot while trying to escape."

At Fort Pickens, Florida, the most dangerous of the hostile Indians were imprisoned 350 miles away from their wives, children, and relatives in Fort Marion. But a majority in both prisons began to die rapidly from bad conditions and unfamiliar food, diseases they had no immunity to, like malaria, as well as from general depression and homesickness. Not until May 1888 were both groups of Apaches finally joined in the pine woods of Mount Vernon Barracks in Alabama. Unfortunately, there they also became infected with the tuberculosis some of their children had picked up at the famous Carlisle Indian School in Pennsylvania, and many more slowly died of this strange disease. By the end of 1889, one quarter of all the

Apaches who had been shipped out to Florida were dead, in only three years!

General Crook attempted several times to intervene with Congress and the White House to get his Apache Scouts released from prison, recognized for their service in the army, and repatriated to their Southwestern homelands, as he had originally promised them when they surrendered to him. He was never successful. Finally, in the fall of 1894, eight years after they had been sent east, the last Chiricahuas were again resettled on their own reservation in Fort Sill, Oklahoma.

George Crook later commanded the Division of the Missouri and was promoted to Major General, a rank and posting he held until he died of a heart attack in 1890 at the age of sixty-one. He was among the preeminent Indian fighters the U.S. Army ever produced, and his noble sentiments about their welfare and justice for the Native American tribes echo to this day in Indian/white relationships.

Geronimo and Naiche lived longer, with Geronimo a big tourist attraction in Pawnee Bill's Wild West Show and at the "Apache Village" in the 1904 St. Louis World's Fair. After the death of Sitting Bull, he had easily become the most famous Indian in America, invited by President Theodore Roosevelt to ride at the head of his inaugural parade in 1905 and even publishing his cowritten autobiography a year later. He died in the winter of 1909, after a drunken fall off a horse left him on the frozen ground all night to contract pneumonia. Geronimo went into his grave at age eighty-five with supposedly fifty bullet wounds and battle scars on him, secure in his "vision" while a much younger man that no bullet would ever kill him.

Naiche took up art, and his scenes of Apache life painted on deerskin are still preserved at the Fort Sill Museum. At the turn of the century he joined the Dutch Reformed Church and was a good Christian until he died of influenza in 1921 in New Mexico at age sixty-five, preceded by eight of his fourteen children by his three wives.

After twenty-seven years as prisoners of war, by far the longest confinement served by *any* Indian tribe in American history, the Chiricahuas were finally freed in 1913. Two-thirds of the only 258 Chiricahuas still left (down from 1,675 in 1873!) moved west onto the reservation of their sometime allies, the Mescalero Apaches, near Ruidoso in southern New Mexico, where they remain today, divided between there and Oklahoma. The Jicarilla Apaches were also given their own reservation by the U.S. government in their homelands in northern New Mexico, as were the Western Apaches on the Fort Apache and San Carlos reservations adjacent to it in the White Mountains of eastern Arizona.

But not the Chiricahuas. Hard feelings against them by their powerful white enemies still run deep. To this day, by state law, a Chiricahua Apache is not allowed to own one square inch of land in Arizona.

General Nelson Miles eventually set up 33 heliograph stations across Arizona and New Mexico Territory, even down into Old Mexico. These observation posts helped coordinate pursuit and resupply columns to exert constant pressure on the few still wild Apaches fleeing an occasional border raid back into Mexico. They operated until one final field exercise expanded to 51 temporary stations in a two-thousand-mile network over two weeks in 1890, after which they were taken down for good. After the turn of the century, the U.S. Army's heliographs were replaced by a new system of military communications, the wireless radio. Today the heliograph is seldom remembered and only four of the original instruments still exist on display in military museums.

A century's later analysis by army historian Bruno J. Rolak showed that only *once*, on June 5, 1886, did a heliograph post at Antelope Springs, near the mining town of Bisbee, observe a party of Apaches emerging from the Whetstone Mountains and heading south. The operators flashed this information on to Forts Bowie and Huachuca, which in turn flashed it to Captain

Henry Lawton and his large patrol, who were camped on the Santa Cruz River. Capt. Lawton sent several detachments in hot pursuit, and one of these, led by Second Lieutenant Robert Walsh, surprised the raiders in the Patagonia Mountains of Mexico, capturing their stock and equipment. The hostiles fled on foot.

Significantly, after this one instance of an observation post locating a war party and sending a strike force after it, the Apaches from then on knew what the heliographs were used for and avoided areas where they had been installed. Miles's communications network *had* established a protective barrier across southern Arizona and New Mexico, which the renegades now knew they could not penetrate unobserved during daylight hours, and Apaches were always reluctant to travel at night.

The heliograph was therefore more than just an "expensive toy." The southern line of flashing mirrors denied Geronimo's and Naiche's raiders access to the Apache reservations and provided security for settlers north of the border as well as prevented troops from going out on useless investigations of every spooked rancher's report of large dust clouds or strangers passing by. General Miles deserves credit for establishing the most elaborate and effective communications network in the army's history until that time, superior to any system in use by foreign armies then, except the British. But Miles's heliographs' extensive use probably didn't end this longest American war one day sooner.

On October 17, 1894, Troops B and L, Second Cavalry, marched out of old Fort Bowie and left it to be sold. As late as March 1896, ten years after the Apache War's supposed end, following small-scale attacks in southeastern Arizona, troops of cavalry and Indian scouts were again sent out from Forts Grant and Huachuca to trail a small band of still-wild Apaches back into their lair in the Sierra Madres, where they finally found them and captured their stock and equipment, scattering the hostiles. These renegade Apaches wouldn't bother any Americans across the border again, and the summer of 1896 is considered the final end date of the Indian wars in the Southwest.

Charles Lummis quit the *Times* because of exhaustion after returning to Los Angeles. He lived in the Pueblo of Isleta in New Mexico for five years, regaining his health while learning the language and customs of that Indian people. He founded *Out West Magazine* in 1894, influenced fellow Harvard classmate Teddy Roosevelt on Southwestern matters during the latter's presidency, was the Los Angeles librarian for six years, and founded the Southwest Museum there in 1907. Lummis published a number of books about his travels, his poetry, and the folktales of the American Southwest he did so much to popularize. He married three times, but each ended in divorce because of his recurring extramarital affairs.

General Miles went on to preside over the massacre of the ghost-dancing Oglala and Brule Sioux at Wounded Knee on the Pine Ridge at the end of 1890 and more successfully when, as Commanding General of the army, he oversaw the invasion of Cuba and actually led the American troops' smashing victory in Puerto Rico in the Spanish-American War. But Nelson Miles's oversized ego and intemperate remarks to the press didn't serve well his ambitions to achieve high elected office, and he died of a heart attack in 1925 during the playing of the national anthem while attending the Ringling Brothers' Circus with his grandchildren. He died a rich but widely ignored and criticized General for his still outspoken opinions, at the time when the Army of America had moved into the much deadlier mode of modern mechanized warfare.

ACKNOWLEDGMENTS AND SOURCES

"The Attack on the Mountain" is the original title of *The Sergeant's Lady*, when it first appeared as a three-page short story by my late father, Glendon, in the old large-format *Saturday Evening Post Magazine* on July 4, 1959. My dad was an American military history buff, having served as a Sergeant in the Third Infantry Division in World War II, and had read all the old issues of the *Cavalry Journal*, the magazine of the U.S. Horse Cavalry. His authentic research on the frontier army embellished "The Attack on the Mountain," as well as another short story about the aftermath of the Custer debacle, "A Horse for Mrs. Custer," which became one of Randolph Scott's better B-Westerns for Columbia Pictures back in 1956—*Seventh Cavalry*.

Two elements made "The Attack on the Mountain" notable and original. First were Glendon's descriptions of the U.S. Army's use of the heliograph, a mirrored system of communication, which it tested and used in the field for twenty-five years, beginning in the early 1880s, when General Nelson A. Miles took over command of the Department of the Columbia. From his headquarters at Vancouver Barracks on the Columbia River in Washington Territory, Miles began testing a heliograph on the summit of Mount Hood, sending sunlit messages back and forth, fifty miles away. The results were so satisfactory the General quickly instituted full-scale use of the heliograph when he took over command of the Department of Arizona in 1886. The army's then-new heliograph system had never before been used as a backdrop for a Western story, and the details about what it hoped to accomplish in the Apache wars and how the heliograph was actually utilized in Arizona should be unusual material for today's Western history buffs.

Second, the original author's introduction of a strong female character, the rancher's middle-aged sister, who could ranch and shoot and handle Indian trouble better than any of the soldiers assigned to this miserable Arizona mountain lookout post, was innovative for Westerns written in the late Fifties. Miss Martha Cox is so tough and forward that it's *she* who proposes marriage to the gruff army Sergeant Ammon Swing. Strong frontierswomen characters were fairly unusual in Westerns written during what's known as their "golden age." The horse cavalry background and hit-and-miss love affair between this different Sergeant and his aggressive sweetheart also prefigured the same key love match in Glendon's later comic Western novel, *The Tin Lizzie Troop*, which actor Paul Newman bought to turn into an almost-made motion picture for Warner Brothers/First Artists back in the Seventies.

In the Apaches' final attack on the army men in "The Attack on the Mountain," Glendon didn't dwell on the violence and bloodshed, but paid more descriptive attention to the Sergeant's arrow wound, another unusual literary device and a physiological writing technique he refined to perfection in describing the hero's bullet wounds in *The Shootist*, his Western masterpiece, sixteen years later.

I always felt "Attack" would make a good low-budget Western film and set out to adapt it into one in the late nineties, changing the title, however, so as not to give away the ending.

By the time I'd finished my screenplay I'd done so much additional research and added characters and secondary plots to the story, that I belatedly realized it ought to be expanded into a Western novel.

The original short story, "The Attack on the Mountain," on which this new novel is based, is now back in print in a new collection of all of his fine stories entitled *Easterns & Westerns, Short Stories by Glendon Swarthout*, which is available from Michigan State University Press in East Lansing, Michigan. Refer to *www.msu.edu/unit/msupress* or *www.bn.com* for ordering a hardcover edition.

In writing this first novel, I'm indebted to my dear mother, Kathryn, for her undying love, encouragement, and support. Jeff Hengesbaugh, an expert writer/mountain man from Glorieta, New Mexico, vetted my original screenplay to correct my usage and descriptions of some of the arms and survival techniques of that historical period. Tim Simmons, a firefighter friend from Phoenix, Arizona, has known and written about Apaches virtually all of his adult life, and his corrections of and suggestions for some of the material regarding the fighting Apaches, as well as his loan of a partial Apache language dictionary, was invaluable for this story's authenticity. My literary agent, Nat Sobel, of Sobel/Webber & Associates in New York City, also gave very valuable notes that helped me achieve a publishable draft. Nat also thought up this title, *The Sergeant's Lady*, which he felt would reflect the romance at the heart of this frontier adventure. Editor Bob Gleason at Forge Press also contributed good suggestions to enhance the final polish, and publisher Tom Doherty of TOR/Forge gave me this first shot at breaking into print. I am grateful to them all.

And, of course, my late father Glendon's original short story gave me the great basic plot and characters with which to begin. I owe him *everything*, and always will. Further information about Glendon Swarthout's prize-winning novels and the movies made from them can be found on the Internet at his official literary website, *www.glendonswarthout.com.*

For readers who would like to learn more about the real historical background to this story of the Apache fighting, certainly the most well-documented of all the Indian wars because it went on for so long and ended last, begin with the firsthand accounts of the action, Captain John G. Bourke's *On the Border with Crook* and Lieutenant Britton Davis's *The Truth About Geronimo.* Other excellent primary sources are Eve Ball's fascinating interviews with famous Apaches' descendants in *Indeh, an Apache Odyssey* and *In the Days of Victorio: Recollections of a Warm Springs Apache.* Dan L. Thrapp has written many excellent recountings of the Apache campaigns, especially *The Conquest of Apacheria.* Thrapp's three-volume *Encyclopedia of Frontier Biography* is also exceptional for its concise listings of the personalities involved in this long war.

Geronimo: A Biography by Alexander B. Adams covers the life of the legendary war leader of the Apaches. The very best of the recent historical studies about this last of the great Indian wars is *Once They Moved Like the Wind: Cochise, Geronimo, and the Apache* Wars by David Roberts. A fine overview of all the branches of the Apache tribe, with photos and illustrations of them and their equipment as well as the army men and Scouts who chased them, can be found in Thomas E. Mails's big book, *The People Called Apache.*

The best information on the use of the heliographs in this campaign is found in Bruno J. Rolak's 1976 article for the *Journal of Arizona History.* "General Miles' Mirrors." E. Lisle Reedstrom's *Apache Wars, An Illustrated Battle History,* is also particularly thorough on the heliograph, with great photos of Apaches and soldiers and color drawings of all the equipment the army used during this endless war. *Fort Huachuca, the Story of a Frontier Post* by Cornelius C. Smith, Jr., contains interesting chapters on the heliograph, the Apache War, and the Apache Scouts who fought from that famous fort. Louis Kraft's *Gatewood and Geronimo* covers the lives of these two preeminent figures in the Apache War well and has some of the best photographs of the Apaches as well as maps of the campaign.

For a fascinating history of soldier life in the frontier army, check out Don Rickey's *Forty Miles a Day on Beans and Hay*. Emmet M. Essin's recent *Shavetails & Bell Sharps* is the only good history of the use of the U.S. Army mules in desert combat. Robert Wooster is the ranking expert on *Nelson A. Miles and the Twilight of the Frontier Army*, and certainly the General's own two-volume autobiography, *Personal Recollections & Observations of General Nelson A. Miles*, is worth perusing. Glenda Riley is the expert on women's hard lives on the American frontier, which she has covered in a number of good books, including *The Female Frontier: A Comparative View of Women on the Prairie and the Plains.*

Charles Fletcher Lummis was a well-known Los Angeles journalist for the *Los Angeles Times* who was right on the scene at endgame for the Apaches and wrote *The Land of Poco Tiempo* about his extensive travels through the Southwest. Lummis's dispatches from the battlefield in Arizona Territory in 1886 were edited by his daughter, Turbesé Lummis Fiske, into a book that was published by Northland Press eighty years later in 1966, *General Crook and the Apache Wars*, selections from which were used verbatim in this novel. These same battlefront dispatches were more thoroughly compiled and introduced in a later volume by Apache War expert Dan L. Thrapp, *Dateline Fort Bowie* (1979). Mark Thompson has also written a fine new biography (2001) of the feisty historian, *American Character, the Curious Life of Charles Fletcher Lummis and the Rediscovery of the Southwest.*

Famed historian Robert Utley gives a good account of the

goings-on at that same army headquarters in *A Clash of Cultures: Fort Bowie and the Chiricahua Apaches*. This last great Indian war represents a fascinating era in America's late frontier history that is well covered in all of these fine histories of the Southwest.